HORSEMAN

A NATE TEMPLE SUPERNATURAL THRILLER BOOK 10

SHAYNE SILVERS

ARGENTO PUBLISHING

Shayne Silvers

Horseman

A Nate Temple Supernatural Thriller Book 10

The Temple Chronicles

ISBN 13: **978-1-947709-16-4**

© 2018, Shayne Silvers / Argento Publishing, LLC

info@shaynesilvers.com

For updates on new releases, promotions, and updates, please sign up for my mailing list on **shaynesilvers.com**.

CONTENTS

BOOKS IN THE TEMPLE VERSE

CHRONOLOGY: *All stories in the Temple Verse are shown in chronological order on the following page*

NATE TEMPLE SERIES

FAIRY TALE - FREE prequel novella #0 for my subscribers

OBSIDIAN SON

BLOOD DEBTS

GRIMM

SILVER TONGUE

BEAST MASTER

TINY GODS

DADDY DUTY (Novella #6.5)

WILD SIDE

WAR HAMMER

NINE SOULS

HORSEMAN

LEGEND (TEMPLE #11) - *COMING DECEMBER 2018...*

FEATHERS AND FIRE SERIES

(Also set in the Temple Universe)

UNCHAINED

RAGE

WHISPERS

ANGEL'S ROAR

SINNER - *COMING SEPTEMBER 2018...*

WHISKEY GINGER

COSMOPOLITAN

OLD FASHIONED

DARK AND STORMY -

MOSCOW MULE - *COMING FALL 2018...*

CHRONOLOGICAL ORDER: TEMPLE VERSE

FAIRY TALE (TEMPLE PREQUEL)

OBSIDIAN SON (TEMPLE 1)

BLOOD DEBTS (TEMPLE 2)

GRIMM (TEMPLE 3)

SILVER TONGUE (TEMPLE 4)

BEAST MASTER (TEMPLE 5)

TINY GODS (TEMPLE 6)

DADDY DUTY (TEMPLE NOVELLA 6.5)

UNCHAINED (FEATHERS... 1)

RAGE (FEATHERS... 2)

WILD SIDE (TEMPLE 7)

WAR HAMMER (TEMPLE 8)

WHISPERS (FEATHERS... 3)

WHISKEY GINGER (PHANTOM... 1)

NINE SOULS (TEMPLE 9)

COSMOPOLITAN (PHANTOM... 2)

ANGEL'S ROAR (FEATHERS... 4)

OLD FASHIONED (PHANTOM...3)

HORSEMAN (TEMPLE 10)

DARK AND STORMY (PHANTOM... 4)

STALK ME ONLINE!

To get a free copy of **FAIRY TALE** (a prequel novella with Nate Temple), news updates, book release alerts, and other secret bonus content...

SIGN UP for my NEWSLETTER:
http://www.shaynesilvers.com/l/38599

And...

FOLLOW and LIKE my FACEBOOK PAGE:
www.shaynesilvers.com/l/38602

I respond to all messages, so don't hesitate to drop me a line. Not interacting with readers is the biggest travesty that most authors can make. Let me fix that.

CHAPTER 1

$\mathcal{I}$ straightened my suitcoat, studying myself in the mirror. Dark circles showed under my eyes from lack of sleep, faint but permanent fine wrinkles spreading out from the corners, and a slight redness to my sclera. My hair was growing longer and losing the occasional lighter streaks of blonde. I hadn't shaved in a while, leaving behind an unkempt scruff over my cheeks and neck. My skin was pale, because I hadn't seen enough daylight lately. Hell, Alucard saw more sunlight than me these days, the sparkly bastard.

"I still can't get over how vain you are," Callie teased gently, touching up the makeup, concealer, foundation, and whatever other magic she needed to make me look like I wasn't stumbling out of a bar at sunrise after a three-day bender. "Use these eye drops before you go on stage. They feel like napalm, but they're incredible." She handed me a tiny bottle with a strange name on it, and I nodded.

"I'm not vain, just…" I trailed off, not knowing how to put it into words.

"Vain," Callie grinned, putting the word in my mouth. But she placed a hand on my thigh and squeezed compassionately. "You just need to slow down. You're not sleeping, running from ancient library to ancient library, sticking behind the walls of Chateau Falco. You've been a hermit these last weeks. It's not good for you, and it's making your friends nervous."

I grunted. "Making the *city* nervous, you mean. Have you heard about the uptick in graffiti pieces throughout St. Louis lately? *The King is Dead.* *#NotMyKing.*" I gestured vaguely with my hand.

Callie nodded. "I heard about that. But don't pretend they're all negative. I've heard just as much about the ones praising you."

I grunted noncommittally. "And the Regulars don't know what to make of their local billionaire suddenly being nicknamed *King* Temple rather than *Master* Temple. Why I'm suddenly a topic of interest to the graffiti community. They think it's all some publicity stunt on my part."

"Well, that's one benefit of tonight, right? To answer to the people? To feed them a comforting lie rather than admitting to being an arrogant wizard who fights monsters in the night and keeps them safe by claiming St. Louis as his own sovereign nation?" I nodded. "But don't forget to appeal to the Freaks in the audience. You need them as allies." She waited until I nodded again before shoving me gently back into the chair, rather than sitting on the edge like I had been, getting worked up about the speech.

I smiled faintly as she leaned closer, smudging more goop under my eye. With her so close, I couldn't help but inhale the scent of strawberries and sunshine. I commented on it absently. "You smell nice."

She paused, her hands cupping my face. She didn't make eye contact, just continued staring at her applications. "Nice..." she said in an *oh so gentle* tone, resuming her work a little more forcefully.

I grinned. "You smell *purdy*," I teased. "Like fruit and sun rays."

This time, she did pause, the corner of her lip rising. "Well, you smell like alcohol." I scowled at her. She gripped my chin with her thumb and forefinger, and my skin suddenly throbbed with cold. She jerked her hand away. "Sorry. I forgot about..." she moved her hand so that the ever-shifting ring of shadows over her thumb didn't touch my skin any longer.

The ring where she had trapped an Angel.

"You know, I would really like to inspect that soon," I told her. "Just to make sure there isn't any risk in you wearing it." She also wore a long, thick chain around her neck, and on it hung a large silver signet ring. The Seal of Solomon. Something just as dangerous.

Callie rolled her eyes, leaning back to the table to scoop up another tube of tan cream. "You want to weaponize it."

I opened my mouth to argue, thought about it, and then sighed. "Well, that, too."

She was silent for a few moments, humming to herself as she rifled through the never-ending collection of creams and powders. "It's probably a good idea," she finally said.

And I could tell that was as far as the topic was going to go tonight, so I dropped it.

She leaned in close, another whiff of her perfume – or maybe it was just her natural pheromones translating to a pleasant smell in my mind. "Do I really smell like booze? Because I'll probably run into the Mayor, and that's not the impression I'd like to give him."

She laughed lightly. "When I said you smelled like alcohol, it was actually a compliment."

"Oh? You're into alcoholics?"

She gave me a stern look. "Careful, or I'll mess up your eyelash extensions." I stiffened in horror. She was giving me extensions? She burst out laughing, placing a hand on my shoulder. "I'm only kidding. But your scent, it's more... earthy."

"Now you're talking. Boozy *and* dirty—"

She growled, and I saw her eyes flicker with an almost chrome sheen. "It's an herbal thing. You smell like..." she leaned back, glancing down at her hands. "I don't know how to explain it. It's a romantic concept *beyond* smell. Like... anise and fennel. A musky, natural whiff." Seeing my grin grow, she sighed, closing her eyes to think about it. She opened them after a moment, looking more committed. "It makes me feel like we're stuck on an island, and that you know how to take care of anything. Like confidence and protection. Earthy – like you are one with the land. Musky – like the prey you hunt. Savage. A wild protector..." She sighed, setting the tube back down. "I'm fumbling here, but... it just makes me feel *safe*, and I'm not accustomed to looking *elsewhere* for safety."

I nodded, thinking about it. "I had some absinthe earlier. Maybe your brain is just trying to translate that into an emotional response," I suggested. "Like me saying you smell like strawberries and sunshine."

She placed a finger over my lips. "Or, you smell like a sexy caveman, and this cavewoman likes it."

I grinned. "Yeah, that sounds bett—"

Someone rapped on the door politely – my five-minute reminder – interrupting me. Callie burst out laughing. "That!" she giggled, pointing at my face. "That look matches the scent *perfectly*." She tugged the tissue paper from between my shirt collar and skin – a precaution to not stain my white shirt – and rather than tossing it in the trash, she incinerated it with a quick flare of fire, using her magic openly.

She leaned in, adjusted my tie slightly, and locked eyes with me. "I want you to look at me three times while you're on stage. Try to seduce me from afar."

I grinned wolfishly. "Oh?" This was new.

Callie nodded, her white hair tickling her jaws. Her white and silver dress made it look like she was wearing chrome body-paint. Not that it was inappropriate, but more that she just owned the dress so completely it seemed a part of her, transforming her into an avenging angel. "It will keep you focused and make you appear confident to the cameras."

My confidence deflated, ironically. "Oh."

"And who knows, you might just catch a girl's attention." She shot me a wink, and pulled me to my feet, her eyes latching onto a book on the table. *A Tale of Two Cities*. She'd bought it for me recently, setting off all sorts of alarm bells, because I'd had a bizarre dream not too long ago, and Callie had been in it.

In the dream, I'd said the phrase *Tale of Two Cities*, using it to describe the strange setting of the place. Then, not long after, Callie shipped me that exact book, making me believe that it had been more than a dream, and that perhaps Callie really had been in it, or that we'd shared the same dream.

Or some other magical crap.

To be fair, the dream had happened while I was helping her out with some crazy stuff in Kansas City regarding the heavy, prominent ring now nestled between her breasts. I'd been so concerned about her that I'd kidnapped her to prove my undying loyalty. Then I'd handed her over to an Angel to be interrogated. The bill for that decision hadn't come in the mail yet, but I was betting Callie had all sorts of opinions on it.

Callie noticed me studying the book, and suddenly looked just as hesitant. "Like the book?" she asked softly.

I nodded slowly, studying her face for clues. "Yes. It hasn't left my sight since I got it," I admitted.

She blushed. "Oh. I thought you might like it." She took a deep breath, the motion doing all sorts of pleasant things to her cleavage, but I pretended not to notice. I failed, judging by her instant grin. "Remind me to tell you about a dream I had…" and she was instantly blushing again.

My heart abruptly thundered in my chest. Could it be? Was she talking about the dream I'd had? For fear of sounding like a love-sick puppy, I hadn't wanted to bring it up, first. I could just imagine it. *Hey, Callie, I had this vivid dream about you topless in a strange bedroom. Want to talk about it?*

She glanced at the clock on the wall, grimacing. "Later," she sighed. Then she frowned regretfully. "We always come back to that word, don't we?"

I nodded woodenly, suddenly very interested, but also... nervous. Because the dream had felt so real, like a vision of the future. It had been both alarming and... exciting. "I look forward to it... later," I told her cautiously. Was I reading too much into the comment? Or maybe she was just messing with me. Callie had a knack for mental manipulation. It wasn't magic or anything, she was just a walking psychologist, able to read, assess, and decipher almost anyone she came across – instantly seeming to know their strengths and weaknesses, and how to exploit them all to her benefit. It was one of the reasons I enjoyed spending time around her. She kept me on my toes, always guessing if our conversations were really about something entirely different than they seemed at the time.

But if she really had shared the same dream as me... Well, I wasn't sure if that was terrifying or exciting. Both, surely, but which trumped the other? The fact that we had been in a bedroom together half-naked, or that beyond that bedroom had been an Apocalyptic wasteland?

Being a healthy male, I told myself that the bedroom thing was the clear winner.

The land beyond the bedroom hadn't really been *that* Apocalyptic, just a little war-torn around the edges...

CHAPTER 2

I heard the door click and realized Callie had left to take her place at a table in the audience. I sighed regretfully as I walked up to the tall, standup mirror, making sure I didn't have any makeup smudges on my light gray houndstooth suit. I studied myself, trying to get a glimpse of that savage man-beast Callie saw in me. I guessed beauty – or beast – was in the eye of the beholder.

Enough about Callie, I told myself. I needed to focus.

I checked my earpiece, which was a communication network Othello had given all my attending friends, who were currently loitering in the audience at strategic locations, blending in. It was pretty neat technology. Tap your jaw twice and your earbud would activate, letting you speak with your partners across the room. Hold down on the earbud itself, and you could leave the communication line open so that the rest of your team heard a live feed of your activities.

Obviously, since I'd been in a private dressing room with Callie, I'd turned off the live function.

I'd been to too many events where things went sideways, and I'd needed to alert my friends to a supernatural threat. Yelling *werewolves are about to attack!* out loud in a crowded room usually didn't make people calm down. Especially at a speech where I was denying the existence of such things.

So, nifty comms hardware from Othello. Check.

I checked my phone absently and sighed at the article Othello had sent me. Tomas Mullingsworth – an old dragon-hunter pal of mine from back in the day – had gone missing and was presumed dead. I'd tried a few secret phone numbers I had for him but hadn't had any luck. I'd told Othello to dig deeper because he'd been a good friend, and it didn't sound like the local authorities in London were giving it much attention, judging by the article, anyway. I turned the phone to silent and slipped it into my jacket's inner pocket.

There would be a lot of wealthy people present tonight, so maybe I could even turn my speech into a plug for *Shift*, the school for wayward children I had helped open with Tory. Really, it was a place for shifters without parents to learn self-control, and I had a Beast Master running the place. She could shut down a shifter with a look – any shifter, no matter how old. Well, as far as we'd discovered, anyway. It wasn't like we had walked the country searching for ancient shifters to challenge or anything, but her track record was pretty damned good so far.

St. Louis was hosting this event to bring to light the overwhelming flood of reports, online videos, and blog articles shouting that magic was absolutely real. It had gotten so much attention lately that people were taking it seriously. By that, I meant politicians were, of course, wanting to put an end to it, and what better way than to be seen attending a VIP dinner with a speech from the local billionaire.

Me.

I considered the irony of denying the existence of magic in my speech, and then using my speech to do a plug for a school of were-animals – shifters who needed to learn self-control so they didn't go on a killing spree at Wal-Mart or a public park. Not that any Regulars actually knew Shift was a school for shifters. They all thought it was for wayward kids.

Half-truths built empires, folks.

Thanks to Othello's network of eyes and ears, I also knew I would have two audiences in the crowd. The Regulars – non-magical humans – but also the heads or representatives of the major supernatural families in town. They all had a vested interest in this topic, and after me sending shifter dragon delegates all over St. Louis to declare to everyone that I was their new King, they probably wanted to get a personal feel for me.

Many already had a personal feel – both for and against – judging by the graffiti.

Tonight was all about calming people down. I needed to appease them and the Regulars, both.

So that I could get back to my own drama.

Mordred was out there somewhere, probably doing something nefarious. And it was my fault, since I'd busted him out of Hell. I hadn't heard a word about his actions, and that made me very nervous. Everyone who knew about it had seemed so horrified that he had broken free from Hell – obviously categorizing the illegitimate son of King Arthur in the *not a nice guy* category – so I had expected instant chaos and destruction... somewhere. But I hadn't heard a peep – from gods, legends, or any of my fellow monsters – about him. Maybe he was taking a vacation, to start. He'd been locked up for centuries, after all.

Hell wasn't known for its golf courses or mixed drink specials.

I did know for a fact that he wanted to decimate anything related to Camelot and its memory. I glanced up at the clock and cursed. I was on in one minute. Ready to address the growing topic of misinformation and truth in media. Numerous online videos were popping up like weeds after a storm – all showing magic or monsters on film. Either the monsters were getting careless, they were *purposely* letting themselves be recorded – which wasn't a good thing – or it was inevitability at work. Everything was on camera these days, so it only made sense that monsters would occasionally make a cameo.

My goal today was to discredit the clips. Since I was the poster child for getting caught doing stupid stuff on camera and garnering a lot of buzz about the recent street art, it made sense they wanted me to appear in public. Also, I'd once been outed as a wizard during an eclipse convention a few years ago. It had died down soon after – I'd killed the man who put me in that position, Alaric Slate – but now it was back in everyone's minds. I was probably the only one to have any credibility on the matter, if for no other reason than because I'd once been called a wizard at a public event.

Tonight I was going to be cool, calm, and collected. Change the narrative.

I opened my dressing room door and approached the stage entrance. I waited in the wings, listening to the announcer give a quick biography of me. I would deliver a quick speech, shake some hands, and then I could get back to my research.

Because I had much more important things to do than public relations.

8

Mordred was out there, with the Nine Souls he had stolen from Hell. I didn't know who the Nine Souls actually were, but I knew they had been in a solitary confinement of sorts, always spoken about in hushed tones. But for Mordred to have stolen them meant he had bad things planned.

Soon.

If I couldn't find Mordred, I needed to find out what he was after, which I assumed was anything to do with the destruction of Camelot. My ancestor, Matthias Temple, had recently kidnapped one of King Arthur's supposed Knights, and had him holed up... somewhere. Maybe it was time to visit.

I had found very little concrete information about Mordred. Stories abounded about him, but almost all were contradictory. He was allegedly the illegitimate son of King Arthur and his enchantress half-sister, Morgause, but sometimes he was referred to as more of an adopted son or nephew. Gotta' love that Medieval Spin, right? *Oh, no. I didn't sleep with my sister, we just found the boy...*

I couldn't fault Mordred's bone-deep hatred, just where he directed it.

Some stories said Mordred had died at the Battle of Camlann, but not before giving Arthur a fatal wound. Some said Mordred was a wizard. Others, a knight. Some said he had been a better ruler than Arthur. Some said a traitor.

Since I'd met him in Hell, I had a pretty good idea of where he fit on the bad versus evil spectrum.

The announcer called out my name, and I heard the seated audience burst into applause.

I stepped out of the wings and through the curtain, smiling confidently. The bright lights were a little excessive, so I waited a moment for my eyes to adjust. It would be embarrassing to stumble on my way to the podium...

My smile faltered momentarily as I noticed the announcer carrying the podium away. Instead, a rectangular table sat in the center of the stage, overlooking the fifty or so round tables of St. Louis' elites, all wearing sparkling dresses and crisp suits, and surrounded by bottles of wine and platters of exquisite food. I spotted Callie, and she looked ready to murder everyone in the room.

A man sat at the table on the stage, and he was patting the empty chair beside him, smiling invitingly for me to join him. A microphone sat before each seat, and a placard on the front of the table told me in all capital letters who my new co-speaker was.

MOE DREDD.

NATE TEMPLE.

I stared at the name in disbelief, then at the man, somehow maintaining my smile for the audience. Any hesitation on my part could easily be answered by no one having told me I would have a co-speaker. But this was so much worse than my pride taking a body-shot.

Moe began to clap, flashing a beaming smile out at the crowd, and then back to me. His eyes flickered with amusement – he was basically laughing in my face.

He looked a lot better than when I had last seen him breaking out of Hell.

Mordred cleaned up well, apparently.

Tonight had just gotten a *hell* of a lot more interesting.

CHAPTER 3

I sat down next to Mordred, instinctively ready for a magical fight even though we were in front of a dozen cameramen, photographers, and several hundred of St. Louis' wealthiest citizens. Was Mordred intending to answer the topic of the night with a big display of show and tell?

Or did he have another motive?

Mordred was no longer a smudged charcoal stain, but a tall, fit, dark-haired, middle-aged man with icy green eyes. His jaw was harsh and angular, and his long hair was tied back in a bun, looking like it would reach his shoulders when let down. But those eyes... they danced with shadows, zipping back and forth behind his obviously fake, round-lensed spectacles. It was something a wizard like myself could easily discern, and I wondered if other Freaks would be able to pick up on it. His three-piece tweed suit made him look like nothing more than an adjunct professor slumming it with the elites. Just an academic let out of his cage for the night.

The crowd continued to applaud, and my eyes locked onto Callie – who had masked her anger, and now sat on the edge of her seat. Mordred leaned in close, and there was nothing unassuming about the waves of power I felt emanating from him. He was strong as hell. Quite literally. "It is so good to see you again, Nate. I had no idea my savior was so distinguished." He placed a very warm palm on my shoulder and patted it twice, smiling out at the crowd.

"What are you doing here, *Moe?*" I hissed, emphasizing his bullshit name. "I had hoped you would find a quiet place to resume your calligraphy hobby. Maybe sell your creepy wall-art online," I said, referring to the names he had carved into the walls of his prison cell about a billion times. I was sure to maintain my smile for the crowd, even though I felt like I had just stepped into a boxing ring. "I thought you wanted to destroy Camelot?"

He chuckled good-naturedly, not a flicker of menace on his stark features. "That's exactly what I'm doing, Temple." Up close, I could see a tightness around his eyes, the tension of restraining the abundance of power the Nine Souls were pumping into him.

The audience quieted and I noticed a felt pen on our table. I abruptly uncapped it, took my name placard, and wrote KING in front of my name. I carefully repositioned the placard in front of me, smiling absently at the audience. "If enough people say it, maybe it will become true," I said in a not so humble tone. I heard several cheers, but most just laughed politely, turning to my co-speaker.

Mordred took the pen, thought for a moment, and then swept up his own placard, drawing a large letter R between his two names, MOE R. DREDD. He capped the pen and shrugged humbly. "I don't have a crown, but I do have a middle name," he said into his microphone, using his finger to push the bridge of his glasses up, smiling wide.

The audience began to clap, adoring the nerdy little wanker.

I nodded my head in resignation, waiting for the announcer to begin. Was this some kind of debate? Or was it still about the public concerns over inexplicable online videos? I hadn't heard a whisper about having a partner on stage, which made me think I had been set up. But who would have agreed to such a plan? Effectively putting a celebrity like me in the crosshairs without prior warning. That was a career-ending move.

Or a career *starting* move. Mordred had been busy, because I knew he had to be involved. A man with no ties to the community could have only gotten a seat beside me with a lot of money changing hands, or a lot of blackmail and extortion.

The announcer cleared his throat. "I'm so glad you were able to join us this evening, Mr. Dredd," he said warmly, smiling at Mordred, who nodded back politely.

"It's a pleasure to be seated beside Master—" he hesitated, glancing up at the placard I had modified. Then he leaned closer to the microphone as if to impart a secret, "*King* Temple," he corrected with a wide grin. The words boomed through the room like a cavalry of invading horses, and I winced. He blushed at the technical faux pas, as if he hadn't known full-well the microphone was perfectly calibrated. *King Temple* echoed in the room, and the audience looked truly uncomfortable for a heartbeat before smiling at the apologetic look on Mordred's face. I gritted my teeth, pretending to smile.

"I think the St. Louis Police Department appreciates your generosity even more," the announcer said.

Mordred nodded soberly. "Our Knights in Shining Armor deserve more than they get. I'm just trying to help." Many in the crowd clapped lightly, especially the Commissioner and Mayor. This was their language – politics. Mordred had just made two new friends. The bastard.

It was very difficult for me to maintain my smile and not grit my teeth. I managed a happy medium that I hoped no one picked up on. He had made a hefty donation to the police department. That explained things. He'd greased some palms to get here and looked like a saint doing it.

But why?

He could have met up with me at any point if he had wanted to. I'd been searching him out for some time, now. He had to have a different motive for tonight. This event was public, which meant he had a message to deliver, whether everyone knew it or not.

My eyes latched onto the various representatives of the supernatural community in the audience, and I suddenly felt a pit of fear in my stomach. Did this have to do with them? Was he… rallying an army?

The announcer was speaking again, more to the crowd than us. Mordred leaned in, and I had to fight not to flinch away. "Remember to smile, Nate. I'd hate for them to think we're not old friends. I'd hate to have to tell them how we met. Maybe *show* them how we met… I rather like my newfound freedom, and it would be inconvenient for everyone if a few Calavera coincidentally appeared to take me back home. I might even devolve to violence. In self-defense, of course."

Then he was leaning away, smiling at the announcer.

I grimaced inwardly. If that happened, many would die. Also, it would pretty much put a pin in the conversation about magic not being real. He had me by the short hairs. Play ball, or today might go down in history as the day the world lost their collective shit – in that monsters and magic were very real.

"There is much talk about false news," the announcer began, reading from his notes, "inaccurate articles shared online, or doctored videos going viral, the authors publicizing them strictly to incite fear in our great city, let alone the nation."

What had Mordred posed as, other than a philanthropist? A politician? Was he in agreement with my planned stance, or opposed to it? I took a breath, clearing my head as the announcer continued in an uplifting tone, playing both sides against the middle, riling up the audience.

I noticed several familiar faces in the crowd. Many of my friends were present. Many of them were also on my comms network, but no one was using the earbuds at the moment, not wanting to distract me.

Raego Slate – the king of the dragons, or Obsidian Son – sat near the front, leaning back in his chair, ankles crossed and arms folded as if incredibly bored. Raego was like a long-haired James Dean. His tie was loose, and he hadn't bothered with a suitcoat, just a dress shirt and vest. His slacks were carefully tailored to his exact size, and he wore very expensive crocodile skin dress shoes, which I thought might have been disrespectful, but apparently were not.

Beside him sat Baron Skyfall and Enya – a woman so beautiful and deadly, she needed no last name.

Enya was pale with long, strawberry blonde golden hair and emerald eyes. Her green cocktail dress glittered like scales, flattering her already perfect body beyond realistic expectations for most women. And she knew it. She probably looked good in whatever she put on. Or took off.

Baron, on the other hand, was a robust, English black man. He wore a sharp, white suit, complete with an orange pocket square that would have matched his irises if he hadn't been wearing contacts to conceal what he was. Because dragons had *horizontal* slits for pupils – like demonic goats – rather than the vertical pupils of most serpents. Very noticeable.

The colors of their irises also told you – kind of – what flavor of dragon you might be dealing with, and what their powers may be.

He was bald as an egg, and sported dark freckles on his brown cheeks, just below his eyes. Compensating for his shiny dome, he had a dense, but short white beard. He was a tall, buff bastard, easily twice as wide as most men, and had a thick neck. He was larger than Gunnar, but differently proportioned.

Tory Marlin – the Headmistress at *Shift*, our school for orphan shifters – was seated at a table of politicians. She wore a flashy pantsuit, her hair tucked back in a bun, making her look like a harmless school principal. Which she was. And wasn't. She was a Beast Master, able to control shifters at will. She was also abnormally strong, like 'swing a motorcycle with one arm,' strong.

Gunnar Randulf – the alpha werewolf of St. Louis – also leaned back in his chair as if lounging. Ironically, he wore a silver suit, his thick blonde beard covering up most of his tie. His stone eyepatch reflected the light, and I caught many women sizing him up hungrily. Luckily for them, his wife, Ashley, wasn't present or they would already be dead. She was likely watching over the pack in his absence. I knew his lieutenants, Drake and Cowan were lurking about somewhere, but I didn't see them.

Because none of us had considered tonight's event all that important, as long as I said my piece on live camera. Just putting a bandage on an age-old topic. Again.

Point for Mordred – intentional or not.

What concerned me were the *other* faces in the crowd, those I didn't have a personal connection with, but were obviously representatives of various supernatural families in town. Othello had done some research into the attendees, even though I would need to have a hard talk with her about missing the surprise guest.

The announcer finally finished up his introduction and addressed me, asking my opinion on the numerous videos. He even played a few on the screen behind us, the lights in the room dimming. Mordred and I both turned to watch along with the audience. I was sure to chuckle and shake my head for appearances but kept quiet as they played. More than a few depicted dragons flying across the skies of St. Louis a few weeks ago.

From when I had declared St. Louis as mine and sent emissaries out to the ruling families. The very same night I had broken Mordred out of Hell.

I smiled good-naturedly as the lights brightened, turning back to the microphone. "It seems we have a talented kite-maker in town. If he comes forward, maybe I can hire him to work for me at Grimm Tech. We're always looking for innovators. Perhaps he's the next Leonardo da Vinci."

Mordred considered me in silence, and I held my breath.

CHAPTER 4

Finally, Mordred nodded his agreement. "I, too, think the simplest explanation is usually the most accurate. Then again, it would be wonderful if such creatures truly did exist. Just imagine, knowing you are sitting beside a dragon…" his twinkling gaze scanned the crowd, resting on Raego for a moment. The king of the dragons, the Obsidian Son, pretended not to notice, suddenly pouring another drink and laughing with his friends, Baron and Enya.

I was glad the shifter dragons were wearing contacts to conceal their strangely colored eyes – and their horizontal pupils. That would have made things awkward.

Several members of other supernatural families looked decidedly uncomfortable.

The two dragons shook their heads good-naturedly, and Baron even flapped his hands dramatically, like wings. "Rawr!" Those at their table chuckled, turning back to the stage. But I saw Raego's eyes. They were cold and ruthless as he sipped his drink, peering over the rim at Mordred.

Mordred winked back playfully.

The announcer brought us back on topic. "Several years ago, we had a convention here during a solar eclipse. The topic was brought up – after a series of… unfortunate events you were involve—"

"Allegedly," I said in a dry tone. "They never proved I was a malevolent wizard, much to my dismay," I added, shaking my head in mock disappointment. "Or else I would have added *dark wizard* to my card," I said, picking it up to show the crowd.

The announcer's lips tightened briefly, not pleased I had stolen his thunder. "Which is my point. A gentleman named Alaric Slate stated that you were a wizard, but he seemed to disappear after suggesting a coalition of what he called *Freaks*."

I shrugged. "Perhaps he realized how ridiculous the idea sounded after talking it over with his Public Relations team. A healthy imagination can inspire, but oftentimes it's best left where it belongs, rather than involving the rest of the world in your childhood dreams of fairies, trolls, and unicorns." I glanced back at the screen where they had played the video a moment ago. "Or dragons," I added, rolling my eyes.

Mordred smiled, nodding his head in agreement. "I couldn't agree more. Master Temple is a visionary. Why, in my brief time here, I've even seen the beautiful street art showing him posing as a king. Obviously, the city adores him and his heroic reputation. St. Louis' golden child," Mordred said with a sincerity even I almost bought.

The announcer fumbled with his notes, as if considering dropping a few truth bombs about my past in the public eye. Maybe a burned down stripclub or two, a few of my more notorious arrests, or my televised appearance at a big concert getting punched in the nuts by a guy in a kilt.

"I'm sure they meant well, but I hear the crown looks wrong," I shrugged.

Mordred nodded, waving a hand. "True. I've unfortunately seen a few that were… less than flattering."

I smiled with my teeth. "No accounting for taste, I guess."

The announcer piped up. "Where do we go from here, gentlemen? How do we move past these unfortunate fits of paranoia and get the city back on track?" He addressed Mordred this time. "You seem to have made an admirable start, with your generous donation to the police…" he smirked, changing his phrase, "the Knights in Shining Armor, as you called them. You've only been here a short while but are obviously invested in this city. What else do you have in store for us?"

Mordred waved a hand vaguely. "I was just hoping to avoid as many speeding tickets as possible," he chuckled, looking innocently guilty, the smug prick. Was the announcer working for him, or did the guy just not like me all that much? I didn't recognize him, and I knew most of the local reporters, unfortunately.

Mordred cleared his throat, his smile fading, taking the question more seriously this time. "It is true I've only been here a short while. I don't even have a home yet, just hopping from hotel to hotel at the moment, but this means I've *walked* the city streets. Felt the *pulse* of the city. I don't get to just turn it off after a day of work, retiring to my private solitude. I have dinner at a local restaurant, do my dry-cleaning down the street, take Ubers to my appointments. I..." he trailed off, eyes distant and proud. "I talk to the people of this city. And I feel their pain as my own. Which... well, I guess you set me up quite nicely, and it would be a shame for me not to take advantage of a shameless plug for my own charitable foundation..." The announcer waved a hand, smiling brightly, and the crowd grew quieter, leaning forwards.

Motherfucker. He was subtly implying that I was apart from the people of the city. He was efficiently separating me from the population, all while seeming to compliment me.

Mordred turned to me with a guilty smile. "I must confess to a bit of a deception. You see, I had hoped to discuss the matter with you privately—"

"Then you probably should," I advised drily.

But the audience began to protest in a low rumble. No jeering or anything, but very interested in Mordred's announcement.

I relented, waving my hand. "I hope it's not something too controversial, Moe," I said. "After all, I have to answer to my Board, lawyers, and investors. I can hardly go to the restroom without permission these days."

Mordred nodded knowingly. "Of course, and perhaps you are correct. I didn't intend to put you on the spot. More to plug my own organization. Plant a seed, as it were..." he trailed off, and inwardly I cringed.

He was feeding the crowd, and as expected, the protests became louder, very quickly.

Like I was putting a noose around my neck, I nodded. "I'm always open to discussions, as long as you know I may have to refer to wiser minds than mine to make a final decision..." and I let my eyes sweep the crowd, discreetly, but pointedly locking eyes with the representatives of the major supernatural families in attendance. "But I'm strongly against holding the information hostage from the public, so lay it on me."

He smiled like a shark, pretending to roll up his sleeves. He arched a brow at the audience. "I'm a little nervous," he admitted. "I'd never considered myself a public speaker, especially not with such an esteemed audience, or esteemed... adversaries," he said in a dramatic whisper, winking at me.

I rolled my eyes, feigning humility. "Hurry, before the alcohol hits their bloodstreams." I pretended to think, as if I'd just had a sudden thought. I needed to talk with him in private. A diversion. "In fact, maybe it would be relaxing to have a drink together. Pretend we are having a fire-side chat. In some old castle or something. You know, somewhere far, far away." Before he could respond, I leaned back to the server waiting in the wings. He was holding a pitcher of ice water. "Can I get two dry martinis, please? Put it on his tab," I whispered loudly, pretending to hide that I was pointing my thumb at Mordred.

The server blinked at me, glanced down at the pitcher in his hands, and then vanished, not having anticipated needing booze.

I hadn't either.

I turned back to Mordred. "Okay, Moe. You'll have about two minutes before my judgment is impaired," I smiled. "Make the most of it. And remember. No audience in front of us. Just a dusty, empty castle that no one here cares about. We're all alone..."

He gave me a very slow smile, nodding his approval, and definitely getting my not-so-subtle reference – that this wasn't Camelot. "I think we're going to need those drinks."

There was a flurry of activity, and suddenly three servers were rushing up to our table, setting down a bottle of scotch – Macallan.

Fifty-year Macallan. The Huntress, disguised as one of the servers, dipped her head subserviently. "We were all out of vodka, Master Temple. I hope this will suffice. If it's not to your liking, I'll zip right back over like an arrow to discard it."

I nodded absently, pretending not to recognize her or to pick up on her subtle threat. The Huntress was possibly the best bowman in the world. Ever. At least the best I'd ever seen. She had a bow – stolen from a Greek bastard of the highest order named Bellerophon – that could be drawn as easily as breaking a cobweb with your fingers. She was a ruthless killer. And she'd just offered me a free assassination, courtesy of the house.

All the best waiters usually did.

I scooped up the bottle and inspected it. "Only the finest when my new friend is paying the price," I smiled, thanking her. The audience chuckled.

Mordred grinned, holding up his glass. I poured him a few fingers, then a healthy splash for myself.

I set the bottle down between us, lifted my glass, and spoke into the microphone. "Bring down the lights, please. We're in a faraway castle, remember?" I said, arching a playful eyebrow at the announcer.

His lips thinned, suddenly realizing he had lost control of the situation. To be honest, I wasn't sure who *was* in control of the situation either, but I was trying to throw down as many obstacles and double-meanings as possible.

Because this wasn't just a showdown between Mordred and me. This was a message, delivered to both the Regulars of St. Louis, and the supernatural factions suddenly latching onto our every gesture and word.

A moment later the houselights dimmed, creating a mellow ambience on the stage and cloaking the crowd in murky darkness. Like what I imagined would happen if Mordred had his way. I studied the crowd, trying to catch my friends' attention. If I focused, I could just make them out. Perfect. This would also give them a measure of privacy to converse amongst themselves without fear of their neighboring tables eavesdropping or spying on them.

Because I was confident Mordred had his own people in the crowd, just like I did.

Two self-appointed kings surveying the field of battle, imagining the blood and carnage to come.

I lifted my glass to clink with his in a gesture of peaceful camaraderie.

"To the Round Table Initiative," Mordred said in a proud cheer, right before locking eyes with me and clinking our glasses together.

I almost dropped my drink but masked it well. I think. The Round Table Initiative? Mordred wasn't very subtle, either.

The game was a-fucking-foot.

CHAPTER 5

I took a very healthy sip of my drink, thinking furiously as I waited for Mordred to begin. He took his time, giving me a moment to process the situation.

He had planned this out to the letter. I had wandered in, dreading a boring social event where I would have to reassure the public that teens with GoPro video cameras and decent editing software were having a little fun at our expense, making us believe in monsters.

Mordred, on the other hand, had considered how to use the topic to his tactical advantage. He had turned it into an opportunity, while I had treated it like a chore.

Was that because... he knew what it was like to be a king? What it truly took? How to manipulate the various lords and ladies of his court to push forward his agenda? Because so far, it sure didn't feel like he had stumbled in, found a way to capitalize on the situation, and used momentum to coincidentally manipulate me.

No. This felt... well, classy. Suave. Debonair. Mordred was clever as shit. Smooth. He wasn't just playing *me*.

He'd played the announcer.

The Police.

The Regular audience.

The supernatural audience – the Freaks.

I felt that no matter what I did, I was simply walking down the path he had cleared for me, like a lamb led to slaughter. That he had meticulously considered every move or turn of events possible, and had a ready-made response to each, and that they all led to his ultimate success.

I'd never really been a humble guy. Neither was I – despite contrary rumor – ignorantly arrogant. I was proud, sure. But I also typically knew when I was being outclassed and had, so far in my life, been successful at reacting in a way that turned the tables in my favor. I used my arrogance like armor, letting people assume what I wanted them to assume, because in that way, I knew how they were likely to react, and how to lead them by the nose.

But Mordred… well, he knew nothing about me, as far as I knew. And I knew next to nothing about him, other than old stories found in T.H. White's *The Once and Future King*, or Sir Thomas Mallory's *Le Mort D'Arthur*.

But that hadn't mattered. He had focused on the solution, not the problem. Basically, it felt like he'd held me in the highest respects and planned accordingly. Like… what he would do if he was going up against himself.

He had set up multiple battle fronts to distract me, lining me up for the sucker punch.

This *Round Table Initiative*.

Did Mordred know about the Round Table at Chateau Falco? I shivered at the thought.

"In your experience with Temple Industries and now Grimm Tech," Mordred began in a clear, thoughtful tone, "I'm sure you learned quite a bit about hostile takeovers. How the media can fan the flames if they focus on inaccurate information or purposely-inflammatory news, making an initially peaceful discussion potentially hostile."

"Is that what you think is happening? A hostile takeover? From some YouTube videos?" I said carefully, frowning for effect. "I'm not usually one for conspiracy theories, and I left my tinfoil hat at home."

"Heavens, no! I want to *avoid* one! With all the talking points focusing on these videos, I see the potential for violence between the believers and the non-believers. I want to prevent that. The Round Table Initiative would be an open discussion to bridge the gap between both sides."

I nodded hesitantly. "You still haven't elaborated on that. Intentions are great, but what exactly are we talking about? Specifics make the wheel go 'round…" I said, taking another sip of my drink.

"I think the peoples' concerns need to be heard and addressed. On both sides of the issue. By a team of individuals who can objectively decide how best to move forward, after hearing both sides of the topic. Not just on these YouTube videos, but on all sorts of things. Public safety, discrimination, civilian rights..." he trailed off, waving a hand.

The crowd seemed to be holding their breath. I nodded in agreement, otherwise I would look like a callous billionaire. "I think everyone can agree on that, but it's the means I'm asking about."

Mordred nodded his agreement. "I greatly appreciate you leaving it up to me to mention that we've worked together in the past. You met me at a very dark point in my life, but you still reached out and helped pull me out of my own personal Hell. I wouldn't be here without you," he said meaningfully, and I felt my pulse climbing as the audience began to murmur amongst themselves. "But your humility to not mention it to them is truly admirable. Letting me stand on my own two feet, as it were. To win over the citizens of St. Louis on my own merit, rather than riding in on your coattails. You don't ask for thanks. You want others to stand for themselves. Make their own decisions. Never taking credit where credit is due. You are a clever one, Master Temple, and my Round Table Initiative could benefit from one such as you," he said, bowing his head and taking a sip of his drink.

I felt like I'd just taken three body blows. For anyone who knew who he *really* was – Mordred, not Moe R. Dredd – he'd just announced that we'd once been allies, that I'd busted him out of Hell and hadn't told anyone. And as a result, had just shot up my credibility with the supernatural families in town. If I'd been in league with him in the past, why was I against working with him now?

My chances of uniting the families was dying a slow death, and no one even knew it.

I nodded. "I think a man *should* stand on his own merits. Make his own mistakes and pay for the consequences of his past decisions. Even any... *unintended* consequences."

Mordred nodded seriously. "Exactly. Like you. I've seen old media reports about your past mistakes – no disrespect intended at all – and you've turned them all around, owning up to them." I had to bite my tongue to prevent myself from launching a fireball at him. But that was obviously part of his game. I couldn't physically react without putting the lie to my earlier statements about magic. "And look at you now! St. Louis' playboy is now known as the uncrowned King of St. Louis! That's quite a rebrand. This city adores you *for* your past flaws!" He shook his head in wonderment. "It takes a special kind of man to earn that admiration." Then he waved a hand, chuckling like everyone's favorite uncle. "Here I am, fangirling. You're no stranger to being a celebrity. And that could help my cause. Let you be the face, and I'll be the..." he flashed a grin at the audience, "wizard behind the curtains, so to speak."

Many in the audience chuckled at him bringing the conversation back to magic. But the Freaks in the crowd looked ready to bolt. "It sounds promising," I said, thinking. "Not to be blunt, but what do *you* bring to the table? Other than the idea, and money, of course."

Mordred nodded. "Fair question, and this is exactly why I need an enforcer like you." I gritted my teeth. He was subconsciously making everyone see me as a grunt, a brute – beneath him, even when I was questioning his authority. "You have resources, Temple. You're a billionaire, of course. I'm wealthy myself, thanks to favors owed to me, but *nothing* like you. And that's the crux of it. I bring *people* to the equation, Temple. *So. Many. People.* They understand my cause and are devoted to it with a passion that even *I* blink at. You could be our benefactor. Our public face."

He had just subtly threatened having an army. Disguised as volunteer philanthropists, but there was no arguing what he really meant.

"For example, I was considering calling your fiancée's mother for a position. Indie Rippley's mother..." Mordred – very casually – glanced directly at Callie in the audience, and I barely restrained from incinerating everything within a one-mile-radius to ashes.

My earbud suddenly crackled with urgent whispers from Gunnar, telling Tory to get Indie's mom to safety.

I realized I was just staring at him. Behind the façade of his eager smile, I saw the cool, calculating gaze of a King. And he'd just said *Checkmate*.

CHAPTER 6

I cleared my throat. "We are no longer engaged. Haven't been for quite some time, now…" I told him, not bothering to hide my anger.

Because all I saw was red. I was seriously considering throwing down with Mordred. Right here. Right now. Despite Indie's bad decisions in the past, bringing her innocent mother into the equation was unspeakably cruel. And it was a warning. He'd done his research on me.

And, now that I thought about it, I realized I hadn't checked up on Indie's mother. Did she even know her daughter was dead? I'd sprinted from one fight to the next, forgetting all about it. Not of my own choice, necessarily, but out of necessity. I'd spent the last few years only reacting.

And I was beginning to see the difference between Mordred and me.

He never had to react to anything. He anticipated and prevented bad outcomes. Even if I – and the King of Hell – saw him as evil, he was a better king than I was. At least, more competent.

But to bring her mother into this was beyond cruel. He was figuratively holding her hostage, and he was dangling her in front of my face, disguising it as generosity and goodwill for the crowd.

Mordred looked aghast. "Oh, dear. My apologies. My sources must be dated."

"Incorrect information can be a nightmare. That's what we're all here about, right?" I said, hoping to bring an end to the conversation and give the announcer a moment to take over again.

Mordred smirked, eyes flicking to Callie again. "Hard to stay in a committed relationship when you're so famous, I guess. Luckily, I've never been that popular."

I gripped the table with my fingers, on the verge of ripping it to shreds with my magic. In front of hundreds of cameras. "It was a mutual agreement. I'm just glad we realized it before we tied the knot. Because marriage vows are sacred, and I couldn't *imagine* breaking one apart. I mean the guilt alone would destroy me. There is a special place in Hell for those who betray it."

A not-so-subtle reference to his dalliance with Guinevere, his daddy's wife – when they'd played their own game of *sword in the stone* behind closed doors.

I noticed Tory stand, murmuring whispered apologies to those at her table, and then leaving. Mordred didn't miss a beat, but I swore I saw his eyes tighten for a millisecond at my comment. "I'm glad to hear there were no hard feelings between you two. Perhaps it's best if I don't call her. Bad blood can ruin a family."

I waved a hand, trying to conceal that it was shaking, but I knew Mordred noticed. "No bad blood, but she doesn't live near St. Louis."

Mordred nodded, still managing to look embarrassed for the audience.

Good god. He wasn't just stabbing me in the back. He was twisting the knife. Coming between me and Callie. But how did he even know about her? Why was he planting himself in my way? It had to mean he wanted something from me. And that couldn't be good, because that meant the Round Table.

In my silence, Mordred pressed the advantage. "And I'm proud to see you taking a solid stance on all this wizard confusion. Could get people hurt. Start a war between those who feel differently from others. Alienated. Isolated. Alone. We families," he enunciated the word, glancing out at the crowd, "need to stick together in times of crises. I think we can all agree there has been quite enough division these days. Which is why I find the Round Table Initiative so important."

"Why not leave it to the government?" I asked, trying to switch gears.

He sighed, shaking his head. "I fear – unfortunately – that this is beyond their ability to control." *They can't stop me,* I translated his words in my mind. "I once knew a homeless veteran who thought he was a wizard. Called himself Merlin, of all things. I helped him find a new vocation since his previous government had done him ill." He sighed sadly, lifting his glass in honor of Merlin before taking a sip.

I ignored his comment about his association with Merlin. "Are you implying this is the government's fault? Didn't you just make a sizable bribe to the police?" I asked, frowning.

"Donation," the announcer interrupted abruptly, the weaselly bastard. He had no problem helping out Mordred, which pretty much clarified he was on the take, too.

Mordred was shaking his head. "I think this requires a more grassroots movement. At least initially. The world is changing, and those who see themselves as different need a voice to represent them. To empower them. Give them the courage to make the Capital listen to them. That person could be you, Master Temple. My organization could use your talents. If you would consider working with us. I'd hate to be rivals. I wouldn't be here without your help, after all..."

"I think those in positions of power are listening pretty closely," I said. "As is the rest of the world. And they're not liking the developing situation. Not at all..." Mordred shrugged, a hopeful look on his face. "Perhaps we could discuss this in more detail in private," I said, begrudgingly. Because he was neutering me in this arena, and I knew when to throw in the towel.

"That would be amazing. Perhaps I can see your ancestral home I've heard so much about. Chateau Falco, is it not? Big houses can be Beasts on the maintenance expenses, I've found." He shook his head, chuckling. "My calendar is suddenly open tomorrow."

I shivered, gritting my teeth in a smile. Another trap. Inviting him to the one place in the world he wanted to go. Where I'd stashed the Round Table. "I'm not sure that will work. I'd have to—"

"Two days, then. I'm at your disposal. We can drink tea and discuss this like gentlemen. Maybe even bring some of your *family* friends who may be interested in hearing what I have to say." He turned to the audience, wiping figurative sweat from his brow. "I just earned an audience with the king!" he whispered theatrically.

They chuckled at him, but not at the moniker. More at his act. They were buying it hook, line, and sinker. Well, all but the stoic faces of the supernatural families interspersed in the audience. They looked like they trusted neither but wanted more information. Now.

Seeing he had backed me into a corner, with the whole world given the chance to see me as a heartless elitist who was hesitant to help a charity, I nodded. "It would be my pleasure," I said, smiling. "We can discuss cleaning up the streets of St. Louis while we're at it. I've seen reports of all sorts of hoodlums running around with delusions of grandeur, causing problems. Like these videos we were *supposed* to be discussing..." I shot him a faux stern look. "I think we've wasted enough of the taxpayers' dollars on our little chat—"

"Oh, this isn't on the taxpayers' dime," Mordred chuckled, waving a hand.

I blinked at him. Of course it was. It had been planned months ago, and no donation to the police would change that. Had I finally caught him in a mistake?

"I'm afraid I wrote a check to the city to cover tonight's event. On behalf of the Round Table Initiative. I wanted to... put my money where my mouth is, so to speak," he admitted. "I wouldn't have brought up the charity otherwise."

Wow. This guy was a political marvel. I nodded. "Well said."

The announcer piped up, interrupting me. "Before we wrap up, could you give us a soundbite on the Round Table Initiative, Mr. Dredd?"

"The Round Table initiative..." Mordred thought out loud, scratching at his cleanshaven chin. "Much like the fabled King Arthur brought a handful of uniquely different, but respectable, honorable men together, I aim to do much the same. Representatives from a handful of families that represent St. Louis, given equal voice so we can come together as one. I'm a hopeless romantic, you see. I always fancied myself a knight."

But I heard what was said in subtext. Pull the families – supernatural families – together under one banner. *His* banner. With me as his enforcer. His Black Knight.

The announcer pounced, sensing the approval of the crowd. "Would that make you King Arthur in this example?" he teased.

Mordred leaned forward, scratching his chin again. He glanced over at me, and I just knew he was roaring with laughter inside. "Why, yes. I guess it would..." he said distantly. "But don't worry, I'll be a benevolent king," he said with feigned pompousness. He glanced over at me abruptly.

"And look! I've already found my wise advisor, Merlin!" he said, pointing at me.

"If only Alaric Slate had been right... If magic was real, I might have been able to find a way through your clever schemes unscathed," I said, smiling good-naturedly.

"How is Alaric these days?" Mordred asked me conversationally. "He didn't look well last time I saw him. But he spoke very passionately about a mutual acquaintance before we parted ways."

I nodded, masking my anger. So that was how he'd learned about me. But who had Alaric mentioned? I'd hardly known the bastard. Had Mordred infiltrated the dragons?

I gritted my teeth in a fake smile. "He was down on his luck, unfortunately. Couple of bad business decisions he never learned from. I helped teach him that the definition of insanity is doing the same thing and expecting a different result. I think he took the lesson to heart."

Mordred flashed me a knowing smile, having the time of his life. "That is good advice. I'm glad I never play the same game twice. You're a wise one, Master Temple..." he cocked his head, "or I guess I should say *Merlin!*" He winked at the crowd. "I so look forward to our meeting in two days. I'll have you signing agreements before you even get to serving the tea," he promised. "I must warn you, despite my sad attempt at public discourse, I'm a mean negotiator behind closed doors," he smiled, shaking his fist at me, somehow managing to look weak and pathetic, and owning it entirely for the crowd.

"I've handled a few intense meetings before and always came out on top. But I think we can come to a mutual understanding. Like I did with Alaric. Now, I think everyone is ready to see the band and have some refreshments."

The announcer – the little shit – waited until Mordred nodded before asking the crowd for a round of applause. Mordred finished his drink and waited for the applause to die down before leaning into the microphone, looking over at me. "Don't forget our photo opportunity," Mordred smiled, pointing at one of the cameramen – who had indeed set up an area for us already. He even had a fake crown and a staff for props.

For King Arthur and Merlin.

Grinding my teeth in a smile, I noticed the Huntress standing in the crowd, shooting me a questioning look. "Say the word and he'll be drowning in blood," she whispered into my comms. "It won't look like an accident, but I'll make sure the cameraman gets a good... shot."

I shook my head discreetly. An assassination would only make everything worse.

I joined Mordred in front of the cameraman, ready to take a quick picture and then get as far away as possible. I remained very still, hoping the Huntress listened to my advice.

Which was why I wasn't paying attention when Mordred handed me the wizard's staff. He already had the fake crown on his head.

I politely declined and, without hesitation, he scooped up a second crown I hadn't noticed. He held it out for me and I heard the cameraman clicking behind me like a shotgun.

Getting a picture of Mordred handing me a crown.

A subtle message that he was in complete control, and this was his ultimate plan. To have me set up as a king under his rule.

Just like... I had done with all my friends.

It was... humbling. I hadn't considered how grating it would feel, but now I had a unique perspective on how my friends and allies must have initially felt. For a second time, I politely declined.

"Fine, spoilsport," Mordred chuckled. "We can just take a boring picture shaking hands," he said, rolling his eyes. He held out his hand, and I took it. Better than the alternative.

He pulled me in for a tight hug, surprisingly strong, and I could feel him chuckling. Then, he opened himself up, letting me feel the storm of power currently raging through him. I gasped into his shoulder, thankful that a cameraman hadn't gotten a picture of my face.

Or they would have thought I'd been stabbed.

I'd never – ever – felt someone so powerful. Not even the gods I knew. Not even Athena, the god I had killed. Mordred was practically vibrating with power. My teeth threatened to rattle from my gums.

In the heat of the discussion, I had entirely forgotten about the Nine Souls inhabiting his body, fueling him. Powering him up. In my ear, he whispered, "This was fun. I look forward to our next chat."

Then he released me and melted into the crowd. I noticed several men following him, obviously security, and they weren't about to let him out of their sight. Which would make abducting him all but impossible.

I immediately pulled my phone to my ear to pretend a phone call, but really, I tapped my jaw twice, opening up my comms.

"Get Callie out of here. Now!" I snarled on the open line. "Spill a drink on her dress. Whatever it takes."

"What? Why don't *you* do it?" Gunnar murmured. "That would look more natural."

"Just do it!" I hissed. "I'm a P.R. nightmare right now, and she's about to have a horde of reporters smothering her. Yahn, if you're close, be ready to make her disappear. I'll pretend to be looking for her, and act upset to hear that she left early."

Yahn confirmed he was close and would be on standby.

"You hear that, Callie?" I asked. But she didn't respond. I casually tried to look for her and my heart froze. Mordred was speaking with her.

CHAPTER 7

I continued pretending to talk into the phone, smiling as I passed Congressmen, police officers, and various other wealthy families from around town. I didn't see any of the supernatural family representatives. Either they were hiding from Mordred…

Or waiting for an opportunity to speak with him.

I was sure to keep Callie in my sights. Mordred was smiling as he spoke to her, gesturing animatedly with his hands. Callie simply nodded occasionally, not smiling, but not frowning.

"Gunnar?" I snarled nervously.

"On it. Shit. Are you seeing this—?"

"Yes, damnit. I *see!*" I snapped. Several guests glanced over at me quickly. I smiled through my teeth, waving a hand. Then I leaned away, speaking in a low tone. "I won't be upset if you accidentally slice his artery with a broken wine glass. In fact, I'll pay you ten million dollars cash and sneak you out of the country if you kill him. Right now."

Gunnar actually considered it. "I… can't," he finally said, and I saw him circling Callie, looking like he was about to burst out of his tailored suit. Even his stone eyepatch looked classy. Like a statement piece.

"I understand," I sighed.

"No, Nate," he urged. "I can't *shift*. He's wearing a Moonstone."

"Someone throw a fucking drink on Callie, NOW!" I growled, turning away from a pair of reporters that had spotted me and were making their way over.

I watched out of the corner of my eye as Gunnar seemed to trip, sending a platter of wine glasses at Callie. Mordred, as quick as a snake, was suddenly shielding her with his body, the wine splashing over his head and back.

And the reporters went wild, declaring him a hero as they snapped a billion pictures.

He looked up at the cameras, smiling, red wine dripping down his face like fresh blood. "I'm not a hero. Just doing what needs to be done. Any man would do the same for a Queen like you," he said, eyeing the ring hanging from a chain around her neck.

But the smile – in my opinion – was entirely calculated and cold. A message.

I continued watching from the corner of my eye, still pretending to speak on the phone, as if I had no idea Callie was near me. I saw Mordred turn to Callie, gripping her hand. I almost broke character, suddenly territorial and protective, but managed to maintain my ruse. I watched, raging, as Mordred kissed the back of her hand, bowing. "My lady."

She smiled politely, but I could tell she was seething inside. "Not in your wildest fantasies."

And Mordred abruptly flinched, his entire arm tensing suddenly. He blinked at her rapidly.

"Sorry. Old souls sometimes bite, even in captivity," she said, lifting up her thumb to glance down at the shadow ring, but careful to conceal it from the photographers. Then she let a slow smile creep over her face, locking eyes with Mordred. "Imagine that. I have nine other fingers... *Mr. Dredd.* Maybe I'll have the complete set, soon..."

His eyes grew entirely too interested, all of a sudden. "That would be a shame..."

The Huntress abruptly stumbled between them, snapping one of her heels in the process, and spilling a tray full of red wine glasses all over Callie's dress. Callie squawked indignantly, instantly demanding to speak to a manager and demanding fresh towels.

Yahn appeared as if summoned, thankfully wearing a suit similar enough to the waiters so as not to cause confusion. He kept his features serious as he apologized profusely to Callie. Then he rounded on the

Huntress, his eyes cold. "Put up your tray. You're finished for the night. I'll have someone else clean up your mess." The Huntress lowered her chin, looking about to cry as she backed away in silence. Yahn turned to guide Callie from the mess, resuming his apologies.

"Got her," he murmured into the comms.

"I'm going to kill that son of a bitch," Callie snarled, also on the comms.

"No, you're going to get the hell out of here and back to Kansas City. He knows who you are, now, and he's fucking powerful," I argued.

Rather than make a scene, they both murmured a vague agreement, and that we would discuss it later. I lowered my phone, tucking it into a pocket, ready to spend a few minutes appearing to look for Callie. I waited a moment to look towards where she had been, standing up on my tiptoes.

To see Mordred smiling at me. He mimed pointing a gun and pulling the trigger. Then he dipped his head as if to say, *your move.*

I smiled back.

Only one of the smiles was genuine.

Guess which one.

Callie actually called my phone a moment later. I shut down my comms before answering, and then I began speaking loud enough for all to hear about how upset I was that she'd suffered a clumsy waitress, ruining her new dress.

"You need to shut this bitch down," she snarled, ignoring my tirade entirely. "We Shadow Walked back to Chateau Falco, but you have a meeting before you can come home."

I blinked, frowning. "A meeting? With who?"

"A member of the Chancery. I talked to her by the bar and convinced her to meet with you. You're to meet at her house in one hour. I'll text you the address."

"You got all that from someone you just met?" I asked incredulously.

"She liked my ring, and I can be very persuasive when I want something," Callie said suggestively. I cleared my throat pointedly, which only made her laugh softly. "And Nate?"

"Yes?" I answered her, already considering my talking points. This was huge. A chance to talk to the Chancery – the Fae who had been banished to Earth for some unknown reason, and had formed their own club, of sorts – had been beyond my abilities so far.

"You need to do whatever you can to convince her you mean well.

Mordred is extremely powerful, and I get the feeling from our brief conversation that he's been working on this plan for quite some time. He may already have some of the Families in his pocket. And you're going to need all the help you can get."

"Thank you, Callie. But you need to promise me you won't get involved with this."

Callie grunted. "I've got the king of Fallen Angels breathing down my neck, so I'll be busy. But you better call if you do need help. This... is going to get messy, Nate."

"I'm the king of messy. Some even call me a hot mess," I told her.

Despite the severity of the conversation, she laughed. And I hadn't realized how badly I needed to hear it. "Stay safe, Nate. And don't waste my favor. Impress them. Eat crow. Bite down on your humility."

I frowned. "That's very specific advice. Like you know exactly what I'm facing for this meeting with her..."

Callie sighed. "You're not going to like it..."

"Spill," I muttered.

She did, and I just stared at nothing for a few seconds, trying to translate what she had said into something that vaguely resembled words I could comprehend. Then...

I began to laugh. Hard.

"Nate, this is serious. I think it's a... test. For you, specifically. She knows you're arrogant, so this is your chance to show her a different side of you."

I nodded, still shaking my head. "I can do this. But I *have* to invite Carl. He might literally kill me if I don't. He will take it more seriously than anyone. He can be my totem to help me get through it alive."

"That's probably fine. Just don't bring an army. Four total, including you. Just a tip, but probably your least arrogant friends... But those still able to hold their own in a fire-fight."

I grunted. "That is a very short list. But I'll take care of it. One hour, you said?"

"Yes. And be careful, Nate. I don't think Mordred is playing the same game as you."

I sighed. "I was on stage. I noticed."

She hung up, and I spoke into the comms, informing everyone it was time to roll out. Because I'm an asshole, I didn't tell them exactly what our meeting was, but that it was incredibly dangerous.

I couldn't let anyone see me leaving, so I pretended to head towards the restrooms. I slipped into a side hallway, and once confident I hadn't been followed, I Shadow Walked into the parking lot to meet up with my crew, but my breath left me as I stared at the gleaming SUV.

No matter how many times I saw it, I always wanted to stop and cackle maniacally.

The Knight XV had been inspired by military vehicles but married together with the luxury interiors of high-end SUV's like the Mercedes G-Wagon. It was breathtaking – both inside and out – and clocked in at over seven *tons*. It had floodlights, night vision cameras, run-flat tires, and really, anything else you might ever consider needing during the apocalypse.

Unlike most armored vehicles – which were upgraded after the fact – the Knight was *born* armored, lovingly handcrafted from the axles up with protection in mind. Since all my friends were monsters with claws, fangs, and magic, and were typically hard on vehicles – what with all the fighting, running, fleeing, and wars – I'd deemed it a necessary investment.

So... I'd bought ten of the hundred they had made.

As a belated wedding gift, I had given one to Ashley and Gunnar. The other nine were in my personal convoy – safely locked away in an undisclosed location – so we were driving Ashley's car.

If they ever had pups, Ashley would be – by far – the coolest, scariest mom in the universe.

Alucard rolled down the passenger window, laughing at the smile on my face. "You're drooling, man."

I shrugged. "I can't help it," I admitted. Talon rolled down the back window, scanning the parking lot for witnesses. Since, you know, he was a bipedal cat warrior. I saw Carl stealthily peering over Talon's shoulder like a creep, thinking I couldn't see him. "How were they?" I asked Talon, ignoring Carl.

"Alu-Carl behaved appropriately, but I did have to break them up a few times."

I ignored Alucard and Carl's sudden vehement protests over the new nickname we had given them – like *Brangelina* for Brad Pitt and Angelina Jolie. I nodded knowingly at Talon. "Cards Against Humanity again?" I asked.

Talon nodded. Alucard rolled up his window, sensing he was going to get no sympathy from me.

I'd kept these three out in the parking lot to watch over the car – not that it needed it – because with all the negative attention I was earning, a car bomb wasn't out of the realm of possibility. Or a tracking device of some kind.

And Alucard hadn't been very open with me about his recent travels – both to Italy and the East Coast – so he was on my shit list until he spilled the beans. I already knew the gist of it, that he'd run into enough trouble to require assistance from Gunnar and his entire pack of werewolves.

But Gunnar had shrugged it off, saying it had been wrapped up in less than an hour, and it wasn't anything to get worked up about.

What I had wanted to learn was *why* it had been necessary to move an entire army of wolves to upstate New York so suddenly. What, exactly, had Alucard done to necessitate that? And did it have anything to do with stories of a forest of trees suddenly appearing on the Brooklyn Bridge not hours later. I trusted Alucard with my life – no question – but I also didn't like him holding back information, so I was punishing him like a child.

Carl, for obvious reasons, couldn't go into a room full of humans. He was a very strange, giant, lizard-man. An Elder. Even if it had been an event for Freaks, they would have all run screaming from the building upon seeing an Elder walking around. The supernatural community had a long memory, and Carl's entire race had been banished from Earth, long ago.

Talon didn't have a human form either, and I hadn't felt like taking a pet cat – his other form – with me into the speech.

So, I'd put Talon in charge of Alu-Carl, knowing they would kill each other if left unsupervised.

To teach Carl social cues, we'd tried explaining what was acceptable in casual conversations. It had been a long, uphill battle, and ultimately, an epic failure. We were now trying a different tactic, resorting to playing Cards Against Humanity with him, in hopes that he might pick up on what was definitely *not ever* socially acceptable.

This usually resulted in fights and arguments when we had to explain why it was not okay for Hitler to be voted best preschool teacher, or any number of other bizarre, twisted outcomes that popped up on the cards during a typical game. Alucard had a very short level of patience with Carl.

Carl, on the other hand, had more patience than anyone I had ever met. Meaning he didn't understand when others were getting well beyond *their* tolerance levels.

Carl still seemed to think the game was about how to overthrow humanity and was desperate to decipher the clues from the horrendous black and white cards.

So, yeah. Talon was supervising them during the speech. My cat in charge of two adult men.

I really needed to find a stable friend, one to keep us all in line. Because together, we were one big hot mess of a family.

My earbud kicked on and I glanced over my shoulder to see Gunnar striding our way from across the parking lot. "We're clear," he said. "The rest will leave in small groups so as not to attract undue attention." I nodded back to him, turning back to the vehicle.

"Want to drive?" I asked Gunnar.

"Nah. Go ahead. I need to think. Keep an eye out."

Alucard rolled down his window as he snorted into the comms, but he didn't actually *say* anything about the one-eyed werewolf being our lookout.

"Shut it, *Alu-Carl*," Gunnar muttered, shutting him up. "You're grounded, remember? No secret meeting for you. Nate's even letting *Carl* go," he teased.

Alucard stared at me in disbelief. I nodded. "Unless you're ready to finally spill…" I asked.

Alucard grumbled unhappily, rolling his window back up. I shrugged, walking over to the driver's seat. We had a meeting with a fairy. I had no idea what to think of the Chancery, but since they were Fae, and most of the Fae I had met either hated or feared me, I expected it to be an after party of tonight's shit show.

But with Mordred pulling strings in the background of St. Louis, I wondered if I wasn't walking into another ambush like this speech had been.

CHAPTER 8

Two days. I had two days until Mordred was meeting me at Chateau Falco.

It concerned me that he'd implied he knew about the Beast powering the house and hadn't seemed the slightest bit worried. What allies or acquaintances of Alaric Slate had he talked to? Someone who obviously knew quite a bit about me. But had they helped Mordred willingly, or had he put them over a barrel, forcing them to serve him?

I wasn't in denial. I had plenty of people who had been waiting for this day – a day where they finally had an ally who might be strong enough to take me down. Mordred walking in, seemingly hell-bent on wrangling me into his posse was like a dream come true for my enemies.

And now, more than ever, I needed allies. Because if I didn't get them, Mordred would.

So, humility was in order. But I wasn't going down with that ship alone. Oh, no. That's what I had minions for. And Alucard – the lucky bastard – wasn't invited.

I settled a heavy glare on Gunnar's single eye, ignoring the quartz-like stone eyepatch that was fused into his other eye socket. "Straighten your tiara. You look positively ridiculous, Princess Padfoot."

He opened his mouth to fire back but thought better of it after a quick glance to my right. At the cute, deadly child sitting beside me. Instead, he straightened his tiara with a discreet murderous glare aimed my way, silently promising me I would pay for this.

"More tea?" the cherubic voice of the young child filled the room like a blast of winter air on a snowy day. She had thankfully ignored our exchange. But I would bet my life she had noticed every detail. She was a beautiful blonde-haired girl, tall and lanky, with big blue eyes. And despite her youthful age, I could already sense a deep reservoir of power inside her.

"Please, my Lady," I said, readjusting the plastic bangles on my wrist – all of them were bright pinks, golds, and purples, and all liberally doused with glitter that I would never – ever – be able to wash off. I had about a dozen of them on each wrist.

They felt like shackles as I extended my shot-glass-sized empty plastic teacup. She topped it off with more of the imaginary tea, and I pretended to sip it, maintaining character.

Carl – an albino, humanoid, lizard warrior – held up a small compact mirror, inspecting his pale, scaled face, which was comically painted with bright purple uneven blotches over his cheeks and ruby red lipstick splashed over his thin lizard lips.

Elders were considered so dangerous and feared that hardly anyone would tell me anything helpful about them. I knew tidbits about him, like not to ever try to manipulate his mind with magic unless I wanted to see what eternal insanity felt like.

I had brought him down to Hell with me. And in those fiery pits of despair, suffering, anguish, and horror, I'd heard Carl sing for the first time. A *Sound of Music* jingle.

As he slaughtered dozens of monsters' intent upon killing us.

He'd also casually shown me that he could tap into my magic, repurposing it to his will. But right now?

The notoriously deadly Elder was having the fucking time of his life. At our tea party with a dangerous child whom we needed to impress in order to get an audience with her mother – a member of the Chancery. I'd spent some time trying to figure out who the group was, and what their intentions were. All I'd learned was that they were the outcast Fae in our world, those not welcome back home in that savage, brutal paradise they called the Land of the Fae.

I was pretty sure Carl was smiling as he closed the compact mirror with a sigh, sliding his plastic teacup across the table for a refill. The child obliged, and Carl turned to the stuffed unicorn sitting at the table beside him, striking up a serious conversation about high heels.

I was equally sure those were bloodstains on the stuffed animal's neck. I shivered, pointedly ignoring that fun fact. Maybe it was just red makeup...

Gunnar muttered something under his breath, folding his thick, beefy arms. The motion almost knocked over our table – since it was barely tall enough for us to fit our thighs under – and I hissed suddenly, shoulders tensing and tiny stool of a plastic chair wobbling as I risked a peripheral glance at the small child beside me.

She was staring at Gunnar now – with disappointment.

Which might just mean his immediate execution, no matter how big and tough he was. No matter how big and tough any of us were. Because this little child was very powerful. I didn't know exactly what kind of powers she had, but she had them in spades.

I held my breath, waiting to see how unstable she was. She cleared her throat, setting down her teapot and meticulously folding her hands atop one another on the table as she regarded Gunnar.

"Now, Princess Padfoot, that wasn't very ladylike, was it?" she said with all the empathy of a firing squad.

Carl was openly scowling at Gunnar, sniffing disdainfully.

"I'm sure it was an accident, my Lady," I offered in a very neutral tone, since that was the only name we had been given. We, on the other hand, had been given Princess names, and we were in her Royal Court. Beneath her station and properly grateful for the audience, of course. "His depth perception is not what it once was. Right, Princess Padfoot?" I asked in a warning tone, glaring at the big, bad Werewolf.

He nodded very slowly before flashing a believably embarrassed frown at the child. "Of course, my Lady. It will not happen again."

"On that," she said, leaning over the table like a creeping shadow in a dark alley, "you are correct, Princess Padfoot." And there was absolutely no chance of mistaking the threat.

The *promise*.

The ensuing silence threatened to smother me.

Ding! I almost soiled my pants at the alien noise, only to realize a second later that it was from the fake oven in the other room.

The child leaned back carefully, but excitedly. "Oh! That will be the crumpets. Please excuse me, Princesses. And do behave in my absence,"

41

she said, somehow managing to make the comment into a veritable threat.

Murmurs of agreement went around the small table, and I risked a glance at Talon.

Well, he was actually in his cat form – a giant Maine Coon – rather than his bipedal warrior form. So technically, he was Sir Muffle Paws at the moment. He was lounging in a plush, glittering kitty throne. But his tail whipped back and forth like a metronome, flared out to the max, especially when the child sauntered out of view.

The tutu around his waist even quivered at his agitation.

"What – *the fuck* – are we doing here, Nate? I don't do tea parties. I'd rather slice her into pieces and play with her vertebrae. I'll gladly switch places with Alucard. No one would even know." His tiara almost fell from his head, and even though he was in his mundane cat form, he managed to straighten it before it could fall, making his threat sound laughable.

Carl frowned, shaking his head. "Nate said the Daywalker is grounded. No crumpets for him."

I glanced over my shoulder to make sure the child was still out of sight, and then I turned back to Talon. "If any of you Neanderthals ruin this for me, I will personally torture and maim you. To get an audience with her mother, we need to give this girl the fucking tea party of the century. So, drink your goddamned tea, fix your fake eyelashes, and smile."

"Fucking tea parties," Gunnar muttered, adjusting the aforementioned eyelashes.

"*Ex-nay* on the *ucking-fay*," I snarled in an urgent whisper.

The silence of my pals made it very obvious that our hostess had returned. Also, the sound of her plastic tray of plastic pastries hitting the floor was a good indicator.

I whirled to see the child panting as she glared at me. "Did someone say... *Fae?*" she hissed.

"Oh, bother," Talon purred in a low, sarcastic tone, his claws digging into the cushioned throne, popping off a few of the sequins. "And I was just getting into character..."

CHAPTER 9

*T*he child was practically hyperventilating, her cheeks flushed. Her hair slowly began to rise, as if she was standing too close to an electric fence. "They took *everything* from us. Our *home!* I *hate* them." Then she slowly lifted her dainty hand, pointing it at my face.

"Now, look…" I began, holding up my hands in a calming gesture. "We weren't talking about—"

"I can't believe you would be so rude," Carl hissed, glaring from Gunnar to me. He had his legs crossed and was still holding his teacup with two claws, his pinky claw extended. I shot him a quick scowl before turning back to the angry, powerful child before us.

I desperately reached out to Wylde, that other part of me that had a deep understanding of Fae magic. We weren't two people, but you could say I had a split personality. My parents had birthed and raised me in Fae, naming me Wylde. I lived there into my teens, gaining a mastery over Fae magic. But then my parents had used some nifty – and highly illegal – artifacts to fuck around with time, so that when they brought me back to the real world here in St. Louis, I was given the chance – unknowingly – to relive my childhood here, on Earth, as Nate.

With no knowledge of already being raised once in Fae.

Talk about keeping secrets.

So, although I had only seemed to scratch the surface in relearning my

Fae gifts, this entire other part of me had recently been revealed – a savage, ruthless, cunning form of myself that thought, acted, and lived like the Fae. Amoral was one way to think of it.

Sociopathic was also accurate.

But since I didn't know what kind of juice this little child could deliver, I wanted a way to squash her temper tantrum without harming her – and pissing off her mother.

Because the whole point of this fiasco was to earn an audience with mommy dearest. So that I could gain her alliance, possibly learn more about the Chancery, and maybe even gather some much-needed information about Mordred.

I had almost overlooked the fact that Mordred's mother was Morgause – a legendary enchantress with ties to the Fae. At least according to a few books I'd read. Maybe the Fae would know a weakness I could exploit.

I carefully lifted my own hands, ready to defend myself, hoping I could use some Grammarie to nullify her attack. Grammarie was the art of making things *be*, as opposed to Glamourie, which was the art of making things *seem*. And right now, I was hoping that Grammarie could also make an attack... well, *un-be*.

But that other part of me must have been napping, because I didn't have the faintest idea where to begin. Sometimes I just knew how to do something really cool with my Fae magic, or that other part of me would kind of guide my hands into doing something like a gentle nudge to the elbow.

But other times, neither of those things happened. Like now. I ended up just kind of facing her with my arms up in an impotent gesture of *don't shoot!*

She flung her hand at me, and an orb of green light sailed right at my face. I had a moment to realize that it looked like she had thrown a pissed-off, neon-green octopus at me. But before I could even react, it fizzled into nothing, and I heard a woman politely clear her throat.

The child spun, face both stunned and horrified. You know the look.

Mommy had just caught her with her hand in the cookie jar.

Or, you know, trying to murder her Royal Court of tea party princesses.

"Mommy, I'm sorry. I was—"

"Enough, Alice. I think you need to go to your room. Think about what you did wrong."

I stored that name away, since it was the first one I had heard here. The mother had answered the door, assessed us from head to toe, and then handed us over to her daughter until she 'had time for us.'

Alice glanced over her shoulder, eyes smoldering as she considered Gunnar and me. But she curtsied to Talon and Carl before stomping out of the room. She slammed her foot down on the plastic tray of pastries and it turned to dust, instantly replaced by fresh offshoots of grass.

Her mother *tsked*. "We will discuss the punishment for breaking your toys this evening. Perhaps a night in the mountains would help cool your temper."

I shared a look with Gunnar. *A night in the mountains?* If that punishment had been on my parents' list when I was a child, I would have become a hermit.

"Whatever…" I heard Alice clearly mutter under her breath.

A new voice suddenly boomed through the room. "Is that how you talk to your mother?" The child froze in mid-stride, whirling to stare at her mother in horror. I frowned, wondering why it sounded familiar, and where the third party was hiding.

Then I saw it. Her mother was holding her cell phone facing the child. She was… Facetiming this? But why had the voice sounded familiar?

The child curtsied so low that I thought she was about to sit down on the ground. She kept her eyes downcast as she meekly replied. "No, Baba."

I blinked. Baba… No way. I burst out laughing. "Mother-loving Baba *Yaga*?!" I hooted. "How in the world do you know—"

I cut off as all three females turned to face me. The child, the mother, and the matron on the phone. Thinking of it in that context – with titles rather than names – made something in the back of my mind start whimpering. I knew these women weren't one of the mythical three-faced goddesses, but…

Boy, oh boy, did it feel like it at that moment. Oddly enough, they all had the exact same look on their faces. They didn't speak, but my sphincter puckered as if they had shouted. Just a little.

"Sorry. I'm new at this whole princess thing," I admitted.

"Leave us, *child*," Baba said in a cool tone.

"Yes, Baba. Thank you, Baba. I'll do better, Baba." Alice curtsied again, and then sprinted out of sight and up the creaky wooden stairs. I heard a door slam before the mother and Baba turned back to us.

I scratched my lip suspiciously as I studied each face. The two women were stoic, no emotions at all. *Too* composed... I finally grunted, tearing the bangles off my wrist and flinging them casually at Carl, who caught them with a hiss of outrage, as if I'd been throwing out real treasures. "We've been had, Princesses," I told my squad of tutu-and-tiara-clad Man-Princesses. "You can probably thank Baba for that," I added, glancing over my shoulder at the woman on the phone.

In unison, Baba and the mother burst out laughing – literally hooting and giggling uproariously. I scowled at the phone, wiping at my cheeks with my sleeve to get rid of some of the makeup.

"I do not understand," Carl murmured to Gunnar. "Aren't pranks usually unpleasant trickeries? But this was lovely."

I heard Gunnar sigh, trying to explain it to Carl, but I kept my eyes locked on the phone, waiting for an explanation.

"That's for not being smart enough to ask *me* for a meeting with the Chancery. And for making me babysit the Knight several months ago."

I growled. "Don't worry, I wouldn't ask you again. You fell asleep on the job."

She hissed so loud that the phone squealed with static. Talon, of course, instinctively reacted to the feral sound, his back arching up, hair sticking straight out, and hopping sideways three times.

Carl and Gunnar both burst out laughing, ignoring Talon as he redirected his hiss at them. He shifted into his bipedal form, a five-foot-tall Thundercat, complete with a veritable beard, and whiskers that trailed down his cheeks. His eyes glowed with a metallic shine as he continued to stare down my friends.

"Surely, there was a better way to handle this," I said. "I didn't do anything to you. My relative did. And look, sleeping beauty is now awake. Like magic."

The mother spoke, cutting off Baba's retort. "We also wanted to see how you would react to humility. Kings can be arrogant. And newly-minted kings even more so."

"You obviously haven't seen my *princess* side," I said with a faint smile. The two smiled back ever so slightly. "Okay, egos aside, you can consider me humbled."

"If you will follow me," the mother said, before turning her back and walking from the room.

I followed her, taking off my tutu and tossing it on the chair. Baba was still talking to the mother. "If that child gets any more uppity, you'll need to send her back to me for a sleepover. It seems she has forgotten her lessons on respecting her elders. And my house is such a wonderful place to learn valuable life lessons..." I shivered at the thought. Baba Yaga was a very powerful and dangerous witch. And her house was technically her Familiar, able to walk around and be her muscle.

When it wasn't walking around as a house on chicken legs, that is.

The mother nodded. "I'll arrange it soon. For now, I can only thank you for this..." she glanced over her shoulder casually, a faint smirk on her perfect cheeks, "experience. But I must go and attend to my guests. You know how princesses can get if they are ignored for too long."

I ignored their laughing goodbyes, imagining all the ways I would get back at Baba Yaga.

CHAPTER 10

*W*e settled in a formal sitting room across the hall from the front door of her home. The three-story house had looked modest and cute from the outside, but inside it felt like a lovingly-maintained museum, complete with priceless artifacts and quality, refurbished leather furniture. It smelled of fresh-cut wood and mint leaves, and I knew it wasn't from any household cleaning solution. No, it was raw and pure, as if the home was freshly built from the healthiest trees from the deepest parts of the forest. Because Fae lived here, and beauty, quality, and the *au natural* factor were big to them.

We were also near Frontenac, a notoriously wealthy part of St. Louis, so no bum neighbors with totaled Pontiacs in the front lawns to be concerned about. I had left my satchel in the SUV with Alucard, but Talon and I had each brought our spears with us to the Fae mother's house, depositing them in the umbrella stand by the front door. I had wanted the mother to see us willfully hand our weapons into her care, a gesture of respect. Then, Talon had promptly shifted into his feline form, a large Maine Coon, another gesture for the mother.

Silently telling her that we felt safe in her home and meant no harm. Even leaving them out of our sight for the tea party had been a calculated and added gesture of trust on our parts.

Then again, we'd brought along a Carl, so maybe inviting an Elder had nullified the rest.

My eyes tracked to the umbrella stand, verifying the spears were still safe. They appeared to have been untouched. The black spear Pandora had sneakily gifted me from the Armory seemed to absorb the darkness, amplifying it somehow. The two-foot long blade on the end was a black-matte spear tip – but shaped like a cross between a sword and an axe, and in the center was a ruby the size of a goose egg. The ruby wasn't currently pulsing with light like it sometimes did, but if you looked closely enough, you could notice that it wasn't all that natural either. One would catch random flickers and pulses of light – as if reflecting a ray of sunlight, even when no sun was hitting it.

It looked like a weapon inspired by a feather from my unicorn. Black with a red orb at the tip. It even had two of Grimm's feathers hanging from the hilt of the blade, although I hadn't found out why or how. Grimm had said *I didn't do it.* But my unicorn was a habitual liar, so…

Talon's white spear – almost an exact duplicate of mine in style – seemed too bright, and was angled the opposite direction, as if the two spears were repelling each other, hanging out opposite sides of the stand. Other than color, the only real difference was that his didn't have a stone in the blade or feathers hanging from the braided hilt fixing the blade to the staff. Otherwise, they looked like siblings. Or as if made by the same blacksmith.

Talon's spear could be invisible, called up at will from thin air, but out of courtesy, he had placed it in the stand, too. We'd also agreed that attending a tea party with spears wasn't exactly very ladylike.

Carl's bone swords – about a dozen different daggers and blades – littered the base of the umbrella stand like a bone altar. I glanced away from them before I drew attention. I didn't want the mother to think I was considering bloodshed.

I didn't even know her name yet, after all.

She didn't seem particularly concerned to be so vastly outnumbered, which told me she was dangerous. If I was smart, this probably would have informed me that maybe *I* should be the one concerned about *her.* But willful arrogance is often the better part of valor. Or something like that.

She reached out to pour a decanter of wine into the five full-bodied glasses already set before us on the coffee table, so I held out a hand, forestalling her. That was pretty much rule number one with the Fae. Don't accept food, drink, or any type of gift.

She sighed, looking directly at me. "You're no fun. What's a little bondage and obligation between friends?"

I met her eyes, politely shaking my head. "We're not thirsty."

"I am thirsty," Carl said. "And she wouldn't dare attempt to obligate an Elder. Again."

I slowly turned to look at Carl. Again? What was he—

And that's when I noticed that the mother had grown very, very still, lowering her gaze to the floor. "Of course not," she said in an almost meek tone. I arched an eyebrow at Gunnar, but he looked just as startled as me. In fact, he looked as if he was seriously considering shifting before huffing and puffing and blowing the house down. I made a discreet gesture with my hand, wordlessly telling him to stand down.

"I think I would like to hear that story…" I said casually. Neither responded. Carl was utterly relaxed, as if witnessing an angry kitten. The mother was… tense as all hell, though.

"Perhaps another time…" Carl finally said, casually crossing his legs as he leaned back in his chair. I blinked at his feet. Where the hell had he found red-heeled, knee-high, pirate boots? And how had I not noticed them until now? "Everything shared here holds no bonds, nevermore," he continued. "Elder Carl says it is so."

The mother nodded hurriedly.

Gunnar let out a low whistle. "Well, *this* is awkward…"

Fucking Carl… He could subdue a dangerous Fae Lady with a few words? Whatever Carl had been subtly reminding her of was so unbelievably terrifying that she had been scared into obeying his demands. Interesting. It meant that he knew her, and he hadn't mentioned that to me. But… *how?* This woman would have to be very, *very* old to know Carl, because the Elders had been banished a long time ago…

The Mother turned to me. "My name is Alvara, and refreshments are freely given. No obligation of any sort. Consider this meeting between friends who have no need for chicanery. We will speak as close family. Words, wine, and wisdom shall flow freely." She hesitated. "As freely as possible, unless it broaches a topic that could bring danger upon any of us," she clarified.

"I can live with that," I agreed slowly. "And thank you."

Carl leaned forward, flicking out his tongue a few times over the wine decanter, tasting the air above it. Then he looked at her. "Sample it, my sweet." She didn't even take offense, immediately pouring a small taste into her glass and guzzling it down. Carl waited a few moments, studying her closely. Then he grunted. "Acceptable, but we will take new glasses. Your finest, Alvara. The ones locked away for family only. Not this rubbish."

"Didn't we already determine that we're acting as family?" I asked slowly, wondering if Carl was going to become a liability. I needed her as an ally, not an enemy.

"Exactly," Carl said, not looking at me, but staring straight at Alvara. "Which means we should drink from the glasses of *her* family."

"Of... course," Alvara said. Then she was walking over to her liquor cabinet in the corner of the room. She reached into a drawer, withdrew a key, and then inserted it into a lock on a nearby wardrobe of sorts. When it opened, I sucked in a breath. Bars of gold, piles of diamonds, priceless other gems, and precious metal statues filled the wardrobe.

And goblets and glasses and other dinnerware that had to be robbed from Renaissance Italy or Medieval Kingdoms filled two of the shelves. Talon narrowed his eyes, his tail twitching at all the twinkling reflections. I cleared my throat and he stiffened, pointedly turning away. There had to be dozens and dozens of goblets. All different styles, sizes, and from different eras.

Alvara stood there, her back to us, staring at them, waiting for something.

Carl pointed a long black claw. "Top shelf, third row, second from the back." She silently grabbed the specific glass, setting it down before her. "Bottom shelf, first row, first goblet..." and he continued pointing out random glasses and goblets, Alvara silently obeying his orders as if this wasn't her own house. When she had four, she turned to face us, and Carl nodded. "Serve us, if you please."

I cleared my throat uncomfortably. "Maybe we can cut the theatrics. We already agreed to be peaceful. Am I missing a massive sub-conversation somewhere? I'd hate for Alvara to feel slighted."

Carl leaned forward menacingly, sniffing the air and flicking out his tongue. His blotchy, fire-engine-red lips curled back to reveal long, inky black fangs. "Alvara *should* feel slighted. Alvara *should* thank me – down to her *bones* – that I don't make her strip down naked, slit her own wrists, and

51

then see if she can dance the *Ulukai* before she bleeds out..." he hissed, a fan of spikes around his neck slowly rising with a quivering rattle. Like a reptilian lion's mane.

Talon began to purr. "This is *much* more my speed..." he said, eyes lidded heavily as if preparing to take a nap. He leaned back into the couch, slowly sheathing and unsheathing his claws.

"My Queen *commanded* me to do as I did, Elder Carl, *knowing* that I would fail. Then she *banished* me here for that failure," she said, not apologetically, but with a touch of anger to her voice. Anger at how she had been played by her own Queen. Carl just stared at her. "I was... unable to decline my Queen's request, as much as I wished to do so. I apologize for what I did to Carlos and Carla—"

Carl's mouth opened wide in a roar of outrage I wasn't sure I had ever seen from him, and several spikes fucking shot out of his rattling mane to pepper the wall. One even tore into a priceless painting on the wall, and another shattered an antique vase

"Don't *ever* speak of my parents, you inflamed meat-sack, or I will consume your child with a song so sweet it will rot your soul and obliterate your mind." Then he began a very soft – almost inaudible – hum.

She squeaked in sheer horror, curtsying immediately. Carl trailed off his song, and my ears seemed to pop as he did so. Talon had curled in on himself, his hair sticking straight up, and had his paws clamped over his ears. Gunnar looked like he had been struck between the eyes.

Well, not technically between his *eyes*, plural. Maybe like he had been flicked in the balls.

I shook off the sensation and cleared my throat, holding up my hands. "Obviously, you two have a past. Something we can maybe put on a shelf for later?"

For her to know Carl's parents proved how old she was. But to learn that their names were Carlos and Carla made me very uneasy. I had chosen Carl's name at random soon after meeting him, and he'd accepted it without issue. Was that some kind of intuition on my part? To pick a name so close to his parents? I'd have to ask him about it later.

"I *was* being polite," Carl argued. "I didn't sing her into the eternal sleep and then ride her bleached bones into oblivion."

CHAPTER 11

alon coughed violently, and then began hacking up a monstrous hairball. I kicked his chair and he cut off with a final hack into his elbow, attempting to be polite.

"Right, no riding her bones into oblivion," I said, then winced at the words. Jesus.

"Pour, woman," Carl intoned, setting his plastic teacup from our princess party on the table for her to fill up, only just now bringing to my attention that he'd only asked Alvara to grab four glasses. Because he'd obviously planned to use the teacup. "I will think on your words…"

That was apparently good enough for Alvara. She dipped her head gratefully, and then filled our glasses, seating herself only after Carl gave her a satisfied nod. She let out a slow breath as she slid into her chair, folding her hands in her lap.

"If I may be so bold…" Alvara asked, not meeting our eyes directly, but flicking them first in Carl's direction, and then mine.

I nodded. She needed us to give her something after that mental abuse. Carl nodded curtly, lapping up his wine with his tongue, staring at Alvara with his unblinking eyes over the rim of his pink teacup.

She hesitated. "No disrespect intended to anyone present, but Elder… Carl speaks very openly for one of your subjects. I had been led to believe that *you* were the one to fear. Not that you aren't frightening in your own right, but I hadn't anticipated your allies being so outspoken."

"Wylde's mother taught me the secret of the D. I have made a new Gateway into our realm and intend to bring my people back into this world, under Master Wylde's dominion. He values my service."

Alvara dropped her glass, spilling wine all over Talon's ankles. He hissed instinctively as the mother stared dumbfounded into the middle distance between us, mouth opening and closing wordlessly.

Talon set her glass back onto the table – since it hadn't broken – and then lifted up his leg straight into the air, perpendicular to the ground – an acrobatic feat only felines could do – and began licking the wine from his fur. Gunnar grimaced in distaste, especially since Talon's mooseknuckle was pointed directly at him.

I noticed all this absently, because I was also staring at Carl. "I wasn't aware of all that, Carl. The tree you grew is a Gateway?" Another damned doorway into some dangerous world on my property. Come on!

Carl nodded proudly. "Your mother is truly a master of the D, as you call it here. We also refer to the trees as Elder Portals. My people will serve you, King Wylde, Master Temple. Or they will bathe in an ocean of blood. You will be pleased with me."

I nodded to him, not knowing what else to do with Alvara watching. Then I turned to face her, thinking. I had no ties to the Chancery, knew next to nothing about them, and most of those in the Land of the Fae hated or feared me. Perhaps the banished Fae were different... To gain her trust, I needed to give her something, an olive branch. "Do you know of my... experience in Fae?" I asked her.

She nodded. "Everyone knows about Wylde, the Manling born in Fae. All fear you, and most hate you. No disrespect intended, but your attack on the Queens caused quite the uproar."

I grimaced. "Attack on the Queens..." I growled, taking a sip of my wine to calm down. "*They* attacked *me*. Demanded my servitude. I responded in kind."

She considered that, looking startled. "Oh."

"And not all hate or fear me," I said, brandishing the silver butterfly Barbie had given to me after our last... encounter. When she had given me the lap dance of all lap dances. I was pretty sure she hadn't meant it that way, or not *just* that way. It had been some form of respect, ritualistic, a symbolic act of some kind. And before she had left, after she had mentioned Callie with a sad smile, she had placed this silver butterfly on the ground.

The mother stared at it curiously, her eyes growing distant. "That is... very important. Although I don't know how. I can sense the power vibrating inside of it. She must love you dearly."

I studied her. "Romantic love?"

She considered that for a moment before shrugging. "There are many forms of love. Only she can tell you what she meant by it. I can merely sense the passion behind its creation."

I nodded, studying the butterfly before putting it back into my pocket. "Hopefully, this proves I am not a natural enemy to the Fae. Those who go against me, yes, but I'm not inherently an enemy. Some humans are dicks. Some Fae are dicks. I stand up to dicks, on principle." Gunnar coughed. "You know what I mean," I muttered.

Talon had finished cleaning himself, and seemed to be dozing on the couch, not bothering to drink his wine, but judging by his swiveling ears, he was aware of every word. I listened to the sounds of Alice running around upstairs, laughing as she played with her toys, and I found that I was smiling.

It was good background noise.

"So, was the tea party really Baba Yaga's idea?" I asked, smiling faintly, thinking of anything to bring some levity into the strained conversation.

She smiled. "When Callie Penrose asked me to meet with you tonight, I remembered a conversation I had with Baba a few months ago. I'd asked her about you, if you were as cruel as we all thought..." she said in a soft, wary tone.

Gunnar leaned forward. "What did she say?"

"She told me if I wanted to see what you were truly like, to put you in front of a child that I cared for and watch how you responded." She met my eyes meaningfully. "I thought Baba had been warning me. She doesn't often talk about her work associates, and I knew she had at one point been tasked with killing you, but afterwards had begun *working* for you. I assumed the worst, naturally. That you had subjugated her..."

I nodded slowly, not offering a comment.

"But after the speech tonight, seeing Mordred alive and in the flesh... I realized that perhaps we needed someone as scary as you to defeat him," she admitted. "Still, I remembered Baba's response. Her warning." She lowered her gaze, embarrassed. "I was about to decline Callie's request, but I hadn't counted on her being quite so... convincing." Alvara looked up at me, then, smiling distantly. "She cares about you quite deeply. As much as I've ever seen a powerful woman care for a powerful man. You should consider yourself very lucky."

I smiled. "I do, but don't put the cart before the horse. We aren't..." I searched for the right way to say it. "We're just very good friends."

She arched a brow at me. "Then you, Nate Temple, are an idiot."

Gunnar burst out laughing, lifting his glass to salute Alvara. She dipped her chin primly, but she did clink glasses with him. I sighed, staring into my cup. "You have no idea, Alvara..." I agreed.

She gave me a satisfied nod. "Callie Penrose convinced me with one simple phrase. *Character is who you are in the dark, when no one is watching.*" I nodded slowly. That sounded like Callie. Alvara met my eyes, making sure she had my attention. "Then she told me that if I had any doubts about your character, to put you in a room with my child, with no one watching."

Talon's eyes popped open in disbelief, and even Carl looked properly surprised. Gunnar grunted in approval. I could only stare. Why hadn't Callie told me any of this?

Alvara cleared her throat. "Having two very powerful, very different women say the same thing made me reconsider Baba Yaga's comment about you. That perhaps she hadn't been *warning* me but trying to tell me the same thing that Callie told me tonight. That your character was best seen in your simpler interactions, not in the rumors spread about you. To look at how you treated those with *less* power than yourself. To judge you – not by how you treated your *enemies*, but how you treated everyone *else*. So... I agreed," she said, shrugging.

I was silent for a full ten seconds, taking a sip of my wine as I digested everything. "Was the makeup really necessary?" I finally asked.

Alvara burst out laughing. "I told Alice to do her worst," she admitted, slapping her knee gleefully. Carl, surprisingly, gave her a respectful flick of the tongue – which made me feel all sorts of strange, being able to distinguish between his tongue gestures, now.

"Thank you for testing me, Alvara. I'm glad I didn't disappoint," I told her. "I'm not a great man, but I try very hard to at least be a *decent* man."

"Man-*ling*," she corrected, enunciating the addition. "You do the term justice. Don't let fearful rumors define the word. Let your actions define it.

Make it mean something to be proud of. Something others can be proud of. Something maybe your Callie can be proud of…" she added suggestively. I rolled my eyes, and her face grew serious. "I think it's time for you to become a *legend*, Wylde."

I smiled, nodding in agreement. "I think I can do that…" I said, still thinking of Callie. She had delivered, as usual, beyond all expectations. And she'd done it with a casual comment to a stranger at a bar. It was my job to close the deal.

"Now," I said, leaning forward. "What does a legend need to know about defeating Mordred?" I asked. My friends leaned closer as well, looking radically energized and motivated.

And *hungry*.

CHAPTER 12

*A*lvara considered my question in silence for a minute, digging deep from her long memory, and searching for anything useful. "Mordred, unknown to many, was a very powerful wizard, and a brilliant tactician," she began. "His mother, Morgause, was a very strong enchantress, and passed on her gift of magic, although in an unexpected way, of course. Perhaps that has to do with her Fae and Arthur's mortal blood mixing."

Or maybe it was that *and* the fact that Arthur and Morgause were brother and sister. I wisely didn't voice this, not wanting to offend Alvara if sibling relationships were more... acceptable among the Fae.

"Is Morgause still alive?" I asked instead, fearing the worst.

Alvara pursed her lips, looking uncomfortable. "Morgause is no supporter of Mordred. She holds a position of power in the Fae Courts, and..." she let out a long breath, as if making a difficult decision. "She may even be one of the reasons her son was sent to Hell."

Gunnar let out a long whistle. "That sounds like motive."

I shivered at the implications. Was Mordred determined to take out both his parents? This didn't help me, really. I was persona non-grata to the Fae, so it wasn't like I could just waltz up to her and ask her to help me talk some sense into her son. But indirectly, it could be a good piece of news. Mordred had no allies among the Fae.

Alvara continued. "Despite his estranged relationship with his mother, maybe even as a result of that bad blood, he has gathered an army – and it's growing every day – to march on Camelot. Mordred felt he was betrayed by his city – and his family – and I cannot say he is wrong to believe so. I think he thirsts for vengeance. To destroy everything his parents ever created. Burning Camelot to the foundations, and possibly turning next to the Fae Courts and his mother. To burn out even the memory of his parents' very existence. These are two very powerful symbols in Fae. Destroying them would disrupt the balance that keeps us all relatively safe."

"I understand why the Fae Courts must not fall, but why is Camelot important? Is it even populated, now?"

Alvara sighed. "Camelot is not heavily populated, true. But it is a *symbol…*" she shook her head, eyes dancing with fear, "and destroying those symbols would break the resolve of the Fae. You understand how Fae uses memories, stories, and legends to sustain itself, yes?" I nodded, remembering. The more humans that spoke about Fae, the longer Fae kept its utilities running. We were like a battery for them. "Camelot has many stories attached to it. Losing it… could be cataclysmic."

I nodded with a weary sigh. "I understand." I was getting a better picture of the man. Even with all the contradicting stories, that was one point that seemed consistent. He'd always wanted Camelot for himself. When he felt betrayed by the city he most coveted, there was only one logical reaction. To destroy the symbol of his shame. But was this truly just about his pride? Or was there also some power he wanted to reclaim?

Like the Round Table. Since his first act had been to set up a charity called *The Round Table Initiative*, I was guessing that was a clue.

I doubted he wanted the table for power, because he'd already stolen the Nine Souls from Hell. It had to be symbolic. Destroy his dad's Round Table. And likely… his dad's sword, Excalibur, as well.

Thankfully, I knew I didn't have *that*. I'd checked the Armory, and any other myth I could find regarding its passing through the pages of history. I'd even reached into my satchel, not long ago, thinking of nothing but Excalibur, knowing I had terrible luck like that – that I might find it inside, mislabeled as a letter opener, or something ridiculous.

"Mordred never acts without a purpose, often multiple purposes. If he is also aiming for St. Louis, he has a reason," Alvara continued. "Whether it be to acquire something he desires, to gather an army, or perhaps it is his chosen location to set up his own court – a new Camelot."

The room was silent as we sipped our wine, thinking.

Alvara continued after a few moments, looking thoughtful. "This is likely just his opening move. He sets his foes to panic, looking where he wants them to look, doing what he wants them to do, reacting how he wants them to react..." she said slowly, letting me know – politely – that I was falling victim to his desires.

I cursed angrily, clenching my fist. "It's not like I can just forget about allying the houses. After his talk tonight, they'll fall into his palm without me running interference."

She held up her hands with a sad smile. "You think he did not know this?"

"But why St. Louis?" I pressed, hoping for an objective answer that differed from my theory.

"St. Louis is important to a great number of Freaks," she said carefully. "None know exactly why, but we all *feel* it. Maybe that is his reason, too." She studied me, waiting for a response.

I finally shook my head. "No. He's after something specific. You said it yourself." I gathered my thoughts, thinking furiously. Mordred had made it very apparent tonight that he was interested in me, specifically, even going out of his way to gather intelligence on me. A mutual acquaintance of Alaric Slate and I had been gossiping, giving Mordred ammunition for his attack tonight. But I had no idea who that could have been. Alaric and I hadn't been particularly close. We'd known each other for a few days, tops, before I'd killed him. The pool of potentials was very, very small.

So small, that I couldn't even think of one. I knew, beyond a shadow of a doubt, that it wasn't one of my friends, and wasn't any of the dragons, because we'd just cleaned house with them, recently. Who or what could have pointed a flashing arrow down on me as his target?

Then, a very sneaking suspicion came to mind. "What would Mordred want more than anything?" I asked, finally, taking a calming breath and a sip of my wine. I already knew the answer, but I wanted a second opinion.

Alvara thought about it. "The Round Table and Excalibur, surely. But what if he believes those items are no longer in Camelot? Arthur died long ago, as did Merlin. No doubt some thieving wizard stole these things years ago, locking them away in his personal stash. I hear wizards are notorious for it. Like a crow with their shinies. Perhaps Mordred thinks they are here."

And her eyes slowly locked onto mine like a bird of prey, not accusing, but judging my response.

I kept my face very still, nodding at her words for effect. "You're probably not wrong…"

Her gaze drifted to the weapons in her umbrella stand. Too casually, they came back to me. "Didn't your parents amass an Armory?"

Yeah, if she'd come to that conclusion so easily, I was pretty sure Mordred had, too. Where else would you hide a dangerous sword and a magical table?

Maybe that asshole with the magical Armory.

I was pretty sure why Mordred wanted to be my best friend, all of a sudden.

CHAPTER 13

J met her eyes and nodded. "Neither of those items are in the Armory. I swear it on my wizard's power," I told her, casually using my magic to bond me to the oath. She studied me for any sign of deception, but I was telling the truth. "But Mordred doesn't know that."

Talon had opened his eyes slightly upon hearing me swear an oath and was now watching us discreetly.

"He thinks your Armory has his heirlooms," Alvara breathed incredulously.

Any number of people could have told Mordred about my Armory, and it began to make sense why Mordred hadn't simply come at me with the power of his Nine Souls to lay waste to Chateau Falco to claim control over it. Because destroying my mansion would potentially destroy his only *entrance* into the Armory.

And I'd inadvertently given him an invitation to my home in two days. Practically bringing him to sit at the Round Table for drinks while we discussed his *Round Table Initiative*. Even though his aim was off, his arrow would land dangerously close to his prize – the Sanctorum, where the Round Table actually sat. Unless I did something fast, he was about to *accidentally* hit his target.

And for obvious reasons, I couldn't very well take Mordred into the Armory to prove that what he sought wasn't there. Because he might decide that he wanted to go shopping through all the *other* dangerous magical weapons since he was already there.

Discovering that Armory – the cache of supernatural weapons and fabled magical toys my parents had stolen and locked away over the years – had pretty much been the point when my worldview suddenly turned into an extreme close-up of a big, stinky defecation chamber.

Mordred wanted to use his parents' tools of power to destroy everything they had ever built – poetic justice. And I needed to lock down *my* parents' tools of power in order to keep them from Mordred. Irony was a swift flick in the eyeball, some days.

I needed to tell Pandora to lock down the Armory. Tonight.

Alvara cleared her throat, slowly setting down her glass and looking me in the eyes. "Mordred said some things tonight, and I think I'm only just now beginning to read between the lines. He said you had a past – which is impossible. That you pulled him out of a personal *hell...*" I closed my eyes, deciding not to lie. If Mordred had his way, everyone was going to know soon enough, and likely at the worst possible moment. I needed to get in front of it.

"Yes," I admitted. "I accidentally broke him out of Hell."

She sucked in a breath to hear such a thing actually spoken. Suspecting it was different from hearing it. And I hadn't waffled or dodged the question, something the Fae weren't familiar with.

Open honesty.

Carl scowled at her. "It's not as bad as it sounds."

Her eyes widened. "With all due respect, Elder Carl, I think it's *exactly* as bad as it sounds."

Carl cocked his head. "I disagree. I found Hell quite pleasant. Nothing like everyone says."

Talon scoffed, overriding the stunned look on Alvara's face as he rounded on Carl. "The place was horrifying! I still have nightmares about it!"

Gunnar rolled his eye at the two, maintaining his position between me and Alvara. Like my very own one-eyed secret service. Alvara – if possible – looked even more alarmed. "You were *both* in Hell with him?" she hissed, her hands shaking in her lap.

They turned to her, then to me, not sure how I wanted them to respond.

"I took them with me," I told her. "I trust them with my life. Without them, I don't know if I would have survived. Let alone escaped."

Talon and Carl both grew rather moody at that, because they'd fought over who would remain behind to become Anubis' new Guide to Hell – a required cost that hadn't been explained until *after* we used Hell's tour guide, Dante – the author of the *Divine Comedy*, which had apparently been his memoir. I wasn't sure how he managed to publish it from Hell, though. It was hard enough to get published while on Earth.

Maybe he had self-published. I heard those authors were taking over the traditional publishing model.

I snapped out of my thoughts, noticing Alvara was about to run screaming from her own house, I held up a hand to forestall her, and then gave her a quick recap of the relevant details about our journey to Hell, and ultimately, how I had accidentally freed Mordred.

She listened in rapt attention, pouring a fresh glass of wine and immediately downing it in one pull, her eyes a little wild around the edges. Once finished, I gave her a few moments to collect her thoughts. I didn't like sharing that information, but I knew Mordred would just use it against me later, so it was a necessary decision. I didn't give her all the details, just enough for her to understand the big picture. That this was all my fault.

"I... see," she finally said. "Then Mordred stole these Nine Souls and escaped..." I nodded. She began drumming her fingers on her knee, studying me. "You will confront Mordred?" she asked.

I nodded firmly. "Yes." Even though I had no idea how to stand up to his Nine Souls, or even what that meant, exactly. Did it just mean he had nine lives? Or was he nine times stronger than a wizard?

"You have given me much to think over..." Alvara said. "I believe I will share the story of my night with Wylde Fae with some associates at the Chancery," she said absently, not openly committing support, but speaking as if to herself. I nodded gratefully. That was exactly what I'd hoped to get out of tonight's meeting. But she wasn't finished. "The Chancery will be very interested to hear of your allies..." she said, dipping her chin respectfully at Carl, then the others. "Not to mention Callie Penrose," she added with a faint grin.

"Maybe leave out the tea party part," I suggested.

The corner of her lip pulled up in a smirk, but she didn't agree. It had been worth a shot. Maybe hearing that Alvara had humiliated me would gain me support from the Chancery, and I knew hearing about the Elders backing me – even only *one* Elder backing me – would be enough to cause a panic. Which I was totally fine with at the moment.

"I cannot guarantee their decision, but my voice will give them much to consider. You are a *Manling*, after all. And a *notorious* one at that. Any official alliance would likely require an official meeting between you and them, because a decision like this would impact *all* of us." I nodded in under-standing.

Her eyes locked onto me, and although she'd implied she couldn't sway the Chancery… that look made me think otherwise.

CHAPTER 14

I lifted my glass to salute her generosity. She did the same, eyes calculating. I took a sip and leaned back into my chair content-edly. Since I didn't often do *contentedly*, my friends watched me with open suspicion, ruining my ruse, damn them. But I had just seen an opportunity.

"I've had issues with my Fae magic," I told Alvara. "Sometimes I can use it easily, but other times I cannot even touch it. Do you have any tips or advice for me? Finding a teacher who doesn't run screaming in terror is harder than I thought it would be." And here I was, sitting before a woman who obviously knew a thing or two about Fae magic. Perhaps she could help.

Instead of laughing at my comment or answering me out loud, she just began to stare at me – but in a way that made me feel abruptly self-conscious, as if she was seeing *inside* of me.

She seemed to snap out of it after a few moments, as if waking up from a dream, shaking her head slowly to reorient herself. "You're fragmented," she said, frowning. "I sense vast gaps in you, as if you've forgotten parts of your soul." Something deep inside of me grumbled an agreement, making me tense up. "You need to remember your legend to fully access your Fae side. A re-memory, if you will."

I stared back at her, considering her explanation. Legend was another word for *origin*. And she'd used it a few times, tonight. "Because I can't remember all of my Fae childhood," I ventured.

She nodded. "Once you take care of all this nonsense," she gestured, implying Mordred, "you should go visit Fae…" her gaze grew nostalgic, and I remembered that she was no longer welcome to visit her homeland of Fae – that her advice was to tell me to do something she seemed to want more than anything in the world. "Everything will become clear after a prolonged stay, and you would have done the Fae Queens a great service in defeating Mordred, so perhaps they wouldn't *immediately* hunt you down."

I leaned forward, as did the rest of my friends. I felt nervous, but they merely looked anticipatory – at the chance to test out their wild sides again. But I couldn't just bring an army of my friends to Fae. If I was visiting in order to remember my childhood, I couldn't afford to babysit anyone. I wisely didn't mention that, now. "How prolonged are we talking?" I asked.

"Oh, that *is* a relative question," Alvara mused. "You are attempting to remember an entire lifetime, of sorts, so I would imagine a considerable period of time. Then again… you are an anomaly, a Manling born in Fae, so who knows? And as a wizard, you are no doubt familiar with introspection, meditation, the quiet, natural life…" I nodded eagerly, encouraged by her words. "Then it shall be easier for you, perhaps also quicker. But none of that matters at the moment. You need to handle Mordred, first, or…" she drew a finger across her throat, shrugging mercilessly.

My shoulders slumped in frustration. She had a freaking point, after all. "I have other powers at my disposal. I'll just use them."

She regarded me. "May I offer some advice?" she asked guardedly.

I nodded, not particularly liking her tone. "Please."

"The… gaps in your soul are not limited to your Wylde persona. I sense… other gaps as well. As if you have only dabbled in these various… *powers at your disposal*," she said, enunciating my very words. "Does that make sense?" she asked.

"I think so… I haven't spent enough time mastering my other gifts like I have done with my wizard's magic. These…" I struggled for the right word, then set my elbows on my lap, lifting my hands to my head to support it as I stared down at the table. I needed to be open. This was quite literally a chance of a lifetime, and she seemed knowledgeable enough to help. I'd given her enough clear answers this evening for her to open up to me and speak freely.

Fae didn't do that. I needed to take advantage of it.

"Ever since my parents died, possibly before, I've been subjected to random, inexplainable but temporary access to powers that most wizards don't ever touch. For a long time, I considered it like a weak immune system. That whatever I came across power-wise, I could accidentally contract. To support this theory, I've lost as many powers as I've gained, just like one shakes off a sickness. So, your advice makes perfect sense. I'm a jack of all trades, and a master of none..." I admitted.

"Perhaps your mind is just searching for the right flavors of magic it wants to keep," she suggested.

I looked up at her sharply. "I've never heard of such a thing. Choosing your magic?"

She nodded, opened her mouth, and then closed it, as if considering something. Her eyes touched the ceiling fleetingly before she turned back to me. "Let's make a deal."

I narrowed my eyes suspiciously. There went my chance of an open, honest discussion. "What kind of a deal?" I asked.

Gunnar piped up. "Nate, this is probably not a good idea—"

Carl slapped him in the shoulder, silencing him as he studied Alvara. "Speak, my sweet."

Alvara nodded slowly, considering each of us. "I would like you to take me and my daughter to Fae when you decide to visit next." Talon was sheathing and unsheathing his claws subconsciously as he watched.

"Go on," I said cautiously.

"In return for you smuggling us into Fae, I will assist you in filling those gaps in your memory." Talon leaned forward so suddenly that even I looked over at him. He averted his eyes apologetically, and I turned back to Alvara. "I may also be able to assist with your other powers as well. I know those in Fae who do not wish to be found but may have knowledge that could aid you."

I frowned at her. "Aid me with what, Alvara?" I asked, because her words sounded very specific, as if she was referring to something unspoken.

"Being a Catalyst, of course. That's what is causing all of this. But I will speak no further until we are safely in Fae, and we get your memory restored. You know I cannot lie, so my words are truth. Consider my proposal wisely."

I blinked incredulously, a million questions exploding across my mind, dancing across the tip of my tongue.

Alice suddenly sprinted into the room, startling all of us. I still heard the running feet from upstairs and realized that the girl had used Glamourie – the art of illusion – to make us think she was still upstairs. Judging by the disapproving look on her mother's face, she had also fallen for the ploy, too distracted with our conversation to notice the sneaky eavesdropper.

Before her mother could chastise her for interrupting, Alice ran right up to me and hopped onto my lap. She gripped me by the face, and I realized she was crying, and had been for quite some time.

"Please help us get back home, Princess Sparkles," she whispered. And then she was sobbing into my shoulder, clutching me like her life depended on it. Her tiny body rocked back and forth as she snotted and whimpered all over my neck, and I realized I was gripping her tiny body tightly, stroking her hair reassuringly.

She had knocked my tiara off, but I didn't care. All I cared about was the pain in her voice.

It reminded me of my brief time with Alex as a child. He was fully grown, now – the magic from Fae having apparently worn off to bring him back to his more rightful Earth age. But... we'd had a moment or two just like this. Where a parental adrenaline shot had hit me like a taser when I saw him in pain.

Alice was clutching me like I was some kind of damned hero. A legend that could accomplish anything. And to be honest, the way she gripped me, clinging to me with her fingers like I was the edge of a cliff…

I kind of began to believe it.

Alvara was watching me thoughtfully. I nodded slowly, continuing to pet her daughter's hair. I had already made my decision, even before Alice's emotional plea. If Alvara had a way of helping me get a grip on my powers, I was going to take it. There really wasn't anything to think about. It was the only bus out of town, so to speak. So, I looked Alvara in the eyes, over her daughter's shoulder, and nodded. "Deal."

Alice squealed into my neck, thanking me repeatedly as she clutched me even tighter. After a few moments, she pulled back, wiping at her eyes with her sleeves. "Are you really Wylde? The Manling born in Fae? The Manling King?" she whispered, red-rimmed eyes scanning my face as if she would find proof on my cheeks that I was the boogeyman.

I nodded, "but I'm not a bad guy. Just… misunderstood." I remembered hearing that Fae children read Manling Tales, much like we read Fairy Tales, and that they were not Disney-rated. "Maybe I can come back some time, read some Manling Tales with you before bed one night. We can laugh at how wrong they all are." Alice's eyes shot wide open, and she nodded excitedly. "If your mother approves, of course," I added.

Alvara nodded thoughtfully, likely thinking of our potential deal, that those stories just might be told over a campfire in Fae. "You'd likely be the only Fae child to ever have such an experience," she told Alice, knowing exactly how to motivate her. "But you would need to prove to me that you can listen when I speak."

Alice nodded eagerly to her mother before turning back to me to wrap her arms around my neck, grinning as wide as only children can. In those eyes, I saw that we had made our own pact. About those Manling Tales. And in return, I got her unfettered gratitude. I found myself smiling right back. It was a fair deal.

A pact between a girl and a hero.

A fae child and a legend.

A daughter and a father.

Her mother watched us with a pleased, but haunted look. As if seeing me hold her daughter had brought back a happy memory that was now just a lonely ache. A love lost. The child's father. Considering that, I clutched Alice in one more hug.

Then I abruptly burst to my feet, restraining her with one hand as I tickled her with the other, ignoring her sudden outcries of protest and laughter. Then I body-slammed her into the pillows on the couch, gently slapping my tiara onto her wavy hair. "Princess Sparkles always wins," I told her.

Then, I curtsied.

I shot a stern glare over my shoulder at my Drag Queen Divas, placing my hands on my hips in warning. "It will be worse for you if I have to make you do it," I told them.

And that's how a werewolf king, an albino lizard king, and a Thundercat all curtsied to a little Fae child. Alice clapped delightedly.

Then, like badass princess rock stars, we retrieved our weapons and left the house – in search of our dignity but feeling like heroes.

CHAPTER 15

I stopped at the red light, drumming the steering wheel with my fingers, thinking over Alvara's conversation, that she might be able to help me with the Catalyst mystery.

"She's a beauty, ain't she?" Alucard murmured from the passenger seat, caressing the leather seat.

"Don't get your vampire slobber on it," Gunnar growled.

Alucard grunted, tapping his fingernail against the window. "Is this really bulletproof? I saw the video, but have you personally tested it? I think I could punch right through it." Talon, having zero interest in our conversation, had decided to take a cat nap.

"I dare you," I said drily. Alucard grunted. "Why haven't *you* tested it, Mr. Manly Man?" I asked Gunnar.

"Because if it doesn't work, I don't want to have to explain how I damaged the car."

I glanced at him in the rearview mirror. "Get Drake or Cowan to do it. That's the benefit of having minions."

He nodded thoughtfully and I shifted so that he couldn't see my grin. I kind of hoped the SUV didn't live up to the hype, because without a moment's hesitation, I would tell Ashley the truth, that her husband had put Drake up to the task of shooting her wedding gift.

I felt Alucard's gaze and couldn't conceal my smirk. He chuckled.

"What are you two laughing about?" Gunnar growled, leaning between us, checking our hands and then faces for evidence of our suspected crime.

"Nothing. Just admiring the car."

"Armored SUV— Hey! You just ran over that bush!" Gunnar snapped, pointing it out to me.

"Well, if they would fix the streetlights around here, maybe I would have seen it," I lied. I had almost missed my turn, distracted by their conversation – and my own mental replay of our talk with Alvara. I desperately wanted to know how Alvara had known Carl's parents, but now wasn't the time. I was confident her fear of Elders had played a big factor in her deciding to speak to the Chancery on our behalf – that Carl forgot to mention that he intended to bring an army of Elders to Chateau Falco to serve me. I shivered at the thought. That hadn't worked out so well for anyone last time.

"Why are we going to Plato's Cave again? I can't even remember the last time I was inside," Gunnar said. "We had some good times there, didn't we?"

I nodded, smiling nostalgically. "Remember when that dragon burned my book? Raven, the yellow one."

Gunnar nodded. "Yeah. We kicked some serious ass in there. Then Peter killed her."

Silence settled over the car, and Alucard shot Gunnar a dark look. "Gee, thanks for killing the mood."

Gunnar sighed. "Sorry, Nate." The vehicle was uncomfortably silent for a few more seconds. "Hey, remember when you hired Alucard as your manager—"

"I think we've had enough of this trip down memory lane," Alucard interrupted.

"How many times did he get zapped by religious artifacts?" Gunnar hooted, gripping my arm with one hand and slapping Alucard's shoulder with the other. The Alpha werewolf's grip made me swerve the vehicle a little, but I was grinning at the memory.

Back then, Alucard was a run-of-the-mill vampire, and hadn't been able to touch religious items. Since my bookstore was more of an arcane and occult novelty shop as well as a bookstore – and that most everything else was directly tied to a spiritual belief of some sort – basically everything in the store had been toxic to a vampire.

And he couldn't talk to the customers, because all he could think about was drinking their blood. Or it was daytime, and the sun shining through the windows could have burned him.

Also, my old employee, Greta, had taken it upon herself to send me about a dozen religious pamphlets a week in the mail. So, on a daily basis, Alucard would unsuspectingly get smited by God.

But he was a Daywalker now, and had lost that aversion to religious items, sunlight, and all sorts of perks.

"What was the final tally?" Gunnar pressed, as if suddenly remembering something. "I know you were keeping track, Nate, but I'd forgotten all about it."

Alucard slowly turned to look at me, face disbelieving. "You... were keeping track of the number of times I was injured at your bookstore?" he asked incredulously.

I shrugged guiltily. "Nine-hundred-forty-four," I told Gunnar. He slapped his knees, roaring with laughter. "What about the ratio? Did you win?" he asked, gripping my arm again.

Alucard was scowling but seemed suddenly curious about the question. "What do you mean, *did you win?*"

I let out a sigh, pulling up to Plato's Cave, smiling distantly at the sign above the shop. I shifted to park before turning to look at Gunnar and Alucard. "Six-hundred-eighty-eight," I said. "In the Nate column. The rest were lucky happenstance."

Alucard was staring at me. "Wait... you *personally* sabotaged the shop in *addition* to the accidental ones? And then kept *track* of it all?" He folded his arms, shaking his head. Then he snapped his fingers, remembering something that must have been bothering him for a long time. "What did you do to the counters?" he demanded.

"Holy water in the cleaning solution," I admitted.

"Wow... I can't even. You just took asshole to a new plane of existence, Little Brother."

"Thank you?"

He tried to scowl, but after a few seconds, he finally let out a laugh. "You know... that really fucked with me back then. But right now? All I can do is laugh about it. Because you helped me realize something about myself. How to embrace my inner monster," he admitted, speaking softly. "Without all your poking, prodding, and pranking, I may have tried harder to stick more to my guilty human side..."

I nodded. "Yeah, I didn't want you to do that."

He frowned. "You... considered that?"

I shrugged. "Sure. That's why I tried to keep you on your toes. I knew you wouldn't be complete if you tried to become normal."

"Then why did you let me *try?*"

I arched an eyebrow at him. "You wouldn't have listened to my advice back then. You needed to see it for yourself. So, like any good friend, I was forced to sabotage you at every opportunity."

Alucard was studying me like he had never met me before. "You're full of shit."

Gunnar cleared his throat. "Actually, he's telling the truth. I called him an asshole for it, but after a few days of thinking about it, and getting to know you better, I thought it was a pretty good assessment of you. Definitely an asshole move, but... a *friendly* asshole move."

The sign to the bookstore cast a pale glow over the dashboard. "Just to be clear. I would have totally fucked with you even if I hadn't had an altruistic purpose behind it. I'm not a saint."

Gunnar and Alucard were facing me, so didn't see Carl's pale, shining face slowly lean forward from the third row, close enough to nibble Gunnar's earlobe.

"What are we doing here?" Carl asked in the loudest whisper I'd ever heard. Like a stage whisper for an audience at a play.

Gunnar snarled instinctively, flinching back from Carl's snout and slamming his back into the door. I burst out laughing.

"What the *fuck*, Carl?" Gunnar roared. "Why the hell were you so close? You could have asked that back from the third row, where you *belong!*"

Carl narrowed his eyes and flicked out his tongue, slapping Gunnar in the cheek. Gunnar recoiled, looking on the verge of pummeling the Elder. Then he thought about that, and probably remembered how terrified Alvara had been of Carl. I know I was still thinking about it.

"Why are we not driving?" Carl finally repeated, this time turning to look at me.

"Othello told me there was a package waiting for me inside."

We sat there in silence, listening to Talon's purring snore. "We're still not driving," Carl noted.

"I don't think it's a good idea to leave you three unsupervised in the car," I admitted.

Alucard folded his arms. "I'm never going inside that place again." Then, as an afterthought, he added, "Asshole."

"It's my car. You can't make me leave," Gunnar snapped. Everyone turned to consider Talon, who was still sleeping, but we were all smart enough not to try waking the cat warrior.

Carl nodded seriously. "I will grab Nate's package. I will hold it close and keep it safe—"

"Jesus…" Alucard groaned. "Just go grab the damned mail, Carl. Stop making it weird."

He cocked his head, not understanding the nuance of what he had said. Then he leaned in very close to Gunnar's face, about three inches away, staring unblinking into the werewolf's eye.

Gunnar stared right back, but finally demanded, "What?"

"I need your help with the door," Carl said, showing us his long black claws. "I don't want Ashley upset with me for scratching her skin."

"He means the leather," I sighed. "Just open the door for him, Gunnar. It's easier."

Gunnar finally complied, hopping out of the SUV eagerly to get away from Carl. The streetlights hit his stone eyepatch, glinting faintly as he scanned the street out of habit. Satisfied, he handed Carl a hooded trench coat. "Pedestrians across the street. Can't let them see you clearly," he told Carl.

Carl slipped out of the car like a snake, tugged on the knee-length trench coat, flipped up the hood, and then strode up to the door. He tried the handle, his claws having an awkward time with the knob, but I knew he was able. Then he stepped back, scowling angrily at the door.

I rolled my window down, realizing I had forgotten to give him the key. "Hey, Carl—"

"Someone is trying to keep me from grabbing your package!" he hissed.

A hipster had rounded the corner in time to hear the strange serpentine shout and spot the shady silhouette of a hooded, trench coat-wearing, Lord Voldemort sounding creeper lurking in the darkened doorway of the shop. He spun and ran away screaming.

Carl ignored it and kicked the fucking door down, instantly setting off the alarms.

I blinked in disbelief, and Alucard burst out laughing, slapping the dash way too happily. "*Classic* Carl!"

I grimaced, pulling out my phone to text Othello that wherever she was, she was about to get a call from the police or the alarm company and that she would need to make an appointment for someone to replace the door in the morning. The very *expensive* fucking door.

How hard was it to pick up a package off the counter?

I heard a loud crashing sound from inside, and realized Carl was destroying my bookstore in search of my package. Or he was looking for an intruder. Whoever had locked the door, because he apparently wasn't aware that you locked up buildings with valuable inventory when no one was present after hours. So, a locked door implied a direct threat to be annihilated, deboned, and then repurposed into a new set of ivory daggers.

Obviously.

Alucard was actually crying with laughter, now, and Gunnar was leaning his back against the hood of the car, shaking his head in disbelief. I muttered a curse, climbing out of the SUV. "Thanks for running in there to tell Carl to calm the fuck down. Means a lot."

He grunted. "You let him creep out on me."

"I didn't *let* him do anything. It was just Carl being Car—"

And that's when Carl's body flew through the shop window amidst a shower of broken glass, slamming into the windshield of our SUV, right between me and Gunnar. I had a split second to realize that the SUV wasn't even remotely damaged, much to Carl's dismay and Alucard's stunned face. The vehicle rocked slightly as Talon woke from his nap, probably freaking the fuck out. Hopefully Carl hadn't broken his back or anything. He was just lying there, breathing heavily as he stared up at the night sky.

Alucard and Talon stared through the windshield at Carl's back, mouths hanging open.

"I grabbed Nate's package," Carl wheezed, clutching a paper-wrapped bundle to his chest. Then he finally passed out.

I was already running into the bookstore, assuming it had been the griffin statues I had left behind for night security, and that I needed to deactivate them or calm them down before they went on a rampage. I heard Gunnar and Alucard arguing with Talon, probably demanding he stay in the car, because the pedestrians across the street were pointing or fleeing for their lives.

Othello was going to kill me.

CHAPTER 16

I burst through the open doorway, eyes sweeping the chaotic scene for the Guardian gargoyles. The silver glint of a big ass hand-cannon flicked my way, and I dove on instinct over the splintered door to take cover behind the nearest stand of books and trinkets. An intruder really *was* in here! What sounded like a 44 Magnum boomed through the darkness, shattering the piles of books behind me in an explosion of confetti. I kept sneaking around another shelf, and then another, trying to find out who the hell was in here, and how I was going to sneak up on them.

I whipped up a nasty bit of magic that probably wasn't well-known by the Academy – something I'd come up with thanks to my training with Wylde. Not Fae magic, but a hybrid of sorts. A black orb of power that would hit a target and wrap entirely over it, encasing it in a sticky web of shadows, trapping them entirely. I didn't want to use anything elemental and accidentally ruin my merchandise by lighting things on fire or zapping them with electricity or a vortex of wind.

I heard the creak of a floorboard and risked a glance to see the dark silhouette of the shooter at the base of the steps leading up to the loft above the store. The loft had once been my bachelor pad before I had moved into Chateau Falco after my parents had died. Someone was trying to break into the loft.

I leaned back against the bookshelf, took a deep breath, and readied to lean out and tag the shooter.

"Do you have *any* idea who owns this store?" the shooter snarled. "Nate Temple! And I have every right to pump you full of lead, right now—"

"Othello?" I blurted out in disbelief. I thought she had been out of town!

There was a very long, significant pause. "Um... Nate?" she replied, sounding just as surprised.

"Yes, it's me—"

Which was when Gunnar decided to jump through the already broken window in full beast mode, making sure he hit every piece of unbroken glass Carl had missed. He landed atop a display table, shattering it, but maintained his balance, claws out, lone eye seeming to shine with malice.

He even sported his favorite pair of Underdog spandex underwear. The street lights outside illuminated him from behind, making him look all the more threatening. He was a majestic fucker, about seven feet tall, and a mountain of shaggy white fur, jaws wide enough to bite a man in half.

He'd barely touched the ground, already opening his mouth to howl, when a Biblical force punched him in the chest so hard that he flew right the fuck back *out* the window, slamming into Ashley's wedding present, presumably beside Carl.

"Everyone stop! Friendly fire!" I shouted as loud as I could, before Talon and Alucard decided to give it the ol' college try.

A cloaked figure turned to look at me and, even knowing who it was, I took an instinctive step backwards. An aged ivory skull stared back at me, eyes of purple flame flickering in the depths. Even from this distance, in the darkness, I could see the impact craters from where some very heavy artillery had struck his Mask at some point. His cloak was made of what looked like a funeral shroud and patched with cobwebs. Skeletal hands peeped out from the sleeves of his robes, and they were flexed in tight fists, the bones creaking and groaning as he stared at me.

Death, the Horseman of the Apocalypse.

I waved at him jovially. As soon as I'd heard Othello's voice, I'd assumed Death wouldn't be far away. I hadn't known Othello was using the place to sleep in – she had rooms at Chateau Falco, after all. Was she using my bookstore as her hidden love-nest with Death? I hadn't known she was even back in town. She'd been traveling an awful lot lately.

"What are you doing here, Nate?" Death asked, yanking off his Mask.

Which left a very toned, older, naked man staring back at me. Definitely not as frail as he had been when I'd first met him, but then again, I'd learned that he appeared to you in a way that matched your personal perception of Death, the reaper of souls. The more I got to know him, the more my image of him adjusted. Never changing entirely, but constantly evolving. Since I saw him as more dangerous with each passing day, he began to reflect this in actuality. So, he looked like a backwards aging version of Hemingway, the man I'd first met in Achilles' Heel a few years ago. His long, iron gray hair just brushed his shoulders, and eyes of pale gray like chips of polished steel assessed me... accusingly?

"Well, this is *my* bookstore, in case anyone has forgotten that part..."

"Who the hell kicked the door down and set off the alarms?" he asked, bewildered. Then he grunted. "It was Carl, wasn't it? Fucking Carl..." he muttered, shaking his head.

I nodded. "Yeah. The door was locked, and he thought someone was keeping him from entering. He's having a bad night. Even for him."

Death sighed. "Mind telling him I'm sorry? I don't think I'm up to one of his conversations right now."

I smiled, approaching him. Most of my friends liked Carl. Enjoyed having him around. But at the same time, they'd all learned firsthand how difficult some conversations could be for him. He just wasn't the same as a human. Didn't understand social etiquette, nuances, or a billion other subconscious things humans do in a conversation without even realizing we're doing it.

Also, despite their annoyance, every single person I knew was terrified of him on some instinctual level, even if they didn't openly admit it. Even Death, a Horseman of the Apocalypse.

And I had Carl picking up my mail.

"Sure," I said. "We just swung by to pick up the package Othello told me about," I told him, trading grips with him.

Realizing I'd forgotten all about Othello upon recognizing Death, I glanced over his shoulder.

And got a beautiful eyeful of familiar, boob-tacular breasts. The only stitch of clothing she wore was a pair of lacy, boy-shorts lingerie. Like a deer in headlights, I froze. Not because I was leering, but because her mystical, womanly boobie magic entranced me with a power I could not stand against.

Death slapped my cheek lightly, but firmly.

I dropped my gaze. "Right. Hey, Othello. Didn't mean to stare. What's, erm, up?" I asked awkwardly.

"Well, *something* was up, before you ruined the mood, obviously," she muttered, waving her hands at her present state of undress. She still held the 44 Magnum in one hand, liable to blow a hole in the ceiling if she wasn't careful. The Guardian statues were awake and watching us thoughtfully, not having even bothered to stand at the chaos.

Probably because they were the only ones who had sensed that we were all friendlies.

"Nice shooting, Annie Oakley," I finally sighed. "You almost bang-banged me."

"Been there, done that. Shame we couldn't have had a sequel," she muttered, stomping back up the stairs as I heard a phone begin to ring from the loft above. I blinked. Well, that had sounded rehearsed, as if she'd been waiting to say it for quite some time. I shook off the thought, especially since Death was scowling at me – both for my arrival and her comment.

I shrugged at him. "Yeah, I've got no comment on that, except to say good luck, and sorry," I told him, watching her walk up the stairs. She was answering a call from the security company. Or the police.

"I need to take these calls," she grumbled from over her shoulder. "Hemingway, get everyone out of here, and then get your ass back in bed. I wasn't finished with you." She paused at the top of the stairs, turning to look at me over her thin shoulder. "Nice seeing you, Nate. But next time, dress appropriately. Everyone else is in their birthday suits."

Then she slammed the door.

My jaw was hanging open. Not because I had been paying very close attention to her movements, making sure she made it safely up the stairs. Not at all. Her comment had cut deeply, and I don't know why. Perhaps because it had sounded genuine, not just snarky. We'd had a brief romance in the past and seeing her in all her splendor had brought on a pang of memory I didn't particularly need at the moment.

Also – probably more likely – a pang of *Nate hadn't gotten any in a long while.*

Luckily for me, Death had been transfixed with her movements as well, and hadn't noticed me gawking. He had a hungry, cadaverous grin.

"You guys need to get the fuck out of here. Now," he told me with not an ounce of brotherly love, and not even turning to look at me. Then he was stomping up the stairs. I didn't pay as much attention to his movements. In fact, I briefly considered using magic to trip him up so I could watch him tumble ass over heels down the wooden stairs.

That's right. I thought about tripping up Death out of sheer spite and a shadow of old jealousy. But I took a deep breath, deciding to be the better man. To rise above it.

"Good seeing you guys—" But he had already slammed the door.

I scowled, thinking very dark thoughts as I stared up at the door to what had once been *my* loft. Then I grunted and walked over to the table that Othello had blasted with the gun. I stared down at the remains of several books, one with a neat hole through the center. I picked it up to see it was a copy of *Atlas Shrugged*.

"God damnit. Why is it always *this* book?" I muttered, remembering back to the time I had seen my first dragon. The one Gunnar and I had been talking about in the car. Raven. She'd lit *Atlas Shrugged* on fire with her magic. I'd promptly kicked her ass for it.

I glanced up at the loft above. This time, friendly fire had destroyed my book.

"Nate?" Alucard called out from the street. "What's the plan? I hear sirens. Are we sticking around?" I growled under my breath and tossed the book back down.

"We're done here. Is everyone else alright?" I asked, hopping over the splintered door that Carl had kicked down.

Alucard met me just outside, nodding warily. "Yeah, just caught off-guard." He appraised me very seriously. "Everything to do with you is just so much... *more*. Even picking up a package at your *own bookstore* becomes an *event*."

I sighed wearily. "Tell me about it." I made my way back to the car, spotting Gunnar and Carl sitting on the hood, shaking their heads as if still dazed. They looked at me and lowered their heads in embarrassment. The SUV had not a scratch or dent on it. Jesus. Worth every penny.

I waved it off. "It was Death, guys. A freaking Horseman. And you were interrupting some very important *personal* business of his. Don't be too hard on yourselves."

Gunnar frowned curiously, then it dawned on him, and he began to laugh. "Ah. Othello is up there," he said. "She's been busy lately, running around all over the country. I can understand her... pent-up frustration," he added, chuckling harder.

I frowned at that. Where had Othello been lately that even Gunnar knew about it and I didn't? I knew bits and pieces of the New York fiasco, but that was about it. All I did was give Alucard a very thoughtful look – enjoying his sudden uneasiness – before I frowned at a new thought. Because I suddenly realized Talon wasn't at or in the car any longer. Which meant he was probably about to do something he would regret if he had gone inside the bookstore, too, should he manage to interrupt Death and Othello a *second* time. "Alucard, I need to find Talon. Get those two in the car. They might need your help. Death clocked them good."

"Gee, I hadn't noticed," he replied drily. Then he pointed at a nearby shadow in front of the broken window before walking off to help Carl and Gunnar off the hood of the truck. Talon was there, staring into the bookstore suspiciously, sniffing the air.

I walked up to him, preparing to catch him up. The sirens were getting louder, and I didn't want us to be here when the police arrived.

Even though I *very much* wanted to see how Othello handled the police if anyone... *prematurely* interrupted her festivities.

Badump bump.

Talon chose that moment to begin *yowling* at the top of his feline lungs.

It was as shockingly loud and physically painful as a human suddenly yodeling right into your ear canal when you were late for work, and impatiently waiting in line for your coffee at Starbucks, eyes more red than white. You know, the sound those alley cats make only at three in the morning when they are right outside your window on a night that you've had trouble falling asleep.

Yeah. That sound. Except much *louder*.

I swatted at his shoulders violently, shushing him. "*Stop!* Are you *trying* to get us killed?"

Talon glanced over his shoulder at me. "They are mating up there. I know it." He tapped his nose proudly.

I flung my hands up. "So?"

"I was paying tribute. It's like..." he thought about it, cocking his head. Then he tried to snap his fingers like he'd seen Gunnar doing a few days ago, but his furry paws just made it a fluffy *thump*, "a high-five," he said, frowning down at his paw pads.

I ran my hands through my hair in exasperation. "You can yowl at him later. In the truck, now. We're leaving."

And I forcefully shoved him back towards the truck. As he was climbing in, Talon spoke, turning to hold up his paw in my face. "I think you could do with a good high five, you know. You seem frustrated. Pent up. On the edge of violenc—"

I slammed the door a lot harder than necessary, hoping to catch his tail. Then I jogged to the driver's seat, climbed inside, and got the hell out of the vicinity, idly wondering if simply *considering* murdering your pet lizard, cat, and puppy was a crime.

Alucard shot me a wink, and then began to whistle to himself. If he'd laughed, I might have added him to the list of to-be-slain pets.

CHAPTER 17

The car was silent for all but half a minute before Talon chimed in. "We should celebrate."

Alucard snorted, turning around to study the short cat man. "Celebrate that Gunnar doesn't have a broken spine? That Death is getting some. Or Carl— Hey! What are you doing back there, Carl?" Alucard snapped, leaning further into the back of the spacious SUV.

I angled the mirror to see, still needing to pay attention to the road since I was trying to avoid any nearby patrol cars who might recognize our SUV from the description of the pedestrians outside Plato's Cave. Carl was tearing into my package. "It smells good," he murmured to himself, tearing his claws into it.

"Hey! Go easy! What if it's fragile?" I snapped angrily.

"It's not," he argued, finally tearing it free. He tossed the paper behind him and inspected... what looked like a handful of leather straps. "Mmmm. Thought I smelled jerky."

I blinked, trying to get a closer look, but he was all the way back in the darkened third row. "What is it?"

Gunnar wrinkled his nose, backing off slightly. "It smells familiar."

"Hey! Is it some kind of trap or something? Who was it even from?"

Since Carl blatantly ignored me, flicking his tongue up and down the leather wad of straps and buckles in his claws, Talon unbuckled his seatbelt and went for the packaging. He finally came up with the shipping label. "Darling and Dear in Kansas City," he purred, sounding suddenly very interested.

"What did you order from them? Have you even met them yet?" Gunnar asked.

I frowned, shaking my head. "No. I haven't met them, and I definitely didn't order anything. Maybe Callie bought me something?" I said uncertainly.

Carl let the leather contraption unfold, like unrolling a small rug by holding the corners.

And we all stared in stunned silence to see what looked suspiciously like some sort of bondage gear outfit. Not a full bodysuit or anything, but something that looked designed to restrain someone. Like a Mad Max straightjacket that would leave more skin uncovered than covered.

"Ummm…" Gunnar began, shaking his head. "How much does something like that cost?"

"If you have to ask, you can't afford it," I muttered angrily. What the hell was going on here?

Alucard gasped in disbelief. "Callie bought *that* for you? Wow. Okay. I wouldn't have pegged you as—"

"It said it was from Darling and Dear, not Callie. That was just a guess. Maybe they thought I would find it useful. Callie told me they were a strange couple. Pals with Dorian Gray," I added, which should have explained it all. I still hadn't met the bastard, but he'd approached us about televising our Fight Club at the Dueling Grounds. The legendary King Midas – cleverly disguised as *farmer Midas Kingston* – had seemed very interested in the prospect, since he loved making money, but Achilles and Asterion had not been as excited. The fewer who knew about our Fight Nights, the better.

As usual, Midas saw only the opportunity for gold – figuratively speaking. I had even signed over part of my investment portfolio to his care, because as far back as I knew, he had never made a bad investment. Probably because he would just walk into a company that failed and turn the building into solid gold – enough to make a small return, at least.

"Is Callie stopping by later?" Talon asked, casting a suspicious look my way. Alucard burst out laughing.

I snatched the address label from Talon's paw, reading over it. "Look. It's addressed to Grimm Tech, not me. If Callie was interested in a bondage experience, I doubt she would have sent it to my company. The company I'm hardly ever at. I'm dense, but I'm pretty sure I would have picked up on a bondage fetish if she had one."

"You're probably right," Gunnar said in a neutral tone. "I mean, it's not like a guy would ever send a discreet package to his business rather than his home. Especially when he knows a ton of his friends sleep at his house regularly and would definitely pilfer his mail. A man would have to be an idiot to use a discreet shipping address to hide his deviant hobbies," Gunnar said, still with a straight face. I glared at him and he finally grunted with laughter. "I was in the FBI, man. This is textbook."

"You two put the *freak* in Freaks," Alucard grinned.

"It's not—"

They interrupted me with an impromptu chorus of disjointed sing-song phrases mocking me for my extracurricular hobbies.

I snapped my fingers loudly, a skill I had learned from my father as a child. It sounded like a bone snapping in half. It was a skill Talon had been unsuccessfully trying to master for a week or so.

Apparently, it was also some kind of signal for the bondage gear, because it suddenly came to life, hogtying Carl in an instant. Alucard gasped in disbelief, leaning away from the contraption. Gunnar was staring at Carl in shock, hands up to slice any straps that might lunge his way.

Talon leaned closer, sniffing the Elder cautiously. Carl blinked back at us, eyes wide.

"Do you have anything else to say, Carl?" I growled, pretending I had intended this.

The Elder paused. "Sorry, Master Temple. I've been a bad Elder. A bad, *bad* Elder."

And even though he had meant it to be genuine… since he was wrapped up in bondage gear and acting submissive, the statement sent the car into fits of crying laughter. I snapped my fingers again, and a ball gag snapped into place.

Talon leaned closer and began batting at a dangling buckle of leather hanging from Carl's jaw. Carl gagged, trying to snap his teeth at Talon, but the restraints prevented him.

I sighed, focusing back on the road. Thankfully, the rest of the car ride was uneventful. At least, my friends were too busy poking and prodding

Carl to bother me. Every now and then, he struggled to break free, and knowing how powerful he was, how much he was feared by pretty much everyone I had ever met – even Gods – I'll admit I was impressed at the gear's craftsmanship.

I'd have to find a way to free Carl, now. *Then* I'd have to hide the damned thing before my friends decided to use it for a series of pranks on each other. Maybe it only responded to *my* snap. I'd dig through the packaging to see if there were instructions or anything, but at the moment, I didn't want to let them see me doing so, because then they might find the secret way to command the device.

I really needed to meet Darling and Dear, to learn what kind of twisted psychopaths they were. Because if I was judging by their products, they were the freakiest pair of beings ever created.

But that would have to wait. Because I had a meeting with the Obsidian Son that I was late for. He'd been blowing up my phone ever since the event with Mordred, and I'd texted him back after Alvara's to say we were on our way after a quick stop at the bookstore to pick up my mail.

After the fiasco with Othello, I didn't have time to drop off my friends, so they were along for the ride to see what the king of dragons wanted from me. And I was fine with that.

Backup was smart. Since I didn't know how to free Carl from the bondage gear yet, we would leave him in the SUV. I checked him in the mirror to find that he seemed completely at peace, and I sighed.

Why couldn't I meet any *normal* Freaks?

CHAPTER 18

I stood in the manicured front lawn of Raego's mansion, surrounded by dozens of obsidian statues of life-sized creatures, humans, and other dragons.

They were life-sized because, well, they had once *been* alive. These weren't stone replicas. They were living beings who had offended Raego at some point, and he'd decided to turn them into obsidian statues.

His lawn ornaments were literally his fallen enemies. Talk about a super-villain vibe.

Raego was a very rare black dragon.

Dragons came in all shapes, sizes, and colors. Depending on the color and the type, they had access to different magical gifts. I'd killed a silver one who could manipulate your fears and shoot silver spikes like a suicide bombing porcupine.

I'd also met that yellow one who could use lust against you and spit oily, napalm flame.

Basically, they all had some kind of mental manipulation power, latching onto some human emotion and distorting it or enhancing it.

But black dragons were different. Although not as large as some of the others, they had the ability to basically shapeshift into *anything*. Not just dragon or human. Also, their magical ability was twofold – they could spit black fire that burned like dry napalm or emit a black fog of smoke that turned their victims into stone.

They could also dominate other dragons' minds. At least, they had a lot more mental power than their brethren.

Which was why Raego was their king. Or, the Obsidian Son, the prophesied leader of all dragons, in hopes that he could lead them out of the dark ages and into the light. Make them more legitimate. Apparently, dragons had faced a pretty severe culling in history, with dragon slayers hunting them down mercilessly. They'd been forced to go into hiding, but enough time had passed now that they weren't as afraid, and since they could hide their obvious telltale signs of horizontal pupils when in human form – thank the heavens for contacts – they could wander the world without anyone the wiser. Blending in.

I'd helped Raego earn his throne when I'd helped kill his father, Alaric Slate. The bastard had wanted to become the Obsidian Son himself, and had coerced one of my old friends, Peter, to help him achieve this task.

Which was why, right now, I was standing before a very familiar statue.

Peter.

In the chaos of fighting Alaric, Raego had seen an opportunity. He'd glanced at me for my permission, and damn it, I'd nodded. He'd immediately blasted Peter into a statue, turning the tide for our fight.

Peter had deserved it, and I didn't necessarily feel bad, but a lot of time had passed since then, and seeing him now as a helpless human statue made me feel a bit... uncomfortable. My personal wounds and desires for vengeance at his betrayal had healed or scarred over.

Was he still alive in there? Raego had sliced his throat right before turning him to stone, spilling his blood to ignite the spell prematurely – the spell that allowed him to take over the mantle of Obsidian Son.

So, if he was alive, and we unfroze him, would he just bleed out thirty seconds later? Maybe it was more benevolent to let him remain—

"See anything you like?" A cool voice asked from directly behind me.

I flinched, spun, and prepared to incinerate the voice.

Only to realize it was Raego. "Good god, man. Creep around much?" I snapped.

"I don't creep, I stalk," he replied, cocking his head with a grin. Then he glanced past me at Peter's statue.

I sighed, glancing up at Peter's statue as well. "Is there an expiration date on your spell? Will he just unfreeze one day, back to terrorize us all some-how?" I asked, recalling Mordred's knowledge of my history.

Raego scratched at his jaw, thinking. "I'm actually not sure..." He scanned the lawn, considering all the enemies decorating his property. "Maybe it is unwise to leave my enemies like this," he said, frowning.

"Ya' think?" I asked, drily. "You should probably destroy them all, just in case. You know how much carnage that would be, to have all these traitors wake up and rise against you? All conveniently located at your front door," I said, staring at him meaningfully. Because the more I thought about it, the more realistic the fear grew. What if Mordred had stolen one of these stat-ues, waking up one of our mutual enemies, and that was how he had learned so much about me... That the statue of Peter right in front of me was just an illusion, not the original.

Mordred could have an army of our old enemies waiting for us...

Raego finally turned to face me, looking annoyed. "If we have to start fearing my lawn ornaments, I'm hanging up my crown," he growled, indicating the statue of Peter. "Don't let fear cloud your judg-ment, Nate. Fear is a dirty syringe full of a poisonously addictive street drug, and revisiting old history is you slipping the needle into a vein and slamming down the plunger. Don't give in. Mordred is fucking with you. There is *no way* Mordred could have done such a thing." He rapped a knuckle against Peter's statue arrogantly. "This bitch is *mine*."

"It's the anniversary, you know," I told him, changing the topic. I would just come back some other time and destroy them all myself, whether he wanted it or not. It would help me sleep better, at least.

He grunted, obviously well aware. It had been the night we murdered his asshole father, after all. The day he'd become the king. "No solar eclipse this time, though."

"No, thank god. But tonight's social event may have been worse than Alaric's plan. Lot of Regulars in attendance, and Mordred played to their fears..." I muttered, thinking about that aspect of the talk, not just my own personal issues with Mordred.

Raego grunted. "Good thing we don't need to waste our time with the affairs of mortals, then, eh?" Then he spat on the ground, a sizzling black stain that froze the grass into ebony spikes. "We need to talk about Mordred. He's a problem." Raego was walking back towards the house before I could comment. Likely to make sure Gunnar and my friends weren't being eaten by his dragons.

I sighed, took one last glance at Peter, and then followed after him, but he must have run, because I no longer saw his silhouette.

I saw two familiar Asian dudes standing on either side of the open door leading into Raego's darkened mansion. They hadn't bothered to turn on the lights for us. The two late teens were wearing their usual Chinese suits, and they were exquisitely tailored. I'd heard a dozen names for the cut and style, but basically, the suits didn't have lapels – almost like those Kung Fu jackets Bruce Lee used to wear.

They were brothers – and although not twins, they could have easily passed for one another at a casual glance. And, wait for it…

Their names were Fook and Yu. And their father, Chu, had been one of the dragons resisting my decision to become King of St. Louis – as well as being heavily involved in a plot to take down Raego as king of the dragons. Fook and Yu were not pleased with their father for that.

"Fook," I said, dipping my head to the one on the left, first, "Yu," I added, doing the same to the one on the right of the doors.

"You got them backwards," they grumbled in unison.

"Listen up, Yu, Fook," I said, glancing from left to right again. "You need to dress differently. Or always stand with Fook on the left. Otherwise it ruins all my joke material."

They shared a look with each other, then switched places so Fook was on the left. Then Fook lifted his middle finger at me, holding it steady with a smug grin.

I scowled, turning as I saw Yu pointing his index finger at me.

I looked from one to the other, suddenly realizing what they were doing. They were telling me their names. Fook holding up his middle finger, and Yu pointing at me. Like a mime saying *fuck you.*

I grinned. "Fook *me*? Fook *Yu!*" I laughed, duplicating their hand movements.

Surprisingly, they grinned, nodded, and then suddenly froze, shoulders stiffening in abject horror for some reason.

"If it's any easier, I could freeze their respective fingers into obsidian so you always know which one is which," Raego offered, standing in the shadows of the open doorway. I hadn't even noticed him.

He took a step onto the porch, between the guards, and turned to face

Fook. "Hold out your middle finger." The young man gritted his teeth in shame and fear but complied. Raego turned to Yu. "Hold out your index finger. This will only hurt like hell for an hour or so."

They obeyed, grimacing in anticipation. Raego just stood there, and fog began to drift out from his nostrils, even though he was in human form.

"I was just giving them a hard time, Raego," I said carefully, not wanting them to pay the price for my teasing.

Raego cocked his head. "Hmm. Maybe you two could start wearing different colored jackets, like I've mentioned..." he darted his head forward, black fog puffing out of his nostrils like smoke, "three times, already," he finally snarled.

They nodded, and in an instant, were both tearing off their jackets until they both stood there in identical white dress shirts. I let out a sigh. Kids these days, right?

"Make it work!" Raego finally snapped. I blinked. Really? A Tim Gunn reference? I was impressed. "Or my previous solution stands," he added. "You have two minute—"

All three dragons were suddenly staring past my shoulder in disbelief. A wolf howled, and I heard a crashing sound from within the house. Then the three dragons were lunging for me, all sporting claws. "This will only take a minute," a cold, sinister voice said from directly behind me. Then thick arms grabbed me around the torso and I was yanked into a black world.

CHAPTER 19

$\mathcal{J}$'d experienced abductions like this way too many times over the years, so had devised – and practiced religiously – an immediate, instinctual response to knock everyone in my proximity to their asses before they could strap me to a chair, surround me, or otherwise be big, fat meanies.

I built up my power, fueling it like a tiny reservoir inside my soul. Then I unleashed it in every direction, using every element at my disposal to unleash a repercussive supernova that would do no real lasting harm, but would daze everyone around me. Like a magic flash bang grenade – but using *every* element just in case my abductors had an immunity or protection from one or two of my usual flavors of mayhem.

My reaction was non-fatal, because many people thought this was a good way to get my attention – a casual abduction – but they might not necessarily be enemies. They were just terrified to talk with me on an even playing field, like they assumed I had some kind of temper or something.

This was my new way of showing them I was willing to listen with an open heart and mind.

The force ripped off my jacket and sent my abductor flying. I spun on my heels, holding up my hands in case he really was a bully of some flavor, ready to blast his jaw into the concrete.

My blood instantly coagulated as I heard only foreboding laughter and a chorus of strange boiling teakettle whistles. I really took note of my surroundings and realized my night had just gone to hell. We were in a world of roiling black fog.

And I was surrounded by a ring of about a dozen Candy Skulls – Calaveras – the Wardens, or Prison Guards, of Hell.

Shit.

That meant…

A figure slowly rose from beneath the fog where he had landed after my flash bang move. I saw the tall, pointed, black ears first. Then the long, dark snout of a jackal just below a pair of fiery indigo eyes – like windows into a different solar system. His bronze torso was well-muscled, but his abdomen was wrapped with white gauze, impeccably clean. He sported intricate golden bands around each bicep, looking like they could never be removed. As if placed on him at birth, and since his arms had grown so large, could now never be taken off. Ironically, I didn't remember them from the last time we had met.

His golden kilt appeared last, the sapphires dull and flat in this dark world, as he finally stood to his full-height – which was taller than anyone else present.

Anubis. King of the Underworld. Or Hell, as many knew it. Only now, I knew that Hell was more a general term, not only encompassing the Christian version with fiery lakes of brimstone and eternal woe. No, like those late-night infomercials, Hell had many added bonuses.

But wait, there's more!

Hell was comprised of *every* flavor of the various Underworlds across pantheons and belief systems. Greece's Elysium, Tartarus, Egypt's Field of Reeds, Christianity's Pearly Gates and Hell, and everything in the middle. Both the pleasurable places and the horrible places.

And Anubis had been employee of the month one too many times, earning the chance to rule the entire corporation. And he was kind of my boss.

Because I was his new Guide to Hell, and I'd kind of no-call no-showed him.

"Hey, Annie," I said, straightening my suit jacket. A button had popped off and I knew I had zero chance of ever finding it in the shifting fog. "Long time no see. What's new?" I asked jovially, furiously thinking of any possibility at escape. He had Shadow Walked us to this middle… place. The last time I'd been stuck here, I'd seen a window that led to the exit. But I sure didn't see one now.

"Annie?" Anubis grumbled hungrily.

"Annie Ubis. It's something friends do. Give each other nicknames."

"Surely, Temple, you don't think we are friends..."

I narrowed my eyes suspiciously, wondering if he'd really just mocked me by calling me Shirley Temple, or if he was being serious. His emotionless black mask gave me no answer.

Right. Time to switch tactics. "Is this like an employee appreciation event? Did you guys bring cupcakes or anything?" I asked, holding out my hands at the Wardens surrounding us.

"We did. But they melted. Our kitchen was too hot, apparently," he said drily, grinning as he stalked closer. The Calaveras quivered back and forth in unison, emitting their whistling, keening wail like a hive mind. I'd almost forgotten how creepy they were, what with their random, spasmodic twitches, and jerking movements.

"Well, I was kind of in the middle of something—"

"Imagine that," Anubis interrupted me. "Ironically, you're now still in the middle of... *something*." Anubis gestured a hand at the circle of Calaveras surrounding me. "It's time for us to go home. It would be flat out embarrassing if someone happened to want a Guide through Hell only to realize I didn't have one on hand."

I shivered. "Maybe I could be an on-call Guide. A work from home kind of arrangement. I have some things to take care of on the upper levels."

"This is my compassionate face," Anubis said lazily. "The one that shows you exactly how much I care about your to-do list." He stared at me, unblinking.

"I need to take out Mor—"

He was suddenly gripping me by the throat with his furry, black paw, and the Calaveras were all suddenly gone.

My nether regions instantly began to sweat, because the temperature went up by about six-hundred-and-sixty-six degrees.

Celsius.

And the pungent, syrupy-thick scent of sulfur was shoved into my nose like a wet rag, making my eyes instantly water. Then I was slammed onto a skillet, instantly ironing my suit free of wrinkles and almost breaking my spine.

I lay there, staring up at the ebony jackal, and thought that the black and red clouds limning him from behind gave the scene an altogether overly sinister feel.

Tortured souls wailed in anguish, like they were reciting the Pledge of Allegiance, but sadder.

I pledge allegiance, to the flag, of the United Pantheons of Anguish. And to eternity, for which it lasts. One miserable existence, under Anubis, with torture and agony for all...

I was on a rock island in a sea of lava.

"Hell, sweet Hell," I whispered.

CHAPTER 20

*A*nubis released me and climbed to his feet, walking away without an iota of concern for my ouchies – no kiss to make them feel better, and no Band-aid with a cartoonish superhero depiction of Cerberus. I waited a few beats before I stood, confident he wasn't waiting to just swat me back down. "Is it something I said?" I asked, brushing off my pants as I turned to look over at Anubis. He had waded out into the lava like it was a sunny day on the beach and he was cooling off his paws.

Except, you know, the soothing saltwater was molten lava.

Black pillars climbed up from the lava in places, crumbling even as I watched. Bolts of lightning from a mass of black clouds sluggishly drifting on the horizon slammed into the magma ocean, erecting fresh black pillars to replace the collapsing ones.

He waved absently at a figure who was drifting in what looked suspiciously like a bass fishing boat – complete with sparkles and flames painted onto the hull – a few dozen yards away from the shore of our rocky island. Charon, the Boatman to the River Styx – even though this wasn't the River Styx – dropped the can of beer he'd been pouring on his face, spraying his robes with a jet of light beer.

Charon was a bit of an alcoholic. He wiped the booze off his leathery, sewn-up lips, and waved back hesitantly, holding a skeletal hand over his eyes as if to verify we weren't an illusion or hallucination. Anubis was easy for Charon to distinguish, but the Boatman seemed to be uncertain who I was. I waved at him and he froze. Then he rushed to the back of his boat and flicked on what was definitely a trolling motor, guiding his craft our way.

What the hell? A bass fishing boat motor? In lava? At least he wasn't wakeboarding this time.

Anubis sighed impatiently, folding his arms as he waited.

Charon drove his fancy boat up onto the shore of our lone island, and I heard a collection of agonized groans as he did. Looking to the side of his boat, I noticed a rope tied to the hook, the other end dipping below the lava. I frowned, watching as the rope jerked and twisted spastically. Charon calmly picked up an oar and beat at the lava – at whatever was submerged below the surface attached to the rope. He splashed lava all over his robes in the process, but the splatter didn't scorch him.

The bubbling groans died down, and the rope stopped quivering. Charon grunted through his sewn-up lips and nodded self-importantly. That's when it hit me. Those were souls tied to the end of his rope. Like a string of fish. As he was joy-riding around the ocean of lava, he was dragging souls along behind him. I wasn't an expert. Neither was I the kind of guy to tell a man how to do his job, but… that seemed a little cruel to me.

Charon stepped onto shore, lost his balance, and promptly fell onto his face in a drunken stumble. Anubis sighed, turning his back on the both of us to survey his kingdom in silence.

Charon stumbled back to his feet, risking a sheepish glance at Anubis, but seeing he wasn't about to be reprimanded, shot me a grin that dangerously stretched the twine sewing his lips shut. I shivered but smiled back. "Hey, man."

"Temple! It's so great to be working with you!" His voice was like a nest of rattlesnakes on dry leaves in a windstorm. Also, his voice was in my mind, his lips unable to fully open thanks to the thick, twine stiches sewing them shut.

I ignored that last bit with a tight grimace and pointed at the rope. "What'd they do?"

Charon glanced back and chuckled. "Oh, them? They're just asshole politicians. We let them choose where they wanted to go, Heaven or Hell."

I blinked back at him. "They *chose* this?" I asked incredulously, waving my hand vaguely at the obviously unpleasant vacation destination.

Charon grinned, one of his stitches actually tearing through his ancient leather cheeks, making me wince uneasily. "Technically, yes. We—" he shot a look at his boss' back, changing what he'd been about to say, "well, *Anubis* had a grand idea. We took them on a tour, first. Like one of those timeshare salesmen. We let them spend a day down here, but we showed them a bunch of cool places from Elysium and Nirvana. We let them hang out with their departed friends and family, attend a rock concert, and threw more booze and drugs at them than they could deny. The next morning, we asked them to make their decision. Pearly Gates with a bunch of stuffy do-gooders, or Hell. After their tour, they obviously chose Hell."

I nodded slowly, pointing a finger at his string of souls hanging from the boat. "Then why are you dragging them through lava?"

He grinned, straining his stitches and making me grit my teeth in imagined pain. "You know, that's the best part. They asked the same thing on their first official day here, right after our first orientation course – *Endless Torture 101.* Crying about how it was nothing like the tour we had taken them on." Anubis chuckled to himself, the sound sending a shiver up my spine. He wasn't facing us, but his stance reeked of smug pride. "We told them that the tour with their friends was *election day*, and that we had needed their *votes*. But this was the day *after* elections, and we could do whatever the hell we pleased, now."

I shook my head at the cruel justice but couldn't help smiling. "Wow. That's... hardcore."

He nodded. "They did the same thing to their constituents on Earth. Seemed fitting." He shot a glance at Anubis' back, looking respectfully proud of the jackal. "He's a good boss. Harsh, but fair. You'll see. And just think, you'll get to see your parents." Anubis cleared his throat pointedly, and Charon lowered his gaze. "Well, you'll have the chance. Maybe... in passing."

I ran a hand through my hair, glancing up at the rock ceiling hundreds of feet above our heads. It was so high up that the patches of dark clouds weren't just pockets of smoke, but Hell's own weather system.

Charon nodded, following my gaze. "It will rain Hellfire soon," he sighed. "But as an employee, at least it won't harm you. Hurts a little, but you get used to it after a few decades."

"Charon..." I said, speaking lower. "I messed up. I let..." I hesitated, recalling how Anubis had reacted when I'd almost said his name a few minutes ago, "someone out of here, and I need to make that right. Or the world will suffer for it. If I have to come back after, I'll do it, but I have to convince Anubis to give me... well, enough rope to hang myself. It's not like he has anything to lose. If I die, I'm pretty sure I'll end up down here anyway."

Charon had gone entirely still and was staring down at the ground, kicking the ash and gravel absently, like a child pretending to be innocent when a mother catches him doing something sinister. I had perfected those movements over the years.

"He's right behind me, isn't he?" I asked, letting out a slow breath.

"Yes. *He* is," Anubis growled.

I turned to look up at him. He was a tall son of a bitch. Much taller than me. Which meant if I wanted to attempt a headbutt, I would get a face full of furry man chest. Still, I tried to make my look politely defiant. "I want to fix my mistake. Not out of any personal gain, but because it's on my shoulders. My responsibility."

"I know it is. But you failed once already. And then failed again tonight."

I sighed angrily but nodded. "I know."

"I gave you every opportunity to prove yourself. Searched your bag. Searched you. Even set it up for one of your friends to take your place as my guide. Why the sudden change of heart, if you're so noble?" he asked, already knowing the answer.

And he had done those things. I just hadn't been willing to allow Talon or Carl to sacrifice themselves for me. Because my parents had reminded me that Temples paid their own debts. Always. I let out a breath. Like I'd shown humility to Alvara, I needed to show honesty to Anubis. "From the beginning, I was planning on finding a way to break out," I admitted.

He watched me, waiting. Then he gave me a respectful nod.

"Was that you agreeing with me?" I asked, hopefully. "Because that would be super-duper—"

He snorted. "That was me acknowledging your *honor*." His gaze swept over his domain, as did one of his claws, as if needing to remind me of where we stood. "Although *honor* lives here – I run the place by it, after all – there is no *hope* here. Did you forget my sign out front? *Abandon hope, all ye who enter here...*"

I slowly reached into my shirt to lift up my thick, braided silver necklace where he could see. I'd gotten rid of the leather cord, deciding it was too flimsy to risk wearing something so valuable, and upgraded to a solid, rope-like silver chain.

To hold my Horseman's Mask prominent. I was the Fifth Horseman – the Horseman of *Hope*.

Because carrying an actual Mask around in a pocket was awkward, the Four Horsemen had all chosen a memento of some kind to conceal their Masks – Death had a scythe keychain, and War had a small amber plaque. I wasn't entirely sure what Conquest and Famine disguised theirs as though.

I'd chosen a silver coin. I could change it to other things if I really wanted, but anything other than a coin took a lot more effort – probably because a coin was what I had first chosen to conceal it. But I could change the *type* of coin, no problem. I'd been partial to a Silver Dollar, initially, but now had modified it to a Greek Drachma, for aesthetic reasons, and also a nod of respect to all my Greek allies.

And I'd added a decoy coin alongside the authentic Horseman's Mask coin.

Because ever since Mordred's escape, I'd been terrified that someone would steal it away from me, absconding with my Horseman's Mask. I'd found it to be a legitimate concern after testing the theory with Talon. If he yanked off the necklace, he would have the Mask in his paws.

As a result, I'd taken to spending a bit more time in learning how the Mask worked – on a very basic level. If I focused intently, I could make the coin appear in my pocket, even though Talon held the chain in his hand. I could now do this without any effort, imagining the coin wherever I wanted, and I didn't even have to use magic to do it.

The problem with that being Talon could instantly see that his stolen necklace no longer held the coveted coin. Which would give away my advantage in a real-life scenario.

So, I'd added a decoy coin. This way, I could retrieve my Mask, and leave the bad guy thinking he had succeeded. A little bit of illusion magic, and I could make the authentic coin invisible for a few hours, leaving the decoy as the only visible coin on the necklace.

Of course, I could have taken to simply not openly wearing the coin. But... so many people knew of the coin, now. What it signified. Whenever I met someone new – or ran into an old friend, even – they would instinctively glance down in search of my necklace and be on their best behavior.

It solved a lot of conflicts before they could ever happen. Like walking around with a flaming sword on my back. And if they didn't see me wearing it openly, they might search my pockets.

I jangled the necklace to Anubis, meeting his eyes. "Looks like I brought a little contraband with me," I said politely.

CHAPTER 21

*A*nubis sniffed it absently, not getting too close. He knew what it was. "Tell me how you broke out. How you broke Mordred out. You shouldn't have had the power to do either, let alone *both*. And I *tested* your power. It wasn't enough. That is why I accepted you as the Guide, because you weren't who I thought you were. Who I..." he paused, smiling wickedly in both disgust and amusement, "who I had *hoped* you were."

I frowned at him. He was making it sound like he had done me a favor, but he had been a raging dick when I'd met him.

He had definitely acted shady when we first met, obviously hoping to find something in my satchel that would benefit him – which he hadn't – and he'd even tried to give me a free trip to Hell without taking the long, grueling walk we had taken – by offering his Calaveras as a Lyft driver of sorts. I'd never learned his true motivations, or whether they would have been something harmful or helpful to me, but I'd assumed the latter since it had ended with him tossing me in a cell with a couple of Hell's biggest assholes.

He had also spied on my meeting with my parents, depriving me of vital information, and forcing them to give me only very vague, cryptic insinuations – that the three items they had left me were vitally important to the world.

The Hand of God.

The War Hammer.

The Hourglass.

They said – and many agreed – that there was some world-ending war coming – the All War – and the three inherited items were incredibly important. As were three people: me, Talon, and Carl. And she'd sure made it sound like we were vital to Alex, that he had a major part to play in all of this. Or that he was vital to us.

But if Alex was so important, why did people keep calling *me* the Cata-lyst? In my current position, I didn't really feel like asking Anubis for help. Instead, I considered his words, now.

And found myself frowning as a very vague suspicion emerged. "No way..." I breathed.

"There she is..." Anubis yawned. "Always late, but *maybe* worth the wait."

"You... were conning me. Playing the long game? But... what was your *angle*? All you did was make everything harder. Worse," I growled, having no idea how to fit his actions into a rational plan, and I was usually pretty good at that sort of thing. I was a schemer. A con-man, if I was being honest. I played people. Nowhere near as well as Callie Penrose did, but I was no slouch at it.

"You still don't get it..." he sighed. "And I can't afford to explain it. Or, to put it differently, if you have to ask, you can't afford to know it."

"I said that earlier..." I said, frowning accusingly.

"Gee, I wonder why I chose that phrase. Maybe because I've been following you. Weighing my options. Considering the infinite number of outcomes of this very discussion, the plethora of ripples that would roll across the universe. That you would come asking for another chance, and whether or not I wanted to double down on a lost cause. You owe me a debt. Owe me your very *soul*. I can find you *anywhere*. *Anytime*."

And he flexed his fingers into a fist. My chest felt like I suddenly had no air, and that he was squeezing my inner organs, leaving my flesh and bones pain free. I instantly hunched over, gasping like a fish out of water.

Wylde, that inner part of my psyche began to scream in a way I had never heard before. Like a man being burned alive. Slowly.

"And I'll get two souls for the price of one, which doesn't aid your cause." Then he released me by unflexing his fist. I sucked in a deep breath, not realizing I had fallen to my knees.

I took a moment to shake off the bruised feeling to my organs, regaining my composure. My choice was either to accept my new job in Hell or try to persuade Anubis to double-down on a two-time failure. I needed to carefully come clean with Anubis, whether I wanted to or not. I slowly climbed back to my feet and, sensing them both watching me, I let out a resigned breath. "Can we take a ride in the boat? I'll tell you a story, but I'd like to get a taste of my future. Might motivate me to be... more open."

Anubis grunted. "I hate standing still, so that's fine. But know this. I don't give two shits how *motivated* you are. I *own* your souls already. You better be very fucking convincing."

I nodded uncertainly, turning my back on him to follow Charon, who had already climbed into the boat. He opened a battered tackle box, and I felt tendrils of cold air emanating from within. There was no ice, but I heard a faint, tortured wail from inside, making me shiver. He had some poor soul tucked inside...

To keep his beer cold.

Noticing the casual nature of both Charon and Anubis not even really registering the sound of agony, I took a measured breath. That was my future, here. Even knowing the soul probably deserved it for whatever he had done, I didn't ever want to be armored by such callousness.

The Boatman snagged a couple cans and slammed the lid closed, cutting off the haunting lament. He held a can out to me with a smile, the gesture pulling the stitches covering his mouth tight. I managed not to wince and took it like a man dying of thirst. Anything cold would do in Hell. Charon pounded his in a blink, dumping half of it over his face like he was taking a pledge at a fraternity house, and then used his oar to shove the boat out into the waves of lava.

One drop splashed up onto me, scorching through my pants. I hissed in agony, desperately swatting at it to put it out before it ate through my flesh to the bone.

"Pour your beer on it," Charon offered.

I didn't even think about the ridiculousness of his suggestion, dumping my beer on the smoking wound. Anything to at least alleviate the pain would be welcome. As the ice-cold beer touched my skin, the pain instantly disappeared as if I had only imagined it. Even more surprising, I watched the wound wash away with the beer as if it had been no more than a smudge of dirt. I gasped in disbelief. There was no wound, and no burn mark. I still had a hole in my pants, but I watched as another droplet of lava slapped the damp, beer-soaked part of my pants. It puffed up with a little steam, but other than a slight pressure, I felt nothing. And my wet pants didn't burn.

The healing beer also made me fireproof.

I desperately reached into the makeshift cooler and pulled out three cans, ignoring the desperate soul within. The cans were home-made, and Charon had simply written *not-beer* on the face. I popped all three lids and took a light-beer shower like Charon had done, careful to cover my entire body. Doused, feeling safe, and noticeably better, I took another one out of the cooler to actually *drink*. Surprisingly, the cooler still held the same amount of... *not-beer* as when Charon had first opened it.

Charon noticed my surprised look and chuckled. "Freaking awesome job, right?" He saw me reading the label again and nodded. "Makes my passengers feel safer. They get squeamish about drinking and driving."

I stared at him for a moment, wondering if he was kidding. "Sure, Charon. Sure..." I finally said, deciding that some things were just better left unasked. I gazed out at our surroundings curiously, no longer concerned with any splashing lava. Thankfully, I noticed that even when the beer dried off from the extreme heat, I was still immune to the lava. Kind of like Achilles being doused in the River Styx, and immune to all harm.

I jolted, glancing down at my can in disbelief. "Where... do you get this beer, Charon?"

He grunted, flicking on his trolling motor. "Oh, I brew it myself."

I nodded woodenly. "You use the water from the River Styx, don't you?"

He cocked his head like an owl. "How did you know?"

I chugged my beer in one pull. "Just a lucky fucking guess, Charon." I was drinking beer made from the water that had essentially made Achilles immortal. Sweet Jesus. Instead of mentioning this, or trying to confirm it, I let it go. Whether the effects were permanent or not, it was keeping me alive just a little bit longer. Long enough to potentially persuade Anubis.

Now, it was time for my scheme, and to convince Anubis I was worth a third chance. I pointed absently to our right where I could see cliffs rising up in the distance. There were cliffs all around us, but these looked familiar. "Let's go that way," I suggested with a shrug. "Now, let me tell you how I broke out of Hel—"

"You think you're so fucking clever, don't you? You're used to being the smartest, richest, handsomest, strongest bastard in the brothel," Anubis suddenly snarled, not bothering to turn around and face me. He stared ahead of us like a lookout.

Thinking on the accusation, I nodded. Honesty was needed. Games and trickery would not work. Anubis was all about honor, and probably a lot cleverer than me. "Yeah. I guess so."

"Just know that most of us had to work for what we have. Entitlement will get you nowhere with me. I judge you on *your* actions, not the consequences and benefits of your *parents'* decisions. If you want to drive by their worksite, just fucking ask. No more games, Temple." This time, he actually glanced over his shoulder at me, and I saw his indigo eyes flickering with shadow. "Or my patience will expire."

"I'm sorry. It's a habit from up above," I admitted. "Can we drive by my parents' worksite?"

Anubis nodded, pointing the opposite direction from where I had intended. "They are that way. Not the same place you saw them before. I've heard all about your special memory and acted accordingly. I moved them to a new location. Depending on how this plays out, I might even let you talk to them again someday. But it better be a very good story. And a very *honest* story..." he slowly lifted a paw up in the air, still not bothering to look at me. Then he slowly began closing it into a fist in warning. A reminder.

"Okay!" I gasped before he could close it. "Got it. I'll tell the truth. The truth as I know it, anyway. Because I don't understand half of it myself."

Charon appeared to be devoting all his attention to driving, but I could see by his body language that he was mentally recording every word and gesture. "Better start talking, Nate..." Anubis reminded me after a few seconds of silence.

I took a deep breath and scooped up another beer.

CHAPTER 22

*a*fter I'd told him everything, I waited patiently, studying the cliff to our right, scanning the mass of souls swinging pickaxes into the rock. Each swing really didn't do much, maybe producing a few pebbles. So, either the rock was unbelievably tough, the pickaxes were dull or blunt, or this was Hell, and Anubis was just screwing with them. Like giving them plastic knives to cut down trees.

Like he was screwing with me now by not commenting on my story.

"Break!" a crystalline voice called out, and I was suddenly lurching to my feet in the boat.

I knew that voice. I opened my mouth to shout out my mother's name.

"Speak, and we're finished here," Anubis murmured. Even though he said it under his breath, the force of the command was enough for my words to die in my mouth.

Instead, I silently scanned the crowd, trying to find her. I finally found her seated on a palanquin with my father at her side. They were...

Eating pomegranate seeds.

The army of souls dropped their pickaxes and began to sing, locking hands to dance and frolic about in the break in work my mother had called out. Everyone looked... deceptively happy.

I frowned at Anubis, who was watching me, now. "What kind of sick joke is this?"

Anubis' lips pulled back in a mildly annoyed smile as he surveyed his souls. "Your parents were promoted."

I blinked at him. "You promoted them?"

Anubis sighed. "Actually, no. They uncovered a plot against me from their previous taskmaster." He shook his head absently. "Since then, they have saved me considerable time and resources. Their team produces more with less effort and punishment than any other team."

I just stared at him for a few moments, dumbfounded. My parents had introduced... what, capitalism? In Hell? "And what exactly are they *producing?* I didn't realize you had any trade partners down here."

He slowly met my eyes, and I found myself sitting back down under those merciless eyes, like staring into two black holes. "You really, really don't want me to answer that." He continued staring at me for a few more tense moments, then added, "Yet."

I nodded slowly, not entirely sure what I was nodding to, or why I might someday need to know what they mined in Hell. Or who it was sold to. I was entirely sure that I wouldn't like the answer, or that the knowledge might cost me a bit of my naivety.

"Thank you," I told him, turning to watch my parents still feeding one another. My father abruptly popped a pomegranate seed into his own mouth, and then flipped my mother onto her back to tickle her. I silently begged them to look our way, just one time, but they didn't.

I felt a few tears trailing down my cheeks as her laughter echoed above all other sounds in the caverns of Hell, even the singing voices of their crew, the gentle hum of Charon's trolling motor, the fiery splash of lava against the boat...

Then my father ceased his attack, stared down at her, and gave her a very slow kiss.

I shuddered, my heart dropping into my stomach, and stared down at my boots.

I wasn't sure if I was sad that it wasn't happening up on Earth at Chateau Falco, happy that they had found at least some tiny sliver of joy in this fiery world, anger at Anubis for punishing two wizards who had walked the world with the best of intentions, even if they often hadn't anticipated the consequences, or honored that he had allowed them to wield a position of power.

Or maybe it was a combination of it all. Seeing them briefly loving the hell out of each other with abandon – harboring no concern or fear. Turning their dull existence into a corporate retreat.

When I lifted my gaze, Anubis was watching me. He nodded his head infinitesimally.

"Your story… I have a few questions, but primarily, what were you *thinking*, unleashing an unbound Beast into the world?" he demanded, face entirely serious.

I grunted. "It was an accident. How was I supposed to know Kai would – or even *could* – knock up my house and bring a baby into the picture?" I snapped, shaking my head.

Because that was exactly what had happened, and the only reason I had been able to escape Hell was because that Baby Beast had come to save me, knowing only that his mother was concerned about a man wearing the Temple Family Crest. On Earth, B had followed my friends in search of the Crest, in search of the man who wore it, thinking it was his father. I studied the brand on my palm thoughtfully. Somehow, I'd been privy to B's visions anytime I fell asleep, dreaming what he saw. I'd watched – not knowing it was live footage rather than a trippy dream – as he'd traipsed through Hell, all alone, scared to death, but more concerned with protecting his daddy.

Well, the man he *thought* was his daddy.

Me.

Because my palm was branded with the Temple Family Crest.

Anubis leaned forward, inspecting the brand on my palm. Then he grunted, leaning back. "Brave little shit," he said, shaking his head.

I smiled. "Yeah. He thought I was his dad…"

Anubis shifted on his seat uncomfortably, eyes considering the satchel by my feet. "Show me how it works. I did sense that your purse could hold more than it should, but I didn't realize it could *hide* things." I gritted my teeth, preventing myself from correcting him.

It was a *satchel*, damn it.

I'd kept some things out of my story to Anubis. Not to lie, but because it literally had nothing to do with him, and I didn't exactly know where he stood on the whole good-guy-bad-guy spectrum. He sure seemed like an honorable guy, and a potential ally, but that didn't mean our motives would align. I hadn't told him about the three special items my parents had left me.

I held the satchel out to him. "Reach inside and grab my staff."

His face grew darker. "Really, Nate?" he asked in a low growl.

I sighed. "Slip of the tongue. Just try," I told him.

He did, reaching in up to his elbow, but after a few moments, pulled his arm back out without the prized staff. "No staff."

I nodded, reaching inside to pull out my long, black spear.

Anubis hit me like a linebacker, slamming me right into Charon, sending him cartwheeling off the boat and into the lava, his beer splashing all over my face. Anubis towered over me, blocking much of my view, but held me pinned to the floor of the boat by my throat with one paw. I'd dropped the spear to the floor of the boat, and there was no way I could reach it before he simply crushed my jugular. I saw him snatch up my satchel and fling his paw out over the lava, tossing it overboard. He was snarling down at me.

But all I could think about was my satchel sinking to the bottom of the lava ocean.

Seeing I no longer held the spear, he let go and stepped back. I rasped out a breath, and instantly scrambled to the side of the boat, staring down into the lava, searching for any sign of my satchel in the shifting, molten rock. I felt no heat, but instincts are hard to ignore. This was fucking lava, not water.

Before I could think too hard about it, I took a deep breath, and then shoved my hand into the fucking lava. Anubis watched me thoughtfully, making no move to stop me. I frantically grasped, sweeping my hand from left to right, wondering if the lava had simply burned the satchel out of existence in seconds.

My hands touched something, and I let out a gasp of relief, instantly lifting it up from the depths. Too late, I realized it was one of the souls tied to the boat, and he had grabbed me right back, latching onto my forearm. With a snarl, I yanked my hand out of the lava to find a balding man with a congress-issued grin staring up at me, fingers grasping onto the side of the boat for dear life. "Look," he pleaded in a rasping voice, "I can make you a deal. I can—"

I reached down, grabbed my spear, and swiftly stabbed him through the throat on instinct, not even consciously deciding to do it.

My spear... gobbled him right up, the massive ruby flashing once before the soulless soul of the senator winked out of existence. Remembering Anubis' dislike of the spear, I tossed it back into the boat, and reached out even deeper into the lava, desperate now to find whatever remained of my satchel.

Because the items inside were all I had left from my parents. I couldn't just let them go.

And… Callie had given me that satchel.

I had never – before this moment, my arm submerged in lava – really considered how much that gift had meant to me. That she had bought me such a rare gift was great, but more than that was the fact that she had gotten me a satchel, *at all*.

Callie had arrived at my door one night out of the blue, and had told Dean she needed me in Kansas City at a hotel – the same hotel where we had almost kissed…

Then she had promptly left before Dean could respond or go get me. Thinking she was in danger, I'd arrived half-dressed, ready for war, clutching a tattered satchel full of dangerous weapons to help me save her. I hadn't even hesitated to answer her call.

And I'd found her – absolutely not in danger – sitting on the roof of the hotel. She'd teased me about the satchel absently, and then we'd spent some time drinking and talking. She hadn't been in danger at all – she'd just wanted to bounce some ideas off of me.

And seeing me arriving ready for war with a torn satchel, she had silently decided that I needed a new one.

She could have bought me a Mickey Mouse satchel for all I cared. Quality wasn't the point. A friend – one who knew me barely at all at that point in our lives – had gotten me one of the most thoughtful gifts she could think of. Not something that I said I *wanted* – anyone could do that – but something she knew I *needed*.

People don't normally do that. They discover your interests and find something super flashy and cool that you would probably like based on those interests. Or they just flat out ask you.

But to silently observe someone, pick up on the subtle nuances behind the person, silently dissecting what made them tick, and what meant the most to them, and then to nonchalantly buy them the thing they wouldn't have ever asked anyone for…

That was an attention to detail rarely seen. And to do that for someone you hardly knew…

So, yeah. I realized in this moment that the fucking satchel was pretty fucking important to me, for multiple fucking reasons.

And hanging out of Charon's boat in the deepest levels of Hell, with

Anubis sitting beside me, having just obliterated a soul with my mysterious new spear, and shoving my arm up to my armpit in an ocean of lava, a funny thought flittered across my mind.

Maybe, *just maybe*, this was what love felt like.

Not the ocean of lava aspect, but the emotion fueling me to shove my arm *into* the lava without concern for the consequences.

I was waving my arm back and forth, now, panting as I stretched, reaching, the molten lava rolling over my fingers like warm syrup, when Anubis cleared his throat behind me.

I glanced over my shoulder – still searching with my other hand – and froze.

Anubis dangled my satchel in his claws, letting it swing back and forth. He was grinning as I stared at him, my mind short-circuiting. I'd seen him throw the satchel…

"I always wondered," he said conversationally, "what it felt like, pretending to throw a ball and then watching as your dog took off in a dead sprint, chasing down the ball…" he grinned wickedly, "that you're really still holding in your hand. It makes more sense, now," he admitted, tossing the bag at my feet.

I stared into the dog-like god's soulless eyes. "You… are an asshole." I couldn't believe I'd fallen for it.

Anubis ignored my accusation, giving me a very deep look, his eyes narrowed as if he hadn't truly seen me – or recognized my level of insanity – up until this point.

Something brushed my hand – the one I had forgotten about in the lava – and I shrieked instinctively, jerking it away and splashing lava all over me in the process.

Luckily, it didn't burn, and I turned to see Charon treading lava, staring up at me with a concerned frown. He had reached out to touch my hand, scaring the shit out of me.

"It's couture," I muttered, shaking lava from my fingers.

I let out a faint shudder, my brain only just now beginning to process what I had done – submerging my entire arm in lava. I should be dead. Good thing Charon's beer hadn't worn off.

I reached out a hand, pulling Charon back into the boat. He was staring at me wonderingly. "I'm really glad your beer kept me from losing an arm," I told him, laughing shakily. I felt slightly dizzy, the adrenaline wearing off and likely sending me into a form of shock.

He stared at me, shaking his head. "The beer wore off ten minutes ago," he told me softly. "I thought you knew that when Anubis pretended to throw your satchel into the lava."

I jolted, staring down at my arm.

And saw a faint flicker of gold where my veins were visible under my skin.

Anubis grunted, staring at my arm thoughtfully. "Looks like I guessed right... You do have a little god in you..."

CHAPTER 23

Charon kicked the motor back on, not speaking or drinking as he did. Which let me know just how bizarre the situation had really been.

"I needed to test your heart," Anubis told me, obviously not a question. He held up a paw, pads aimed at me, and closed his eyes, murmuring something exotic under his breath, probably Egyptian. Or Jackal-ese.

"And my mortality, apparently," I muttered, studying my hand. The flickers of gold were faint, maybe one or two a minute. A weaker form of what they had been directly after I had killed Athena, when they had shone like permanent glow sticks for a short time.

"I don't understand," I finally admitted. "You saw, I barely had any last time I was here, and I used the last of it to power up my hammer and fight Alaric, accidentally breaking Mordred out of his cell. Why would you put me in that room, anyway, knowing Mordred was locked up in there?"

Anubis studied me, thoughtfully. "Thank you for finally telling me about the hammer…"

I winced inwardly, realizing that I'd just slipped up.

But Anubis just chuckled. "I knew about the Key from the beginning," he said, waving a paw dismissively. "Odin told me about it before you first came to Hell. But when I searched your bag and didn't find it…" he said, locking eyes with me, "I thought we'd been wrong. That you weren't the one to take out Mordred."

I did a whole lot of staring, remembering that Anubis had seemed desperate to find a Key in my satchel. I hadn't known what he meant at the time, but to hear that he'd known about it all along… that Odin had told him about my hammer…

Made me feel very concerned.

Odin didn't just talk hammers with anyone. Only one hammer really held his interest…

Anubis continued, saving me from panic-inducing introspection. "My original plan had been that you had enough god juice to kill him outright. When I realized you didn't, and had no Key, I saw no harm in tossing you in the cell." He lifted his eyes to mine. "But look at you now…"

"But what does all of this *mean*?" I demanded.

"I think it means you're the fucking Catalyst. You already claimed your Devourer," he muttered, kicking the spear that still sat on the bottom of the boat. "Although you failed to fucking *use* it when you had Mordred sitting twelve inches away from you," he growled.

I frowned. "Devourer?"

Anubis sighed. "Souleater, Devourer, Neverwas… More of them than I'd care to admit floating around on Earth. They go by many names. But before you play with a Devourer, I recommend you regrow your Ichor."

I frowned at him, then down at my veins, wondering what I wanted to ask him about, first. "The gold stuff? I thought it was only called Ichor when inside a god."

Anubis arched a brow, his silence speaking volumes. "We already talked about this…"

I was already shaking my head. "Nope. I'm not a god. My parents are right over there, remember? In your chain-gang."

He waved away my comment. "Semantics. A Godkiller *becomes* a god by default. In a way. It's all very complicated for your tiny, almost non-existent, speck-of-dust-sized brain, so let's just leave it at the fact that you're techni-cally a god. And technicalities can win *Wars*."

I studied him. "The Catalyst thing…" I said out loud.

He nodded. "That's a part of it. Or, that's the whole of it, depending on how you look at these types of things."

"Right. *These types of things*. Like wondering why hot dogs come in packs of ten, but hot dog *buns* come in packs of eight," I mused. "Just a pointless debate. Fun for a laugh, but ultimately, not that big—"

I cut off as he abruptly lifted his paw, reminding me of his ability to fist me into oblivion.

Well, *use* his fist to crush my heart, not the *other* kind of fisting.

Realizing that was all he was going to say about it, I scratched at my chin. Was that why the lava hadn't harmed me? Just to be safe, I reached into the cooler for a few more beers, dumping them liberally over myself. Satisfied, I set my elbows on my knees.

He met my eyes. "I applaud you on deceiving me, and I forgive you for it."

This was him doing me a very big favor, judging by the look in his eyes. I nodded gratefully. "Thank you. So... how do I regrow my Ichor? I thought I used up the last of it to beef up the Hammer."

"The Hammer. Right." He was watching me very intently, that smug grin on his face.

"Yeah. The big fucking stone hammer, or *Key*, as you called it," I explained. Part of me wondered if the Hammer was some sort of Devourer, since I'd seen it eat Alaric's soul. But it didn't have a stone on it, and it hadn't eaten every soul it came across, where my spear sure had.

Anubis was silent for a few minutes, eyes distant, coming to some decision. "You are going to go back to your realm," he said, turning back to me, and seeming to speak very deliberately, choosing his words carefully. "You are going to use every tool in your precious little treasure box, your Mask, Ichor, and every speck of magic you can beg, borrow, or steal. Maybe this will give you the strength to destroy Mordred. The table and sword are not what you think, and he must not get his hands on them. You are going to make an example of him. You will return my Nine Souls. You are my emissary in this. You are my hand. I own your soul—"

Charon popped the tab on another beer, ruining Anubis' threatening speech. I was finding more and more reasons to be happy that I had always paid homage to the alcoholic, scarecrow-looking reaper. "I think he gets it," Charon muttered drily, taking a healthy gulp of his beer. "Maybe you should calm the fuck down."

The resulting silence was as brittle as glass. "*What* did you just say?" Anubis snarled, leaning forward.

Charon, with the patience of a priest, downed the rest of his beer, then crushed it on his forehead, tossing the empty out into the lava. I guess it wasn't littering when the can would dissolve in milliseconds.

Charon gripped the paddle in his hand and climbed to his feet. He thumped the butt into the boat and I shivered as I felt a pulse of power emanate from it. Then I blinked to see that the paddle was suddenly a rough, but deadly looking iron spear, of sorts, like an iron leaf, but each of those nicks and gouges as sharp as any razor. Like someone had made a paddle into a blade, sharpening the edges, beating it against thousands of other blades, and then retooling each scarred indentation. The beauty was in its function, not its perfection.

Anubis sat very still, lips curled back defiantly, challenging Charon and his spear with respectful wariness. I realized I was in a very shitty location for this family feud.

Right in the middle.

And what was Charon *thinking*? Wasn't Anubis his *boss*? I didn't want to have the Boatman's death on my conscience.

Charon slowly lifted a hand to the stitches on his mouth and tugged one free. Then another, until half his mouth was open. Anubis might as well have been a statue, no longer looking as aggressive. I don't exactly know how to describe what emanated from Charon's mouth, but it was like silvery fog, and it was as cold as liquid nitrogen.

Charon was like Mr. Keystone. I had never thought I would hero-worship cheap light beer, but in this moment, sitting on his boat in the middle of Hell, watching the Boatman flex his muscles for the first time against Anubis, I suddenly realized that frat bros across the universe actually had a spokesperson – a god listening to their drunken prayers.

All those lonely, desperate frat bros praying for women with lower standards, stronger protein shakes, popped collars, new Axe Body Spray scents, and more *s-medium* sized muscle tees.

Charon spoke. "You're on my boat, Anubis. I think you just might be overplaying your hand, here. Temple has shown you nothing but respect, even impressed you, as impossible as that is to believe. Perhaps you should extend the fucking courtesy." He lifted a hand to another set of stitches, and I realized that this last knot was one solid thread.

The last stitch that – if tugged free – would open his mouth entirely. Which, judging by the dog-headed god's *I just crapped on the living room floor* face, wasn't a desirable outcome.

"I could give this a little yank..." Charon said, pinching the twine between his fingers.

Anubis lifted a hand, stalling him. He didn't look pleased, but he did look defeated. In fact, he looked... humbled. "Well played, Boatman. One so easily forgets that you are formidable in your own right. Always sitting back, drinking your brews, cruising the lakes in leisure. Perhaps I had forgotten why you were hired," he admitted, dipping his head slightly. "My apologies." He turned to me. "To the both of you."

I nodded, remembering that I really wasn't in the physical position to get out of the way if they threw down, and although my Ichor had prevented the lava from melting my arm off in point-three seconds, I wasn't sure I was up to testing it out with a swim to the shore while the two duked it out.

"But my demand still stands. You will do this thing," Anubis said in a gravelly tone.

"Then he shall get something in return," Charon pressed.

Anubis studied him. "What did you have in mind, Boatman?"

"Relieved of his debt to you, and he gets two get-out-of-Hell-free cards," Charon said, as if he had planned this out well ahead of this conversation.

Anubis blinked at him. "Two..." he said, glancing thoughtfully at the cliffs we had left behind, where my parents had been working.

My heart suddenly skipped a beat in realization. Wait... what the hell was going on here?

Anubis smiled way too emphatically for me to feel entirely good about it. "Agreed."

"Agreed," Charon said.

When I hesitated, Charon nudged me with his wicked paddle, and I felt a bone deep frost flick my soul, causing me to yelp as I jumped clear. "Fine. Agreed," I shivered.

Anubis gripped me by the shirt, pulling me close. "I'm warning you... pull no punches against Mordred. If you think, for just one moment, that you are overpowered, you will realize the error in your judgment. Overkill is your only salvation. Use every tool, every *Key* at your disposal, not just your Devourer. It's not strong enough to hold all Nine Souls, so make sure your cat's Eyeless gets a Devourer, too. I recommend a blue one," he said with a meaningful wink. "Maybe then, you'll stand a slim chance of survival."

I blinked at the rapid fire. "My cat? What the hell does that mean? Talon?"

Anubis nodded. "His spear. It's just like yours, but it is missing its Devourer, so it's Eyeless at the moment."

I blinked at him. "Talon... his last *name* is Devourer," I said, freaking out a little.

"Huh. Imagine that," Anubis muttered, smirking. "Almost like it *means* something."

I shook my head, clutching my satchel and spear anxiously. "No. *I* named him Talon the Devourer. As a *child*. There is no *way* I could have known it meant something more important. I was just a stupid fucking kid giving my pet a name," I snapped, realizing that I was panting, shaking my head furiously in denial.

"From the mouths of babes," Anubis chuckled.

I was shivering, hugging my toys to my chest like a security blanket. My temples began to throb, not helped by the fact that I was still jerking my head back and forth in denial. I had just been a kid naming a cat Pan had brought over. An orphan. Coincidences like that didn't exist. I felt like I was drowning, spinning out of control, my memories of my childhood in Fae – the moment I had met Talon and named him – merging with my current predicament, and the importance of these Devourers in killing Mordred, in taking away his Nine Souls.

I panted, inhaling great deep breaths, my head throbbing harder now.

And like a good friend, Anubis decided it would help to pick me up and hurl me out of the boat and into the ocean of lava while I was in the middle of my panic attack.

I squeezed my toys desperately, begging for help like a lost boy, alone in this scary place. Anubis waited until the last possible moment to rip open a Gateway beneath me – when I was only scant millimeters away from splashing into the bubbling waves of lava. Which meant I was already a few seconds into a very manly scream, wondering where the Gateway was going to deposit me.

And if I would be safe there.

If my pet cat would be there to hug me and protect me.

Where my parents were.

If... Pan would be there to help with this sudden blinding headache threatening to rip my skull in half. *Where are you, Pan!*

CHAPTER 24

I slammed into the arms of a big, meaty, black man with all the force of a wet towel.

Not one of my top three ways to wrap up a Saturday night. I was panting, shaking, and maybe freaking out a little bit, flashing back and forth between my Fae childhood and my sudden trip to Hell. And my head was pounding, making me dizzy and sick to my stomach.

The big black man pried a white satchel from my hands and quickly draped it over my head to rest on my shoulder. The strap was chain, which was odd.

Forged metal was… dangerous, wasn't it? Wood was much safer.

Then the man was propping me up with both hands, shaking me gently to look into his face. He looked familiar, his eyes glowing a burnt orange color, and his irises were very strangely shaped, like horizontal bars. He looked desperate.

And he looked to be a disciple in the school of violence.

He shook me again, causing my headache to bloom with new intensity. "You keep repeating yourself, Temple. *Where is Pan?* I can help if you just tell me who Pan is!" he pleaded in a strange accent. "We've been looking everywhere for you, mate!"

At his questions, a moment of panic flashed over me, and then rage, and then… confusion.

What the hell was going on with me? I knew this man, didn't I? Why had he and his allies been looking for me? And why did he want Pan?

A bone-deep fear settled into my fingers, making them ache. I was shaking... literally.

This man... terrified me, for some reason. But where had he come from? How had he found me? Hadn't I just been in a boat? I shivered with fresh horror at even the idea of that.

Boats were bad. Very, *very* bad. *Everyone* knew that.

The man repeated his question, and something inside of me just snapped. Anger and fear took over me in a roaring wave, and I unleashed every emotion into one desperate blast.

I screamed a feral cry as I flung out my free hand and sent him flying a good dozen feet into a stone wall. I was suddenly gripping a stick in my hand.

I stared down at it, frowning as I tried to remember what it was, why it was both familiar and not familiar.

It was crackling with red lightning, crimson smoke curling around a giant ruby in the blade, and it felt both content and eager. I studied it, stroking the hilt, silently talking to it, gaining its trust. It stiffened abruptly, surprised that I could talk to it.

They always were, the first time I spoke back to them.

I smiled, realizing it hadn't spoken to anyone in a while. "Oh, you just ate," I said to it, nodding. "And you're still hungry."

I heard the dangerous man getting back to his feet. He was staring at me, holding out his palms carefully to show me he had no weapons. I glared at him. "You have no idea what I've been through!" I shouted at him.

"Easy, Temple," he said. "I wasn't trying to hurt you. I was just trying to calm you down. You've been gone for hours."

I hesitated, feeling suddenly confused. "Temple..." I repeated, thinking desperately.

He cocked his head uncertainly. "Yes. Let me help you, Temple. I think you bumped your head..." he said, taking a few slow steps towards me, hands still out.

I cringed the moment he said *Temple* again, gasping as what felt like a blade scraped the inside of my skull. Then it was gone and I rubbed my head with my free hand. I was... injured. And I was missing something.

Something was lost. I was lost... I blinked a few times, massaging my neck. What had I lost?

I glanced down at the bag on my hip, and then to the hungry spear.

Then I suddenly noticed what was wrong. "Where's my Shadow?" I demanded. I couldn't remember *why* it was important, but losing my shadow was a death sentence.

Maybe the big man walking towards me had seen it.

Wait... did I know him? Had he given me his name? Why was he coming closer?

Now that I thought about it, watching him approach with deliberately slow steps, I didn't like the fact that he was an adult. A sneaking, creeping adult, his hands out to *catch* me. Adults, other than my parents, were enemies, here.

The man had cocked his head at my question, pretending to be confused. "Your shadow? Probably behind you..." he said. He was good. Was this a trick? They were always trying to trick us, the skulking bastards.

"No, he's... missing," I told him, feeling a wave of dizziness roll over me, and forgetting who was missing. I placed a hand on my head, closing my eyes as the headache began to throb like a deep drum, my eyes feeling like they were bulging with each *thud* of my heart.

I sucked a breath through my teeth, gripping the hungry stick in my hand. Hungry stick... That sounded familiar. With a faint *ticking* sound like a clock in my mind, I recalled it. A giant tree. Friends were near that tree. I swept the area around me, seeing no familiar trees. Where was it? Where was I? How far had I walked if I couldn't see the damned tree?

"Peter told me to catch him..." I mumbled, spinning in a slow circle, searching for the tree.

All I saw was a giant building made of stone.

And grass. *Green* grass. I frowned. Why wasn't it purple?

And why wasn't that small bush chiming in the wind? Metal bushes were supposed to chime and jingle. And I didn't see any telltale flickers of flame that implied pixies or fairies dancing about on their nightly sentry duties.

Or any of the other boys.

I was alone. With an *adult*.

"Where... is... my... cat...?" I whispered desperately. Talon could help me. He never lost his way. He was my brother. My family. My friend.

I snarled, curling my lip as I hunched low, ready to run from the man. "What did you do to my cat?" I hissed. "He will *devour* you…"

The big man stared back at me, and his eyes glowed like twin bonfires in the moonlight. "I think you need to come with me…"

"No, no, no, no…" I said as another wave of pain struck my mind, making me drop the spear in my hand. I was panting desperately. "My Shadow. My cat. Where are they, you filthy pirate?" I wheezed.

He began walking closer, holding out his arms to capture me.

In sudden desperation, I jumped up, anxious to escape to freedom.

I rose a foot off the ground and then fell to my rear.

The man was moving much faster now that he realized I was weakened, land-locked, and vulnerable. In fact, he was running, and shouting for reinforcements, calling out strange names.

"Star light, star bright, first star I see tonight…" I whispered, shivering so hard my teeth were clattering. But he was moving so *fast*. I had to stop him. Before he woke the others. "I wish I may…" he was so close, now. "I wish I might…" he reached out to me, hands like claws. "Have this wish… I wish tonight," I wheezed.

And the man flew up into the air, spread-eagled, gasping in disbelief. He began to roar in outrage and fear. I felt a cold front in the distance and pulled it close like drawing up a blanket over the warmer air, here, creating an instant vortex of wind as the two clashed against each other. The wind ripped at his clothes, sliced into his skin, and bit at his eyes with dust and debris.

I lay on my back, staring up at him. In defense against the wind scoring his flesh, great scaled wings suddenly exploded from his back, attempting to protect himself from the torrent of power, making him look like a winged crocodile. I *knew* he'd been dangerous.

"Where. Is. My. Cat?" I snarled, loud enough for him to hear over the vortex of wind tearing at him from every direction.

I began stretching out his limbs, ready to rip him to pieces, weaving beams of moonlight and affixing them to his appendages, ready to rip the wings off this fly. All the while, my wind pounded, tore, shredded, and hammered at him from every direction.

I would do anything for Talon the Devourer. My best friend.

"Nate, STOP!" a booming voice shouted.

I ignored them, wondering if my victim was named Nate.

I was going to make an example of this one.

"He doesn't understand!" a familiar voice snarled. "WYLDE! GAME OVER!"

And I released the man from midair, letting him collapse to the ground. My cat, Talon, had finally shown up to help me. To save me. Moments later, he was hovering above me, thumbing back my eyelids.

"Hey, Tal," I whispered. "I got him. Filthy pirate. But I think I lost my shadow..." I admitted, beginning to cry. "Help me find it? You're better at catching them..."

Tal gasped inwardly, and I saw tears flowing down his furry cheeks. But something was wrong. He looked so... *old*.

None of us looked old.

Well, except my parents. But they were safe.

"Yes, Wylde..." Tal breathed. "You got him. Thanks for saving us. But never fear. Your Shadow is here. *I'm* here, brother..." and one of his tears hit my own cheeks.

I grabbed it, plucking the tear off my cheek and watching as I rolled it back and forth over my knuckles playfully. Then I made a fist, drinking it into my heart.

Tal gasped, sobbing openly at the gesture of undying loyalty.

Finally, feeling safe, I closed my eyes to sleep.

It was a good night to sleep under the stars. It had been a few days since we'd done that.

Something Tal had said tickled a memory, but I was too tired to grasp it.

"Never... never... never..." I murmured as Tal scooped me up in his arms and carried me to shelter.

But I fell asleep before I could finish the thought. I'd ask him at Mess in the morning. After our food fight, of course...

125

CHAPTER 25

$\mathcal{I}$ stood in a cavernous marble forest – the pillars were too wide for me to wrap my arms around and they climbed so high that I couldn't see what they supported. Silver and black veins streaked the white marble, and as I looked closer, I even spotted a few golden traceries. Despite the place being empty and devoid of inhabitants, no dust covered the pristine marble pillars or floor – they were clean enough to reflect the flames of torches in their richly-embellished silver sconces.

My mind flickered between confusion and amused recognition, back and forth like a metronome, my very brain seeming to throb.

I began turning in a circle to study my surroundings but stiffened at the sound of scraping stone. I waited, ready for an attack, but the sound had ceased the moment I caught onto it. I resumed my slow circle, and the sound returned.

Directly behind me.

I spun, hands out to grip and shred the inferior form of existence with my bare...

I blinked, staring out at my hands. Because they were not *hands*, but *claws*. Wicked, stone claws of black quartz. And I knew—

I immediately cringed, rolling my shoulders like some unseen person had just trailed a cold fingernail down my spine. A warm, relaxing sensation rolled over me in its wake, and my headache vanished in a heartbeat.

The brief concern I had felt was abruptly replaced by idle amusement. *Had the Smiths forged me some new gauntlets?* I thought to myself. I inspected my hands, turning them this way and that, but frowned as I realized they were *part* of me, not a Sung Armor piece. I studied myself more directly, finding that my entire form was this stone flesh, and the sound I had heard behind me was...

A pair of long, skeletal wings extending from my shoulders – but there was no membrane between the spines to aid in flight. *Curious...* I thought to myself. The stone spines looked to be cracked and fragile. I couldn't discern if it was an injury, or something trying to break free from within. It didn't hurt, so I dismissed it.

An idle thought came to mind. *This was a Dream Orb.* It had to be. One of my siblings was playing a prank on me, turning me into a monster while I slumbered in the Ether.

I let out a laugh, shaking my head. I'd return the favor eventually. With nothing else to do until the Dream Orb popped, I decided to explore. I began to walk onward, choosing a direction at random. This Song wasn't complete, but rather shadowy and dark at the edges where the Singer had chosen not to flesh out the myriad of harmonies required to make Dream Orbs so authentic so as to force the victim to mistake them for actual reality.

There was a fragile, enclosed feeling to the place, letting me know I wasn't outdoors. "Shoddy work," I muttered, shaking my head. I'd been in this Dream Orb before. I knew that much, even if I couldn't recall the details of my earlier visits. A soft voice – like a memory of a dream, whispering on the currents of time – drifted into the edge of my thoughts. Upon acknowledgment, it was suddenly a shouted Song.

HORSEMAN!

I jolted, a sharp pain lashing my temples. I crouched down, hissing as I clutched my head between my palms. The warm, soothing sensation over my neck had simply fled, replaced with an alarmed sense of panic.

"What... the fuck is a Dream Orb?" I whispered out loud, my voice echoing slightly in the midst of the marble columns. The headache faded and I stood, blinking slowly. What had that been about? Those hadn't been my thoughts... Hadn't been *me*...

"I am Nate Temple..." I murmured woozily. I didn't remember arriving at this place, or how I had traveled here, but my mind was a murky fog, full of half-remembered euphoric dreams and half-forgotten debilitating nightmares.

I studied my surroundings warily. Someone was here, messing with my mind. But the harder I tried to discover the source, the more severe the aching throb in my head grew, warning me not to think too hard in this... place.

But focusing on my wings had helped kick him out of my head. Because I knew what they were. My Horseman wings. I latched onto that thought, letting it ground me firmly.

"I'm the Horseman of Hope," I said aloud, feeling that enticing sense of relaxation struggling to subsume my body and mind, but it rebounded on contact with my rock-solid belief and acceptance that I was a Horseman.

"Horseman of Hope," I repeated defiantly, gritting my teeth. The sensation of that other being departed in search of easier prey. I hoped...

I shivered involuntarily and resumed my walk, wanting away from this area. Torches popped to life ahead of me and extinguished behind me, but I felt no whispers of magic causing it. They just changed. I altered my course, angling to the right between more columns, and the torches lit in different sequences, the flames in slightly different, muted, chromatic hues.

The sound of my stone wings dragging across the floor echoed as I moved. Was... my Mask trying to protect me from... whatever that other being had been? The one trying to use my body like a puppet? I began flexing my fists, the sound of grating stone like a constant reminder of who I was, preventing that other... thing from taking over again.

I soon came upon an arcing ring of three steps descending down into a luxurious royal suite of sorts. A titanic bed built from precious metals sat against the far wall – the first border I had found in this place of fog and mirrors.

Then I saw *her*.

My heart shuddered out of rhythm, then kicked back into overdrive to make up for it.

Callie Penrose stood on the other side of the bedroom area, leaning out over a balcony, her back facing me. She wore some kind of white toga, her pale hair seeming to glow. She was shaking her head piteously at what she saw. *Storms, War, damnation, chaos...* I thought to myself, somehow knowing what she was seeing.

Because... I had seen it before. A shredded, beaten down castle on the horizon, armies on the march to demolish the last remnants of an already failed and forgotten kingdom.

Camelot.

"A waste of manpower," I whispered under my breath, not consciously deciding to speak.

Callie spun around, stepping into the shadows as she searched for the source of the sound – the echo of my voice. But she apparently couldn't see me, just like I couldn't make her out clearly in the shadows. The balcony behind her looked damaged, as if struck with a powerful force, small piles of rubble on the ground where she had stood. Had she done that?

I remained silent, not wanting to spook her as she approached the room, slipping from shadow to shadow. She looked as if she hadn't realized anything beyond the balcony existed before my voice had alerted her. But she stopped at the top of the stairs, distracted by the room between us, still not noticing me opposite her.

She wore a bandage around her head, covering her eyes, and twin silver trails streaked down her dirty, scratched cheeks. I tensed instinctively, suddenly furious that she had been attacked, but she didn't look to be in pain. She wore a brilliant white toga, leaving one shoulder bare, and her forearms were wrapped in stained gauze.

I devoured her with my eyes, my fingers flexing subconsciously.

It was a primal sensation, not a purely physical one. As if her very *being* was drawing me in, not just her beauty. I followed her gaze, studying the room in an effort to peel my eyes from her allure.

Her gaze tracked to the exotic, priceless bed – large enough for a dozen people – and then the wall behind the intricate headboard. The wall was some form of natural spring because crisp, tantalizing water dribbled down the surface in an eternal flow.

The air was warm, and I noticed the fireplaces on either side of the bed – one of white flame and one of black. The crackling fires and gurgling spring had an overall soothing tone, a harmony of sorts...

And in my distraction, that warm sensation rolled back over me, this time like a waterfall.

I rolled my shoulders, shaking my head slowly at the familiar transition.

Much better, I thought to myself.

I knew I could join in that harmony of sound, creating a Song like the world hadn't heard in millennia. But I no longer felt like Singing. It had been a long time since I had Sung...

My jaw clenched at even *considering* using my voice to build something beautiful.

Never again... I promised myself, and the tension evaporated like a puff of dandelion.

The woman – *my* woman, I decided hungrily – turned to face me, and my heart thundered louder than the first peal of thunder I had Sung at the creation of time itself.

She held a crackling white spear with two bands of shifting black rings on the haft, breaking it into thirds. I felt the dull throb of resistance growing in my mind but fought against it. Persistent host, this one was...

I studied the spear again, and the resistance intensified. Confusion even began to drift over me, an emotion I hadn't felt in eons. Although impressed, I squashed the host's resistance, growing annoyed.

I called out to the spear, demanding to know its story. It retaliated, refusing to answer my call, and I frowned harder. All I could tell was that it was powerful, had been broken, and then re-forged – although inexpertly.

The woman, as if suddenly noticing me, turned to face me directly, her shoulders squared, defiant, and uncompromising.

That blindfolded look struck out like an invisible wildfire.

I rocked back slightly, the alien sensation fleeing my mind.

I blinked rapidly, clenching my fists. I was *me* again. *Nate Temple. Horseman of Hope*, I thought to myself, mentally screaming the declaration as loud as I could. Whatever Callie had done with that look had sent the thing screaming from my mind.

I felt it circling me furiously, searching for another opening to invade, some chink in my mental armor that would allow it to take over again. It wasn't happy that it had been knocked out of me. Wasn't familiar with being knocked down.

Horseman of Hope. I'm the Horseman of Hope! I thought furiously, repeating it again and again in my mind. With a savage hiss, the entity left me, heading back to the columns.

Even thinking of it seemed to draw its attention, inviting it to enthrall me again, so I walled up my mind with a looped chant of *Horseman of Hope, Horseman of Hope...*

As a backup, I began flexing my claws – anything to help keep an anchor to reality.

Callie stared at me, not seeming to notice the mental assassin stalking me.

The way she faced me, assessing me up and down, let me know that despite the bandage over her eyes, or the silver tears on her cheeks, she could still *see*.

She took a hesitant step down the stairs, closer to me and the suite. Then another.

Like a mirror image, I advanced a step. Then another.

When she stopped, I stopped, wondering if she was also fighting some foreign entity in her mind. If so, I didn't want to alarm it.

Callie took a last step down into the bedroom, and I mirrored her movement. She stared at me, sucking in a quick breath. Did that mean she recognized me, but was scared of my Horseman's Mask? My wings? Or... Maybe this *wasn't* Callie, but a mental invader like I'd been fighting.

She lifted a hand, even though she wasn't close enough to touch me.

I smiled hopefully, mirroring the motion.

She looked slightly relieved, taking a step closer. If she was enthralled, she never would have looked at me with relief. Again, I mirrored her, taking a step closer.

She frowned, then, glancing down at her ankles. She grew suddenly tense, as if only just now seeing her own attire. Her own form.

"Who are you?" she asked in a cautious whisper, glancing back up at me. I clenched my claws again, reminding myself who I was, not giving that other entity a chance to swoop in. Because Callie didn't seem to know me. More than anything, I'd *needed* Callie to *know me*. Even more than I needed the Mask to remind myself who I really was...

Callie abruptly shuddered, as if asking the question aloud had snapped her out of some daze.

I stared, hoping desperately... Then it hit me. She needed to see my *face*. I tore off my Mask flinging it onto the bed angrily, repeating a different mantra in my mind. *Hope, hope, hope, hope*, to remind myself who I was.

Because I wasn't defined by the *Mask*. I was defined by the ideal *behind* the Mask.

Hope.

At a faint breeze, I glanced down to see I was suddenly bare-chested, wearing only a kilt of braided white and silver leather strips. I knew I hadn't been wearing that before... My entire body had been that quartz-like stone. But now... I was flesh and bone.

"Callie..." I whispered anxiously. "What are *you* doing here?" And before I consciously thought about it, I was sprinting towards her. The marble floor crunched under my feet, shattering upon contact, as I reached out a hand to grab her and protect her from whatever lived here, those mental invaders.

Everything froze in mid-step, and even the flames in the fireplace halted. As if I was now staring at a room-sized snapshot of what I had just experienced. Between my outstretched hand and Callie – only a few feet away – was what looked like a glass wall, casting back a reflection of my anguished face.

Callie seemed to notice her own appearance for the first time. She let out a gasp, reaching up to touch her cheeks, wiping at the silver tears. After a few moments, she shook her head stubbornly and stared *through* her reflection, slowly reaching out her hand to touch the glass keeping us apart. Our fingers touched the glass at the same time and it imploded in on itself in a cascade of shards. The debris evaporated almost instantly, as if it had been imagined.

And – like time had spun back – we were on opposite sides of the bedroom again, staring at each other from the top steps.

I shook my head, realizing I wore the Mask again. I snarled, yanking it off furiously.

Callie was facing me openly, her lips plump and inflamed as she licked them absently, her tongue touching the silver tears.

She reached up to her blindfold and tore it off as violently as I had my Mask, letting it flutter to the ground beside her. In an instant, her outfit also changed.

She wore a white diaphanous silk skirt, almost transparent, and fluttering faintly in the unseen breeze. And like me, her chest was bare. Her eyes were pools of liquid silver, and the molten chrome tears dripped down her cheeks a little faster without the bandage. She lifted both hands to her cheeks, touching the silver tears with her fingers, and then stared down at her chrome fingertips.

I watched as several tears fell from her jawline to her breasts, splashing over them like silver paint, and I heard myself growling hungrily as I devoured her with my eyes. She looked up, noticing my reaction, and grinned in appreciation. She took her own time in gobbling up her own eyeful of my body, and I found myself panting in response.

On some unspoken cue, we both began walking towards each other. She arched her shoulders defiantly, clenching her fists at her sides, as if daring the scene to freeze again, daring *anything* to keep us apart. I clenched my jaws, feeling the same desire to destroy anything standing between us.

She strode with the confidence of a warrior queen, and my respect for her trebled with each step. Like two animals, we stalked closer, waiting for some obstacle.

We stopped, both our shoulders tight, only inches apart. And we locked eyes as the tips of her breasts touched my heaving chest. She stiffened at the same time as I did, like some electric current had zapped us upon contact, and the shudder of her body only made me wilder as her breasts quivered against my chest.

Unable to take it any longer, I slowly lifted my shaking hands to her cheeks. Nothing was going to stop me from holding her in this place. I would burn the universe to ashes, first.

In response, Callie set her hands on my chest, leaving smudged silver hand-prints over my body, as if she had needed to confirm that I, too, was real.

I gripped her face and leaned closer, my breath low, shallow, and rapid as I stared into those infinite pools of chrome.

Blue and green pockets of light suddenly bloomed around us, limning us in a cool, soothing light. Then they began to rotate, spinning in bobbing circles around us like reflections from a disco ball. She squeezed her fingers into my chest possessively, refusing to let me slip away. She stared back at me, gritting her teeth. *Mine*, the look said.

I couldn't tell if she was claiming me or challenging me, but I was pretty sure I was giving her the same look. A wild tension, unrestrained and nuclear, stormed between us as the fireflies whirled faster and faster, our hair whipping back and forth at the steadily increasing vortex of power they left in their wake.

"What is this?" she whispered raggedly, digging her fingers tighter into my chest.

My fingers were slick with the silvery tears dripping from her eyes, but I cupped her jaws, my fingers gripping the sides of her neck below her ears, and my thumbs tracing slow circles through the chrome tears painting her cheeks.

I held her in the palms of my hands while she clutched my heart and soul.

And the world raged around us in a vortex of light.

Neither of us cared about that at the moment.

"A tale of two cities..." I whispered back, smiling harshly as my gaze flicked beyond her shoulder at the chaos, storms, war, and fallen kingdoms beyond the balcony. I'd seen different depictions of that war-torn scene, but never in such... captivating company.

As if my words had been a Catalyst, fire suddenly rolled over us, immolating the entire world in green and blue flame.

Silver and gold flame.

White and black flame.

CHAPTER 26

I woke up with a groan – an Apocalyptic set of blue balls threatening to obliterate me. I'd relived my strange dream with Callie, which was surprising. Those in the supposed *know* said it was impossible to have the same dream twice.

Which meant they were either wrong, or I'd just proven that my dream was not just a dream.

Which was both exciting and terrifying. Because that meant that strange sinister presence fighting to take over my mind from the dream was…

Real.

As if I hadn't had enough to worry about.

I stared up at a familiar ceiling full of painted stars, planets, constellations and other space-themed swirls of color and darkness. I stared at it, surprised to find myself smiling, despite the re-dream. I hadn't been in this room in years.

My old room from my childhood.

My parents had redecorated the room itself but had never wanted to paint over the ceiling. Too many fond memories of us lying on my bed together before bed, pointing out galaxies, constellations, and laughing about which planet we would like to live on some day. You couldn't just paint over memories like that.

I glanced to my right and saw a few of my old comic posters, probably worth a few bucks now that they were adapting everything into movies. My parents had kept staples of my childhood décor and made the rest of the room work around it. To be honest, I hadn't been back here since my college days, opening the door once or twice to look in and have a good laugh with my new love interest, Othello.

With a grimace at the thought, I slowly sat up. I didn't have any romantic interest in Othello but seeing her naked recently felt like salt in old wounds. Just a reminder that she had moved on and I was still kind of floundering in bachelorhood.

I stared down at the floorboards, and carefully placed my foot on the third plank out of habit. I grinned, shaking my head at the muscle memory. The first two planks creaked, but the third one was safe. I knew that fact like every child learns the secrets of their home, if they live in one place long enough. How to sneak out, or at least how to sneak down to the kitchen for a late-night snack, when the parents were sleeping.

For fun, I pressed down on the third board, and only heard a faint creak. Then I pressed down on the first two and winced at the familiar groan and strain – which in the middle of the night, might as well have been an alarm.

"It only creaks now because you weigh more," a familiar voice said from a chair in the corner.

I jolted instinctively at the sound, turning to see Gunnar sitting on the old gaming couch on the opposite wall – where we had stayed up countless nights watching movies, playing video games, or hatching some plan. "You've put on more weight than I have, chubs," I told him.

He nodded, but his smile was forced. Judging from the look in his eye, I decided I wasn't going to tell him about my dream. The first person to hear about that would be Callie. Period. And even that made me feel anxious. Maybe her take on the dream was a little different than mine.

"We called Darling and Dear, found out how to free Carl," Gunnar said, as if struggling to make small talk.

"Oh," I said distractedly. "That's good. Thanks."

I rubbed my temples absently, sensing a faint throb. I pulled my fingers away, checking for dried blood but didn't find any. Was that from my dream, or last night? I frowned, realizing I couldn't remember how I had gotten here. And trying to recall it was making my head throb more insistently.

I looked up at Gunnar. "What happened? Was I hit in the head?"

Gunnar watched me with his one eye, debating how much to tell me. "We don't know. You must have been, because you weren't making any sense. What do you remember?"

I thought back on it and winced, my headache coming back in a thunderous warning. I could remember speaking with Anubis... but that was it, unless I wanted to entice my migraine. "It's a little fuzzy," I lied.

Gunnar, knowing me too well, frowned, leaning forward. "Try," he said, and it wasn't a request.

I sighed. It wasn't that I wanted to lie or keep things from him, but I knew explaining what I did remember wouldn't make much sense and would apparently bring me closer to a debilitating migraine, which I didn't have time for. Still, I'd promised to keep him in the loop.

So, I told him about my quick jaunt to Hell, how I'd been abducted in front of Raego and his two guards. And I didn't hold anything back as I hit the point in the story where Anubis ejected me from Hell.

I climbed out of bed. "And then I saw..." I struggled to remember the next part, my headache rolling over the back of my neck and shoulders with a vengeance. "And then I was... *back*," I mumbled, trying to mask my sudden headache with a walk over to the window that we had used to sneak out of the house as children.

Gunnar was silent for a time, digesting my story. The doorknob jiggled, and I turned to see Gunnar already pounding towards it in a dead sprint like he was protecting me from an assassin. He slammed a shoulder into the door, eliciting a surprised shout from the other side. Gunnar had a fire-poker in one hand, and he simply stabbed it *through* the edge of the door and deep into the trim, effectively deadbolting the entrance. He studied his handiwork, his back to me. His shoulders rose up and down, fists flexing open and closed at his sides as he panted.

I frowned, trying to make out the argued protests from the other side, but a hushed conversation ensued, and the sounds quickly cut off.

"I usually just yell through the door for Dean to come back later..." I said. Gunnar grunted in response, not turning to look at me. "Do I need to use the window escape?" I asked.

"You're safe. No one will interrupt us."

"I meant to escape from *you*, Gunnar. You seem a little... on edge."

He stiffened as if I had struck him. Then he took a deep breath and slowly turned to face me. His lone eye was bloodshot. I hadn't noticed that from across the room.

"What's going on, Gunnar?" I asked carefully.

"Long night," he replied, closing his eye for a moment.

"What did I do?" I asked uncertainly. Had I done something terrible after returning from Hell? I couldn't remember. Every time I tried, that headache came back. I tried again anyway, gritting my teeth over the pain. I remembered running into… someone. A big person. I let out a shaky breath, abandoning the attempt. That was it. Had the big person tried to attack me? Had I killed someone? I opened my mouth, taking a step closer.

Gunnar waved a hand dismissively, seeing the concern in my eyes. If anything, it seemed to deflate his own concern. Marginally. "It's okay. We stopped you. But I need to know what you remember. This is important."

They had… *stopped* me? That sounded all sorts of bad. "Why do I feel like I'm being interrogated?"

He smirked crookedly. "Because I used to be an FBI Agent, and I'm interrogating you. Idiot." And even though he was attempting to make light of it, there was a sense of seriousness about his words. This *was* an interrogation. Just a friendly one.

"I…" the headache came back sharper this time, and I fell to my knees, groaning. Gunnar was there in an instant, propping me up.

Which was when I made my move.

I rammed my shoulder into his neck, knocking him on his ass. I reached out for my magic, wanting something to restrain him before he used his superior muscles to throw me around like a rag doll. And that's when I realized I couldn't touch my magic.

I glanced down to see a wooden bracelet on my wrist, and I snarled like a wild animal, trying to break through it with my Fae Magic – like a dog willing to chew off his leg to escape a beartrap. "*Never—*" I cut off, gasping involuntarily as a sharp flash of pain abruptly arced up my neck.

Gunnar began to struggle, preparing to toss me off of him. I blinked through stars in my vision, spotting the tattoo on his wrist. I took a gamble, panting through my pain. I flung out my hand – the one with the Temple Crest branded into the palm – and slapped it over his tattoo. "Family," I hissed.

Gunnar went entirely still, gritting his teeth, but obeying me.

I let out a breath, and fell onto my back, lying on the ground for a few seconds, rolling my shoulders to shake off the pain. Whatever that stab of agony had been slowly faded. Had I injured myself? Hurt my neck or something? I slowly climbed to my feet, and then shambled over to the couch. "Sit beside me, Wulfric."

He did, shooting a last look at his makeshift deadbolt, as if only now realizing he had sealed his own fate.

"Oh, don't be such a drama queen," I snapped. "But maybe you should think twice before mistreating me in my own home," I said, waving my wrist to show him the bangle. "Really? I did something *this bad*? Enough to warrant *house arrest*?" I hadn't even known he had found where I'd hidden this cursed thing – cuffs able to prevent a wizard from using his own magic.

Gunnar sighed from beside me on the couch, placing his elbows on his knees, and resting his face in his palms. "Kind of. Almost, anyway. I really need you to try to remember, Nate. It's not that I don't want to tell you, but that you need to try to remember it for *yourself*. The fact that I see you wince in pain every time you try to remember should tell you something… It will answer a lot more questions if *you* can remember, because what *we* saw isn't very helpful."

I frowned. "What's the difference between you telling me and me telling you? You obviously remember a whole lot more. You didn't pass out after." He sighed, glaring down at his tattoo, his own handcuffs.

To be honest, I was just as surprised as Gunnar that the last-ditch attempt had worked. The first time I had found this loophole, it had been when he and I were not on the friendliest of terms, and I was coming to grips with a Beast dwelling inside me.

Kai had ridden the Nate train for a little while, giving me access to all sorts of powers as a Maker – a symbiotic relationship with a Beast – exactly like how my mansion was bonded with its own Beast, Falco.

But I was no longer a Maker, so perhaps my mastery over Gunnar's tattoo had had nothing to do with being one. But that didn't help me. That just gave me *more* questions. My parents had given Gunnar the tattoo, after all, and I'd recently learned that they were liars like the world had never seen before.

"In the name of Chateau Defiance," Gunnar finally said. "If you can't tell me what happened last night, I will cut off my arm and this tattoo, and I will leave St. Louis forever," he whispered. He wasn't threatening me, he sounded terrified.

I blinked at him incredulously, not sure how to respond. "You're calling up the oath from our old tree house?" I asked softly, recognizing the severity of the situation from that comment alone. It was about as sacred and old of an oath as we had between us. It sounded ridiculous, but we'd always promised to hold it up as our highest standard of honesty. It was sacrosanct.

He looked up, finally, and in that bloodshot eye was desperation. "Yes."

I let out a breath. "Okay. I'll try... But only because you invoked the sacred oath," I muttered.

"Thank you."

I leaned back into the couch and closed my eyes. Since I had found only pain anytime I tried to recall the details of last night, I decided to try a different tactic. I called upon my Memory Palace.

My parents had taught me how to construct an imagined place where I could store an unlimited number of memories, knowledge, and facts. We had come up with the solution after I'd told my parents about having constant migraines. After some consideration, they had theorized that it had something to do with my memory, that since I could recall even the most mundane of details about a place, event, or person, that my mind was simply having trouble storing it all.

They believed I had an eidetic memory. But I'd learned there were different levels of eidetic memory. Some better than others. The more severe cases had near instant recall, and often had antisocial behaviors, living too deeply in their memories, unable to relate to their peers.

Others compartmentalized things, basically archiving everything until it was needed at some later date.

My memory was somewhere in the middle of those but leaning more towards the former.

It was one reason why meeting Gunnar had been so vital to me. A means to escape the data dump in my mind. With Gunnar, I had been able to forget all that, and instead use my imagination to... well, *imagine.*

We built our treehouse. Made slingshots. Pretended we were monster hunters. Pretended we were monsters.

Kings.

Princes.

Angels.

Demons.

You know, kid stuff. Delusions of grandeur.

And those growing bonds of friendship had helped to keep me grounded. Helped drown out the noise.

But on top of that, my parents had thought it beneficial to help me build a mental library, so that instead of remembering every detail chronologically, I could attach them to objects and tuck them away on a dusty shelf for later.

For example, I could mentally create a schoolroom inside my Memory Palace, and anything associated with school or learning would be stored there. A set of imaginary beakers where I could toss all my science lessons.

An abacus to store all my math homework.

Things like that. All I would need to do was 'visit' my mental schoolroom, pick up the abacus, and *wham*, I could delve through specific details related to any math lessons I'd ever had.

As one could probably guess, my Memory Palace had quickly grown beyond one room.

A living room to recall all the time spent with my family – full of pictures, photo albums, and movie stubs, and even an arcade token. Pick one of these up, and I could relive the moment.

A conservatory for my dreams and worldly adventures.

A library for my favorite books and authors.

All in all, my Memory Palace was now considerably larger than my real mansion, Chateau Falco, which I had used as the basis for my imagined construct.

And... I hadn't been there in a very long while. Really, maybe since my parents died. At least habitually, anyway. Maybe it was time I took a stroll, dusted off some shelves. Took a trip down memory lane.

Because memories never hurt anyone...

CHAPTER 27

I stood before the massive front door to my Memory Palace. A large crest emblazoned the door, the Temple Family Crest. I glanced down at my palm, seeing the identical brand.

A shield with a point at the bottom and split vertically by a jagged lightning bolt. On one side of the lightning was a pair of mountains, and on the other, a feather. The top of the shield was bordered by a strip of eight stars, and a clenched fist rose above the top of the shield, and beneath it were the words *Non Serviam*, meaning, *I will never serve*. It was a quote made famous by Milton's *Paradise Lost* when Lucifer told the Angels he would no longer be a blind devotee.

Diagonally crossing behind the shield were two polearms. One was a spear of sorts, and a strip of cloth furled out from it with the word *Arete* on it – Aristotle's famous lesson to Alexander the Great to strive to become the best possible form of a thing, whatever that *thing* was. Basically, to be the role model for anyone else behind you. If you chose to be a wizard, be a notorious one. The most legendary wizard the world had ever seen.

The other polearm was a scythe, and a similar strip of cloth dangled from the haft with the words *Memento Mori* – remember you will die. Live life to the fullest, because at any moment you could die.

Below the shield, the butts of the spears extended out a little, and on each was a raven with the names Hugin and Munin beneath them – Odin's Ravens, Thought and Memory.

I shivered at a breeze.

Then I belted out a laugh, realizing what I had done. The Crest always humbled me, because it embodied so much, had been a symbol for the Temple Clan for centuries. And it sure seemed more than a little prophetic to me. I wondered if that was something every Temple had felt at one point in their life. Like the Crest had been designed specifically for them.

Or if I was just a special flavor of arrogant.

Regardless, the Crest made me uneasy, so I had imagined a cool breeze here in this imagined realm. I turned to look back out at the rolling hills of trees and manicured lawns that ringed the property. It was uncanny.

I glanced at the spot where a tree now stood, and smiled as one popped into existence, fleshing and building out like a photoshopped image in fast-forward. A titanic white tree covered in scales, and a tiny white treehouse perched high above.

Carl's Mighty D, as we'd taken to calling it.

In the distance, I saw Chateau Defiance, Gunnar's and my treehouse. It was much larger than in real life, because most of my childhood memories took up too much space. All our adventures.

I sighed, shaking my head, and turned back to the front door. Then I walked inside.

Here, Chateau Falco was much different than reality. Because I had removed anything not pertinent to my specific needs. I strolled down the marble halls, about three times wider than they really were, and admired the artwork. I strolled past a section of painted portraits of past Temple ancestors that my parents had acquired. They weren't all here, but any my parents specifically sought out had been found, and a few they had only seen pictures of – because I had added them to the walls.

I paused before Matthias Temple's portrait, frowning.

He'd been banished to the Fae Realm long ago after his friend had betrayed him, pinning the blame for the influx of Brothers Grimm in America on him. Matthias had been in Fae for so long that he'd taken to believing himself the real Mad Hatter. Since his prison had been entirely white, I made the painting also entirely white, even the man himself, like a textured painting in milk. Then I added a fancy fedora and a red ascot, because I could.

Even though Matthias was borderline insane and had caused me any number of headaches – like kidnapping the only Knight of the Round Table we had found still living – he meant well. I think.

So, I didn't draw a wang on his face, out of respect. But it was a faint respect. Very, very faint. If he didn't give me back my knight, I'd come back with a sharpie to vandalize this portrait.

I continued on down the halls, wondering what I hoped to find here. I knew this place like the back of my hand. Was I just hoping it would clear my head, or that I would actually find a memory of last night?

Whatever I had done that had been so bad I had repressed it.

I slowed, thinking. Maybe there was a way to find the answer here, after all.

I let myself *feel* the place itself. The temperature was a little stuffy, so I made it cooler. The familiar smells of my father's Gurkha Black Dragon cigars permeated the air – not the smoke smell, but the crisp vibrant smell that always wafted up the next day. I savored it, recalling the times I had spied my father working late into the night, hunched over his desk in his office.

Then, I focused on the *opposite* of that feeling.

Discomfort. Uncertainty. Fear.

And, in a heartbeat, I felt it. Like a creeping tendril of black fog leading towards a dim hall. I frowned, staring at it. I followed the hall, realizing I had created it at some point, but had left it incomplete, almost hazy, and if I looked away, it began to fade.

I followed the hall, seeing that it ended in a set of creaky stairs, leading up. I paused at the base, imagining the area lighter, but the Memory Palace fought me, the entire place quivering slightly.

And I saw a figure staring back at me from the top of the stairs, an entirely black shadow.

With blazing white eyes.

We stared at each other for a few moments, and then he bolted like a rabbit, pounding up the stairs. I hesitated for all of two seconds before I took off after him. I ran, and ran, pounding up the steps two at a time, the staircase spiraling in on itself again and again and again. I had to have climbed a dozen flights before I spilled out onto a hallway of silver chrome. I skidded to a halt, not seeing the shadow.

But the tendril of darkness was thicker here, leading onwards.

I walked cautiously. I was in uncharted territory. Even in my own mind.

Which... shouldn't have been possible. Well, I knew it was, obviously, but it was still alarming. My subconscious had made some renovations without me.

And judging from the extravagant gleaming hall, my subconscious was apparently a suave, classy, but creepy asshole. My surroundings glittered with opulence, decadence, and arrogance. Silver busts of myself in dramatic poses. Every single fucking trophy I had ever won, cast in gleaming silver. Models of the cars I had owned. A blueprint for Plato's Cave. Every speeding ticket framed and displayed in a position of prominence.

Life-sized portraits of every pretty woman I had ever encountered, all smiling and deliriously happy, and I could tell that they were smiling at me. How I imagined they felt about me.

Tory. Ashley. Indie. Othello. The Reds' mother, Misha...

And a full bodied, life-sized statue of Callie Penrose, hands held together in prayer, smiling adoringly at me like an Angel. She was gloriously naked.

I ran past that one faster than the others, but her eyes followed me. If she ever found out, she'd kill me.

I began staring at the floor as I pounded my feet, unable to witness anymore false idols of my pride and arrogance. My self-imagined world of how I believed everyone should see me.

I had enough arrogance for a thousand men, because even the chrome floor tiles were odes to my achievements. Each tile was carved with minor accomplishments, grade cards, awards, diplomas, degrees, and even the napkin notes my mom had tucked into my lunch boxes as a child.

Calling me things like...

Her tiny godling.

Her knight in shining armor.

Her cute little Manling.

I set my jaw, growing angry.

It was a Hall of Vanities.

And I finally realized what I was actually seeing. It was a security system.

A visual replication of everything I had ever done that made me feel good about myself. Every defense mechanism I had ever hidden behind. Every flaw I had worn like a badge of honor. Of course, many were legitimate accomplishments, but there were enough of the false depictions of prideful achievements to make me snarl.

An area of my Memory Palace carefully designed to reassure me that I was awesome. To distract me from venturing further. I began to run faster, because whatever lay beyond this area had to be *dark*.

The hallway ended in a floor-to-ceiling chrome mirror, but my reflection was a suave, perfectly polished version of myself. No scars. No scruff on my cheeks. No torn clothes. No pain in my eyes. Nothing but sheer joy at everything I had accomplished, at how perfectly incredible I was.

I punched the mirror as hard as I could, clocking that cold, arrogant motherfucker right in the jaw. And like the world was made entirely of glass, everything before and behind me shattered, and I stared down at the blood running down my knuckles, panting heavily.

"I'm Nate Fucking Temple, and I'm *nobody's* hero," I snarled, stomping through the mounds of broken glass, leaving bloody footprints in my wake.

I felt resolved – and calmer than I could ever recall feeling.

As if a great weight had been lifted from my shoulders – the weight of my own prideful arrogance.

I ground the shards of glass beneath my feet, eager to destroy even the dust of that world beneath my heels.

CHAPTER 28

The shards of glass sliced and bit into the thin skin of my feet and toes, drawing blood, but I gritted my teeth and pressed on. Other than the heaps of broken glass, the world beyond, above, behind, and below looked as lush and comforting as black velvet, begging me to run towards its comforting embrace.

I ignored it and purposely made sure to walk on nothing *but* the glass.

After a few minutes, I glanced back behind me curiously, wondering how far I had walked. As far as the eye could see was nothing except broken glass, and a lone, crimson trail of my blood leading to me. Surely, I hadn't walked that far…

I growled and pressed on.

What felt like an hour later, I was staggering, dragging my feet through the glass now, weakened from blood loss. Everything abruptly changed between one shuffled step and the next, and I found myself on a roof.

Stone gargoyles lined the edge to my left and right, and on closer inspection, I realized they were Guardians, like the ones that I used to protect Chateau Falco.

This became obvious when they turned their heads to stare at me, or ruffled their feathers, or pawed the rooftop with long, stone claws, letting me know I wasn't welcome here.

I grunted, dismissing them as I stared upwards. The thunderstorm of the century tried to bat me down, the skies black with pregnant, bloated clouds, and never-ending bolts of red and blue lightning crackled from cloud to cloud, frequently erupting down to touch the rooftop I stood on. I didn't flinch, wiping the water from my eyes, squinting through the walls of water hammering the earth.

I stared ahead since there were no Guardians in that direction, only the edge of the roof.

And I saw the shadow I'd been initially chasing standing on the edge of the roof, limned by the flashes of lightning. He had his hands on his waist, arms akimbo, and he was staring at me.

I smirked defiantly and continued on. The Guardians snarled, growled, shrieked, and hissed at me, snapping their jaws and beaks at me, dragging their claws across the concrete in threatening gestures.

I ignored them, holding up my hand to shield the rain from my eyes – fearing the little shit would run away again and I'd lose track of him for good. He watched me in silence, his eyes – one red and one blue, now – were merciless, cold, and demanding. As I got closer, I realized he was too small. Like a child.

I also realized that he wasn't wearing a cloak, because each peal of lightning and thunder that rattled the rooftop didn't so much as faze him or illuminate him. In fact, I could see his shaggy, unkempt hair waving in the wind, and it was also pure black, like every other part of him. Because he was one solid color.

Superblack.

As I got within reaching distance – almost – he startled me by smiling. It was the sudden flash of perfectly straight white teeth that really caught me off guard.

Then the little shit flipped me off, flung his arms out wide, and then stepped backwards off the damned building. I stared in disbelief, waiting to hear a yell, or a sickening splat.

Instead, I heard a faint voice through the storm.

You'll never learn to fly if you don't first learn to jump...

I stepped up on the edge of the roof, and realized I was grinning. I turned to look back the way I had come.

The Guardians had all stepped off their perches and were staring at me in neat, orderly rows, like a military unit waiting for their King's demands. As one, they dipped their heads, and knelt.

I laughed, the sound eerily real in this place, overriding the veritable hurricane.

Then I threw up two middle fingers.

For the Guardians…

The trail of blood I had left behind…

The Hall of Vanities…

And I stepped backwards off the ledge, laughing. I spun myself around, reaching out a hand to grab that insolent little shit of a shadow by the ankle and teach him a thing or two about flipping off his elders.

My shadow was only just out of reach, even though he had jumped long before me. And he was laughing at me. The ground raced up to meet us, and right before we hit, I managed to grab him by the ankle and tucked him in close, rolling so that I would hit the ground first.

Because shadows were important. You had to hold them close or they might just run away.

Or get themselves hurt.

And what was a man without a shadow?

Or a shadow without a man…

CHAPTER 29

J gasped frantically. Gunnar suddenly loomed over me, his face pale, and horrified.

"I got the little fucker!" I hooted at the werewolf, lifting up my clenched fist. Gunnar snarled, jumping out of sight. I glanced down to see I actually held a fucking shadow in my fist.

My fucking shadow. I released it, and felt it snap back into its proper place. I let out a breath of relief, as if taking a languid stretch after a long sleep. It wasn't that I hadn't had a shadow before, but that I had been missing my *entire* shadow. It all made so much sense now...

Well, in a strange euphoric sense, anyway.

Like trying to explain an acid trip, I couldn't really think of a way to put it into words, but I felt... better. More myself. Raw, sure, but honest.

"What the *hell* just happened?" Gunnar asked, staring at me uncertainly.

I realized something. "I'm even more awesome that I ever knew," I told him, shaking my head proudly. But it was a clean, *honest* pride. My subconscious had tried to drown me in *false* pride, but I'd beaten it – destroyed my secret Hall of Vanities. No one ever needed to know about that. Surely, such a feat made me even cooler than the lies I had hidden behind my entire life, right?

I opened my mouth in an attempt to put words to it because Gunnar looked like he'd just been neutered with a rusty nail and no anesthesia.

The door suddenly blew inwards, flying across the room and shattering the window. The fire-poker deadbolt slammed into the wall where it stuck, vibrating in a humming chime.

And in stormed Callie Penrose.

She looked *pissed*.

She stared at us, arcs of white lightning crackling over her fists, and eyes seeming to faintly glow silver. She stared at Gunnar and let out an unimpressed sniff. Then she turned to me, and her features broke with alarm.

I realized – quite rapidly – that she hadn't looked pissed before. That had been her adopt-a-puppy face.

"Why is he covered in *blood*?" she demanded, rounding on Gunnar. "What did you do to him?" And suddenly he was slammed into the wall, the sheet rock shattering on impact. She held him there with her magic, and bolted my way, kneeling at my feet, grabbing me by the wrists.

She snarled at the manacle on my wrist and snapped it in half with a precise crack of white lightning in her palms. Then she was cradling my hands, inspecting them. I hadn't realized they were covered in blood. So were my bare feet. That shouldn't have been possible. That had happened in my Memory Palace.

Then again, I'd smuggled my shadow from my Memory Palace, and that hadn't fazed me.

But my injuries were a distant thought as I observed Callie kneeling before me, clutching my hands. I felt suddenly giddy as I recalled a vision Pandora had shown me recently, where she had made herself look like Callie in a very similar position to what I was now experiencing. Except Pandora Callie had been naked. Now, I wasn't complaining about the current wardrobe situation or anything, but... I'll just say this.

Pandora Callie had done a bang-up job, and I found it almost impossible to wall off the memory – failing to prevent myself from superimposing Pandora's Callie over the here and now.

Then I recalled that bizarre dream – the one Callie sure seemed to have shared, judging by her cryptic actions lately, like giving me the book, *A Tale of Two Cities*. Thinking of that gift, I realized I had left it in the dressing room. Hopefully, someone had picked it up for me.

A stray thought managed to creep into my mind, and I felt myself blushing.

Not hours after Pandora's free illusion, a pixie friend, Barbie, had given me a new definition for the term *hugging*, and that had *also* been quite... *memorable*.

But it wasn't the video replay of her overexuberant hug that I was remembering now.

I bit my lip as I reached inside my pocket, ignoring the pain from my wounds as they scraped over the fabric. I found the item Barbie had given me. I pulled a silver butterfly from my pocket, remembering that Alvara had said it was powerful and meaningful. Barbie hadn't left any advice on what it was for, but we'd been talking – quite in depth – about Callie immediately before she gave it to me.

Callie had given me two gifts... My satchel and the book.

I held the butterfly out to Callie, now. She froze, staring down at it in surprised confusion.

"I got you a gift," I whispered. "You're very important to me, Callie. I don't know if I've ever actually told you that directly or not."

She gently set down my other hand and accepted the butterfly in a shaking hand. Then she lay her cheek on my thigh and began to sob, gripping the butterfly as if she would never let it go, staring at it as she cried.

If she had laid her head down any higher, things might have gotten awkward really quick. I lifted my hand to pet her hair, and then hesitated. My hands were bloody, and her icy white hair was so beautiful.

As if reading my mind, she grabbed my hand and placed it on her jaw, closing her eyes as she took a deep, satisfied breath, as if she'd waited for this moment for a long, long while. Then, eyes still closed, she kissed my palm right on the center of the brand. If I had to guess, I would have said her lips touched the feather on my Family Crest, but maybe that was just my imagination.

"You are very special to me, too, Nate..." she whispered softly.

Gunnar cleared his throat. "That's great. Really. I feel very special and appreciated, too. All pinned up on this wall and everythin—"

Callie blushed and Gunnar suddenly dropped to the floor with a grunt. She masked her embarrassment with a cool tone and a frosty look. "Go get bandages. I'm going to dress his injuries," she told Gunnar, not lifting her head to command him.

"I'd rather stay close in case you need help—"

He slammed back into the wall with another, harsher grunt, plaster and drywall raining down upon his shoulders this time. I arched an eyebrow at him and shrugged.

"I'd do what the lady says. I think we can handle any monsters under the bed."

His boots hit the floor a second time, and rather than arguing, he stomped out of the room, muttering unhappily under his breath.

I let my thumb trace slow, tentative circles on her cheeks, smiling as I closed my eyes, savoring the moment. I felt her do the same, letting out a heavy breath as she began to hum to me.

I found myself grinning silently as I recognized the tune.

Star light, star bright. First star I see tonight. I wish I may, I wish I might, have this wish I wish tonight...

CHAPTER 30

*I*n Gunnar's absence, Callie had simply laid her head back down on my thigh, closing her eyes and listening as I caught her up to what had happened since the speech, up to my meeting with Anubis and our new agreement for killing Mordred.

Retrieving the Nine Souls for my freedom plus two get out of Hell free cards.

When Gunnar returned with the bandages, Callie had silently taken them from him to begin cleaning up the cuts and scrapes with alcohol pads and fresh gauze. None were deep, but they were all crusted over. Mallory wasn't at Chateau Falco, or he could have easily magicked away my mild injuries.

Callie didn't let Gunnar speak while she worked, so he was practically quivering after about two seconds.

I used the time to clear my head, because my Memory Palace had definitely brought back last night's events with Baron Skyfall – how I'd almost killed the dragon ally out of fear that he was a pirate, thinking he had harmed my *Shadow*.

I'd only calmed down once Talon had arrived – a friend from my... other childhood in Fae.

And really, Talon was the *cause* of what had set me off in the *first* place – Anubis informing me that I needed to use my spear – my *Devourer* – to take out Mordred, and that me naming him Talon the *Devourer* in my Fae child-hood was no coincidence.

My mind had cracked – or perhaps, splintered – at the revelation, sending me into some unknown memory in Fae where I had needed my *Shadow* – Talon's self-appointed title as my protector – to save me from a pirate.

But apparently, *Shadow* had also meant a few other things, considering my sudden fear of adults, a belief that I could fly, pirates, and a fixation on a word starting with *Never* that I had been unable to fully articulate...

The headache I had felt – much like my shared dream with Callie – had been a warning sign, and ignoring it had almost cost Baron his life.

I had the sneaking suspicion that my parents' idea of a Memory Palace might have served dual purposes – as a way to help me compartmentalize my second childhood in Fae – as Wylde – keeping it hidden before I was ready to accept it, lest it break me. Maybe my eidetic memory was some consequence of my double-childhood.

Callie placed a hand on my wrist, applying gentle pressure. I looked up and smiled sheepishly, not having realized she had finished. "Sorry."

"You were shaking, and getting worked up," she said gently.

I nodded. "I was just trying to digest it all. I have to sacrifice power to my other organs when I fire up my brain. It's why I don't do it often. Reacting on emotions is so much simpler."

Gunnar grunted. He was still mildly upset by Callie manhandling him. Or womanhandling him. He was used to being the big bad wolf, and this tiny white-haired girl had put him in his place without any real effort.

I took a deep breath, and then began to talk. "It seems that in my delirium after returning from Hell, and the stuff discussed with Anubis, I may have suffered a severe flashback. Maybe I inhaled too much sulfur down there."

Neither spoke, waiting for me to tell everything, rather than wheedling it all out of me piece by piece.

"When Anubis threw me back here through his Gateway, I was shaken by our conversation, and when I tried processing some of what he'd said, I realized my head was aching. So, I tried harder. But with each attempt, I lost more and more of myself, and..." I let out a deep breath. "I think my mind reverted to my childhood. My, erm, *other* childhood."

Gunnar grumbled unhappily.

"From what I've heard," Callie said, speaking up before Gunnar could do so, "you didn't use your wizard's magic on Baron Skyfall when you almost ripped him limb from limb. And you did it without any apparent effort, not even realizing what you were doing. Like a child plucking the wings from a butterfly..."

I nodded. "Fae magic... from my other childhood. With Talon."

She studied me. "I thought you didn't recall much of that. Only bits and pieces..."

I nodded. "The flashback hit me like a truck. I thought I was back in Fae. In danger..."

Gunnar leaned forward. "You remember it all, now?"

I shook my head, running my hand through my shaggy hair. "No. Not all. Like I said, it was just a flashback. I don't know what led up to my flashback, why I was so scared, or what happened after."

"I don't understand. I thought you and Wylde... merged," he finally said, grasping for the right word.

I shrugged. "I don't know what to tell you, man. It's not like there's a guidebook to this. I'm pretty sure I'm the only Manling ever *born* in Fae. When I told you Wylde and I had teamed up, I was pretty sure I was telling you the truth. But apparently, it's not so easy to merge two lives into one body. Or one mind. Maybe it's the only way for me to stay sane. To take the memories in bits and pieces. Too much, and I crack. Like..." I sighed. "Well, last night is a pretty good example."

Callie began rubbing my wrist with her thumb reassuringly, not commenting on my tirade. "We're all confused by this, Nate. You more than us, I'm sure. What do you need from us?"

"I want to know why he was desperate to find his shadow," Gunnar said, overriding Callie. "And then, how he fucking *caught* it while meditating, bringing it back *here*."

Callie let out a mildly perturbed breath, but waited for me to respond on my own, rather than standing up to defend me. And to be honest, I appreciated that. I didn't need a bodyguard, and Callie was subtly letting me know she wouldn't be one. I was my own man. She was her own woman.

I let out a breath, shaking my head at how it was going to sound. "Couple reasons, as far as I can guess. The obvious one being that in my flashback, *Wylde* needed a friendly face, someone to help him fight off a pirate. But the *Nate* part of me knew something was wrong and that I needed an anchor to snap me out of the hallucination..." I met Gunnar's eyes. "Talon was my only friend in Fae, and he calls himself my *Shadow* – my protector. Coincidences suck," I muttered.

They were both silent for a few moments. "And the non-obvious reason?" Callie asked.

I decided not to sugarcoat it, and told them all about my Memory Palace, and the shadow I had been chasing. I didn't share specific details on the Hall of Vanities, just the general concept. And there was zero mention of the life-sized statue of naked Callie, but I did make the mistake of mentioning depictions of all the *other* pretty women I had met in my life. She arched a brow at that, and I could tell it was something she would bring back up – at length – at a later date.

I told them about destroying the Hall of Vanities, indicating my bloody hands and feet. Then I told them about the roof, the childlike shadow, and jumping off after him. About grabbing him and keeping him safe, and then waking up still clutching my shadow.

Gunnar still looked confused, not understanding how it tied together. I sighed, taking a deep breath, knowing how crazy this was about to sound, and silently hoping they would immediately poke holes in it.

"I think last night was me reliving an actual memory in Fae where a pirate was trying to catch me... And visiting my Memory Palace, only to chase my own *shadow*, was a metaphor... I think I spent some time with Peter Pan and his gang of Lost Boys in Neverland. I can almost remember them..."

There. It was out. *I do believe in Fairies.*

It just goes to show you how truly great my friends are. Neither laughed. They just stared at me for a good ten seconds, nodding slowly as pieces of the puzzle slid into place.

"And there was that whole thing with Peter Pan and his shadow..." Gunnar said, nodding slowly. "He was always chasing it. And you caught yours..." I nodded, waiting for someone to laugh. "I guess... that actually makes sense. It would explain all the pirate comments, too," Gunnar added, scratching at his beard. He didn't look entirely comfortable with it, but I had just convinced an ex-FBI Agent, which was saying a lot.

Damn it.

"So, Neverland is in Fae," Callie said pensively.

"Apparently." The room was silent as they considered it, but the more I thought about it, the more convinced I was. I could recall – like a montage – talking to Peter, having a food fight with dozens of young feral boys, laughing as Talon chased my sneaky shadow in what felt like a familiar game.

I let out a breath, closing my eyes. "When the *hell* did my parents find the time to take me on a trip to Neverland? No one has *ever* mentioned that to me. Yet another secret withheld by my loving parents."

No one spoke. Finally, I heard Gunnar climb to his feet. I was pretty sure he was debating storming from the room. He took the best friend title pretty seriously, and it bothered him to know Talon had obviously come before him in that category last night.

I listened to his boots thumping across the floor but was surprised when a fist grabbed me by the shirt, yanking me up off of the couch. I opened my eyes to find Gunnar holding me up and glaring at me with his bloodshot stink-eye. "Stop feeling sorry for yourself. Get up, iron your green tights, and let's figure this Mordred shit out. Neverland can wait, you stupid fairy."

I snorted out a laugh against my will, and Gunnar smiled, looking relieved to see it. "You're right."

"Anubis gave you a job, and it pays pretty damned well. We take out Mordred's Nine Souls, and you no longer have to be his Guide to Hell. And you get two free passes at Death." I didn't bother correcting him on that. I wasn't entirely sure what I would use those passes for, but that only mattered if we won. If it made Gunnar feel better to think I had two extra lives – like a video game – well, he'd been through enough for one night. I wasn't going to burst his bubble. He shook me, sensing my wandering attention. "That's a fucking bargain if I've ever heard one. And if the price was to go a little crazy for a minute…" he shrugged. "Baron's a big boy. He'll deal with it. I'll go have a beer or two with him, reassure him."

I found myself grinning wider. "Charon was kind of a badass. I wish you could have seen it."

Gunnar smiled faintly. "Look, I might have a minor jealousy streak—"

Callie snorted, cutting him off. "More than most girls I know," she teased.

"Quiet, woman, before I say something that makes me have to let you slam me up against that wall again to prove my undisputed dominance," he muttered, rolling his eye.

Callie giggled. "Fine." She turned to me. "We should probably reschedule our dinner. I've got some pressing matters to take care of in Kansas City, as you know, and you look like you have your hands full."

I opened my mouth to protest, picking up on the disappointment in her eyes. "I'm sure—"

She placed a finger over my lips. "Later, Nate. You'll just have to make it up to me. I expect a thorough attempt to do so." Her eyes seemed to flicker, and I could tell she had something else on her mind, but it was a private matter, and she wasn't going to mention it in front of Gunnar.

"Hey, Gunnar. Can you give us a min—"

He threw me onto the couch, almost knocking the breath out of me. Callie gasped in surprise, but before she could react, Gunnar shoved her on top of me. "Yabba-dabba-doo!" he crowed, bolting from the room before either of us could retaliate.

I very quickly realized Callie had no intention of retaliating, because she was staring at me with a smoldering gaze. My bloody fingerprints still painted her jaws from earlier. She slowly leaned close to whisper into my ear.

"Be careful with me, Nate... Or I'll kill you," she breathed.

I agreed in a hoarse, caveman grunt, drawing deep from my Neanderthal roots.

She nipped my ear playfully, her breath sweet like fresh-cut fruit. "Eve made the same mistake, you know. Having a taste of the forbidden fruit..." she warned.

I was actually growling until I realized she was laughing softly. She pulled back, her hair cascading over my face, and our noses brushed as she leaned down to touch her lips to mine as gently as... a butterfly's wings. Her lips were inflamed, scalding to the touch, and neither of us breathed for an eternal second.

And then she kissed me deeply, caressing my tongue with hers.

I groaned, my mouth exploding with a tingling sensation that physically made my eyes roll back. My brain immediately commanded me to grab her and pin her to the couch, but she had already slipped out of my grasp.

I saw her standing before me safely out of reach, and panting, her legs shaking ever so slightly. Her finger slowly rose to her smiling, plump lips, touching them as if to make sure it had all been real. Her gaze was distant and dreamy, and she closed her eyes slowly, letting out a pleased sound of appreciation.

I just stared up at her, panting raggedly, digging my fingers into the couch as I touched my teeth with my tongue, tasting strawberries and sunshine.

"That... okay, yeah," she whispered. "You need to take care of business, because we *really* need to come back to this..."

I studied her. "We could get a nice preliminary discussion going right now."

She was already shaking her head. "Oh, no... I have a feeling *preliminary* isn't really in our vocabulary..." she said distractedly, still touching a finger to her lips. "And I'm supposed to be babysitting some toddler werebears. And *you* have an errand for the King of Hell. This... was just a reminder that you have..." Then she grinned ruthlessly. "Dinner waiting for you when you get home from work."

She let out a malicious giggle as I lunged to grab her, but she Shadow Walked from the room before I could snatch her. I chuckled, both happy and angry. Then I decided I was going to take a long, arctic shower.

As I made my way into the bathroom, I found myself humming that damned song.

Star light, star bright...

CHAPTER 31

Still shivering and clutching my childhood Thundercats bathrobe in a wad over my junk – my suit from last night had been bloody, full of burned lava holes, and generally filthy – I walked the halls of my mansion, naked, making my way back to my own rooms and some fresh clothes, hoping no one would spot the Master of the house essentially streaking.

"Hey, sailor," Othello called out from a suite I had just shuffled past. "Shipping off soon?" she purred, jogging out of her room.

I grinned instinctively, glancing down at my indecency. I felt like a gazelle who had just been spotted by an overly-friendly lioness. "I thought you were heading out of town?" I asked.

She shrugged. "Some assholes broke into the shop last night and dealing with the cops took a few hours. Especially trying to convince them – despite the excessive damage – that it was all a misunderstanding. They seemed pretty adamant about searching the shop to make sure I hadn't hidden the bodies or something, since I answered the door with my 44 Magnum and my registration for it. They didn't approve of my nonchalance. Then again, the way Hemingway was glaring at them could have increased their suspicions. We hadn't finished our... *meeting* before they arrived," she grinned salaciously. "He was rather frustrated about that. But not for too long. The police *eventually* left, of course..." she said, chuckling mischievously.

I burst out laughing. "Asshole robbers. At least you taught them to knock first."

She slapped my ass – since I had no way of defending myself – and then used my surprise to link her arm through mine before I could do anything to reclaim my virtue. I silently noted that her linking arms with me, while I was using both hands to cover up my danger-zone with the tiny Thunder-cats robe – put her in an awfully good position to yank my arm away and leave me open to leering.

Othello was a bizarre one. A constant tease, even to those not sexually involved with her – but to those who *had* once been sexually involved with her, she was a constant source of sexual frustration. She was just one of those possessive, playful types. It was adorable, frustrating, funny, and maddening.

Really, she was kind of like a different flavor of myself. Maybe that was why we'd gotten along so well back in college.

"So, I saw Callie earlier..." she said casually.

"Yeah..." I said stiffly.

"Your arms are cold. You even have goosebumps." I felt her studying my face in my peripheral vision. "You poor thing. Cold showers are the worst."

I groaned. "Thanks, Othello. But you know what's worse? Being reminded of cold showers. After bragging to me about your booty call last night. Which happened in *my* old loft."

I felt her suddenly relax, as if realizing she had pushed me too far, and we walked on in silence for a few moments. I wasn't mad at her. I wasn't even jealous. It was just the combination of everything. I was kind of all over the place lately. Seeing an old flame naked in my old loft with another man, getting abducted to Hell, having a flashback of a forgotten childhood, realizing how deep my feelings for Callie just might be, and then getting only the briefest taste of Paradise on my tongue before being abandoned again. Then, running into Othello. Again. But this time, with *me* naked.

All in less than twelve hours.

"You okay, Nate?" she finally asked in a soft voice.

I let out a loud breath, nodding. "Sure. Just a lot on my mind."

She tugged hard at my arm, making me fight to keep myself covered. "Nate..." she warned.

"Fine!" I snapped, repositioning my make-shift loin cloth. And I gave her a brief update.

"Wow..." she said after I'd finished, no longer struggling against my arm.

"What about you?" I asked. "You've been traveling a lot, lately."

Her arm stiffened slightly. "Oh, that's nothing."

I stopped, planting my feet. Like an idiot, I hadn't considered the physics involved, because Othello kept walking, yanking away my arm and making me drop my robe. She caught it before it fell to the ground, but she kept her distance, a mischievous twinkle in her eyes as she stared down at the wad of damp fabric.

I stood there, naked, and quickly decided that the only course of action was to maintain character.

I placed my hands on my hips as she finally looked up at me. She assessed me from head-to-toe appraisingly, not an ounce of shame. "Oh, Pharos is back..." she teased, bringing up her old nickname for me. It had been a while since she had used it. Since she had met Hemingway. "You're pulling out the big gun to make me talk..." she teased.

Carl walked around the corner to find me naked, hands on my hips like I was posing for a statue, scowling at Othello. He turned to Othello, then back to me, considering something.

"I see..." he said, and then casually turned around to walk down the hall.

Othello watched him for a moment. "What do you think he'll make of that?" she asked.

"Something very creepy, most likely," I mumbled. "But don't dodge the question, Othello. Tell me about New York. Whatever you and Alucard have been up to."

She sighed. "Okay. I've been working with a girl in Boston."

I frowned. That was better than I had assumed. What with the army of werewolves needing to help out of the blue not long ago. "Why?"

"She's a good thief. And even better than good at finding the more obscure things you're usually interested in. I recruited her after she success-fully stole something from Grimm Tech." I felt my shoulders tightening in anger, but Othello held up a hand. "It was an accident, and I took care of it. Calm down. I've sent her on a task or two and she's done well. Just an asset in Boston. Thought she might be useful for Plato's Cave or Grimm Tech," she shrugged.

I thought about that. "A thief..." I wondered if she could maybe help me find a Devourer for Talon's spear. A blue one, like Anubis had suggested. "Why don't you send me her details."

"You can't bully her, Nate. I'm serious. She's dangerous."

I frowned. "I wasn't going to." Othello arched an eyebrow doubtfully. "Okay, maybe a little. But what do you mean *she's dangerous*? I'm dangerous, too," I said, realizing I sounded petty.

She pointedly glanced down at my current threat level, and found it wanting. "Magic doesn't affect her."

I blinked, recalling an encounter I'd had in Boston not long ago, when I had jumped into an Uber to meet up with Callie for a dinner. The girl in the Uber had given me a high five and zapped my power away from me on contact before speeding away. "A feisty redheaded Irish girl?"

Othello nodded slowly. "Yeah. That one. Quinn MacKenna."

"Why did you send Gunnar and a bunch of others to New York not long ago? Around the time that forest abruptly grew out of the Brooklyn Bridge?" I asked.

She nodded carefully. "I sent Quinn to acquire a seed from the Tree of Life. We ran into a few obstacles. I called in backup."

I blinked at her. "What exactly are you doing over there at Grimm Tech these days? Do I need to get some kind of weekly briefings or something?"

"It's probably better that you don't, but I do tell you about all the successful missions."

I scowled. "So, Quinn took the seed for herself instead of giving it to you?" I asked in a very cold tone.

Othello held up her hands, shaking her head. Then, realizing she still held the robe, she tossed it back at me. "No. Someone else took it and used it to grow that forest."

I positioned the robe over my goods as I studied her, wondering if she would lie to me. Then I let it go with a frustrated sigh. I had enough to worry about already. "Okay. But I want to meet her. Soon."

Her phone began to ring, and she pulled it out of a pocket. "Sorry, Nate. I need to take this. I'll email you the stuff on Quinn. Oh, I beefed the hell out of your security system on the Gate and the entire perimeter wall. I almost pity anyone stupid enough to attempt a breach. Your security team each has a tablet with a full dossier on any reporter out front, and they are casually walking around amongst them, bringing up sensitive matters in passing.

Talk to you later," she said sweetly, answering the phone and heading past me back to her suite.

I snapped my teeth at her as she walked past, and for my trouble, she slapped me on the ass again with her free hand, full palm, and since her hand was wet from the robe, it was a resounding, echoing *crack* in the mansion. I hopped instinctively, scowling over my shoulder at her... only to notice Carl's head peering around the corner, having witnessed the whole thing. He stared me in the eyes and slowly withdrew from sight, his tongue flicking out twice, as if assuming I wouldn't notice him if he moved slowly enough.

I sighed, and continued on to my room, wondering what security measures Othello had installed. Reporters? Was she talking about tomorrow's meeting with Mordred? Likely, they were both physically fatal and combined with electronic surveillance deterrents. And my security team? Who had she roped in for that? I had a brief image of Achilles walking around with a tablet, casually bringing up proof of affairs, extortion, and other blackmail-worthy schemes with the reporters, all while loudly sipping his fat-free-skim-sugar-free-mocha-frap-a-latte. Othello was one of the most unassumingly dangerous people I knew, especially when anyone tried to uncover something she considered private. And she considered almost everything private, hoarding intel like a dragon hoarded treasure.

As I walked, I found myself considering ways I could make use of Quinn. If she was as good as Othello thought, maybe she would know where to find a blue Devourer, not that I had the faintest idea of where to begin my search. And I didn't have time to go hunting for one. My meeting with Mordred was tomorrow.

The advice for a second Devourer was too little, too late.

I did have a decent collection of stones in the Sanctorum and Armory. Maybe I already had this Devourer...

All in all, I had a daunting to-do list. I wanted to talk to Talon about my flashback. He'd been suspiciously absent since last night. Had he ever even heard of a Devourer? Or those other names Anubis had mentioned – a Souleater. A Neverwas. And more importantly, had Talon known the significance of his name, Talon the *Devourer*?

Anubis said I needed to find out how to rejuvenate my Ichor, my borrowed god-juice.

I had to unite some of the other Families under my banner.

And I wanted to dig some dirt up on a Knight currently being watched over by Matthias. At least, the last I knew, Matthias had kidnapped him, drugging Baba Yaga and Van Helsing to achieve it.

But first, clothes.

CHAPTER 32

Dressed and ready to conquer the day, I tightened my satchel on my shoulder, and stormed out of my room in search of Talon. I had an errand to run, and I wanted him with me.

I snagged an apple off the counter of the kitchen and caught a bit of news on the television for my trouble. Mordred had found the time to do an interview after the speech last night.

"Master Temple fancies himself a modern-day Batman, what with his impressive technology company, Grimm Tech. Maybe I can help him turn his illusion into a reality to help this city," he said with a smile.

"Mr. Dred, do you look forward to your meeting?" the reporter asked him, gobbling the whole topic up.

Mordred nodded eagerly. *"I'll only miss that meeting if I'm dead and buried. Even then, I would do my best to sneak out of the underworld to make it. One doesn't stand up a meeting with a King, after all,"* he said, winking at the camera – winking at me, specifically. He was also telling the entire world that our meeting was happening, no matter what. Which meant I couldn't simply kill him before that time. I realized I was clenching my fist, the apple forgotten in my other hand. *"You won't find me disappearing like Alaric Slate did..."* Mordred trailed off thoughtfully.

The reporter pounced. *"Are you suggesting that... King Temple,"* the reporter asked with a wink, *"had something to do with Alaric's disappearance?"*

Mordred replied with a wave of his hand. *"Oh, not at all. But when you're as famous as Temple, sometimes your employees, attorneys, friends, family janitors, or even secretaries can feel... overprotective."* He shrugged, waving it off. The bastard had just casually mentioned a bunch of my friends. Obviously, his research hadn't been limited to me. But who was his source?

The television abruptly flicked off, and I turned to find Dean sneering at it.

"Did you need anything else?" he asked, not meeting my eyes.

I sighed, shaking my head. "No. Thank you, Dean."

"I've taken to target shooting," he said as I turned my back. I stopped, frowning back at him. "I hope that is permissible."

I nodded slowly. "Sure. May I ask why? You're safe here."

He arched a brow at me, silently reminding me of all the times the mansion had come under attack. I shrugged sheepishly. "It's the damned reporters lurking outside the gates. Waiting for this meeting tomorrow," he grumbled.

I frowned, growing concerned. "You're not shooting the reporters, are you?"

He gritted his teeth. "Much to my dismay, no. I am shooting the sudden influx of pigeons roosting on the wall. Coincidentally, they are in close proximity to the reporters on the other side..." he said, face impassive – but for him, it was a maniacal cackle.

I grinned. "Oh, right. We can't have that. Um... shoot away. Give them a warning, though. Just in case."

"Of course. I announce my intentions on the intercom at the gates... precisely seven seconds before I begin my irregularly-timed, hour-long shooting sessions. I checked with Turner Locke, the family attorney. This is private property, outside City Limits, and we are within our rights to use firearms on the grounds. Turner Locke arrived in the middle of the night to personally speak with every reporter, threatening them with the end of their careers and personal lives if anyone so much as considered trespassing. He also hinted that the entire news network would be slapped with legal repercussions they would never wade out of if even *one* of their reporters went rogue. Our privacy should be guaranteed, at least from the Regulars."

I shook my head, trying not to laugh. "For a butler, you're pretty cool sometimes, Dean. High five?" I asked, holding up my hand.

He grimaced distastefully. "I hear you were wandering the halls naked again this morning."

I lowered my hand. "I wasn't *wandering*," I argued. At his look, I sighed. "Yeah. Old habits die hard."

The kitchen was silent for a moment. Then Dean casually unbuttoned his suitcoat, revealing a pistol on a shoulder-rig. "I've also been practicing my marksmanship with these air-soft guns. I can do so indoors. It's remarkably efficient at eliminating the bad habits of any pesky residents."

I studied him. Was he threatening to shoot me if I was found naked in the public areas? I gave his unblinking face a slow nod of understanding. Then I lifted my hands in surrender, slowly backing out of the kitchen.

One of these days, I would get a high-five from someone without having to argue about it.

It took me a while, but I finally made my way outside, not finding Talon indoors. I took a breath of fresh air, gazing out at the Gate in the distance. Dean had been right. About a dozen vans were parked up and down the street, and a handful of reporters were huddled in tight groups, surprisingly well-behaved. They leaned against their vehicles with cameras dangling from their necks. Some were pointing up at the massive white tree climbing up into the sky, snapping pictures of it, likely wondering why it glittered in the sun.

Well, that was because it didn't have bark. It had scales, like a lizard. Like Carl. I frowned at the tree, recalling Carl's comment about it being a Gateway to his dimension. From this vantage, the reporters could see the front door, and several with long scopes began snapping pictures as soon as they saw me exit the front door. But they didn't suddenly rush the gates. Who the hell had Othello put on security? They were obviously doing a great job.

Still, I didn't like it. Mordred had effectively trapped me, leaving my comings and goings a matter of public record with reporters surveilling Chateau Falco and her residents. I sighed, walking down the steps.

Luckily, there was a ton of trees, landscaping, and even a steep hill blocking the lower fifty feet of the tree from the reporters' view. Because that's where I finally found Talon speaking with Grimm – my unicorn.

The reporters would have lost their collective shit seeing those two. Maybe Dean had the right idea about keeping them on their toes with the target practice. It likely reaffirmed that they probably didn't want to risk a late-night climb just to get a fresh photo. Then again, the walls were lined with Guardians like in Plato's Cave.

I just hoped it was enough, because Mordred was up to something. I just knew it.

I walked up to Grimm and Talon, wondering where I wanted to begin.

Grimm wasn't exactly the cute, My Little Pony edition.

He was like the washed-up child celebrity that had turned to drug smuggling for the cartels, rock and roll music, major felonies, maybe a bank heist or two, and he'd joined a biker gang for community service.

I don't say that to imply he was out of his prime. Oh, no. He was just a dark son of a bitch.

And I loved him for it.

The black feathers of his mane and tail caught the sunlight, seeming to shine, drawing the eye towards the blood-red circles at the tips. His horn was a gnarly, thorn-covered bone, one that looked as if it would be more painful coming out of a wound than it would be causing one. His eyes flickered with fire, and as he snorted at whatever Talon had just murmured to him, slight flame flared up from his nostrils, kind of like the propane on a gas stovetop – always there, but flaring brighter when you cranked the dial.

My pussycat had just cranked up my pony's dial.

Grimm pawed at the earth savagely, his silver hooves tearing into the manicured lawn. Then again, this section wasn't all that manicured any longer, because Grimm and Pegasus liked to hang out here, sparring or attacking the hundred or so rainbow reflections cast upon the earth by the giant crystal I had hung from one of the tree branches high above.

Still, the grass was persistent.

Lawncare pro-tip – regularly water your lawn with the blood of your enemies for the spongiest grass. Several hundred creatures had died painful, excruciating deaths in this spot over the last few years. I had over fifty acres – most of it undeveloped behind the property – and all the shit always seemed to go down right here.

Like the giant tree Carl had grown with a haunting song and some small blood sacrifice.

Grimms, Elders, Greek heroes, monsters of numerous flavors, humans, and even a freaking Maker and Beast had died in this area.

I swept the lawn, frowning. Not this *area*, but literally right fucking *here*.

Was that why Carl had been able to grow his Gateway here? He was convinced that my mother had taught him the secret of the D – a running joke that had ultimately backfired on us. Maybe all that death, all that blood, had set the stage for this tree to grow so suddenly. Within a few minutes, it had grown a couple hundred feet tall.

Grimm neighed loudly, catching my attention and snapping me out of my thoughts.

I frowned when I saw one of the feathers hanging over his forehead, looking suspiciously styled. It was painted in the seven colors of the rainbow, but as I walked closer, I realized it didn't look like a dye job. It was still wet, almost as if literally painted only a few seconds ago.

He saw me frowning at it and neighed proudly. "Rainbow. A twelve on the Fuck-Roy scale. I painted my mane with its blood for all to know and fear my duty. My devotion."

I blinked at him a few times.

Talon cleared his throat. "Something about a guy named Roy G. Biv. Your Alicorn seems to despise him immensely. Much like how you judge the strength of hurricanes and tornadoes, Grimm has come up with a scale for rainbow sizes." Grimm preened, batting his eyelashes as he nodded one time.

"Roy G. Biv…" I said slowly, reciting the colors of the rainbow in my mind – *red, orange, yellow, green, blue, indigo, violet.* "The acronym for the colors of the rainbow?" I asked.

My alicorn slammed a hoof into the ground, launching a clod of grass into the air. "No. He's the motherfucker that *created* rainbows. Asshole prances about in Fae, concealing his movements while he tries to beautify everything in his path."

I blinked again, and finally shook my head. "Sorry, man. He's not a real person. It's just an acron—"

"Don't tell me what I know and don't know, Rider," Grimm snarled. "Why do you think I hunt his spawn at every opportunity?" He didn't wait for me to answer, so it must have been rhetorical. "To draw out the bastard. I will get him one of these days. Do you know how long it took me to even discover his name?"

"I can honestly say I have no idea," I said, careful to keep my face neutral.

"Well, the Reds told me his secret name, and now I have power over him. They told me the name has been passed down from generation to generation in their family. And only after learning my devotion to hunting him down, did they decide to share it with me. They saw how depressed I was to discover that Yahn wasn't the Father of Rainbows, so they told me the bastard's real name, and his nefarious legend."

"Ah, I see. I didn't know that," I said, keeping my face serious. The Reds were becoming a problem, pulling more pranks than even I had as a youth. Then again, Grimm had seemed pretty set on murdering Yahn, and it seemed like the Reds had some kind of polygamous relationship with the glass dragon shifter. So, turning Grimm onto this imagined Roy G. Biv assassination contract seemed harmless enough.

Then again, an innocent prank much like that had erected this giant, scaly white tree, that looked suspiciously like Carl's own skin.

"Grimm, can you give us a minute? I need to talk to Talon." He didn't reply, just shook his head from side to side, waving his rainbow forelock of hair at us, and then trotted away.

CHAPTER 33

$\mathcal{T}$alon was staring at the ground, shoulders slumped. "I'm sorry, Wylde," he whispered, sounding as if he wanted to open a vein.

I grunted, deciding to let him stew in his discomfort for a minute as I surveyed the grounds. It was strangely peaceful. The workers had finished fixing up the landscape after the most recent battle here between dragons and werewolves a few weeks back, and surprisingly, it felt… empty. Likely a result of all the reporters at the gate. Mordred's plan in action.

I was used to shifters training and sparring on the grounds. Werewolves lounging about. My Guardian gargoyles sweeping over the perimeter to make sure we were safe, or Pegasus and Grimm racing each other over the house. Maybe even a dragon or two. Achilles and Leonidas sparring.

Carl lurking about, practicing his social skills to disastrous effect.

Or Hugin and Munin trying to shit on Talon—

I quickly looked up, fearing an aerial assault, but let out a breath when I didn't see the pair of beady black eyes staring down at us. I relaxed, but wasn't entirely comfortable with the realization that I hadn't seen them in a little while.

Talon noticed me studying the tree and pounced on the opportunity to speak. "I keep looking over my shoulder for them, too."

I didn't say anything, letting him squirm a bit longer as I turned to look at the mansion. Chateau Falco loomed over us in the morning sun, all

17,000 square feet seeming to stretch like a sunbather, curving with the landscape as if the Earth had formed around her.

"You know," I finally mused out loud, "I had a pretty good upbringing here. Plenty of room to cause trouble without fear of neighbors seeing magic. Gunnar could shift whenever he pleased. A good home for a boy."

"Not much different from Fae, if you think about it. Freedom, and your parents got you a... pet."

I glanced at Talon thoughtfully, and finally nodded. "Yeah. I guess you're right. But a *friend*, not a *pet*."

Talon followed in silence as I patted my satchel and began to walk towards the labyrinth. I didn't intend to walk through it, but around it, to the back of the mansion and the ponds and water features. "How many flashbacks have you had, Tal?" I asked, pretending to not notice his sudden startled flinch. "You looked entirely too interested when Alvara mentioned helping me reclaim my memories."

Talon stiffened, jerking his chin towards me. I nodded slowly. "You notice everything," he whispered. I let him believe what he would as I continued walking. I'd only remembered it in the shower, having wondered why Talon had gone from bored and sleepy to suddenly intensely interested when Alvara had mentioned it.

"I felt like we were back there," Talon finally murmured, studying the green walls of the labyrinth as we walked on the stone path leading between it and the side of the mansion, blocking out the sun. "Your flashback was one of the last times we saw each other before you left..." he whispered, voice raw with emotion. "But I only just remembered it." His eyes flickered towards me, meeting mine for a heartbeat. "After our trip to Hell, incidentally..."

I grunted.

Talon nodded. "It's why I was able to react so quickly last night. That was pretty much the first memory that came back to me, too, after..." he waved a hand vaguely, implying our first trip to Hell. "We were leaving Neverland and got separated from your parents for a few hours. Ran into a pirate and escaped. After finding your parents again, we said our goodbyes for the last time." He grew quiet for a few moments. "Then Pan wiped my mind and delivered me to Oberon to begin my service."

"Neverland," I breathed, shaking my head. It was almost too much. Peter fucking Pan and I had played together beneath a giant fucking tree, fighting pirates and chasing our shadows.

My headache began to come back, and I closed my eyes.

"The headaches fade," Talon said, noticing the pain in my features. "But do not press them. Just let them come back organically. I tried fighting them. It didn't end well for me. I had a migraine for days. Had to hide in the Sanctorum. In one of those dark rooms."

I frowned at him. "I thought you were just hiding from Hugin and Munin," I murmured.

He shook his head. "I tried to force the memories back, and could barely see straight, let alone walk for a few days. After that, I just let them hit me on their own, but was sure to keep to myself if I felt them coming on. A faint throb to the temples, and you should go find some solitude."

I growled. I had hoped to pepper him with questions, but even now, I felt my headache returning, throbbing harder the more I tried to press the fragmented memory. I remembered the events, but not the circumstances leading up to it. I could remember knowing Peter Pan, but not our first actual meeting. I remembered Talon being with me and keeping me safe after a pirate had stumbled onto my path through the woods at night. I remembered my parents being the only safe adults. All the others were deadly. But nothing before or after, especially not my final goodbye with Talon.

My brain began to throb harder, and I let out a breath, relenting.

"Damn it," I muttered, scuffing the ground with my boot in frustration.

Talon nodded, flexing and retracting his claws absently. "Yes. Like a shiny just out of reach." He abruptly cleared his throat. "I mean, I know it is frustrating."

I thought about the situation for a few moments, careful to keep far away from specifics. "You think the flashbacks work backwards? The most recent events coming back first, and the others following in order?"

Talon was silent for a few moments. "I thought so, at first, but I think I may have discovered a pattern..." He waited until I waved a hand for him to continue. "Mine all seem to relate to some important moment. Rather than moving chronologically, the memories move more in order of significance – a major lesson of some kind, or an unexpected moment of compassion, or a danger we overcame together." He let out a breath, sounding frustrated.

"Something that changed you somehow, you mean." Talon nodded eagerly, glancing over at me as we finally reached the back gardens. The ponds glittered like sapphires and emeralds in the sunlight, and the constant burble of flowing water was soothing. I saw we weren't the only ones back here. Alex was sparring near one of the outer ponds. "More related to the heart..." I said, angling us towards Alex. Because I needed to talk to him, and Pandora, too. To shut down the Armory, and possibly put a lid on whatever hobbies they'd decided to pursue. Or at least get some kind of explanation about it. The Armory might have the Devourer, too. Glancing over at Talon, I decided to wait a few minutes before bringing that up.

Talon thought about my comment. "Yes, but both good and bad memories of the heart. Not just nice memories. Anything that seemed... momentous."

"What about all the stuff in the middle?" I asked. "Like, you remember our goodbye, and then probably another event some span of time before that, right?" He nodded. "What about the period of time between the two memories?"

He was already nodding. "That stuff just kind of fills in on its own time. A few days after my second memory, I realized I recalled bits and pieces connecting the two. Enough to help me put a length of time between them, at least. Before that, I felt rather overwhelmed. Recalling two random moments, but not knowing *when* they happened in relation to the other..."

I opened my mouth to ask why my flashbacks had been delayed, but my cellphone rang. Out of habit, I answered, putting it on speaker. Alex was closer, now, but was too focused on his sparring to take notice of us.

"Hello?" I asked.

"Hey," Alucard said, voice sounding annoyed and pompous. "I'm ready to spill."

It took me a moment to catch on. "About your trip to Italy? And New York? Maybe a feisty redhead?" I asked, frustrated he had held back this long, even though he was apparently ready to cough up the details, now.

The line went silent for a moment, and I could tell I had caught him off guard. It also gave me proof he had been working with Quinn in some fashion. The plot thickens.

"Sure, if you hurry. But if you take too long, I'm going to start decapitating the locals." I heard a lot of angry curses and threats in the background.

"What are you talking about?" I asked, frowning, but also picking up on the seriousness layered in his flippant comment, which had obviously been worded in order to get a reaction from whoever was around him.

"I'm sitting here with the..." then he let out a laugh. "The Desperate Vampires of St. Louis," he said, still laughing. "Just as dramatic, and just as cancerous as those reality TV shows."

Shit. That wasn't good. I needed their allegiance, not hatred.

"Don't kill them yet. I'll be right there. Where are you?"

"Well, I tried to get them to join me under the Arch for some sun, but they weren't having it. You could say they're a little grouchy. It's past their bedtime." Because it was afternoon.

"Literally none of that helps me. Where are you?"

"Check the Drop Zone," he said, and my eyes immediately shot over to an area about a hundred yards away, beneath a giant willow tree near where Alex was sparring. I scowled, spotting Yahn and the Reds lurking near the trunk, looking suspiciously prepared to go somewhere, but standing still, staring at the Willow tree as if waiting for something.

We had set up the spot as a Drop Zone for Gateways – that way we didn't accidentally slice someone in half when any number of people used the Tiny Balls I had Grimm Tech producing like candy. I jerked a thumb at Talon, motioning him to follow me as I began jogging over towards the Drop Zone.

"They don't look suspicious at all," Talon said, keeping pace as he studied the three young dragons.

I grunted my agreement, especially when they noticed us coming and flinched simultaneously. "A little more warning would have been great, Alucard," I snarled into the phone.

"Is that *Talon?* Oh, this is going to be a *hoot*," he chuckled. "And I *tried* to talk to you this morning. Maybe you should put your dog on a leash." Alucard's Southern drawl dripped like molasses into my ear. "Get ready, Little Brother. In three... two... *one.*"

I was suddenly sprinting, holding my satchel tight to my hip. In the background of the phone, I heard a faint sound of shattering glass followed by shouts of alarm and Alucard laughing uproariously like a psycho.

A Gateway suddenly ripped into existence beneath the Willow tree.

"How long will it remain open?" Talon demanded, sprinting beside me and motioning for the dragons to join us – even though it was obviously what they had been waiting for, judging by their complete and utter lack of surprise to have a Gateway erupt in front of them, right where they had been staring.

I shrugged. The Gateways made by the Tiny Balls weren't all entirely consistent. Sometimes they remained open for a few seconds, and other times for longer. "It all depends on how old Alucard's Balls are," I shouted between breaths.

The Reds burst out laughing.

I shot them a stern look. "Gee, fancy seeing you three here," I snapped. "Almost like you knew about it."

Yahn grinned. "Toe-tah-lee, yah? Porcu-shine asked us to help and stuff."

Then they were jogging beside us, the Reds dressed in new-age grunge tees and ripped jeans. They had dark circles under their eyes, as if they hadn't slept a lot recently. Yahn let out a breath, eyes glinting with anticipation, and suddenly shifted into his dragon form, a small, candy-painted dragon the size of a few Bull Mastiffs mashed together. For a dragon, that was small.

With each step, his scales began to change hues, merging with the scenery around him, until he was practically invisible by the third step. Then he was simply gone, right as we reached the front of the Gateway.

"Jump," I snarled.

And we all leapt through the Gateway, ready for... well, I didn't know what.

Maybe the *Desperate Vampires of St. Louis Reunion* episodes.

But would it be the usually calmer and polite part one, the chaotic part two, or...

The Apocalyptic *Reunion – Part Three.*

CHAPTER 34

The four of us who were visible, skidded to a halt, eyes darting back and forth for immediate dangers. Yahn was presumably beside us, hopefully, because the Gateway winked out a moment later. I let out a sigh of relief that it hadn't closed while we were mid-jump.

I realized we were in a large antiquated room, and we were standing atop one of those long, elegant thirty-person dining tables. At our feet, in the center of the table, was a staked vampire lying on his back.

His own severed head was neatly placed on his chest, and the head wore a white fedora. He looked surprised, startled, and generally unhappy to have his head detached.

About two dozen vampires sat in chairs lining either side of the table, staring up at us like we had just interrupted the evening prayer. Alucard, seated at the head of the table, began a very slow, steady clap.

I kept my face impassive, regarding Alucard for a few moments in silence. Then, I nodded my head slightly. I turned to the vampires glaring up at us. They looked anxious and pissed. Especially at my companions.

Because Talon was standing beside me with the butt of his milky white spear resting on the table's surface, right in the glowing pool of blood oozing from the decapitated vampire's body. He glared down at the vampires, lip curled back faintly. Then he knelt, dipped a paw in the blood, and slowly drew two faint lines from his forehead down to his cheeks, bisecting his eyes.

Finally, he held his paw to his mouth, and licked off the last of the blood, purring loudly.

The Reds stood still, hands at their sides, their faces entirely blank, as if emotionless statues. No one looked pleased to be here, especially not at the way Alucard had greeted them – I glanced down at the body quickly – in such an extravagant manner, decapitating one of their own.

"King Temple, I thank you for joining us," Alucard drawled in a loud, booming voice, dipping his head again. "And Talon the Devourer, always a pleasure to meet a kindred spirit," he murmured, leaning forward with a sinister grin. Alucard's eyes drifted to the unassuming Reds, and he smirked playfully. "And two… feisty redheads," he said, discreetly meeting my eyes. "But we can get to them later," he suggested meaningfully.

I nodded slowly, getting the hint. He had something planned, and he didn't want me ruining it. I'd play ball. Because he'd set the table for me, and it would be incredibly rude to disrupt his dinner party.

Alucard glanced to either side of the table, addressing the vampires. "We should be on our best behavior, my friends. They're only children, after all. And obviously not right in the head."

I glanced back to find the Reds flanking me on either side, a pace back. They stared blankly at nothing, as if they were blind, deaf, and dumb. I was going to have to play catch-up, because the Reds were the exact opposite of emotionless, so they were obviously in on Alucard's game. Several of the vampires sniffed disdainfully, maybe disappointed that the Reds weren't appetizers – peace offerings.

I swept the room, taking note of everyone present. They represented all factions. Some old, some young, and dressed entirely different from one another. They kind of looked like a random sampling of people you might spot in a quaint coffee shop – all different professions, ages, shapes, sizes, and colors. A college professor type, several in suits, a handful of young adults, a tattooed heiress of sorts, and even a few gray hairs. One woman in particular looked older than the rest, her hair entirely white, but her dark mahogany skin was as flawless as her companions. Vampires were the worst. They aged so beautifully, so when I said a few were gray hairs, they still had a twenty-something's perfect skin complexion.

The elderly woman watched me very intently. Not angrily or malevolently, but very… aware. Then she smiled faintly, dipping her head. Usually, with monsters, that was not a good development. But only time would tell if her gesture had been amusement or a threat.

Not seeing the point in staring down at everyone any longer, I hopped off the table, and held out a hand to the Reds. They each took it graciously, stepping from the table to a chair, to the floor, faces dumbly blank. Then, they silently stepped back behind me, resuming their earlier positions.

Talon leapt off the table in an effortless backflip, his spear whirling beside him, and landed in a crouch, slamming the butt of his blade into the floorboards, making the white blade quiver in the air like a tuning fork.

My eyes flicked to the vibrating blade, lingering on the place where a Devourer would likely fit. *Eyeless*, Anubis had called it. I could almost make out a faint circle where one would fit. Or… maybe where one had once been set into the blade. Presumably, a blue one, if Anubis was to be believed.

I set my hand on my satchel, ready to grab my own spear if necessary. I could fit any number of things into my satchel, and had taken to stashing my new spear there, along with a dozen other dangerous items I had personally acquired over the years. The three items from my parents, for example, although I didn't talk about them with anyone.

I wasn't used to grabbing a weapon when shit went down, but I'd been thinking about the spear a lot since I woke up. Anubis had been very adamant about it being vital to defeating Mordred, so I'd decided to keep it close. And, magic in a dim confined room with so many people around us could result in friendly fire. But with my backup, I highly doubted my spear would be necessary. With three dragons, Talon, and hopefully Alucard, I was confident we could kill two-dozen vampires in a minute or two, max.

From what I'd heard, the vampires of St. Louis were fragmented without a Master, and ripe for the picking. Enter Alucard, head of the table. It looked like he was ready to claim his throne, whether in blood or with an easy smile was yet to be determined. But the decapitated centerpiece on the table seemed like a good indicator of his plan.

To follow in my footsteps and become King Fanger with a wooden stake for an exclamation point.

So, it was probably wise to be ready for a scrap. Because many of these vampires *looked* old, and supernatural things that *looked* old were usually *much more powerful*.

I was mildly surprised no one had seemed to pick up on what the Reds truly were, or that a third, chameleon dragon was lurking unseen around us.

I waited for the festivities to commence. After a few moments, heads began slowly swiveling to Alucard, growing anxious and impatient as well.

"All the big-shots are present, yes?" Alucard asked, loud enough for all to hear, absently drumming his fingers on the table.

Everyone at the table murmured their agreement, but it was pretty obvious old feuds were alive and well – hateful, malicious looks passed back and forth between what looked like the most unlikely of fellow vampires.

One man, who looked like the stereotypical vampire overlord – long blonde hair, metrosexual clothing, and smug arrogance permanently etched onto his features – seemed to be getting a lot of discreet sidelong glances. Both fearful and hateful.

I dubbed him Blonde-Angst.

The little old lady was getting a whole lot of non-looks, people pointedly avoiding looking at her so bluntly that they might as well have shouted they were paying very close attention, and that something was up.

"Great," Alucard drawled, kicking his boots up onto the table. "Saves me time. Now, everyone is going to write down the name of the most hated person present, excluding myself, naturally," he chuckled. His was the only laugh. "Oh, and our guests. This is a fanger-only vote."

"And why do we have *guests* present? This should be an internal discussion," the beautiful raven-haired heiress purred, adjusting the shoulder strap of her flowery sundress, and fingering her hair coyly. "Unless he intends to share?" she added, turning her smile to the Reds.

They didn't even blink back, just stared ahead into the middle distance like automatons.

I smiled at her. "Sharing is my favorite," I told her, and something about my tone made her wilt slightly. The elderly black woman chuckled huskily, shaking her head at me, somehow earning the ire of her fellow vampires, even though they still weren't looking at her directly.

The Blonde-Angst vampire gripped the table hard, his nails biting into the wood. I rolled my eyes at him, and turned back to Alucard, wondering exactly what he was up to.

"It's cute…" Alucard began, slowly turning to look at the raven-haired heiress. She smiled hungrily at his faint grin. "That you think this is a discussion," he finished in a soft tone.

Her smile withered away and died. No one else moved.

"Well?" Alucard asked absently, shuffling through a deck of large cards he had apparently pulled out of his pocket. When no one spoke, he looked up, frowning. "If you can't handle a simple request like writing a fucking name down, you'll probably get to see your first sunrise soon," he told them in a bored tone. "I promise, it's truly unforgettable."

"We don't have any paper," the older black woman said with a grand-mother's smirk. "Or pens." She somehow managed to say it politely, not appearing to be mocking him for his obvious oversight.

Alucard climbed to his feet with a frown. I was already reaching down into my satchel to see if I had anything that might help, when I heard a loud *thud* and a splintering *crunch*. I looked up to see Alucard had torn a massive painting of some Victorian Lord and Lady from the wall, letting it drop to the floor. It was easily ten-feet-tall, and the frame was now ruined. He splayed his fingers to reveal claws, and swiftly sliced vertically through the painting a few times, tearing it into ribbons. Then he sliced again in the opposite direction, effectively making scratch paper for everyone.

From a painting that had to have been worth thousands, if not hundreds of thousands of dollars. Who owned this place, anyway? And where was it? Maybe that was why Alucard had chosen our method of transportation, knowing it prevented me from pinpointing the address on a map. Clever.

Alucard scooped up the pieces, ignoring the indignant squawks from several of the vampires seated at the table, and then he began walking from chair to chair, handing everyone a piece. He ended up near the body of the dead vampire and reached into the man's lapel pocket where a pen was poking out the top. He frowned thoughtfully at the body, clicking the pen several times absently, and then he grinned. He plucked the hat off the vampire's detached head, dropped the pen inside the fedora, and then slid it across the table at Blonde-Angst. The vampire caught it, using the motion to flip his hair back like a shampoo commercial, but his lips were set in a thin line.

Alucard walked back to his seat. "Pass the pen when you're finished and toss your paper into the hat. I'll tally them in two minutes and announce the winner."

"Winner?" a man in a suit spoke in what sounded like a sophisticated air, absently checking the ruby cufflinks on his sleeves.

Alucard waved his hand vaguely, focused on inspecting and shuffling the deck of cards in his hands. "Less *talky*, more *writey*," he murmured distractedly.

Talon shot me a questioning look, but I shook my head, not having an explanation for him, and knowing I was unable to voice it even if I had understood.

"I want to know who the fuck you think you are," one of the younger, hipper vampires beside Blonde-Angst said. "Why are we playing his games?" he snapped, turning to his fellow vampires.

Alucard paused his shuffling and slowly looked up, locking eyes with the kid. Well, not kid, but I guessed I was turning into an old man, because he looked to be barely into his twenties, and that seemed horribly young to me. Since he was a vampire, he was likely a few decades older than me, but there was no way to be sure other than asking him outright.

"He didn't want to play my game either," Alucard said in a hurt tone, slowly extending his finger to point at the dead vampire on the table. The room grew silent. "Sixty seconds," Alucard said cheerfully, resuming his shuffling of the deck. The pen quickly began passing down the line, the vampires suddenly realizing that the two-minute time limit had actually been a command, not a suggestion.

I watched them thoughtfully, noticing that Mr. Blonde-Angst was subtly shooting threatening looks at those writing down their chosen names. I didn't say anything out loud, because I was just a spectator, and didn't really care, but it was obvious he was trying to manipulate the vote somehow.

The elderly grandmother was at the end of the line, so she began to knit as she waited her turn at the pen. The needles looked suspiciously like bone, and not the cute, store-bought type of bone. I was pretty sure I saw blood-stains and toothmarks on them. I shivered involuntarily. Grandmas were scary, but bloodsucking grandmas were something else.

She finally got her turn, and scribbled down a name without hesitation, tossing it into the hat and resuming her knitting. The pretty raven-haired heiress scoffed at the old lady and stood to retrieve the hat, horribly put-out that she'd had to do anything other than look pretty.

She walked up to Alucard with the hat, careful to sway and roll her hips as she moved.

He didn't even look up from his cards, just gestured for her to set it down before him. I saw her jaws clench, but she silently obeyed before returning to her seat.

Finally, Alucard sighed and set his cards down on the table. Then he began rifling through the papers, putting them in stacks, presumably tallying up votes for the written names.

I found myself very interested in the cards, because he had left them face-up, and they weren't traditional playing cards. They were Tarot Cards of some flavor. They didn't feel magical or anything, so I relaxed.

Alucard lifted up the hat after a few moments, shaking it out to show everyone it was empty. Then he slapped it on his head, ignoring the blood spatter on the brim as he tilted it at a rakish angle. He leaned back in his chair and kicked his boots back up onto the table, surveying all the faces watching him.

He settled his gaze on the little old lady, but she didn't bother looking up. With every head in the room turning to follow Alucard's gaze, she obviously noticed. *Click, click, click...*

Alucard shrugged apologetically. "I thought it would be you," he admitted, sounding sad. She nodded absently, still not looking up or ceasing her knitting. She looked entirely at peace.

Alucard dropped his boots with a sigh and then walked over to her, rolling his shoulders in preparation, clutching the deck of cards in one hand. I bit my tongue, reminding myself that I had no say in the matter. The vampires needed their own Master. If that was going to be Alucard, I couldn't swoop in and overrule him during his first meeting with them. In what was essentially his coronation festival.

His boots thumped across the floor in a measured, steady beat like a death march.

Grandma Fang kept right on clicking her needles, and I began to wonder if she was playing a game as well. If she was about to lunge up and stab Alucard in the heart or something. Maybe those stakes were *wood*, not bone...

CHAPTER 35

The air in the room was tense, several scooting their chairs back slightly from their fellow vampires, but no one voiced a word of protest. Blonde-Angst was one of the only smiles in the room. Alucard reached the old woman and let out a resigned breath.

Talon's tail began to twitch impatiently, flicking back and forth, and even the Reds were discreetly paying attention, now.

Alucard leaned over and placed a hand over hers, ending the incessant clicking. She slowly looked up at him, not a flicker of fear in her eyes.

Then Alucard was kneeling beside her, and he lifted her hand to his lips, kissing the back of it as gently as one would kiss a sleeping baby's forehead. Her eyes widened at the gesture, but even more so when Alucard slowly leaned in for her neck. Her chin quivered, but she did open her neck for him to bite her, or whatever flavor of execution he had in store for her.

Instead, he whispered something into her ear. Then he withdrew, staring into her startled face.

She blinked a few times, but then slowly lifted one of her sewing needles to point to…

Blonde-Angst.

The overlord-lookalike scowled back, face a thunderhead. "What madness is she spouting now? How the younger generation has no idea how to be *true* vampires? That's her usual shtick," he muttered, shooting his threatening glare around the room at his fellow vampires. They murmured their agreement, flinching under his glare whenever it landed on them.

But Alucard was already circling the table, staring down at the deck of cards in his hand as he read them and then discarded them onto the table or floor with a casual flick of his fingers. He paused, did a little two-step, and continued on, humming to himself as he continued dropping cards, completely unaware of the growing argument among his dinner guests.

I blinked. Was he… yes, he was definitely dancing as he walked. I almost burst out laughing, but the level of anxiety was rapidly growing as everyone wondered exactly what was happening, murmuring to each other.

Blonde-Angst wasn't bothering to be discreet anymore, but loudly muttering to his pals about the charade. "What is the meaning of this?" he finally demanded, glaring first at Alucard and then the older lady, who was smiling approvingly at Alucard's rear as he danced, paused, spun, did another quick two-step, and then continued on, shaking his hips absently, as if he'd forgotten anyone was in the room and he was just jamming to some soul music.

"I lived in N'awlins," he finally murmured as if talking to himself, still dropping cards one by one. "Had shitty parents, and an even shittier sister. Woe is me."

I grimaced at that casual comment. I'd had the misfortune of meeting his sister once. Even helped Alucard kill her. As I looked about the room, I realized that no small number of the vampires had also recognized the reference, possibly having known Neveah on a personal level, and were now likely wondering if they'd just realized how fatal that relation might end up being.

But Alucard continued, still flicking cards to the floor after a quick glance. "There's a reason that matriarchal societies function so well, historically speaking. Must show the women respect," he said solemnly. He paused, flipped a card over, and then flung it to the ground. "Because if Mama ain't happy," he smiled, shooting a glance at the older lady, "ain't nobody happy."

"Tell it to 'em, Morningstar," she chuckled under her breath, shaking her head jovially.

I briefly wondered if I had maybe encouraged Alucard a little too well in embracing his inner monster, his darker side, because this was just cruel. I knew vampires loved their games, but even I was getting fidgety, and the Reds were breathing faster – a fact that several of the vampires were also noticing, although trying to be discreet about their hungry looks. I was just glad no one had jumped to their feet screaming *dragon!*

"I picked up a thing or two – Tarot, Voodoo, and whatnot..." Alucard said, still checking and then flicking cards to the floor, the table, the fireplace. Then he paused upon seeing the next card, a smile stretching across his face. "Ah, *finally!* Here it is."

"Here *what* is?" Blonde-Angst snapped. "Just kill the lying bitch already!"

Alucard looked up, cocking his head as he assessed the room. "I want you to look at this very closely..." he said, holding up the card for all to see. It was the Nineteenth Major Arcana – the Sun Card, and it showed a child riding a white horse with a sun dominating the sky.

The vampires cringed in unison, obviously not devout fans of the sun.

But as everyone stared at the card, I realized Alucard was no longer sharing his glance with every vampire in the room, only Blonde-Angst. He took two, carefully measured steps to the right, as if lining up something. "Oh, my apologies," Alucard told him, noticing the frown of confusion on Blonde Angst's face. "You probably can't see it very well from over there. Here, catch." And Alucard flung it with two fingers.

The card burst into flame halfway across the table and then sliced straight through Blonde-Angst's neck, leaving only a faint black line before it struck another priceless painting hanging on the wall behind him.

"Ta-da!" Alucard chimed, and then took a bow. The flaming card managed to burn a small hole in the painting before extinguishing itself.

When no one laughed, Alucard frowned. "Oh, don't worry! We can get a new painting," he said dismissively. The room was eerily silent as we all stared at Blonde-Angst, who was staring back at Alucard with wide eyes. Then, with a sickening *squelch*, his body fell forward and his head tumbled into the center of the table. The wound was cauterized, leaving no gore to clean up. The young vampire who had hitched himself to Blonde-Angst earlier looked about ready to soil himself.

Alucard was shaking out his hand, extinguishing the fire dancing over his fingertips. He finally looked back up at the room of frozen vampires. "Anyone else want to get a closer look at the card? I'll have to tug it out of the painting. That might give you a few seconds head start to run screaming from the building. Run screaming from St. Louis..."

Everyone shook their heads stiffly.

"Really? No one?" he asked, smiling beside the beautiful pretend-heiress.

"Last chance… Imagine how funny it would look to see a kiss of vampires running from the building and bursting into flame as soon as they opened the front door…" He leaned over, pinching her cheek playfully, "Because it's a grand, sunny day, *mon cher*," he told her, chuckling at her full-body clench.

As Alucard continued on past her, she deflated like a wet rag, shivering, and pointedly ignoring Blonde-Angst's motionless body. Either they'd been an item, or she had just witnessed some plot of hers die a sudden, violent death. Alucard's flashy card trick and pinching her cheek had just told her that she was on thin ice, and that her usual tricks would obviously not work on him.

The Daywalker cleared his throat. "I'm the new Master Vampire of St. Louis. Discuss." He folded his arms like a bored college professor that was too hungover to teach his students on Monday morning.

His new students didn't discuss anything. Didn't even make eye contact with one another.

Just like college students, I thought to myself absently.

CHAPTER 36

*A*lucard grunted when it was apparent the discussion was dead in the water. "Okay. Discussion over. Now, this sweet little thing," Alucard finally said, pointing at the knitting lady, "is my foxy proxy for when I'm doing..." he gestured pompously, "other things. Like sun tanning." The old woman beamed happily. She had this cute twinkle of carnage in her eyes that let me imagine her baking cookies during the End Days.

One vampire, the sophisticated guy in a suit, cleared his throat gently, keeping his eyes lowered. "With all due respect, does the Sanguine Council know of this? I know we recently approached you about becoming Master of St. Louis, but in your delay and then absence..." his eyes briefly touched upon the Blonde-Angst's dead body decorating the table, "opposing factions began to speak up." He finally met Alucard's eyes very briefly and gave him a respectful nod. "I, for one, would prefer your ruthless stability, but it's a fair point..."

Alucard drummed his fingers, slowly leaning over the table to peer down at the outspoken vampire, looking like nothing but a pitbull debating whether or not to rip an intruder's throat out. A subtle message that Alucard wasn't so easily won over by a compliment. The vampire lowered his eyes again, and although obviously terrified, he hid it well. "The old wine-sacks in Italy gave me a choice. St. Louis or New York."

The man glanced up sharply. "New York? Why?"

Alucard smiled distantly, pausing to shoot me a brief glance, letting me know this answer was also for me. Finally, I would hear an answer on exactly what the hell had went down during his fang-cation.

"Remember Roland Haviar, the Vatican Shepherd from Kansas City? The legendary vampire hunter that voluntarily chose to *become* a vampire? I invited him to our last party together." The vampires were eerily silent, probably wondering if it was a rhetorical question. "You remember, the one who still has access to his wizard's power." It was obvious from the very first mention of the name, that they remembered *exactly* who Roland was. Alucard was just being overly dramatic to incite fear. A great tactic at times. Alucard slapped the table loudly, his hand bursting to flames and scorching the wood. "Well?" he demanded.

They couldn't nod fast enough.

"Thank you. Roland and I had a road-trip on our way back from our meeting with the Sanguine Council. Might have caused a vacancy for the Master of New York position, but in my defense, I'd had a few too many drinks that night."

Judging by the sudden flinches, that statement struck a chord in them. They either knew who – and how dangerous – Roland was, and that he was Alucard's friend. Or, they knew exactly how powerful the Master of New York had been, and that Alucard had gotten a little tipsy and killed him. Whoopsies. Party foul.

Just one of these comments would have been enough to solidify his rule. But combined? Especially after his card trick moments ago? He had them in the palm of his hand.

Another sneaky aspect of Alucard's statement was that, out of the two options, Alucard had *chosen* St. Louis over New York. The honey to the great swinging club of a stick he had used on the two vampires now lying on the table. He had just told them he thought them more important than New York.

"Did… Roland take New York, then?" the pretty raven-haired vampire asked, likely considering applying her wares on the East Coast.

Alucard frowned at her. "Nah, he likes the Midwest. I think he's hanging around Kansas City for a while. He's friends with Callie Penrose. You've heard of her, right?"

Stiff, jerking nods circled the table like the wave at a sporting event. They didn't like thinking about Miss Callie Penrose. Not one bit. But they also feared her. I wondered what rumors were being whispered on the streets about her to make them react so strongly.

"Well, Roland – that big, bad sonofabitch – considers Callie to be his adopted *daughter*. Taught her everything she knows. And she's regularly in the company of..." he held out a hand, pointing directly at me, "*this* motherfucker."

Everyone slowly turned to face me, concealing their true feelings. But each look also held a whisper of fear, no matter how hard they tried to hide it.

"Nate Temple. The King of St. Louis." When no one moved, Alucard continued in a very soft, chilling tone. "You should probably bow down to him or something."

The vampire closest to me – a portly, unassuming accountant type – was suddenly lunging at me, claws extended to rip through my chest. I hadn't even really noticed the guy, he had been so bland and silent during the show.

Talon yawned loudly, even covering his mouth with a paw.

I held my ground, locking eyes with my attacker, and smiled. I felt a rush of wind at my side and watched as a glass man suddenly materialized between us, having been invisibly stalking the room up until now.

He'd brushed my sleeve a few times in passing to let me know his position, and so I wouldn't accidentally back into him and seemingly trip over nothing in front of a bunch of predators biologically wired to attack at any sign of weakness.

Yahn had foregone his dragon form for this, apparently. His fist slammed into the vampire's cheekbone, shattering one of his fangs and stopping him cold. His cheek actually fractured like a cracked vase – even sounded like it, too. *Crunch!*

The vampire dropped to the ground in a limp pile, unmoving. Alucard grunted absently, not looking remotely surprised. I toed the two-inch-long tooth lying on the rug beside his face. He didn't move, even when I nudged his nose with my boot. I turned to Yahn with an arched eyebrow.

"Jesus, man. How hard did you *hit* him?"

Yahn frowned back at me. "What do you mean?" He glanced down at the pile of vampire. "I hit him as *hard as I fucking could*, of course. Did you expect me to *slap* him or something?"

I sighed. "No, it's just… I don't know if I've ever really seen someone take a punch like that. Not from this close, anyway." I shrugged, crouching down to scoop up the tooth and tuck it into my pocket. I looked back up to find the vampires all staring from Yahn to me. "Oh, sorry. Go ahead," I told them.

Yahn cleared his throat and clothing suddenly exploded behind me as the Reds burst into their dragon forms, shredded fabric raining down over me. I casually brushed off a shoulder, then the other as spitting snarls flanked me, challenging the vampires. "The dragons serve King Temple," Yahn said in a cold, imperious tone.

Talon's harsh features, only emphasized by the bloody lines he had painted down his face, swept the room, his ears swiveling back and forth.

The vampires gripped their armrests or the table in front of them with sudden black claws, looking on the verge of panic, not having sensed the Reds up until this moment. I'd have to ask how they had pulled that off. Vampires had impeccable senses and should have noticed three shifters in their midst.

Before anyone else could do anything stupid, Alucard clapped his hands twice to halt the hysteria. "You should probably know that I consider King Temple my brother from another mother, so I guess that makes me a prince." He leaned over the table, his fingers suddenly flaming claws again, scorching the wood and cracking the lacquer finish. "And I *definitely* expect you to bow to *me*."

I cleared my throat politely, looking at him. "*Dude…*" I said.

He met my eyes and then chuckled. "*After* you bow down to the King, of course," he amended, dipping his own chin as an example.

And they did. Bowing down to me, and then Alucard. They even looked genuine about it.

I nodded back to them and waved for Alucard to resume dictating his commands to his new Kiss of Vampires.

"Now," Alucard began, kicking his boots back up onto the table. "We have a super-twat named Mordred in town, causing a bother. He thinks he's hot shit. Nate and I disagree. Specifics might change, but generally, we plan on hurting his feelings. This is what you are going to do…"

Inwardly, I was grinning. So far, I had the dragons, the wolves, and the vampires behind me. Possibly the Chancery. Well, I didn't think they'd be staunchly *against* me, which was good enough to smile about.

But how many did Mordred have in his pocket? Or was I simply playing into his game?

"It was a pleasure meeting you. Maybe I'll invite you over for dinner one of these days," I said, smiling politely. Then I ripped a Gateway in the air, motioning for my crew to join me back at Chateau Falco.

Grimm, the sick bastard, was chewing on a wad of rainbow about two feet away from the open Gateway, rainbow blood all over his fangs. He took two steps and stuck his head through the opening and *into* the room of vampires, fiery eyes narrowing as he continued loud, wet chews, rainbow gore dripping onto the floorboards. Then he neighed at them, and his nostrils flared with that deep, inner fire.

I patted him on the neck and stepped through the Gateway. "Easy, Grimm. They're friends."

Grimm snorted indelicately before spitting out a wad of rainbow guts into the room. Incidentally, it hit the face of the vampire head sitting atop the body in the center of the table, knocking it over and sending it rolling down the length of the table, smearing rainbow blood in a long, pretty streak.

Alucard stopped it with a hand, grinning as he leaned close to inspect the blood. "How big was it on the Fuck-Roy scale?" he asked, glancing up at Grimm.

"Oh, hey, Alucard." Grimm said, dipping his head slightly. "Congrats on the king thing. And it was a twelve," he added smugly, licking his rainbow painted lips with a long black tongue.

Alucard grunted. "Wow. New record. Great job."

Grimm slowly backed away. After my crew had all followed me through, I let the Gateway wink shut.

Grimm immediately burst out laughing. "I thought you'd *never* open up the Gateway," he snorted.

The Reds shifted back to their human form, naked as the day is long. Yahn held up a dull, ivory stone, about the size of a large, flattened prune. "I'm just glad this thing worked like Raego said it would. Too bad there aren't more of them."

I studied it thoughtfully. "It hides your nature? That you're shifter dragons?"

Yahn nodded. "Only at a short distance, though, which is why Alucard got them all in that room and closed the doors. I think it masks all shifters in the vicinity, not just the one holding it." He kissed the stone loudly, and I noticed Talon studying him.

I shook my head, impressed. Everyone began to laugh in triumph, even Talon, momentarily forgetting all about Mordred and the shit headed our way.

Laughter was important.

CHAPTER 37

*Y*ahn and the Reds soon peeled off to go do whatever naked dragons did for fun these days, and Grimm was tearing into a hunk of rainbow that resembled a meaty, colorful carcass, using his horn to slash through it before gobbling down another dripping slab.

I made my way over to the sparring area where Alex was now pitted against a trio of Achilles' battle-tested Myrmidons. Talon, as usual, followed at a discreet distance, my Shadow, my protector.

I spotted Ganesh, the elephant-headed Indian god – the remover of obstacles – speaking with Asterion the Minotaur, both seated cross-legged beneath a tree, watching the fight.

But it was the third figure beside them that made me suspicious. King Midas watched Alex entirely too intently. And he had a habit for turning things into gold or finding unique investment opportunities.

I watched Alex flip one of the Myrmidons over his hip, slamming him to the ground and drawing a finger across his throat to symbolize a dagger kill. The two remaining Myrmidons rushed him, and Alex bolted away towards a stump, just out of reach of their hands. He stumbled as his boot touched the stump, and the Myrmidons lunged for him.

But Alex was just as suddenly hanging in the air, upside-down between them, having used the stump as a launchpad for a backflip, his stumble a feigned deceit. He flung out his hands to hammer-fist the backs of their heads, knocking them off balance to headbutt the tree in a double-knockout. Alex did fumble the landing, but turned it into a backwards roll, breathing fast as he climbed to his feet with an impish grin.

The group of waiting Myrmidons clapped their approval, but it was very subdued. Ganesh, Asterion, and Midas, on the other hand were hooting and hollering excitedly.

I'd saved Alex from Fae – a child victim of the Changeling business where the Fae switched out one of their own children to replace a human child on Earth, and vice versa. They had used it as some kind of supernatural battery, the disguised Fae child raised – without the parents' knowledge – as one of their own, thanks to their nifty illusion spells.

The human child would likewise be raised in Fae, typically under less than ideal circumstances.

I'd brought Alex back to St. Louis to raise him. But something about the time that had passed since his abduction in the real world and his return back, had fast-forwarded his growth. So, he was now a twenty-something, in the prime of his life, muscled as all get-out, and thankfully, no longer aging as fast.

Since he was a Regular, and potentially a target as my friend, I had seen fit to begin his self-defense training. I had come up with this grand plan when he had been an awkward pre-teen...

Just a few months ago.

No one had anticipated him looking like a twenty-five-year-old Captain St. Louis superhero in less than half a year. But seeing all the changes, and how quickly he was learning and adapting to his new life, I was beginning to have my doubts about what I thought I had known.

For example, Pandora had told me his given last name was *Arete*, just like the word on the Temple Family Crest that meant *to become the best possible form of a thing.*

In the famous words of Yoda, *checked that box, Alex had.*

And here he was, kicking Myrmidon ass better than maybe even Achilles could. Leonidas and Achilles both had taken quite a shine to Alex, teaching him private lessons in the arts of war and battle. The boy with no parents now had an army of moms and dads taking care of him, looking out for him, and training him to be...

The best possible form of a thing.

So, it was understandable that my spidey-sense was tingling. Names, I was finding, were the word of the day.

Talon the *Devourer* – which apparently meant something very specific and important.

Naming my Elder pal *Carl* – having had no idea his parents were named Carl-*os* and Carl-*a*.

And Alex had recently given Pandora his virginity merit badge. Pandora had done so out of the goodness of her heart, telling me her coitus skills would somehow unlock abilities in Alex that I would someday rely upon for my survival. Her… *Myth-flix and Chill* date nights were obviously helping.

Despite being a Regular – having no magic – Alex hardly hung out with any of them, spending the majority of his time around the most dangerous and powerful people he could find, learning from them. I'd tried hooking him up on a date with Camilla, a chimera friend of the Reds, but I'd found them an hour later sparring in the back yard, with her teaching him how to survive a chimera encounter. She had left without the twinkle of budding romance in her eye, but they had glimmered with a very solid respect for the boy… no, the *man*.

And seeing that same look from Asterion, Midas, and Ganesh right now made me very uncomfortable. Like having football scouts lurking behind trees, watching your son's scrimmage game. Alex didn't just have moms and dads looking after him. He also had three bad uncles, apparently.

"I hope you three arrived discreetly," I told them.

They murmured that they had, chuckling absently as if to tell me this wasn't their first time in prison.

I grunted. "How have you been, Midas?" I asked.

"Oh, passing fair." And then, without any social foreplay, he said, "Alex should come to Fight Night."

My eyes narrowed, and I shook my head. Three new fighters were squaring off against Alex. He took a calming breath and lowered his hands. Then they rushed him, two fanning out and the other sprinting head on at him. "No, Midas. He's too young. He's not entering your Fight Club so you can win a few bets."

"You big idiot," Asterion snorted, startling me. He was usually the most rational of the bunch.

I rounded on him, staring incredulously. "Excuse me?"

"It's quite astonishing to witness, isn't it?" Ganesh said to Asterion.

I frowned harder. "Alright, King Dong. What are you talking about?" I asked Ganesh, miming stroking my face-trunk like one would stroke a goatee.

He rolled his eyes at my low humor. "Training at the Fight Club is technically *less* dangerous than him training *here*. On your property, he could break a leg or crack a rib... But at Fight Club, the Dueling Grounds keep him safe."

I stared at them for about ten seconds, my face expressionless. I opened my mouth, thinking of the carnage of Fight Nights – the magic, blades, blood, and death, all to the screams of the crowd. I thought about this for another ten whole seconds, because... he was right.

Asterion was nodding. "It makes sense. When you die at Fight Club, your soul is always sent back home, dragging your empty body along with it, and you wake up as good as new. The opposite of Astral Projection, in a way." I blinked at him, not having thought about it in that way before. It actually made more sense than any of my own theories on how the Dueling Grounds worked. "Alex could practice in a more realistic environment against magic and blades, and he would literally be in less danger than he is here, sparring with his hands."

"And I would love to see how he handles himself in a *real* fight," Midas agreed.

Ganesh piped up, and I realized this was rehearsed. I turned, squaring my shoulders and folding my arms as I stared at him. "Sparring is one thing," the elephant-headed god began, "but putting an actual *blade* in a man's hand... *that* will bring out a man's true colors. It's easy to *pretend* to stab someone, but can he actually *do* it? Watch the skin rip and the blood flow?"

I relented, not because of Ganesh's overly creepy comments, but because they were right.

"Hey, Alex," I called out.

He didn't stop his sparring, casually thumping one of the Greeks in the helmet with the hilt of a wooden practice dagger before rolling behind another and dragging his dagger across the back of the Greek's boot, signifying slicing his tendon. "Yeah?" he grunted, not looking at us.

"Want to take off the training wheels and go to Fight Club?"

He swept another opponent off his feet, hammer-fisting him on his way down to the earth. "Sure. Let me finish up here, first."

And that's when he took a punch to the face from the third opponent.

I winced, realizing Ganesh was right. Alex was going to have a broken nose in the morn—

His opponent suddenly cried out, clutching his balls before Alex hip-tossed him to the ground. The Myrmidon let out a manly whimper, clutching his nuts as Alex slowly mimed pressing his blade into the man's eyeball.

Alex stood, brushed off his shorts, and turned to face us. "Okay. Ready. When can I go?" His face was unmarred. What the hell kind of move was that? He walked over to us, wiping the sweat from his brow, strutting like a peacock.

"Tonight is Fight Night," Midas suggested, all too-casually.

"Nothing official for the first fight," I told the three bad uncles. "Just let him train there. He can learn to practice the fatal moves. He doesn't need an audience." Because I didn't want him attracting attention to himself. Freaks held grudges for a long time, and wouldn't be pleased about a Regular kicking their ass in front of a crowd.

They nodded in unison, accepting the win, and confirming my assumption that it had been premeditated. I wrapped an arm around Alex's shoulders and motioned Talon to follow us as we headed back to Chateau Falco.

I hadn't needed to tell Talon to follow us, but it made me feel less pretentious, if that made any sense. Having someone just follow you around all the time, always watching your back, began to grate on your nerves. Made you feel like a target, or like I was overcompensating by shouting to everyone that I was so important I required a constant bodyguard. Telling Talon to follow me made it feel more like hanging out with an antisocial friend.

CHAPTER 38

I glanced over at Alex. "Other than kicking Myrmidon ass, what have you been up to lately?"

He smiled, shrugging, letting me feel the thick, corded muscle flex under his damp shirt. I lowered my arm because he was a tall bastard. And he was sweaty. And it was a strange position for me. I had taken him under my protection, considering him a child I needed to keep safe. Like a foster son. But… that had all evaporated in the course of a few months, and I now had a calorie dumpster who was his own man, in a way.

"I've been spending a lot of time in the Sanctorum. Great books down there," he said. "I'm sure you've read them all, but I'm still a week away from finishing the first few rows. Well, the ones written in English, anyway. Unless I find another secret room full of more books," he admitted.

I nodded stiffly. "The ones written in English. First few rows…" I repeated numbly. "Right. Those are good books. Good words in there…" I said, rambling on.

I hadn't even read all the *spines* of the books on the first few rows of the secret library in Chateau Falco. There were tens of thousands of books in there. Maybe a lot more. And Alex had almost finished off a few full *rows*?

"You're not reading any of the magic books, right? Those can be dangerous." Maybe I needed to restrict his access. I had no idea what he was read—

And that's when it hit me. I was parenting, considering putting parental controls on his internet. But switch *internet* with *fatally dangerous library that a powerful Maker had locked away from prying eyes.*

Alex was shaking his head in denial. "No, nothing like that. Just a lot of philosophy and books on war or ancient heroes from around the globe," he admitted. "If I see any Latin or squiggly symbols, I close it immediately and put a sticker on the shelf, marking it for you. But you've likely perused them all, so would have already taken out the dangerous ones."

I nodded woodenly. "Yeah. Let's pretend that I haven't marked any of them for stuff like that. I didn't realize you'd been spending so much time down there."

"Oh," he said, looking suddenly nervous. "I'm sorry. I just thought…"

I waved off his concern. "Have you found anything about a blue stone in the books?" I asked, feigning casual conversation.

Alex pondered my question, looking down at the grass as we walked. "Doesn't ring a bell," he finally admitted, shrugging.

"What about in the Armory? Seen any blue gems lying around?"

Alex frowned thoughtfully before shaking his head.

"Okay. Can you let me know if you do?"

He nodded firmly. "Sure. I'll check with Pandora…" he trailed off, not bothering to finish.

Maybe he felt awkward bringing her up. "Listen, you and Pandora… I like her a lot, and she's been a great help, but… you need to be very careful with her. Even though she's smart, powerful," I met his eyes, "and ridiculously good looking," I added in a lower voice, making him grin. "She is very dangerous."

He nodded seriously. "I know. I've been keeping an eye on her. But…" he trailed off, thinking. "There's just something about her that attracts me."

I gave him a stern look. "Maybe it has to do with you banging her," I said drily.

"No. It's not like that," Alex argued softly. "It's like magnetism. And not sexual magnetism. She, um, definitely… well, we did do that other thing. Sometimes still do, but more often than not, we just hang out."

I arched a brow doubtfully. "Right."

"No, really," he said, adamantly. "We just talk about things. The books I read. We go on walks through the Armory. Sometimes we do that other thing, but a lot of times she just talks to me. Like I said, it's more of a friendship. Like she's some part of me."

Alarm bells began ringing in my head at his last comment, but I was careful to keep my face neutral. Pandora being a part of Alex... I scrolled through my memory of legends on Pandora, and found exactly zero situations that even remotely had a tie to what Alex was describing, some kind of shared existence.

Like that sinister mental parasite from my dream with Callie. I shivered. Not now.

Maybe I was overanalyzing Alex's description of a friendship bond. One forged in the fuzzy handcuffs of inter-pantheon sex in a magic hot tub in an ancient library full of supernatural nuclear bombs. Or... two young pups who felt alienated from everyone else and had each found a person in a similar situation.

I sighed, patting him on the shoulder. "It's fine. Just be careful. I know you see her as a young woman, but she really is a whole lot more than that. I've seen a few different sides to Pandora, and they always caught me by surprise. None of them were bad," I emphasized, not wanting to turn him against Pandora, "but they were... dangerous. Or had the potential to be very dangerous."

Alex nodded. "I know. She's told me all about herself. All about a lot of people, actually." He turned to look at me. "But you know what?" he asked, face entirely serious.

I hesitated, but tried to cover it up quickly. "What?"

"She loves you more than any other person she has ever met. Maybe even me. Just, you know, differently. Platonically."

Great. He'd just told me I had a supernatural dad-bod, complete with flabby magic love handles. But as I looked past my own ego a moment later, the comment slowly began to hit me on multiple levels.

I hadn't really ever known where I stood with Pandora. We had an odd relationship. Technically, I was her Host. Her literal owner, of sorts. So I had always believed her interest in me had been obligatory.

Hearing otherwise felt... really, really nice.

I also hoped this wasn't Alex's attempt at Oedipus, figuratively stealing his father's wife. But as I looked into his eyes, I was certain this wasn't the case. His interest in Pandora had nothing to do with me. It was entirely genuine. "She's not in trouble, right? I'll take the blame," he said, voice firm.

I chuckled. "No one is in trouble, Alex. I'm trying to *prevent* trouble. I think she's been good for you. So has Baby B." He nodded, grinning suddenly. "And you've been good for both of them, too," I said, patting him on the back. "Thank you for being their friend."

Alex blushed. "Well, to make this *beyond* weird, you remember why I agreed to Pandora's offer in the first place. To help you. That our decision to…" he waved a hand awkwardly, not wanting to spell it out loud, "would help me get stronger, better prepared to help you in the future. I don't really know *how* it's helping, other than the fact that I'm learning a lot, but… she's been very worried about you lately. She even locked down the Armory, but I'm sure she already told you that."

I almost tripped in surprise. "Oh. She forgot to tell me that," I said. "But… it's actually something I was about to go ask her to do." I felt Alex's intelligent eyes watching me. "There is a bad man in town, and he might want to get access to some of her treasures." The words reminded me of Anubis' warning, to use every tool in my *treasure box* to take out Mordred. Had he been talking about the Armory?

Alex's jaws were clenched, but he maintained control, nodding slowly. "That's not going to happen," he promised in a low tone.

"I'll take care of it. Just keep training," I told him.

He nodded after a moment, running a hand through his hair. "I told B I would meet him after sparring…"

"Get out of here, punk," I said, shoving him. "Soon, I'll show you how to fight a wizard. Maybe you can test out a few toys from Grimm Tech to even the odds."

Alex grinned. "That sounds awesome. I'll be ready." Then he was jogging towards the treehouse, calling out for B.

"Oh, and remember we have guests out front, so don't do anything weird where they can see!" I called out to him, remembering the reporters. He spun, running backwards for a moment to give me a thumbs up. Then he spun back around and resumed his jog, making it look effortless.

I watched him thoughtfully. Alex and B had become instant pals, almost always found together, walking, talking, or even watching movies together. I didn't know what they talked about, but then again, a parent isn't always supposed to know what their kids talk about.

And I was glad for it. B was a potentially deadly Beast, and he was not bonded to a human, which supposedly made them safer. He was also kind of like my… brother? We both considered Falco to be a surrogate mother, so it kind of fit.

But before B had entered the picture, Alex had been extremely close with Kai – B's father. Kai had been Alex's lifeline after I saved him from Fae, helping the young boy overcome his fears, offering a shoulder to cry on, and a firm hand to mold him into something stronger. Kai had been a badass.

I sighed sadly, glancing up at the sky, lifting up a small murmur of thanks to Kai. I wasn't sure where he had gone when he died, but I'd seen an epic display of magical dust rise up into the stars, and I liked to imagine he was still conscious up there, smiling down on me.

Or tossing back a beer with the other constellations, laughing at the shit-show that was my grip on this precious gift called life. To see Alex do for B what Kai had once done for Alex was... poetically beautiful.

I watched as Alex reached the tree and slapped at the scaled bark. The door to the treehouse high above opened, and down drifted a wisp of a natural-looking cloud to hover beside Alex, quivering animatedly. I hoped the reporters hadn't noticed it, or had assumed it was just an odd cloud or something – a trick of the light.

I shook my head, turning to find Talon smirking at me. "You haven't read any of them, have you?" he asked.

"Go choke on a tuna can," I muttered, stomping away.

I heard a bush rustle a few feet away and I froze.

CHAPTER 39

I peered at the bush suspiciously.

"You can't see me…" a voice said in an overly theatrical tone.

I let out a breath, lowering my hands. "I *can* see you, Carl. I see your beady little eyes through the branches."

He slowly reached out his milky scaled hands and closed the branches I had pointed out. "*Now*, you can't see me," he clarified in the same wizardly voice, as if trying to put a spell on me.

"Why are you hiding in a bush?" I asked with a sigh. "And please stop trying to spell me."

He finally stood, looking annoyed. "Hiding from reporters. Practicing my stealth."

"Practice harder," Talon coughed.

Carl hissed at him. "Choke on my long bone, smelly cat!" he snarled, drawing one of his longer swords.

I flung up a hand, ignoring Talon's outburst of laughter. "No! Carl, stop!"

He turned to me, frowning. "You just told him to choke on a tuna can. How is my long bone any different?" he asked, sheathing his sword angrily.

Where to even begin. First, the long bone phrase had to die. "It was an expression, Carl. I didn't actually mean it. Expressions are just something you do or say by accident in the heat of the moment."

Carl considered that, scratching at his chin. "An expression is something you don't mean. I understand."

I studied him, wondering what kind of terrible act he would perform with his recent *understanding* of the term *expression*. Thinking of a dozen potentials, I finally let it go. A thought hit me as I watched him slowly sinking back into his bush, never breaking eye contact with me. Then he awkwardly closed the gap in the bush by holding the branches together. "Have you ever heard of a..." remembering Talon was still there, I changed my question slightly, "a Neverwas? Or a Souleater?" I asked the bush.

The branches whipped back into place and Carl poked his head through the opening. "Yessss..."

I waited for more, but got nothing. "Know where I can find one?"

"You already have one," Carl said, retreating back into the bush. "Your spear has a Devourer."

"Yeah, but if I wanted another?" I asked, ignoring Talon's flinch at Carl's words.

"You don't want another. They are quite dangerous."

"I don't want your opinion, Carl. I want your knowledge."

"Are you sure about that, Temple?" he asked in a very chilling tone, and I realized it wasn't his usual flavor of creepy. This voice was a spider ensnaring a fly in a web. I even felt goosebumps on my forearms. Because the way he had spoken reminded me he wasn't just my innocent, socially-awkward, lizard friend. Elders were feared worldwide for their mental abilities, and I didn't quite know the extent of his powers.

"Okay. I don't want your knowledge. It was... an expression," I said, snapping my fingers. "But I do want you to tell me where I can find a Devourer. Or more details on what they are. What they can do. If there are any consequences to using one. Or even how to use one."

"That's a lot..." Carl said after a few moments, still hiding in his bush. I waited patiently. "Can you still see me?" he asked after about ten seconds.

Talon snarled impatiently, but I held up a hand. "No, we can't see you," I lied.

"Successsss..." he hissed in a dry whisper.

"What about my questions?"

He was silent for another five seconds. "I don't know."

"Can I just kill him?" Talon spat, his spear suddenly winking into existence.

Carl jumped from his bush in a perfect flip, landing on the ground between Talon and I in a crouch, his... long bone pointed at Talon.

Oh, and the ground around the Elder cracked as if hit by a meteor, making Talon stumble in surprise, before ramming the butt of his spear into the earth to maintain his balance. Dark fog began to rise up from the cracks, and Carl's Mighty D began to hum in the distance. I spun to see Alex abruptly drop to his knees, clutching his ears, and B suddenly grew larger, wider, and crackled with lightning.

"Carl! Stop!" I shouted at the top of my lungs, slapping my hands over my own ears.

The fog instantly died down, and Carl turned to face me, keeping Talon in his sights. I tentatively lowered my hands to find the humming had stopped. I glanced back to see Alex propping himself up, shaking his head – dazed, but alive. B slowly shrunk back to normal size, but hovered very close to Alex as if inspecting him.

Car alarms blared and wailed from the reporters out front. I turned to Carl, furious and terrified. "What do you think you're *doing*?" I shouted, taking a step closer, ready to kill him.

He cocked his head. "I saw the Eyeless," he said, pointing. "I never really noticed it before you brought it up. I forget things sometimes," he admitted.

I gritted my teeth. "Like knowing Alvara?" I spat.

He nodded. "Yes. Just like that."

I waited. "Well? How *do* you know Alvara."

"It's not important," he said. "Not anymore. Ancient history."

I gritted my teeth, deciding it wasn't worth it at the moment. "What about Talon's Eyeless?" I asked.

Carl nodded, glancing over at it, cocking his head. "It's hungry, but so quiet. Like it's wrapped in a wet blanket, but I can hear it, now."

I blinked a few times, glancing over at Talon's spear. "You can *hear* it," I asked, dumbfounded.

Carl nodded, and Talon looked suddenly very concerned about the spear in his paws.

"What did you just do? That humming thing," I clarified, knowing all-too-well that questions needed to be very specific with Carl.

He glanced back at the massive tree, smiling slightly, although it was hard to tell with Carl. His lizard biology made it look like he was always smirking. "It's more mature than I thought. I didn't mean to call out to it. Your mother truly is a Master of the D."

I held up a hand, stalling Talon's growing fury. "What exactly *did* my mother teach you?" I asked.

Carl shrugged. "A lost song. One she had forgotten remembering." He noticed my rapt attention and cocked his head, his ear holes widening. "Would you like to hear it?" he asked.

I nodded eagerly.

Carl cleared his throat, and his eyes grew distant as he began to emit a soft hum from deep in his throat, his neck bulging slightly like a frog preparing to croak. Then Carl began lifting his claws, one-by-one. The cracked ground began to rattle, and I noticed ribbons of translucent power slowly beginning to twirl around his black claws, guided by his subtle finger motions like he was orchestrating an underwater ribbon dance.

Carl's throat returned to normal, but the humming continued as if picked up by the almost-clear ribbons of power rotating and spinning in slow circles around his claws.

Then Carl began to sing, his voice a surprisingly clear, chiming pell. The words, although not in a typical or familiar tempo seemed to come to life as if transcending a mere song, and telling a story instead.

Memory, re-memory... the Song of creation's chaos.
Hope and despair, entwined in eternal embrace,
Like an infinite web of gossamer lace.
Legends may fall, legends may rise,
But no matter how tall, the Four shall cry.
To bring back a soul, to save a child,
Is to burn all time with the call of the wild..."

Carl's haunting melody trailed off, and I felt like I'd just had my legs swept out from under me. I was openly sobbing, my cheeks drenched with tears. Not at the words, but at... I don't quite know what. The song had ripped at my soul, and I felt a headache abruptly forming.

I shook my head at the look of concern on Carl's face. "There is more... Are you saddened I didn't climax?"

And despite everything, I choked out a laugh, unable to speak for a minute. "*Crescendo*, Carl, not *Climax*," I wheezed. "That was... beautiful. My *mother* taught you that song?" I asked, unable to imagine her singing a song as beautiful and foreboding as that.

Carl was nodding. "It was hidden in her mind. She let me retrieve it. For you, I think."

I blinked a few times. "You… dug that out of my mother's mind?" I asked nervously.

He scratched at his chin. "Well, technically, I scraped it off her soul, but —" He suddenly flinched, crouching as he spun to face the tree, his earholes widening and then narrowing abruptly.

"What's wrong, Carl?" I asked, ready for an invasion.

"I think…" he murmured hesitantly. "I just heard my mother…" he cocked his head, listening. "Yes. I need to leave. I must have woken up the Gateway. And I need to speak with my people before they decide to cross over on their own."

I blinked rapidly, horrified. "You… the Gatway is *open?*" I stammered, seeing the million and one ways that could be terrible for life on Earth.

"Kind of. Maybe not, but open enough for me to go visit." He turned to me, face desperate and nervous. And I could count on no fingers the number of times I'd seen Carl nervous.

"When will you return?" I asked.

"I hope soon, but I do not know." He began to turn away, and then froze. "Give me your blood so that I may find you quickly upon my return. You're always running about." He whipped out a short bone dagger and held it to me, hilt-first.

I took it without hesitation, and sliced my finger. The bone blade began to… drink my blood.

I fell, dropping the dagger and closing my eyes as a headache rolled over me, squashing me with visions.

A giant tree, looking more like the network of roots underground, grasping at the sky.

A ship. Flying in the sky.

A strange, savage little boy zipping about in the air chasing a black silhouette of himself.

Talon batting at a swarm of sprites zipping about his head, playing keepaway with a pod of Fae-nip.

It faded, and I found myself staring up at Tal, who was carrying me through a dark hallway with purple torches. They looked familiar. I closed my eyes again, feeling a throbbing pressure behind my eyes. "I can't do it, Peter," I whispered.

Tal stiffened, and then began rocking me gently, purring loudly, his chest rumbling against my shoulder, lulling me to sleep. "You can do anything, Wylde. Anything... All you have to do is try. Never quit never quitting," he whispered. "Cheat like a bastard to win like a king..."

I think I smiled weakly, nodding. "Okay..." I whispered back.

And then Tal began to hum my favorite song, the one my mother had used to sing me to sleep for as long as I could remember.

Star light, star bright. First star I see tonight...

CHAPTER 40

J woke in darkness to the sound of a crackling fire and harsh
cawing sounds. I looked up to find a field of glittering stars overhead, so I must be outside. There was no wind to speak of, just the scent of
old leather, dust, a faint metallic smell, and fresh water.

"He's not taking it well, is he," a familiar voice croaked from out of sight.

"It's breaking him," another similar sounding voice cawed.

"If I can take it, so can he," Tal growled, sounding on the verge of
violence against the two croaking voices.

"And he asked about the Neverwas?" the first voice said, followed by
another caw and a rustle of feathers. I knew those voices, but couldn't quite
place them, grogginess clouding my mind.

"He did," Tal answered. "We must find a blue one. He seemed sure of it."

"No one would hand another Souleater over to him. Temple is too
unpredictable," the first voice crowed.

"Has he asked the Hatter? He may know," the second voice said.

Tal sighed. "Then that is where I will go. Carl left," he added in a
concerned tone.

"The Elder was dangerous," the two voices agreed in unison.

"*Carl*," Tal corrected, enunciating the name proudly, "is dangerously
loyal. And he found a *Song*—"

I shifted, trying to sit up, but wasn't successful, and the motion alerted the others, ending the conversation. I had a mild headache, but when I tried to remember what had happened, the throbbing intensified.

"Wylde?" Tal asked softly. I mumbled something vaguely affirmative, and Tal was suddenly leaning over me, looking concerned. "How do you feel?"

I coughed, and Tal slowly lifted a glass to my lips. I took a hesitant sip of the water, and then began to guzzle it, coughing and choking as much as I swallowed. I felt dehydrated. How long had I been asleep, and... why had I been sleeping?

"You had a flashback," Tal said, setting the cup down beside me with a thud. And that's when I realized I wasn't sleeping on a bed, but a hard surface. I glanced down to see I was on a wooden floor, not outside. I tried sitting back up, and Tal helped, supporting my weight, murmuring a soft song under his breath. "*Star light, star bright...*"

Hearing that song combined with the sudden change in position sent my blood rushing from my head, and the world tilted woozily until I closed my eyes, taking several deep breaths. That song... made me feel like I had woken up all over again – emerging from a dream. After a few seconds, I opened my eyes.

I was in the Sanctorum, not outside. The stars above had been the gems in the ceiling. I was lying on the Round Table, recovering from an apparent flashback. And the other voices... I swiveled my head angrily, suddenly realizing who they had belonged to. I spotted Hugin and Munin perched on the back of a couch, regarding me silently. They were massive ravens, each the size of a small dog, with feathers as black as night.

"Glad to see you guys again," I muttered, but my sarcasm was lost as I fell into a coughing fit. Talon – not Tal – lifted the cup for me again, helping me take a few more drinks until I felt somewhat human. "Where have you been?" I demanded, glaring at Odin's Ravens.

They shared a look with each other, and then nodded, as if corroborating an alibi. "Scouting."

Talon murmured gently. "It's their job. To give Odin information on the world."

"We had a lot of catching up to do since we've been spending so much time with you," Hugin – I think – said. I'd never really pinned down the art of telling them apart. "Lots to see in Kansas City, St. Louis, Boston."

"Took a while," Munin added. I noticed a faint mark on his beak, a small gouge, but I couldn't tell if the other raven had a matching beauty mark. And it didn't really fucking matter, to be honest.

"Why did I have another flashback?" I asked Talon.

He shrugged. "I think it was Carl's Song."

"You probably shouldn't have let him do that," one of the Ravens muttered before I could press Talon on the issue, because he had seemed to emphasize the word when telling Hugin and Munin about it, as if song was more like *Song, nudge, nudge, wink, wink.*

"Generally speaking, Elder Songs are fatal," the other agreed, preening his feathers with a razor-sharp beak.

Talon shot them a dark look. "He was reciting a song he learned from Makayla Temple, and I don't think it was just a song. I think it was something much older..." Talon shot me a nervous look. "Just a feeling."

I nodded slowly, recalling my dream with Callie, and that parasite's infatuation with *Songs*, making it sound like a power he wielded. Had that parasite been an Elder? I shivered at the thought, suddenly glad Carl had left.

"I think you're right. Carl's Song was different. Some kind of prophecy? He said he scraped it from my mother's soul..." Hugin and Munin both stiffened as if I'd asked them to go duck hunting. "What does that mean? And why did it help grow the Elder Portal?" I asked, latching onto their reaction as I felt my strength slowly returning, enough to prop myself up without Talon's support.

The Ravens shared a long, meaningful look. "We... um, probably should have been around to witness something like that."

I grunted. "Why are you three suddenly buddies?" I asked suspiciously.

Talon's ears wilted back as if I had scolded him. "You asked Alex about blue stones. Then asked Carl about a Neverwas. A Souleater..." He averted his eyes, shuddering faintly. "A... *Devourer.* I didn't know who else to ask, so I called out to them," he lifted a paw slightly, pointing at the Ravens.

Hearing the name *Devourer* had struck him, and with me unconscious... I didn't know if this was the full story, or if their relationship possibly stretched back longer, if maybe they had been friends all along, putting on a show for our benefit. I'd get to the bottom of it later, but right now I needed answers. "Anubis told me I needed another one to defeat Mordred."

"That's not all he said, Temple," a new voice growled from a few feet away. The ravens launched up into the air, cawing and cursing.

"Oh, shit!"

"Black damn!"

I slowly turned to find Odin seated in a chair before the Round Table, leaning back as if it were his throne. I was suddenly glad I hadn't rolled over in my sleep – into the band of flowing liquid metal circling the table like an infinite stream. I also hadn't noticed my satchel on the table, but wasn't pleased to find that it was closer to Odin than me. He leaned forward casually, and calmly reached a scarred hand inside it. I snorted indelicately, not concerned about him finding anything since—

He pulled out the War Hammer and I froze. "How…" I whispered.

"You're not the first one to use a magic purse, Mary Poppins. And I have a thing for hammers…"

I slowly swung my legs off the edge of the table, taking a breath to make sure I wasn't about to collapse. Once confident I wasn't about to make an ass out of myself in front of Odin, I dropped my feet to the floor, still gripping onto the edge just in case.

I turned back to the Norse Big G, considering him thoughtfully. Odin was associated with wisdom, death, royalty, knowledge, battle, sorcery, frenzy, and a host of other things. But what had suddenly struck me was that several of those areas of expertise overlapped – or interfered – with a few recent associates of mine.

For example, one overlapping area of expertise was *death*, and I'd recently learned that Odin was gossip-pals with Anubis, the King of Hell.

Odin was also associated with royalty and magic, and the big dumb wizard leaning on the table right now had recently declared himself a king. As if reading my thoughts, the one-eyed God smirked, casually flipping the Hammer in the air and then catching it by the handle. Again. And again. And again.

"You still have no idea what's really happening, and it's sad," he said, frowning down at my hammer.

"Then *tell* me!" I demanded with unbridled frustration. "Your two fucking birds are on my Crest, so I know we're tied together somehow, Odin. Just fucking explain why or watch me fail. These aren't the old days. I'm not going to pay you fucking tribute or build you an altar to worship you devoutly," I snarled, baring my teeth.

I realized the room was deadly silent, and that Talon was crouching down low, looking resigned to die fighting. But I realized… that I simply no longer had it in me to care. These gods were like grown men shouting at the TV screen during a football game, believing they knew the sport better than the men making millions of dollars per year on the field.

I wasn't necessarily considering myself a pro athlete in that example.

But I was fucking doing the two-a-day practices and hitting the gym with all the other players on the team. I'd at least earned the right to sit on the bench, which was better than the spectators shouting at their TV.

A crazy thought began to emerge from my inner temper tantrum, and I decided to test it, settling my glare on Odin. "Let go of my hammer. Now."

Odin caught the hammer by the large handle and regarded me in silence. "*Your* hammer…"

"Are you missing an ear, too?" I snapped. "Yes, *my* hammer."

"You sure about that?"

I folded my arms. "I don't see *your* name on it anywhere. Finders keepers."

He continued to watch me, and I knew I was probably the only person who had spoken to him this bluntly in quite some time – perhaps ever. But… he was *letting* me. Just like I'd thought he would. Because… he wouldn't be here without a purpose. Something helpful.

He leaned back into the chair and set the stone hammer down on the table, the hilt sticking straight up. "You're under the impression that we don't *want* to help," he said, stroking his beard absently. "But we can only help under limited conditions. A personal favor or obligation. An allegiance," he added as an afterthought.

I thought about his answer, and then about Anubis… Several things began to click into place. Nothing major, but like I had at last found the corner pieces to a puzzle.

I owed Anubis a favor. An obligation. All because… he had set me up. I'd learned that recently when I spoke to him in Hell. But I'd been unable to learn his angle. Combining it with Odin's casual comment, however…

"Yes. You're beginning to see a small part of it. That jackal is a ballsy, clever bastard, I'll give him that."

I sat down heavily, trying to wrap my head around it. "Anubis set me up to be the Guide to Hell, his emissary… So he could skirt around the rules. I'm obligated to him, which lets him *help* me."

Odin nodded. "Not a lot of help, but enough to mention the Devourer. Perhaps a few other morsels."

I frowned. "But... what if I hadn't broken out of Hell?"

"That was the ultimate gamble. If you'd managed to kill Mordred down there, immediate problem solved – *Anubis gets what he wants*. But maybe you ended up *freeing* Mordred, but were stuck in Hell, unable to break out. That would have been bad, but Anubis would have at least been safe in Hell, with you as his Guide – *Anubis gets what he wants*," Odin said, grinning wickedly. "Or maybe you do exactly what you did, proving our suspicions that you are a Catalyst... Anubis now has a path to help you, a tiny bit, which could make all the difference." He slapped the table with a palm. "*Anubis gets what he wants*," he said for the third time.

It hadn't been a perfect plan, but it had been a decent one. "How are *you* able to help me, then?" I asked, eyes latching onto the hammer warily. Did we have some kind of bond that would let him play ball?

Odin snorted, eyeing the hammer in amusement. "I'm just narrating your story."

I rolled my eyes. "Is that Mjolnir?" I asked, pointing at the hammer. Odin mimed zipping his lips shut.

"How do I defeat Mordred?" I asked instead, knowing it was futile.

"Anubis told you about the Devourer already. You need to take away Mordred's souls. How's that for help?"

I blinked, then glanced down at my lap. "I almost got an erection," I said with all the excitement of a potato.

He grinned ever so slightly. "I doubt Mordred wants them anymore, anyway."

I blinked. "What?"

"Well – and I'm just thinking out loud here – but if I was a recently freed soul, I would probably want my own freedom, not a new master. That's just my personal opinion, though."

My eyes darted to the Round Table between us. "*That's* why Mordred wants his father's stuff..."

Odin shrugged absently, and then his massive war spear, Gungnir, suddenly appeared in his fist as he slammed the butt into the floor. The spear hummed with menacing power, the ancient wooden haft carved with crude runes, and the blade itself was wide as my head, not glistening or shining, but an almost slate gray color.

And in the center of the blade was a liquid, yellow stone. "That's a Devourer!" I blurted.

217

Odin nodded. "All the big kids have them. And no, you can't have it." He sniffed the air curiously, ignoring the agonized look on my face. "It smells like blood in here. A coppery scent," he added, sniffing his hands before leaning down to sniff the table. "Did you bleed on this?"

I was too busy staring at Gungnir and Odin's Devourer, thinking furiously for a way to persuade him.

Talon cleared his throat. "No, he didn't injure himself. Just fell unconscious."

I realized they were speaking about my recent flashback, and finally peeled my eyes from Gungnir, wondering why the hell we were talking about blood. I didn't smell anything.

Odin climbed to his feet, his lip curling in disgust as he considered the table again. "Maybe it just needs a good cleansing. It is ridiculously old, after all." He wiped his palms on his pants since he had been touching the table. Maybe he had sensed Carl Ass, since the Elder liked to lounge naked on the table in his spare time.

"What do I have to do to hire you?"

He stopped. Then turned. "You wouldn't like owing me a favor. I would break you. I am not a kind god," he said in a very somber tone. Then he was walking away, calling out over his shoulder. "You can keep the birds. They're on your Crest after all..." he added, way too casually.

Then he left. No fanfare. No flash of light. Just gone between one step and the next.

CHAPTER 41

I sat at the Round Table, thinking furiously, attempting to use the flowing metal stream circling the center of the table to clear my head. I glanced at the War Hammer occasionally, but kept dismissing it at some inner feeling that it wasn't part of the solution. Mordred had already seen it, telling me *It's empty, now* before leaving me behind in Hell. So he obviously wasn't threatened by it.

My cellphone chirped in my pocket and I checked it out of habit, eager for any kind of distraction. It was an email from Othello. I felt a slight burst of excitement as I read the details.

Quinn MacKenna's phone number and address in Boston.

And Othello had said she had a knack for finding things. I doubted she would be of any immediate assistance, but figured it was better to get the ball rolling earlier rather than later. She might be able to find a Devourer for me. I tried calling the number, but it went straight to voicemail. I tapped my fingernail against the Round Table, thinking.

Maybe I could just swing by. It wouldn't take long, just a quick introduction.

"Stay here and watch my satchel," I told Talon, checking the address on my phone, getting a street view from outside Quinn's apartment. I found a nearby alley as Talon began to protest, but I held up a finger, cutting him off. "Just do it, Talon. I don't want to take it with me, and I can't leave it lying around."

Talon nodded stiffly as I climbed to my feet. I ripped open a Gateway right on the spot, stepping through to the dark streets of Boston, distantly surprised, and alarmed to find that it was dark on the East Coast. No one saw me enter the alley, so I didn't waste a moment, walking right up to the apartment building and strolling inside, pretending to talk on my phone in case there was security.

I checked my phone and made it up to her apartment door before slipping my cell into my pocket, straightening my shirt, and knocking. Politely.

No one answered, so I knocked again. Louder. Still no answer.

I considered leaving, but I was already here, and didn't feel like wasting time. So I picked the lock with a little bit of magic, letting the door swing open to make sure it wasn't warded or anything. Nothing shocked, burned, shot, or otherwise injured me, so I strode inside.

I closed the door behind me, latching the deadbolt I had tricked open, and studied the place.

It felt... nice. Not classy or rich by any means, but well lived-in, like an old pair of sneakers that fit perfectly. I checked the rooms, making sure I was alone, and then scanned the counter to verify it really was Quinn's address. I found some mail confirming Othello's details, but nothing overly useful. I wasn't here to steal, spy, or otherwise inconvenience her, so I sat down on a recliner in the living room, taking a minute to relax.

Not having an army of friends waiting on me, sitting in a place where no one else would know me, felt... surprisingly refreshing. I took a few minutes to just process everything I'd learned, even rehearsing what I would say to Quinn if—

The deadbolt jiggled as someone unlocked it. Bingo. I crossed my legs and set my hands in my lap.

An extremely tall red-headed woman entered the apartment, juggling an armload of stuff. I studied Quinn MacKenna in silence, recalling our serendipitous encounter not long ago in an Uber. I'd been in a rush to meet up with Callie and had commandeered her ride. She hadn't been pleased, but I'd talked her into giving me a high five before I let the driver take off.

And upon contact with Quinn's hand, my power – my magic – had just sizzled to nothing. As I studied her, I couldn't get a feel of anything special about her. No waves of power or anything, so how had she nullified me so easily? If I could sense no power on her, how had she neutered me, magi-cally speaking?

And what did she have to do with Alucard? The seed Othello had mentioned her trying to steal? Or needing an army of wolves to come to her aid? I'd sent Gunnar over with his pack, knowing I could trust him to be discreet, but... why had this slip of a girl needed a pack of werewolves? *My* werewolves.

And *my* sparkly vampire.

Now that I thought about it, Alucard had definitely cranked up the monster vibe after spending time on the East Coast. Was that because of this tall woman in front of me?

"Fuckin' Faelin' bastards," she muttered, flicking on the lights and kicking the door closed.

"I know how you feel," I said, unable to help myself.

"Jesus fuckin' Christ!" she yelled, ducking into the bathroom.

I blinked at her reaction, and her foul mouth. Then I smiled, giving her a moment. Well, that had backfired, which made perfect sense, really. A strange man just hanging out in her living room, of all things. "Sorry. I couldn't find the light switch," I lied.

She poked her head out to assess me, and I remained still, letting her see I wasn't a threat. I knew pretty quickly that she recognized me, primarily because her lip curled back in a snarl.

"And just how long have ye been sittin' in me apartment in the dark, ye fuckin' loon?" she demanded.

I forced myself not to burst out laughing at both her intense accent and her penchant for bad language. "Not long. Maybe a couple of hours," I lied, just to see how she reacted. "It's a nice place," I added, taking in the decor. "A good place to collect my thoughts. The last few days have been murder." I turned back to her, letting her see the exhaustion I felt.

Quinn regarded me in silence. "Get out," she finally said.

I arched an eyebrow. Well. I hadn't expected that. Sure, she would be upset, but to kick me out of her apartment, obviously recognizing who I was... That was ballsy. I realized my curiosity was definitely growing, and that I needed to get a better handle on the situation. "Listen, I just wanted to offer you a job, that's—"

"I don't t'ink ye heard me, so I'll say it again. Get. Out." She stepped out of the bathroom and tossed a bundle of clothes on the kitchen counter, then she set something on top of it in a very deliberate manner.

I blinked, recognizing the glass marble. Where had she gotten one of my Tiny Balls? Othello must have offered her some party favors. I realized that accusing her of stealing my stuff after breaking into her apartment wasn't the wisest pathway to earning her friendship, so turned back to her.

Now that Quinn was in the light, I realized she had been beaten to hell, covered in cuts and scrapes, and looking like she hadn't slept in a few days.

"What the hell happened to you?" I asked, my eyes widening.

She grunted, reached under the sink, and pulled out a sawed-off shotgun. Then she very calmly pointed it at me, not a single tremor in her movement. She had no problem with guns. "Get the fuck out."

I narrowed my eyes at her, growing angry. How dare she? She knew Othello, so what the hell was she doing pointing a gun at me? "You don't want to—"

"Now!" she barked.

Suddenly, the front door busted open. She swung her gun to the door, but not fast enough to stop the tall, broad, dark-skinned policeman charging at me like he was trying to sack a quarterback. I let him get pretty close, building up his speed, committing to his decision. Then I flung up an invisible wall of air, watching as he slammed into it. I casually flicked my wrist, sending him sliding across the floor where he couldn't hurt himself again. "He one of yours?" I asked. "If not, I can take him off your hands…"

"You heard what she said, you prick," the policeman said, rising to one knee. "Get out."

"Jimmy!" Quinn snapped. She *knew* him. Interesting. "I've got this under control. I don't need your help."

"It didn't sound like it from out there," Jimmy said, jerking his head towards the open doorway.

"And so ye decided to kick down the damn door? It was unlocked, ye big idgit!"

I grinned. Idgit? Boston was growing on me. The locals were fascinating.

Jimmy began to hang his head, realizing he'd overreacted, but I had a thing or two to say, "Not very bright, this one. I recommend sending the defective ones back." Jimmy's head popped back up in a snarl, and he lunged at me. I batted the Regular policeman away with a tired sigh – mildly impressed that he obviously wasn't scared of being abused by my magic. I absently picked a piece of lint off my shirt. "Batteries definitely not included."

"I swear, if ye don't get the fuck out of me place right now," Quinn snapped, to both of us, "I'll—"

But Jimmy lunged at me *again*, surprising me so much that he actually managed to catch my shirt in – a fucking claw – tearing a hole through the fabric. I dodged a second swipe, ducked, and struck a blow of my own, sending the apparently *not* a Regular Jimmy flying backwards on a small fireball. The man collided against the wall and fell to one knee.

Except he didn't look anything like the Jimmy from a moment ago.

He was now over seven-feet-tall, covered in silver and black fur, and his pointed ears almost touched the ceiling. He was thinner, but with longer limbs, as if he'd traded his bulk for length. He kind of looked like a fox.

I grinned hungrily, eager to hit something after the last twenty-four hours. "Oh, good. I was starting to feel bad for beating up on a Regular. Let's see if that bite can keep up with that annoying bark." I called up my whips, one of fire, and the other of crackling ice, letting the tips rest at my feet.

"Oy! Take it outside!" Quinn yelled.

Jimmy yipped, hunkered down to all fours, and prepared to leap at me. I flicked my wrists, drumming my whips against the floors, taunting him.

A golden light suddenly burst through the room, blinding us all.

"Did you know that someone is home in three out of every ten burglary cases?" a strange voice asked.

"What the fuck was that?" I snarled, blinking rapidly.

"Nate Temple. Master Temple. Would-be King of St. Louis." the voice was matter-of-fact, as if reading from a database. I whirled towards the voice, still blinking, and noticed a potted plant, of all things. "The Rider of Hope. The Fifth Horseman."

"Allegedly," I growled, wondering what the hell was going on.

"Catalyst. Murderer. Friend. Son. Father...no..." the voice drifted off, her tone changing to something softer, gentler. "No. Not father. Tell me, Master Temple...when did you last see the boy?"

I froze, my whips winking out. Alex... was the plant talking about Alex?

I didn't even hesitate, ripping open a Gateway on the spot, ignoring the crackling white fire as I lunged through back to the Drop Zone outside Chateau Falco, hoping to find Alex sparring. I let the Gateway wink shut before the dumb fox got any more stupid ideas. Because right now, I would have simply killed him.

I scanned the dark lawn, looking for...

My son.

But no one was outside. "ALEX!" I roared, panting as I bolted for the mansion. I didn't know what that stupid plant had been referring to, but Pandora believed Alex to be important, and all I'd been able to think about was that maybe Mordred had snatched him up in my absence.

I would never forgive myself if anything happened to him...

I poured on the speed, screaming and shouting his name as I ran through the halls.

This dad would burn the world if he had to. No one touched my family...

CHAPTER 42

*A*fter scaring all the people in the mansion half to death, I found Alex quite by accident. I'd run back to the Sanctorum to recruit Talon for help in my search, and saw Alex reading at the desk and Talon crouched a pace away from my satchel, his Eyeless spear out as if daring anyone to come too close. I skidded to a halt, panting, my adrenaline suddenly flickering out.

"What is it?" they both shouted, jumping to their feet at the look on my face.

I leaned over, placing my hands on my knees, panting. "Sweet baby Jesus. You're okay."

Alex was suddenly gripping my shoulders. "What do you mean? Is everything okay—"

I wrapped him into a tight hug, squeezing him hard enough to produce a grunt, and pounding his back. "Everything is fine, now. I thought you were in trouble," I told him.

He hugged me back, and I saw Talon watching us thoughtfully. As were the Ravens, perched up on the second-floor railing. I finally released Alex and shook my head in relief.

"You look like you could use a drink," he said, frowning at me.

I waved away the offer. "No way. Alcohol is the devil," I told him in mock seriousness.

The two of them studied me, both wanting to demand answers, but sensing I wasn't interested in discussion. To be honest, all I had needed to know was that Alex was okay. If I could have locked him up in the Armory, I would have done so.

But Pandora had locked it down. Which was better anyway. I'd had no reason to think Alex was in danger from Mordred, but with that stupid potted plant's comment, and Pandora believing him so important to *me*, I was done taking *any* chances.

"If everything is okay, I was just getting ready to head out," Alex said slowly.

I looked up at him sharply. "No. I need you to stay here at Chateau Falco where it's safe. There's a mad man on the loose, and he'll do anything to hurt me."

Alex smiled smugly. "Isn't that fortuitous… You want me safe, right?" I nodded, not appreciating the sound of his amused tone. "That's great. Because Midas invited me to Fight Night tonight – as a *spectator*," he clarified before I could pounce. "Not a safer place in the world. That's what you said earlier, *right*?" he smiled triumphantly, using my own words against me.

"Oh," I finally said, coming up with no logical argument to use against my own earlier suggestion that Alex visit the Dueling Grounds. "Just… stay safe," I said lamely, knowing he was right. It really *was* the safest game in town. He couldn't die there. "And always stick close to friends," I added in a commanding tone. That way he couldn't easily be kidnapped.

Jesus. I really was turning into a dad.

Alex nodded, and left the Sanctorum with a little more pep to his step than I would have liked, but he was smart enough not to rub my face in his victory.

I turned to find Talon staring at me, demanding answers. I told him about my brief trip and relished in the stunned look on his face. Finally, he spoke, shaking his head. "We need to keep an eye on her. What do you think her plant meant?"

I shrugged. "I have no idea, man. Maybe it was just screwing with me."

Talon frowned doubtfully. "It would have to know you in order to know how to manipulate you…"

I sighed, harboring vague suspicions on the talking plant. Othello had told me about the Seed to the Tree of Knowledge being stolen. Was Quinn's potted plant really the result of that seed taking life? Had she actually succeeded in stealing it, and then decided to *not* hand it over to Othello? It would explain how it had known so much about me... "I'll look into it later," I said turning away from him as I tried to clear my head. "Right now, we need to strategize."

When Talon didn't respond after a few moments, I turned back around.

He was crouched down again, this time practically at my feet. "You *Named* me, Wylde," he said in a strained whisper. "You. Not my parents. You." His eyes were desperate, frustrated, and frightened. "Why did you give me this name? Talon. The *Devourer*." I hated seeing the hurt, the frustration, the impotence, in those eyes.

We both knew it meant something significant, but neither knew how I had done it. There was no way I could have chosen to name Carl and Talon so specifically. And... my parents, in Hell, had told me that both Carl and Talon were vital to me. It had to be connected.

I clenched my fist, angrily. "I don't *know*, Tal. Without remembering my Fae childhood, I have no idea..." I admitted. "Maybe Pan would know, but he's gone, and I don't know where." Which was probably by design. A subtle hint that he probably knew I would lean on him, perhaps do something reckless to find my answer...

And being Pan, he probably knew my action would only make things worse, so he was removing the temptation, hiding from me. I both hated and loved him for it.

Talon dropped his chin, scratching at the floor with a razor-sharp claw. His gaze drifted to the Round Table after a few moments. "You know Mordred wants that more than anything..."

I grunted. "Maybe we just give it to him."

Talon frowned, slowly turning to look at me. "Never quit never quitting..." he reminded me.

I thought about it. Not his words, but a half-formed plan that had been percolating in my mind. At first, I'd considered it just to let off some steam, a way to trick myself into thinking I wasn't just running around in circles. I didn't really see an end-game in my idea, but it would give me some intelligence on Mordred...

Whatever that was worth.

"I'm not quitting, Tal. But maybe we could use it as bait. To draw him out. All this time, I've been reacting. What if..." I chuckled at the bad pun, "I turn the table on him."

"We can't just hand over the Table, Wylde. What if it makes an already incredibly dangerous enemy even *more* dangerous? We can't gamble with it until we know why he wants it."

I turned to him. "Maybe we should just go ask him what he wants with it. Tonight."

Talon groaned. "Give up our only two advantages? Time *and* the Table?" he asked, exasperated.

I met his eyes, letting him know how serious I was. "Let's face it, Tal. Mordred is too strong. Anubis said I would have to use every tool at my disposal. My magic, my Horseman's Mask, and anything else I could beg, borrow, or steal," I added, quoting Anubis. "And even with all that, I don't think Mordred is going to just stand around as we poke holes in him, leeching out the Nine Souls one-by-one. And what about his *own* soul? Does he technically have *ten*? The Nine Souls *and* his own soul?" I laced my fingers behind my head. "Even if he did stand still, we don't have an extra Devourer to help contain them before sending them back home to Hell. That's why Anubis told me to find another Devourer. Mine isn't strong enough to…"

I trailed off, frowning suddenly. *Souls. Home.*

"What is it?" Talon asked, squinting at me suspiciously.

Never quit never quitting. Cheat like a bastard to win like a king.

If it was all hopeless, then maybe I should just take all hope from the game.

Change the rules.

Cheat like a bastard.

Turn Mordred's very real scheme into…

Nothing *but* a game.

I finally turned to Talon, a very dark smile on my face. "I need you to find Grimm and make sure that – no matter what – Alex does not leave Chateau Falco tonight."

Talon nodded obediently, even though I could see he didn't understand my change of heart regarding Alex.

"Then I need you to round up the boys. We're going to have a night out. We're going to play a fucking *game*, Tal. A game to make even *Neverland* jealous…"

CHAPTER 43

I studied my reflection in the metal elevator doors as it ascended. I wore a pair of dressy, but comfy dark jeans, dark boots, and a black dress shirt. I wanted to look respectable and respectful, but to also *be functional*.

Everything was in motion. All that was left was for me to set the hook. To rattle Mordred's cage. To fling poo at the monkey and hope for the best. My only other option was to sit back and let events unfold as Mordred dictated – at Chateau Falco tomorrow – forcing me to *react* to his no-doubt extensive, meticulously diabolical plan.

And that hadn't worked out too well for me at the speech, my last encounter with Mordred.

The elevator door opened to reveal a swanky Penthouse suite in downtown St. Louis.

Mordred was waiting for me in the massive living area directly in front of the elevator, sitting in one of two oxblood chaise lounge chairs. "Welcome, Nate," he said. "I've been waiting for you to call on me, old friend."

I knew that no one else would be present, because Mordred had nothing to fear from me. He needed to be healthy and whole for our meeting tomorrow. But even if I *was* stupid enough to attack him right now, it wasn't like I was anywhere near strong enough to take on him *and* his Nine Souls – in the center of downtown St. Louis, in the hotel room he'd signed for, after I'd signed in at the lobby downstairs to request a private meeting.

A fight between us would destroy buildings. No way to hide it. So, this really was just a talk, believe it or not.

I tightened the strap of my satchel like it was a gun holster, and aimed a fifty-caliber smile between his eyes. "Me too," I admitted, walking up to him.

He opened a new bottle of twenty-year Ardbeg scotch, poured it into a fresh glass, and swirled it around with one hand. Then he slowly lifted it to his lips, took a liberal drink, swallowed it, and then opened his mouth.

Proving it wasn't poisoned.

Not wanting to swap fluids with someone from the Middle Ages, I shook my head politely, patting my satchel lightly. "No offense, but I'm used to bringing my own just in case the host's selection is sub-par."

He found my comment amusing rather than offensive, chuckling as he motioned for me to proceed. I reached into my satchel and pulled out a bottle of Macallan and a glass. I poured a drink, set it on a side table beside a second oxblood chair, and took a seat.

I sank into the cushions with a pleased sigh, discreetly assessing Mordred. He hadn't flinched, hesitated, or even blinked as I reached into my satchel to grab my drinking gear. Not a flicker of concern that I might whip out a weapon or something. The chair, I also noticed, was almost an exact replica of my favorite chair at Chateau Falco. The one I had placed on my lawn to watch dragons and werewolves tear each other to pieces the same night I had helped Mordred escape Hell.

The same chair I'd sat in after Kai had sacrificed his life to save me.

From the look in his eyes, Mordred *knew* all of this. Neither of us found it necessary to openly acknowledge any of these facts.

"To get the preliminaries out of the way," he began in a polite, but rote, tone, "I have no animosity towards you, Nate. I also have no *fear* of you."

I didn't react to his subtle challenge. I was too busy assessing the painting to my left, nowhere near Mordred. I murmured approvingly at it before turning back to my host. He had a very perplexed look on his face, having expected me to flare up at his overly polite, threatening, non-threat.

I chuckled, lifting my palms in a *whatever* gesture. "*Dude*. Chill *out*." I lifted my glass to my lips, and did as suggested, taking a long, relaxing drink. Then I hung my arm over the armrest, swirling my drink contentedly. "This is nice, isn't it? Two powerful wizards, hanging out at the top of a tower, drinking good scotch, and sharing prison stories. The opportunity doesn't come up as often as you would think."

He watched me in silence, eyes calculating. He was entirely different from how he'd acted during our speech where he'd been in complete control of the situation. Eventually, he repositioned himself in his chair to get more comfortable, more relaxed, and took a drink. I figured he was trying to marry the Nate Temple he saw in front of him with whatever psych eval his source had given him about me.

Readjusting.

Restrategizing.

Calculating a hundred minute variables.

Which was entirely intentional, on my part.

I knew what people said about me, what they thought and felt about me, how I typically reacted to emotional triggers... I'd meticulously considered all that before walking up to his hotel. Mordred's source of intelligence had handed over a big fat personality profile on Nate Temple.

And I was casually lighting it on fire with all the respect for authenticity one would give a tabloid magazine.

To be able to maintain character, I'd had to convince even myself that this was all just a game, a charade. None of it mattered. At least, that's what I needed Mordred to see from me. That his assessment of his foe was grossly incorrect.

In that way, his anger might subconsciously be redirected to whoever had been giving him information on me in the first place, distracting Mordred enough to hopefully fumble into my new game unwillingly.

This was a stage play. And I was both the lead actor and director. I smiled at him, careful to keep my grin care-free, unconcerned, and not remotely arrogant or scheming.

A slow smile split his cheeks. "You know, this is *much* more fun than I had been led to believe."

"*Right?*" I agreed emphatically, patting my armrest and chuckling.

Mordred chuckled along with me, drumming his fingers on his glass as he studied me like I was an exotic purple pigeon he had found in the park. "Why *exactly* are you here tonight, Nate?" he finally asked.

I laughed as if he'd told me an inside joke. "What a funny coincidence! I came here to ask what *you're* doing in St. Louis!" I said, shaking my head at the serendipity. "I figured I should hear it from your own lips rather than relying on hearsay, which is often *terribly* inaccurate..." I added, winking jovially.

No missing *that* reference – how his source of information on me had been nothing but false fluff.

Mordred sighed, hanging his head in admission. "It seems I should have done the same. But it's water under the bridge, now. It's not like I can bring my source back from the dead to reprimand him."

My heart might have fluttered at those words, but I kept my face calm, merely arching an eyebrow.

Mordred lifted a glass in cheers. "To Tomas Mullingsworth," he said in an honorary tone.

And my mind kind of winked on and off a few times as I struggled to keep a straight face. *Tomas Mullingsworth* had been Mordred's source? The dragon hunter? I recalled reading the article about his disappearance, and forced down my instinctive shudder.

"Tomas was quite fond of you, Temple, even to the end," Mordred said in a somber tone, snapping me out of my reverie. He looked slightly frustrated, so I must have maintained my façade. "His loyalty made me resort to more... medieval tactics to learn what I thought I needed to know about you." He let out a sigh. "And to learn that, ultimately, his death meant nothing... Pity. Live by the sword, die by the sword, as they say." He sipped at his drink, watching me.

I managed to cock my head and frown in disappointment. "Out of all the people you could have chosen... you picked a man I hardly knew, from *years* ago..." I said, hiding the very real pain threatening to consume me. "And rather than admitting that personal mistake, you... *tortured* him to death?" I asked distastefully. Mordred nodded, gauging me for any cracks in my composure.

My composure *was* slipping, though, and I could think of only one way to maintain it. I focused on the few funny moments I had of Tomas – when I had snuck into his apartment to leave behind a stalker's board of pictures that sent his date running and screaming from the building, or when his crew of dragon hunter pals had knocked me off the roof of a strip club with a blunt crossbow bolt to the kidney.

And... I laughed.

A belting, eye-watering, soul-deep laugh. For Mordred's sake, I made it insulting, but inwardly, it was me paying homage to the dragon hunter. He'd stood no chance against Mordred, so I held no ill will for him giving away anything on me. The fact that he was now dead told me he had fought to the end.

My laughter finally faded as I noticed the tight look on Mordred's face. "Sorry. It's just… well, it's all rather ridiculous, isn't it?"

And I took a drink, managing not to rattle the glass against my teeth under Mordred's very controlled glare. Tomas hadn't been a saint, but he'd been a damned fine guy, overall. And to feign nonchalance right now felt like the worst kind of betrayal, but I also knew it was a form of tribute. To prove – with my laughter – that Tomas hadn't given Mordred anything useful. If Tomas was up there somewhere, looking down on me, he'd be laughing his ass off, cheering me on.

I just knew it.

And that belief was the only thing that let me pull off my charade for Mordred.

He finally waved a hand. "It seems his death was doubly pointless, then."

"Just for the record," I said, giving him a polite, but stern glare. "I don't appreciate you murdering associates and acquaintances of mine. It's very… sloppy, if I'm being honest." And I gave him my best dad look, silently saying, *I'm not mad, I'm just disappointed…* "Perhaps we can get back to more pressing business…" I suggested, and Mordred nodded tightly. I gathered my thoughts, deciding where to start, first. "Your personal vendetta is with Camelot, where you already have an army on the march." He didn't seem surprised by my knowledge, so I pressed on in a polite, but firm tone. "Why make a spectacle of yourself, here, in St. Louis?"

His jaws clenched briefly at my words, but I didn't let my triumph show on my face.

"My armies *will* crush Camelot. It is only a matter of time. But they don't need me for that. I'm after some items that are… a little closer to the heart and, unfortunately, they are not *in* Camelot. I've already checked. St. Louis is a crossroads of power much like Camelot was in the beginning…" he said, switching topics as he glanced out the window to our right, smiling faintly. "I assumed that if information on my heirlooms could be found anywhere, it would be here." He turned back to me. "Tell me I'm wrong."

I shrugged. "You're wrong."

Mordred smiled sadly. "Tomas did get one thing right. You see… he told me about your parents' Armory. Their fascination with history. How they spent their years acquiring... heirlooms from old families. And I'm very interested in perusing the shelves for one or two items that hold a certain... familial significance."

"Just say it already," I said, feigning bored impatience. "I know you want to. Your charitable foundation kind of gives it away."

Mordred nodded, but for some reason, he didn't look overly happy like I'd expected – that evil villain gene kicking in to make him cackle and laugh as he announced his greatest desires.

"My family betrayed me – my father killing me on the battlefield, and my mother ensuring I was sent to the deepest pits of Hell... My father has already paid for his betrayal. I vividly recall the moment I stabbed him in the stomach, and also the moment he stabbed me," Mordred said, absently touching his stomach as he stared off in the middle distance. "His death was a bit more prolonged, which if I'm being honest, suits me just fine. But Camelot must fall to satisfy my justice. Not just the city, but the *symbol*. Then the Fae Courts, and my dear old mother."

"We already talked about this part," I reminded him. "You were supposed to be telling me about St. Louis, remember?" I offered helpfully.

"Ah, yes. Merlin's treasures. Excalibur and his Round Table," Mordred finally said.

CHAPTER 44

*H*e appraised me silently for a few uncomfortable seconds. "But do you have any idea *why?*"

I pretended to think on it for a moment. "You already have the Nine Souls for power, so I'm guessing you just want to destroy the table and sword for symbolic reasons."

Like a nervous tic, he narrowed his eyes abruptly, straining his neck to the left, as if stretching out a sudden muscle cramp. He... was in *pain*. He noticed my attention and let out a breath. "The Nine Souls chafe. Even now, they writhe inside of my body like oiled serpents, squirming, hissing, biting at each other... biting at *me*," he added, gritting his teeth and rotating his neck the other direction this time. He took a calming breath, mastering himself. "Although they granted me much power, having helped to fully restore my rightful body," he said, gesturing at himself from head to toe, "they grow restless, now. I'd like to be free of them, and I think they're rather opposed to that idea. I can control them, but it is a struggle. They fight to dominate my own soul. Number *ten*, as it were," he mumbled, gesturing vaguely.

Shit. That was one question answered. I had to contend with his own soul, not just the Nine.

I almost told him about my suggested treatment plan to help relieve him of his collection of Souls – the surgery where he stood still as I stabbed him through the throat ten times – but I was confident he wouldn't like the location of the rehabilitation center.

Hell.

Odin's guess had been right. Mordred wanted free of his Nine Souls. How could I use that to my advantage? "Well, why don't you just end the relationship?" I offered, hoping to buy some time to think.

He smiled. "What do you think I've been *doing*, Nate?" he asked, sounding very amused. "Why do you think they are so restless all of a sudden? As soon as you mention my family heirlooms?"

I concealed my shiver. He really did want Excalibur and the Round Table for power, like I had both hoped... and feared. In the long run, this news was very *not good*. But in the short run...

"They're not in my parents' Armory, Mordred. I will even swear it on my power."

He was silent for a moment, using the time to sip at his drink. "I do hate to be rude, but Merlin showed me how to wiggle out of that little oath, so I can't take your word for it."

"There are plenty of other forms of power," I continued on, as if thinking out loud. "Why not just go after them, like I have? Shouldn't you want to destroy the Round Table and Excalibur? The whole symbol thing, remember?"

He didn't look remotely surprised or impressed at my subtle humble brag. "I would love nothing more, but first, I must study the Round Table and Excalibur. Like I said, Merlin was constantly toying with them, modifying them somehow. Merlin was powerful in his own right, I cannot deny it, but he was even more famous for his association with Arthur. *The teacher and mentor to the greatest King that ever lived*," Mordred muttered acidly, as if reciting a commonly-used phrase from his day. "And the people bought it, basking in the radiance of their beloved wizard. They came to worship him, over time, perhaps more than they even worshipped Arthur. But to keep that adoration flowing, Merlin was always tinkering, dreaming up new reasons for the people to love him. Some cure, some magic, some new legend he could birth..." Mordred let out a steadying breath, carefully unclenching his fingers from the armrest. "I need to see what he did with the Table and Sword before I make my decision. Perhaps there is a way to remove and harness his upgrades, granting me freedom from the Nine Souls while allowing me to destroy the cursed heirlooms."

I nodded, appearing to consider the topic academically. "And what will you do with this new power? After you have destroyed Camelot and all that."

Mordred thought about it. "Any number of things. Maybe even set down roots here in St. Louis. The locals seemed to appreciate me."

"I disagree. This crown thing of mine is pretty new, and I kind of want to let it play out," I told him, ignoring his amused smile. "The world is a big place. What if I told you to pick somewhere else?"

He considered it for a time. "I walk these streets, and at every intersection, I taste power in the air. Gods, monsters, legends, angels, demons..." he looked wondrous. "It's incredible, making even my memories of Camelot seem dull and drab in comparison. I'm surprised the city isn't driven mad by it."

"Well, it is a *little* mad," I admitted, thinking on his words. I hadn't noticed power just floating around in the air or anything, but maybe I wasn't as attuned to these types of things as Mordred was. Or... his senses were just overwhelmed. He'd been locked away for so long that even smelling a hot dog might seem magical to him.

But...

He was also not wrong. Gods, monsters, and many other powerful Freaks and legends had been flocking to St. Louis for years. None of us knew why – at least no one had shared any explanations with me – but it seemed everyone always found a reason to move to St. Louis – the Gateway to the West.

I'd always assumed the subconscious magical attraction was related to the Armory. Or, at least that it had been *triggered* by my parents bringing the Armory to St. Louis. But that was just an educated guess.

I finally shrugged. "You can't have St. Louis," I told him. Again, not rudely, but conversationally. I couldn't afford to fight him here in the hotel. I needed to set the hook.

Mordred rolled his eyes. "What are we really doing here, Nate? You know what I want, and why. I doubt you came here just to learn my motives. And you've already sensed my strength. I can assure you that even *without* the Nine Souls, you wouldn't stand a chance against me. You must have a more personal reason for your visit. Some request?"

I made a last-ditch mental sweep of my plan. Mordred's words hadn't really changed anything, merely confirming my suspicions. And I had sensed his power during the speech. All he had done was embrace it for a moment, like flexing his muscles. I wasn't sure about the wizard-to-wizard assessment, without his Nine Souls, but that didn't really matter at the moment. So, I met his eyes and nodded. Then I slowly reached into my satchel and withdrew a small vial the size of my finger.

It was filled with the liquid metal from the stream circling the Round Table – swirls of silver, gold, and copper that never completely blended together. The symbols and runes in the molten metal were vaguely noticeable if you looked closely enough. This part of my plan had made Tal's hair stand up on end. A sample from the Round Table as bait.

Mordred broke composure, gasping in disbelief. He didn't instantly tackle me for it, but he did appear to be gripping the chair as if holding himself back. His eyes also danced with pain, no doubt his Nine Souls were reminding him that *good wizards said no to illegal drugs.*

"*Obey me,*" he suddenly snarled to no one in particular, his voice laced with power that I could feel even from my chair. And the Nine Souls apparently listened, judging by the triumphant look on his face. I wondered where his own soul – number ten – fit in on the pecking order inside his body. Was it hiding in a corner somewhere? Or maybe it had allied with the new roommates.

"I don't know what this is, exactly," I said, swirling the vial in my fingers, "but it seems like you have some idea. I think you can trust me when I say the Round Table is not in the Armory. And if you get any funny ideas about killing me for this, the Table will be destroyed before you even leave this room."

"And Excalibur?" he whispered.

I shrugged. "I wish I knew, man," I admitted.

He let out a frustrated breath. "Why show me this?"

"I propose we throw down in a big, knockout brawl. Like gentlemen, of course. Winner gets the Table."

He looked surprised, no doubt wondering how in the world that could work to my benefit. I didn't stand a chance in a fair fight, no matter what tools I had at my disposal, and Mordred knew about most of them.

I tipped back my drink, finding it barely held one last sip. I stared down into my empty glass, frowning. "Well, that's not symbolic or anything…" I murmured.

Mordred proffered his own empty glass. "How would this work, exactly?

I imagine a fight between us would not go unnoticed," he said sarcastically. Because of all the likely craters, explosions, and destruction we would leave behind.

I pretended to think about it. "You want to go duke it out behind the farmer's shed?" I suggested, wondering if he would understand the reference.

Mordred's eyes twinkled, immediately catching on. "Sure. Tomas told me a little about that place. It's about the safest location for our little wager," he agreed, nodding.

I pretended to ignore the hunger in those eyes as I pocketed the vial.

"Cool," I said, climbing to my feet. "I think it would be good for our relationship to let out some pent-up aggression. Get a good punch or two in, you know?" I asked jovially.

"Sounds productive," he agreed, nodding seriously as he climbed to his feet and set down his glass. His eyes definitely tracked the pocket where I had tucked the vial, but I pretended not to notice.

"I should warn you, though. I don't fight fair. Dick-punches, hair pulling, the works. None of that Knightly stuff for me," I warned him, shaking my head meaningfully. "I have a reputation to maintain."

He smirked, shrugging. "That's fine. No matter how this plays out, are we still on for our meeting tomorrow? Our subjects are expecting it." I nodded, putting the Macallan and my glass back into my satchel. "How do you want to get there?" he asked curiously. "Make a Gateway?"

I shook my head. "I was hoping we could do something dramatic. Get some free press. Do you mind standing over there in front of the window?"

Mordred nodded, smiling curiously before walking over to the floor-to-ceiling glass window overlooking St. Louis. He turned to find me crouching down, dry-washing my hands with an eager grin on my face. "The glass is pretty thick," he commented, not even remotely concerned about my obvious plan.

I grinned wider, feeling adrenaline flooding into my system. "Oh, don't worry. I plan on hitting you pretty hard. I think you can take it, Sir Knight," I told him, grinding my foot into the ground like I was waiting for the start of a race at a track meet. I swung the satchel behind my back, not wanting it to cushion the blow for Mordred. "You ready?" I asked.

He nodded, holding his arms out invitingly. His eyes danced with anticipation. At the knowledge he would soon have the Round Table in his grasp.

"I want you to know that I truly appreciate your class-act," I told him. "It's a nice change of pace."

He chuckled. "What are Knights for?" he asked, waiting.

Without further ado, I sprinted at him as fast as I could, flinging my hands out ahead of me with blasts of air to either side of him.

The glass behind him shattered outwards to rain down on the streets far below, and I rammed my shoulders into Mordred's chest hard enough to make him grunt, sending us both sailing out into the night sky.

Mordred was soon laughing.

I had been laughing upon contact.

The air whipped about us, the shards of glass surrounding us like a cloud of insects. Right when I felt our momentum ebb, and gravity begin to take over, I Shadow Walked us to our spot near a farmer's shed.

Midas Kingston's farm. And behind this farmer's shed was the Dueling Grounds.

Old King Midas had a farm, E-I-E-I-O.

And on that farm, he had a Minotaur, E-I-E-I-O.

We hit the ground on our feet, stumbling slightly, but not tipping over. Asterion stood before us, 100% Greek-Angus Beef. He was much taller than us, and covered in a thick blanket of brown fur. He wore his usual prayer bead necklace – each bead slightly smaller than my fist – a leather skirt designed for battle, and a pair of big ass boots. His stained horns reared up from his temples, the tips glinting in the moonlight, and the thick metal ring from his snout dripped with Minotaur snot. He wasn't surprised by our arrival since I'd told him my intentions earlier, but I knew he believed that a fight between us was both reckless and a waste of time.

I had only shared my entire plan with a few people, after all.

Mordred and I were clutching each other for support, still laughing loudly from the rush of jumping out of a freaking building. As Mordred assessed the Minotaur for some kind of attack or deceit, I slipped the vial from the Round Table into my satchel.

Neither noticed. Perfect.

Asterion watched us with a curious frown, snorting loudly enough to set his thick nose ring to swinging. We probably looked like drunk college roommates. We were supposed to be *enemies*, after all. We still were, but what was the point in letting hatred hold our hearts when we were getting ready to settle our differences in a place where neither of us could really die? A place where, when killed, our bodies...

And souls...

Would return *home*.

So, Mordred and I were laughing for entirely different reasons. He just didn't know it yet.

"Follow me. Everyone is waiting," Asterion finally said, shaking his head again before turning to lead us to the entrance to Fight Night at the Dueling Grounds.

Mordred frowned over at me upon hearing the Minotaur's comment, but didn't hesitate to follow.

I waved a hand dismissively. "I invited a few friends," I told him nonchalantly.

CHAPTER 45

I'd taken a gamble and told Alucard to send his new vampires far and wide, telling everyone that they should really, really consider attending tonight's Fight Night. And they were obviously very persuasive, because more people had listened than even I had anticipated. If things went south, this was about to get very embarrassing for me. Everyone would watch as I got my ass kicked.

No real harm in that. I'd learn a few valuable lessons and wake up at Chateau Falco with only a bruised ego for my troubles.

However...

What if some asshole had *more* than one soul? When you killed one, wouldn't the other eight— no, *nine*, fight to keep the body in place at the Dueling Grounds, effectively banishing the *killed* soul back *home*?

In Mordred's case, back to *Hell*?

I was betting everything on the hope that it would.

The Dueling Grounds was eternally sunset, casting the immediate area in a dusky, crimson tone, thanks to the fiery setting sun raging on the far, far horizon. The space itself, like most sporting arenas, consisted of a massive fight ring – large enough for dragons, even – and then a wide walkway followed by a row of bleachers and benches. A few concessions stands sold a variety of finger foods, primarily consisting of various meats on a stick, and they were doing a brisk business, the smells drifting through the area. I noticed a new shack between two sets of bleachers with a sign above it that said *Carl's Heel*, and a crude painting of a white stick figure lizard wearing red stilettos. They were serving booze, judging by the crowd of Myrmidons lingering beside it, and I found myself smiling at the twist on Achilles' own bar in St. Louis, *Achilles' Heel*.

Several trees dotted the area – hulking monstrous oaks of a sort – but the rest of the Dueling Grounds was grass and dry earth.

About ten feet past the bleachers was a solid perimeter of flaming torches, and beyond that ring of fire was an impenetrable darkness, not even vaguely illuminated by the setting sun in the distance.

In that Dark Land one could hear creatures murdering and slaughtering one another. Asterion had warned me profusely that to enter the Dark Lands was suicide by violent dismemberment from the locals.

Coincidentally, my unicorn had been living in there before deciding to move in with me. And my unicorn was a homicidal psychopath on the best of days. I could only imagine what his old neighbors must have been like – especially if they gave Asterion pause.

I saw Mordred studying the Dark Lands thoughtfully, likely sensing the danger for himself.

Or maybe his stolen Nine Souls had considered it a nice vacation spot, like driving beside a coastal beach.

There were more people in the crowd than even the vampires could have found in the brief time I had given them, meaning that others had blabbed, too, and word had spread that...

Nefarious Nate was going to battle the Magnificent Moe in the Fight of the Century!

Midas had probably had a hand in beefing up the attendance, seeing the revenue potential for a prize fight like this. I shot a look over at him and he shrugged shamelessly, accepting bets from the long line of Freaks waiting their turn.

As soon as spectators began to take notice of our arrival, it was like a fuse had been lit. The air grew tense and thick, and all I could hear were our boots crossing the dying grass. Then we stepped over the line of rocks that marked the fight ring itself.

The bleachers weren't full of people, but they were full of the *right* people.

Alucard's foxy proxy – that cute little old black lady – had a few vampires sitting beside her, literally on leashes. They didn't look happy about it, but they concealed their unhappiness well, holding a parasol and drink for her as she bided her time, knitting happily. She glanced up at my arrival, and my eyes settled briefly on her knitting before flashing her a smile and a thumbs up. She grinned, and I tipped a figurative hat at her attendants.

Alvara, surprisingly, sat beside two ridiculously handsome Legolas types who had obviously been juicing and chugging protein drinks since their victory over Sauron. They watched me impassively, their long, lustrous blonde hair held back by braided leather cords set with dark gems that rested on their foreheads.

Not for the tenth time, my mind began to wander, wondering what terrible act had earned them banishment from the Land of the Fae. Maybe the Chancery had been too *nice* for the merciless Fae Courts.

But it was good to see Alvara pulling through for me – and so quickly. She gave me an almost imperceptible nod, then leaned in close to her companions, speaking softly. I openly waved at her. "Can't wait until our next tea party!" I called out. The three stiffened, and the two men began speaking to her more urgently.

The foxy proxy vampire glanced up thoughtfully, considering the information I had just given up. That I was close with the Chancery. At least, that's what it *looked* like.

Baron Skyfall was there in a typical Englishman's perfectly tailored wool suit. He wore a vest and a paisley tie, roguishly loosened to give his massive ebony tree trunk of a neck some room to turn. Fook and Yu sat beside him – wearing different shirts, I noticed with a grin. I flashed them a thumbs up, nodding and tugging at my own shirt. They grinned crookedly.

"Avast, ye landlubber!" Baron bellowed, and I found myself instantly grinning from ear to ear. He was laughing loudly for all to see, but subtly telling me that we had no bad blood over our last encounter.

And letting the rest of the crowd know that I was close enough to the dragons to have inside jokes.

I didn't need to really acknowledge anyone else, because it was well known I was pals with the werewolves, but I did nod respectfully at Drake and Cowan, Gunnar's top werewolves, who sat a little apart from the others on their bench, glaring openly at Mordred. Drake was a mischievous looking scrawny guy, his eyes always dancing with an inner light that usually made you feel like he'd robbed you blind without ever touching you. Cowan, on the other hand was a tall, stoic man with the emotional capabilities of a statue. Somehow, the two were pals. Not just pals, but more like adopted brothers. I liked them.

There were many faces I didn't recognize from all walks of life – Native Americans in tribal attire, a charcoal-skinned couple in outlandish suits and decorated fedoras, a group of burly mechanics, and many more. Each group stood or sat in small antisocial huddles.

I gave many of them direct, personal, secretive nods – almost enough to flirt with a bow.

Which startled the hell out of them, making them look to the other families I had acknowledged, and cringe at the sudden suspicious glances they received back in turn.

My gestures made it look like I had more discreet connections in the supernatural community of St. Louis, on top of my open alliances with the wolves, vampires, Chancery, and dragons.

I realized Mordred had stopped, and that the crowd was now holding their breaths.

I glanced back, frowning. Mordred didn't look scared, but he did look hyper-aware. "You did warn me you didn't fight fair," he said, smirking faintly. So faint that I couldn't tell if he was annoyed or amused.

I turned around to where he was looking.

Alucard, Talon, and Gunnar were laughing loudly in a small huddle, slapping backs and teasing each other. Like you would expect at a bar. My friends noticed the silence and looked over at us. Then their faces slowly changed, and they made their way towards me, seeming to strut. They looked like someone had just changed the song on the Jukebox, and that they had a very strong opinion on the new song.

I turned back to Mordred. "Oh, them? That's not me fighting dirty. You've just got your Ten Souls, so I figured it was only fair to bring a few friends. You've still got us outnumbered," I added.

"Okay," Mordred said, rolled his shoulders a few times, cracking his neck from side to side to loosen up. "Just surprised me. Made me briefly consider that this might have been arranged beforehand," he said drily, flicking his gaze about the crowd of attendees and King Midas taking last bets in a gruff shout.

"Sometimes coincidences just happen," I told him. "Not everything has to be all mystical and shit."

CHAPTER 46

*A*sterion stepped between us, clearing his throat with an ear-splitting bellow to get everyone's attention. It was entirely unnecessary, because all eyes were already on us, sensing the tension in the ring.

"Welcome to Fight Night!" he shouted, holding up his massive arms as the crowd went wild. "As you have no doubt noticed, we changed the scheduled fight card for the evening. If anyone has a problem with this decision, I encourage you to drown your sorrows at *Carl's Heel*... courtesy of the house."

He pointed a massive, sausage-sized finger at the make-shift bar. Unsurprisingly, a group of Myrmidons were the loudest, cheering and clinking mugs, but a pleased hum rolled over the entire place.

Leonidas and Achilles were conspicuously absent, so maybe they were keeping an eye on the reporters at Chateau Falco.

"We're all about happy customers, here," Asterion continued. He smiled for the crowd – a horrible, wicked look on his bull face – but I sensed it was hollow. He fingered his massive prayer beads absently, a gesture he did only when nervous. He didn't know my plan, but he knew me well enough to expect this event to go very badly, very quickly. But I shrugged it off. The worst that could happen was that Mordred killed us and we woke up in bed, embarrassed at our failed fight.

I scanned the crowd as Asterion continued on, still speaking to the guests about general rules. I'd heard it so many times I could recite it by now, but Mordred was paying very close attention, probably making sure there wasn't some trickery afoot. There wasn't, at least not on Asterion's part. The Dueling Grounds was neutral, and didn't manipulate the fights. Ever. One act like that would ruin its integrity, and the well would run dry.

The Dueling Grounds held many memories for me, both pleasant and unpleasant. My first time here had been when dealing with Alaric's dragons invading St. Louis. Asterion had given me a coin after I beat him in a Duel – a coin given to him by Hermes. *Flip once to save your life, flip again to save the life of another*, he had told me.

I'd had my fair share of not-so-pleasant times, too, but overall it felt good to be back in the ring. Like shore leave for sailors, at the bar with the cheapest beer closest to the docks, but with a lot more violence and magic.

Asterion said something that seemed to catch everyone's attention, so I glanced up. "Tension has been high in St. Louis since yesterday, possibly even before. Many of you know I've had past dealings with Nate Temple, and consider him a friend. That being said, Fight Club transcends all personal ties. That is the entire purpose of the place – to let you guys duke it out without leveling a city or killing bystanders. To have your little grudge matches, settle old feuds, let off steam, and... HAVE FUN!" he roared, lifting his arms again.

Mordred nodded, satisfied with the affirmation that he wasn't walking into a trap.

The Minotaur waited for the crowd's roar to calm down before continuing. "St. Louis is our home, and we all love her savagely. Hopefully, the outcome of tonight's fight will cool some tempers, and make their meeting tomorrow more... productive." Asterion turned to Mordred, then my group, arching a furry eyebrow. "Agreed?" he asked.

But it wasn't really a question.

Mordred bowed deeply. "Agreed. This is all rather exciting. Do you own it with Midas?"

Asterion's face grew impassive. "I am more the bouncer and referee. Midas owns the farmland, and holds it as neutral territory."

Mordred was nodding thoughtfully. "Ah, but I meant *this* place," he said, tapping his foot on the earth. "Not the land that holds the *entrance* to this place. Imagine the chaos that would cause. Anyone with a doorway inside could claim an entire place all for themselves..."

His eyes shot briefly to mine, and I could see what he was getting at. The Armory.

"I don't think you want to meet the *owner* of this *place*," Asterion said, scraping at the earth with a size thirty-eight boot. "I am merely its Warden."

I frowned at that. Warden implied prisoners…

I glanced past the ring of ever-burning torches, at what lived beyond. Asterion's prisoners.

Grimm had been living there, the crazy bastard – about as far from a rainbow as one could possibly get. In the past, I'd heard all sorts of wild, nasty sounds coming from out there, but the beings must have grown accustomed to our Fight Nights since they hardly ever made the sickening song of murder anymore. Either that or we were all accustomed to it, now.

And Mordred was staring at it thoughtfully again.

Asterion noticed and clenched his jaws. "The fight is here. Not out there. Only certain death lies out there."

Mordred blinked, and then nodded. "Of course."

"Is everyone ready?" Asterion asked. I nodded, feeling my friends fan out around me.

Alucard smiled like a model on the runway. He even wore dark sunglasses with his jeans and white tee.

Gunnar winked – or blinked – at Mordred. His stone eyepatch glinted, reflecting the reds, oranges, and yellows of the eternal setting sun.

The last time I'd donned my Horseman's Mask, I'd grown an adorable pair of skeletal wings made of some flavor of quartz-like stone. I'd also sported claws, and from what I'd been told, my entire skin had changed to the same stone-like texture.

And Gunnar, being magically bonded to me as a result of the family rune tattooed on his wrist, had caught some accidental power-up as a result. And it was permanent. Even when I wasn't wearing the Mask, his claws and eyepatch were now that same stone substance, making me think that on some distant level, I was officially a part of the Apocalypse team. But I'd been told that third time was the charm, and that I would hear a great, heavenly bell toll in the skies – announcing to the world that a new Horseman had been born.

The Four Horsemen hadn't offered up a detailed explanation, but they were notorious dicks, so they were probably waiting on some form of official confirmation. A letter from God, or that stupid bell to ring out.

War had told me he wore his Mask several times before it became official.

I had a sinking suspicion that tonight I would hear a big fucking bell. Because I'd felt Mordred's power. He was stronger than anyone I'd ever faced.

Athena.

Kai.

Castor Queen.

Anubis.

Maybe even a few of them combined.

I faced Mordred, no longer laughing. It was time to be Nate. No more façade. I had him where I wanted him.

"Even though this is all fun and games," I said loudly enough for all to hear. "I want you to know that I take great personal offense to you bumbling into my city and stirring up shit. Each resident of St. Louis is under my protection. And whether they want to accept that or not, I will still step in to fight for them. Not because I personally like them, or think they can't take care of themselves, but because this is my *home*, and even if I disagree with some of my neighbors, I won't tolerate some punk teenager driving recklessly through my street, bashing down mailboxes and toilet-papering the trees, thinking he's hot shit with the wisdom of a sixteen-year-old clutching his brand-new driver's license, driving the car his..." I smirked smugly, "*parents* bought for him. Trying desperately to do some-thing outlandishly flamboyant to get some attention, since all the kids on *his* street considered him a joke."

You could have heard a pin drop, and I felt every single eye in the crowd upon me. Mordred, for his part, looked about as furious as I'd ever seen someone look – especially at all the clever analogies and comparisons I'd used to poke and prod at him, mocking his life in Camelot. But he also kept his mouth shut, recognizing that all I had done was stand up for my city, so any comment on his part would only confirm my statement, because he would be mocking everyone here.

Without breaking eye contact, I ripped open a Gateway to my right, about the size of my torso and hovering in midair rather than settled on the ground. "I won't bother giving you my resume, listing all the assholes I've taken care of in the last few years, how much I've bled for this city – whether asked to or not – because you already know all of that. You know, since you killed Tomas Mullingsworth to spy on me," I told Mordred. Several in the crowd gasped in disbelief. Tomas hadn't been a celebrity or anything, but his name had gotten around.

I tugged off my satchel and tossed it through the Gateway without looking. Since I had already slipped the vial from the Round Table into the satchel, I had one less thing to worry about – Mordred stealing it from me during the fight. I began to roll up my sleeves, still locking eyes with Mordred – who looked livid. "And I want you to know that tonight, in front of all my friends…" I said, sweeping the crowd meaningfully, speaking loud enough for all to hear.

I locked eyes with Mordred again, grinning. "I'm going to fight you like I'm the third monkey on the ramp to Noah's Ark," I said, blindly reaching back into the Gateway to grasp a wooden haft on the other side. "And Brother… It's starting to rain."

And I pulled my Devourer into the Dueling Grounds.

My Neverwas didn't shine. The black haft and blade seemed to merely amplify the tone of our play date. But the ruby on the tip looked *hangry*, flickering with crimson lightning and red smoke.

I let the Gateway wink out. My satchel was now safe in the Sanctorum, and I'd given the prearranged signal to those on the other end – that the vial was inside.

Mordred's eyes narrowed dangerously. "You're just a shadow of twenty different flavors," he snarled. "Wizard, Godkiller, Maker…" he trailed off, waving his hand to signify any others he may have missed. "You don't know how to *truly* harness *any* of them."

"But I know how to make a mean mixed drink," I muttered, having expected the comment a long time ago.

"BEGIN!" Asterion said, shuffling backwards to get the hell out of the way.

CHAPTER 47

*M*ordred lifted his palms, and was suddenly holding two great big swords of green flame.

Gunnar howled, clothing exploding everywhere as he shifted into his Wild Side version of his werewolf form – a seven-foot tall monster with matted white fur and finger-thick claws of stone that matched his eye-patch.

The audience roared excitedly to see their local Alpha werewolf – who was fast becoming a legend in St. Louis for how casually he'd dispatched a couple of very powerful werewolves, recently – shift into his exquisitely lethal Wild Side form, but *also* because of the new body armor he wore. *GRIMM TECH* was emblazoned across the front. The roaring excitement of the crowd changed, slightly, or perhaps melded with another harmonious chorus… of gut-busting laughter as some of the audience read the word on the back.

MANIMAL.

The body armor was strong against the usual elemental attacks, and could withstand extreme abuse in the physical arena as well, not that a werewolf really needed much help there, but when standing up against some of the bigger nasties, it couldn't hurt. Claws of all speeds and sharpness sliced off it like chainmail, not that it wouldn't break-down at some point, but it gave that added protection like magical Kevlar.

It was also designed to fit him as a human, but would modify to his new form as a wolf – which had been a tricky fucking thing to nail down, let me tell you.

"I think I'm going to enjoy this," Mordred said, spinning his swords in slow circles, warming up his wrists. "Don't take it personally."

"I was about to say the same thing," Yahn said, materializing out of nowhere to send his glass fist hammering into Mordred's throat like a battering ram. It connected with a sickening crunch, destroying his windpipe, and sent Mordred flying. But surprisingly, Yahn roared in pain as well, now fully visible. He clutched his shattered fist, now just a stump of broken glass.

I ignored Yahn's agonized groans, walling off part of my heart. This wasn't permanent. I had to remember that. We had a job to do and tending to Yahn was both pointless and a weakness, because the worst that could happen was he died and woke up in his bed in a few minutes, probably with a pair of overly concerned red dragons who would be more than happy to tend to his damaged pride.

Instead, I turned to the crowd. Everyone had grown silent at the stunning end to the fight, staring at the scene in disbelief. "For the dragon nation," I told them, my voice echoing in the silence as I lifted my spear in tribute.

Maybe some of them were thinking they had placed the wrong bet earlier.

Maybe, like many lonely wives, they were disappointed in Mordred's ten-second-long performance.

My attention was solely on Mordred, because Yahn had just performed the first experiment of the night, delivering a fatal killing blow to Mordred. Now, we watched for the result. I gripped my spear tightly as I saw Mordred's form shiver involuntarily. He took a desperate gasp of air, despite his supposedly ruined throat, and slowly climbed to his feet, shaking his head drunkenly.

The crowd gasped in disbelief, turning to each other for answers.

I ignored them as I noticed waves of power pulsing around my foe, but judging by their erratic nature, I didn't think it was intentional on Mordred's part. It looked kind of like when it was unbelievably hot outside and you stared out over a patch of concrete at a distant object – faintly able to see visual distortions from the heat radiating off the pavement, but not able to actually *see* those heat waves – just their distorting effect.

He touched his throat instinctively, feeling it twitching and quivering as it began to heal itself beneath his fingertips. Then his eyes took stock of the power waves coming off him, and he looked... mildly alarmed.

He looked up abruptly, eyes locking on Yahn with hatred, and took a determined step.

Then he grunted before he could take a second step, his body stiffening like a board.

The waves of power around him whipped about like a tortured octopus, and his eyes winced with fresh pain and horror. I was practically dancing on my feet, not necessarily with eagerness, but anticipation and hope that something very strange was happening. Mordred reached out a hand, clawing at the air.

And that's when I saw it. The waves of heat were darkening, coalescing to form a humanoid shape outside his body. And like Mordred, it was screaming silently, reaching out a clawed hand towards Mordred's outstretched fingers.

I squinted in disbelief. It looked... like that famous painting where God was lounging on a cloud, reaching out to touch fingers with Adam.

Mordred had just had his Adam's apple crushed...

And was now unknowingly mimicking Michelangelo's famous painting, *The Creation of Adam.*

I laughed at the irony, leaning on my Devourer for support. My laughter might have also been fueled by relief – witnessing proof to my theory. Mordred had entered this ring with Nine Souls from Hell and his own personal soul – for a total of Ten Souls we needed to face down. And my hypothesis was that killing Mordred would force one of his souls from his body, but leave the man behind. From Ten Souls down to Nine – Eight Souls from Hell, and his own personal soul.

Gunnar grumbled as he stepped up beside me. "Is it working?" he growled.

Alucard and Talon stepped up on my other side, watching with blank looks on their faces. Alucard didn't take off his sunglasses or anything, so he mustn't have been that blown away.

Yahn made his way over, clutching his stump with his other hand. Glass shards seemed to be dripping from his shattered fist like blood. But the look on his glass face told me he didn't want to talk about it, just to witness what he had bought with that pain – Mordred's suffering.

I nodded slowly, turning to Gunnar. "I think it's working. Here's the moment of truth…" I said, loud enough for only them to hear me. Mordred was too busy snarling and gasping to overhear us, but I didn't want the audience to catch on yet. That tonight – for the first time in Fight Club history – someone could actually lose more than their dignity.

Since Mordred was cheating, sharing his body with Nine Souls, it was kind of putting a kerfuffle in the natural order of this strange realm – the Dueling Grounds ability to send souls back home *with* a body.

The cosmic judges were going to have to dust off their robes and take a vote, unable to rely on the system they had set in place long ago. If the nine remaining souls in a body were fighting to keep the body *here…*

What happened to the killed soul? Where could it go? It couldn't go back to Mordred's bed, since… you know, Mordred wasn't *in* his bed. Mordred was stuck here, held hostage by his other nine souls. And nine were stronger than one.

At the Dueling Grounds, Mordred's greatest strength might just become his greatest weakness.

We watched the struggle in awe, and I felt my stomach grumble as I caught a whiff of street food from one of the concessions stands. "I really wish I had grabbed one of those hot dogs," I murmured. "I have a feeling this is going to be a long night."

"Or a very short one," Gunnar growled. I wasn't sure if he was implying we were about to pay dearly for what we had done to Mordred, or if he was making some inner promise that he was going to drag out Mordred's torment for as long as possible.

"Sunflower seed?" Alucard asked, holding out a bag. Gunnar snorted disapprovingly.

Mordred was on his knees now, reaching out at the departing soul, but it had stretched longer as if being forcefully pulled away from him. I was about to extend my hand for some seeds when my spear began to quiver. I clenched it with both hands, frowning at it. It must have sensed the strain of Mordred's torment, and wanted to take the soul for itself. It was called a Souleater, after all. I gripped the haft harder, fighting it for a moment before it calmed. I hadn't even considered my Devourer getting frisky. I let out an uneasy breath.

Yahn was smiling darkly at Mordred, unaware anything had happened with my spear, but Talon, Gunnar, and Alucard, had noticed, and were each frowning at it. They looked away as soon as my forearms had relaxed, certain my struggle was over. Alucard shook a few seeds into my hand, and I popped them in my mouth.

With a crack of power like a distant sniper round, Mordred abruptly collapsed, caught at the last minute by his outstretched arms, leaving him panting on all fours, and we watched as the dark soul was yanked into the very ground, silently screaming and clawing the whole way.

Alucard pointed at Mordred with his bag of sunflower seeds. "Look, Gunnar. A bitch in heat. Go nail it."

Gunnar grinned, his fangs glistening. "Looks like that's my cue, lads," he growled, stalking towards Mordred with his claws out like a roman-Greco wrestling werewolf.

I rolled my shoulders, spit out the shells of my seeds, and tightened my grip on my Devourer. Maybe I wouldn't even need it tonight. We just had to kill Mordred nine more times. Maybe I wouldn't even need the coin hanging against my chest. But as Mordred slowly lifted his head, bloodshot eyes locking on Gunnar...

I wondered if I had chosen enough allies. Because he looked ready to burn the world down. As if he had just spotted Arthur, Merlin, and Morgause laughing at a tea-party on a pleasant summer day.

"Yeah, Gunnar's going to need some help," Yahn said in a growl, shaking glass shards from his stump. Talon's fist tightened on his Eyeless, his eyes briefly darting to my Devourer and then back again uneasily. He had spear envy. I hoped I could fix that, because he just might need a Devourer himself if we couldn't finish this off tonight.

We fanned out behind Gunnar, our faces grimdark.

"Let's steal this bully's lunch money," I said in a low, sadistic tone.

CHAPTER 48

*M*ordred spread his hand in an arc before us, and a fan of ethereal swords suddenly floated before him. I rolled my spear over my knuckles, and shoved it into the holster behind my back, letting the blade peep over my shoulder, bathing me in brighter, red, smoking light the closer I got to Mordred – like a homing beacon.

No one had noticed the holster before, because it had been covered by my satchel, looking like part of the strap. Talon grunted. "Mine can disappear," he bragged under his breath.

I ignored him and called out my fire and ice whips just as Mordred began flinging swords at our faces. Yahn exploded into dragon form, darting ahead of Gunnar and slamming his glass wing into the earth like a barricade, protecting us from the onslaught. Glass shards still dribbled from his other stump, like fresh droplets of blood, and I knew he didn't have very long.

The inbound swords slammed into his wings, sending fissures cracking over the membrane.

I drew deeply on my own magic, funneling most of my power into my fire whip. It began to bloat, spitting droplets of liquid fire from the figurative seams, and I slammed it into the ground beside Yahn, creating a small puddle of liquid fire and an explosion of fiery, liquid sparks.

Talon hissed, batting away the embers, but Alucard merely brushed aside the fire, grunting, looking more upset that he'd been forced to drop his bag of sunflower seeds.

Yahn ignored the droplets of fire sizzling against his glass skin and met my eyes with a questioning look. I held up my fist and mimed punching the ground. He stared down at the puddle of lava, the concept finally dawning on him. He stump-punched the molten fire, hissing and shaking at the... heh, *magma-tude* of pain it no doubt caused him. But the glass wound flared orange and then yellow, cauterizing the stump.

Pain didn't matter tonight. Only victory.

Yahn wilted slightly, snorting through his nostrils, and glancing through his wing – which was translucent, of course. In the confusion, Mordred had disappeared.

Gunnar let out a shout to Yahn that I didn't understand, but Yahn apparently did. He instantly made himself opaque to conceal our own movements, and stretched out his other wing on the ground like a long ramp.

Gunnar was already sprinting at him, jumping onto the glass wing in a crouch. The moment he landed, Yahn catapulted the MANIMAL high up into the air. *Way* too high. Crap. Gunnar belted out the most stereotypical howl I'd heard in a long time, the sound causing the hair on my arms to rise up. It was more like a song than a warning bellow. Maybe he was also upset about Yahn throwing him too high.

Mordred suddenly appeared, rising up in mid-air to catch Gunnar by surprise from below.

Which was when Alucard screamed like a banshee, a blur of crimson-soaked robes and wings of fire, to tackle Mordred mid-air, his flaming claws tearing right *through* Mordred's chest. I knew this because Mordred had twisted at the last moment, giving me an unobstructed view of his back.

Which let me clearly see Alucard's flaming claws holding a sizzling hunk of meat the size of a heart, the organ still pumping blood that sizzled and baked over Alucard's flaming knuckles. Alucard had already kicked Mordred's body away in mid-air, still clutching his charred heart as a soul erupted from the wound like he'd been served an eviction notice, slamming into the ground like a comet. The soul spread its jaws wide, fangs as long as Gunnar's as something began pulling it by the feet into the ground. This soul was fighting back, tearing divots in the ground as it fought the Dueling Grounds, but it was losing – only managing to slow down the inevitable.

All of this had only taken a few seconds, at most. I shouted at the top of my lungs, not daring to turn away from Mordred, but still needing to update the crowd. "FOR THE VAMPIRES!"

Mordred's wound sealed almost instantly – much quicker than his throat had – and Mordred gasped as if given CPR after nearly drowning, back on his feet in an instant, even if his eyes were a little wide around the edges from shock, watching the soul being dragged down to Hell.

Mordred was shaken. He was down to Eight Souls.

No slow, drawn out healing and recovery process this time. Almost as if his Eight remaining Souls had held a meeting and decided that they needed to flex and get this fight over with immediately, rather than suffer the same fates as Brothers Nine and Ten.

I agreed with their plan.

I flung out my icy whip to snag Mordred by the throat, hoping to decapitate him – when my body suddenly jerked to the side, making me stumble and cast my whip wide, cracking the tip right in front of Mordred's face to send an explosion of icy shrapnel into his eyeballs rather than beheading him.

My body shook back and forth, and I noticed the red smoke around me was thicker and denser, the pulsing red light brighter. My Devourer. It was trying to gobble up the soul being yanked down to Hell – only the head and claws visible now.

I reached back and gripped the haft, fighting it. The spear stopped the moment the soul disappeared in the earth. But I could sense it practically humming, now.

Maybe taking the Devourer along had been a bad idea. I'd missed the opportunity to kill Mordred for a third time tonight, damn it.

And the sound of twin gasps let me witness what that only-seconds delay had cost me.

Mordred was wielding twin beams of black power like sonic blasters, and they had connected with Yahn and Alucard, narrowly missing Talon, who I saw had singed his back in his effort to escape the blast.

His fur smoldered, but he ignored the pain, eyes latching onto Mordred.

Yahn's wing had been held up to block the attack, but those black cords – whatever they were – had ripped right through the glass membrane, ripping straight through his heart.

Alucard's face was slack, staring with lifeless eyes at the arm-thick bar of blackness piercing his own chest. Mordred had gotten a two-for-one, taking out both Yahn and Alucard.

But Mordred had forgotten about the *MANIMAL* and gravity.

Gunnar – still falling after Yahn's excessive alley-oop – hammered down into Mordred from above, his massive, lethal jaws closing over Mordred's cranium like a bear trap. The cords of power between Mordred's hands and both Alucard and Yahn's hearts winked out the moment the Alpha Werewolf of St. Louis…

Bit.

Off.

Mordred's.

Head.

Yahn and Alucard collapsed into piles of dust that instantly evaporated to nothing, and I let out a sigh of relief to see proof that the Dueling Grounds was still working – they my friends were alive, back in bed. Mordred hadn't found a way to permanently end them, no matter how strong that magic had been.

Gunnar's momentum sent him rolling away from the twitching carcass of King Arthur's cursed seed. And in that chaotic moment, I learned something about my pal, Gunnar. Something I had never wanted to learn about my best friend.

He was, surprisingly, a swallower, not a spitter.

This felt like one of those complicated moments where a person was forced to make an impossible decision.

I might be obligated to tell Ashley, as a good friend, what her husband got into when she wasn't around…

While I considered that moral dilemma, I shouted out to the crowd. "FOR THE WEREWOLVES!"

The soul flew from Mordred's body right before Mordred's head suddenly reappeared as if by magic. Mordred was already back on his feet as if he'd only taken an annoyed slap at a dinner party. Gunnar licked his lips and charged as the departed Soul Number Three slammed into the earth as if drawn by a magnet.

I had been ready this time, so was already gripping my Devourer with both hands when it began to rattle.

Mordred met Gunnar with bolts of silver lightning like he had a thunderbolt Uzi, but Gunnar's vest had been designed for that, thankfully. Still, he attempted to dodge the majority of them, crouching low and bounding back and forth as he ran.

Talon, using the tactics known to wolves fighting in packs, was already running as fast as he could towards Mordred's exposed back, but he was too far away to really help. His pounding paws didn't even elicit a whisper, thanks to his velvet boots, but the roars from the crowd would have drowned them out even if he'd been tap-dancing.

I threw down a Gateway about ten feet in front of Talon, ripping a dozen additional openings around the clearing within Mordred's immediate line of sight, making him momentarily cease his onslaught against Gunnar. The werewolf kept on running, pouring on the speed, his protective armor nothing but shredded cloth, now.

Mordred's eyes darted from Gateway to Gateway, and I was sure to make the first one reflective, so that the others showed mirror images of Talon sprinting at him from a dozen different doorways.

Talon was only a pace away from leaping through and tearing into the one Gateway I had placed just out of sight behind Mordred's back, when Mordred spun towards me in time to see my whips rushing his direction, only halfway there as he was surrounded by over a dozen different attack fronts to consider.

I'd expected him to Shadow Walk to safety, but he just locked eyes with me.

Without even looking, he flung a hand towards Gunnar – who had just launched himself in the air for another fatal attack – and a whip of silvery black chain slammed into Gunnar and wrapped around his torso.

Then Mordred heaved the werewolf at me, crouching down low at the immense effort of hurtling such a large creature so fast and hard.

As a result, Talon ended up sailing right over Mordred's crouched form, his white Eyeless spear whipping through empty air where Mordred's head had been.

I extinguished my whip and flung up my arms to deflect Gunnar's mass from killing me, because his claws were still outstretched, and friendly slicing was a very likely outcome. At least I could deflect the lethality, if not the force.

I heard a clanging of blades, but all I could see was a giant fucking werewolf filling my line of sight. That's why I noticed the chain suddenly tightening around Gunnar's waist, making my best friend's eye bulge as the lasso ripped him in half.

The upper half of my best friend hit me at an angle, sending me spinning rather than crushed beneath the weight, thanks to Mordred's final jerk of the chain. Gunnar blinked up at me, looking like one of those realistic taxidermy wolves, his lower half simply missing somewhere behind me. Then he evaporated.

I spun at a horrific yowling noise to see Mordred slam Talon into the ground, ignoring a stab wound in his side, obviously not fatal enough to kill him and take out one of his souls. Talon's Eyeless spear tumbled a few paces away, but Talon didn't even hesitate, immediately pouncing back up onto Mordred, tackling him to the ground. Then my kitty began slicing and yowling, snapping his teeth like Mordred had attempted to toss him into a bathtub.

Blood flew with the tenacity of Talon's claws.

I began racing towards them, readying my whips for any opening. They scorched and froze the earth at my feet, hungry for destruction. And the Devourer at my back was vibrating enough to almost rattle my teeth, now, no longer needing a fleeing soul to feel agitated. I ignored it as best I could and put everything I had into my sprint. If I could give Talon a distraction, he might just be able to kill one of Mordred's Seven remaining Souls.

Talon sliced at any strip of flesh within reach, biting deep into Mordred's arms, trying desperately to open an artery in order to give us a moment to catch our breaths before he rose back to life again.

Mordred snarled back at him, and suddenly I saw sparks from Talon's blows, because Mordred had turned on a flavor of Stone Skin – an old favorite of mine that I hadn't used in quite some time – temporarily making his skin as hard as rock.

No longer a danger, he gripped Talon by the throat and shoved him off, sending my other best friend straight at me. Talon stared at me with wide eyes, and we both heard the bloom of power behind him as Mordred let loose another blast of his black cord of power.

CHAPTER 49

$\mathcal{I}$ saw a moment of calm clarity wash over Talon's face as he made some silent decision.

He held up a fist, and his spear was suddenly in it, already twirling. In the chaos of the battle, I'd forgotten he could call it to him at will. He hadn't been using claws and fangs on Mordred because he'd lost his spear. It just wouldn't have done him much good in close combat, so he'd chosen his claws.

Talon slammed the butt of his spear into my shoulder, knocking me sideways like I had been clipped by a car. I fell, tumbling and rolling as Mordred's cord of power ripped right through Talon's chest, killing him instantly.

I groaned, flinging out a hand with one of my whips as Mordred stared victoriously at Talon, not having yet realized I was no longer in the line of fire. He'd thought he got a two-for-one special again.

My whip wrapped around his legs, and I yanked it so hard that he fell horizontal to head-butt the ground with a sickening, bursting watermelon sound.

It was a shame that he was too dead to feel me yanking the whip back with his feet still attached.

He was down Four Souls, leaving him with Six. Leaving *me* with Six to contend with, when it had taken all my allies to murder the first Four. Odds weren't looking good for my chances.

"FOR THE CHANCERY!" I yelled tiredly. Then I scrambled to my feet awkwardly, fighting against the Devourer at my back as Mordred's Fourth Soul was yanked out of the hole in his head. This Soul also clawed at the ground with metaphysical fingers, some unseen force slowly tugging it out of its host.

My Devourer began to jerk and tug harder than before, and I felt it suddenly break free of the sheath. I lashed out as it zipped towards the Soul like a magnet, my fingers managing to grasp the wood near the base, sending me running after it like some crazy person, refusing to let go for fear of the consequences of ingesting one of Mordred's souls. Maybe it would bring the Devourer to life in some way, and become Mordred's to wield, like an extension of himself.

Also, I was pretty sure letting my Devourer consume a Soul when our very environment seemed intent on gobbling down the Souls, wouldn't be very polite. I didn't need my spear picking a food fight with the Dueling Grounds, or whatever cosmic power fueled the place.

Because perhaps that might break some major rule, leaving the Dueling Grounds devoid of that unique ability to temporarily grant immortality – meaning that deaths here could become *real* if I didn't let the Dueling Grounds get its fair share.

The price to play was to let it eat away.

Mordred had climbed to his feet to see me skipping along behind my Devourer like a human torpedo, or a wizard lawn dart.

Blessedly, the Fourth Soul finally disappeared beneath the surface of the ground – leaving me to stand against Mordred and his Six remaining Souls.

My Devourer abruptly halted with the Soul's disappearance. And since I hadn't slowed down, the butt of the spear clocked me in the chin, almost knocking me out cold as my fingers abruptly slid up the haft a foot or more.

I collapsed at Mordred's feet, seeing stars. He glared down at me, angrier than I'd ever seen a man. He gripped my Devourer in one hand, yanking it from me, but inadvertently helping me to my feet. Too bad for him that I had sharpened my hand into a claw. As I was yanked to my feet, I buried my clawed fist into his gut.

Unfortunately, I missed any vital organs, merely causing him a great deal of discomfort and, dare I say, agony.

He shoved me away, gasping as my fist left his stomach, revealing a hole almost big enough to see through. He still held my Devourer, but he was wheezing from the injury I had given him.

I met his gaze steadily, shaking off the last of my starry vision. "I've taken four souls from you, on behalf of the Dragons, the Werewolves, the Vampires, and the Chancery…" I said, loud enough for everyone in the audience to hear. "But I think I'll take the rest for myself. I am a King, after all… We can call it a tax."

Mordred grunted, and then slowly began to straighten. I frowned, staring down at his stomach wound, and watched in horror as it began to repair itself. Of course. If given time, he could heal. The only reason the other attacks had worked was because they had been instant kills. But my attack… well, it hadn't been fatal. Just a last-second, opportunistic reaction on my part.

He still had Six Souls left. Damn it.

Mordred hefted my spear, his wound now almost fully healed. "Let's make things interesting, Temple." Before I could respond, he spun, and hurled my Devourer as hard as he could.

If you're wondering, that was about a few hundred yards.

And straight into the Dark Lands beyond the ring of torches.

Asterion bellowed in outrage, stomping into the ring, leaving a very furious-looking Midas on the sidelines, clenching his fists. I was pretty sure it wasn't about lost revenue for taking the fight out of the ring where the spectators were. Pretty sure… Almost sure…

Asterion was panting, his shoulders quivering. "The fight stays in the ring. *Nothing* goes beyond the torches. Worse than death lives out there—"

Mordred grabbed Asterion by the nose-ring and slammed his snout down into his knee with a sickening crunch.

The crowd gasped in disbelief, but I didn't have time to tattle on him for punching the referee, because Mordred had already grabbed me by the shirt, yanking me close. "I'll count to ten, and then, ready or not, here I come," he hissed.

Then he hurled me out into the air like he had with my Devourer, straight into the Dark Lands beyond, and probably just as far away as he had thrown my spear. I heard him cackling uproariously over the confused shouts of the crowd.

And I could also clearly hear each number Mordred cried out as I crossed the demarcation line of torches.

As I crossed that fiery line of safety, my ears abruptly popped, and the air felt thicker – greasier, somehow. The residents were eerily silent, as if waking from a nap. Or acknowledging something even more dangerous waking from a long slumber and giving that thing the first opportunity to welcome the new tourist – me.

After that polite pause, a cacophony erupted. Growls, shrieks, caws, roars, and strange clicking noises of some beings with many legs filled my ears as I watched a smudged, charcoal landscape rise up to meet me.

I wrapped myself up into a ball, encasing myself in Stone Skin, laying it on as thick as possible as I anticipated contact with the Dark Lands. Where Grimm had lived for... he hadn't ever told me how long, actually. But I was betting it had been quite a while.

Mordred reached *ten* the moment before I hit the ground. I bounced and rolled off into a set of bushes I couldn't quite see. I stopped, took a deep breath, and realized I couldn't see because I'd had my eyes closed.

"READY OR NOT, HERE I COME!" Mordred's voice boomed, sounding far off, as if heard from underwater.

I jumped to my feet, blinking rapidly. The darkness slowly began to materialize into vague silhouettes, and I let out a sigh of relief. I could see, kind of. Even a little was better than nothing. I needed to move, now. As quietly as I could, I began to jog, cautious to watch out for any low-hanging branches.

Or tentacles, if that was a thing here.

I heard an impact a short distance away and knew the hunt had begun.

Mordred had landed.

I fingered the coin hanging from my necklace, considering. *Last resort*, I told myself.

Mordred hadn't seemed remotely concerned about the necklace, choosing instead to throw my Devourer here into the Dark Lands. Was there a reason? Did he fear my Devourer more than me donning my Horseman's Mask?

Judging by my trajectory, I couldn't have landed too far away from my spear. I released the coin, focusing intently as I moved. Objects were beginning to shine with an almost dull, silvery hue. Like a very faint night vision, and I wondered if it was my own power, or if this place was giving me a slim fighting chance.

Because... if the place was as bad as Asterion made it sound, the inhabitants were pretty lonely. And wasting their only opportunity in a while to get in some good, old-fashioned hunting shouldn't be squandered. *Give the prey a fighting chance, let it at least see what was coming to rip off its face before gobbling it down alive.*

Yeah, that sounded about right.

And it really didn't matter why I was beginning to see better. I would use it or I would die. Because out here death was very real, and probably very dreadful. Mordred had evened the playing field. We could both lose our Souls, now.

I stared into the dull, chromatic world, and noticed a faint, red-flicker in the distance. Was that... my Devourer? I swept the land but saw no other source of light. It *had* to be.

I huddled low, ignoring Mordred's laughter from behind me, and planned out my route.

Preferably, my route would avoid the three skulking silhouettes of oddly-shaped, bipedal, rhino ostriches bobble-heading in the rocky area about fifty feet away. I still wore my Stone Skin and hoped it would be enough to keep me alive a bit longer. This had the cost of making me louder when I moved, but for now, I would keep it.

Because it might also serve as camouflage if I had to lay down in a pile of boulders, huddled in a badass fetal position.

The area was silent, all the creatures on high alert that the dinner bell had been rung, and it was no longer time to fight each other. It was time to sneak up on fresh prey and get some new flavor of din-dins. And to do that before their neighbors, they needed to hunt and stalk, not roar and charge.

I scooped up a handful of gravel, then another, and hurled one to the left of the creatures. The sound echoed loudly, and the creatures spun, still remaining silent. Then I threw the other, and they promptly darted after it.

Mordred also raced past me, feet pounding as he sought out the source of the sound, which had probably resembled a big, blind idiot scrambling up a gravely hill.

I remembered the time I had cow-tipped Asterion, how I had used a sensory muffling spell to mute the sound of my movements. I did that now, careful to keep an eye out for Mordred. I didn't want him sensing me using magic and spinning around to notice he had just run past his prey.

But as I heard the bobblehead rhino-ostriches suddenly erupt in ear-piercing squawks, I grinned. Mordred had other things to worry about for now, but I knew with his Six remaining Souls, it wouldn't hold him back for long.

I thought about using my Fae magic and instantly felt the dull throb of a headache blooming. I changed course, thinking of my usual wizard's magic, and it faded away. I let out a relieved breath. That would have been the end, having a flashback here. But what other minor wizard's spell could I use to give me an advantage?

And I recalled the first time I had met Callie Penrose. We'd been breaking into a house and she'd casually shown me a variant of illusion that wasn't Fae magic. A way to make you appear more like a chromatic smear, like a charcoal smudge.

Which… was exactly like this place. I grunted silently, shaking my head. Again, with the old memories.

They say you never forget your first time. Maybe they were onto something. Whoever *they* were.

I cast the spell over me, listening to the crashing sounds of Mordred's confrontation with the locals. Either they were chasing him, or he was chasing them, but it meant he was too busy to notice another quick spell. That was three spells I was trying to maintain simultaneously, and I knew it would drain me very fast. I needed to hurry.

I turned to my right and silently sprinted towards my Devourer flashing in the distance. It was my only shot. Get the Devourer.

Get back to the Dueling Grounds.

Or things would end here, in this cold, forgotten place.

The Dark Lands.

CHAPTER 50

*A*fter ten minutes of no attacks, I was twitching at every sound. I'd been careful, going out of my way anytime I ran across the local predators. I was content to determine they were all horrifyingly deadly, and that I didn't need to count their scales or check their eye-colors to confirm my hypothesis had been right.

So, every time I saw something with a pulse, I slowly retraced my foot-steps, and found a new path onward. Confronting anything would only attract Mordred. Time seemed to move quickly here. Or more slowly, I couldn't quite tell. Two minutes into my walk, and even though I was covered in Stone Skin, I began to sweat. It was that nasty, muggy, summer heat I was so familiar with in Missouri – feeling like I had strolled into a steam room by mistake, my lungs instantly heavier, the air thicker, pregnant with water, making it harder to breathe.

Then again, random blasts of frigid, subarctic air would often strike out of nowhere as I made my slow, measured walk through the stilted trees and boulders of the Dark Lands. Those cold fronts were so potent they even covered the ground in thick hoarfrost, which made sneaking about difficult. I paid very close attention to my steps, constantly moving, but not running. Tempting fate by crossing directly over a slight incline was now potentially fatal. If one of those frigid blasts struck while I was halfway up, I might find myself suddenly on a slip-and-slide.

This forced me to take the long way around hills, boulders, and rock walls. The land was still smudged charcoal, but other than the locals, it was pretty uneventful. And since I avoided the locals at all costs, it was almost *entirely* uneventful.

But back to the time thing.

The first minute I'd walked in this place, no distance at all seemed to have changed between me and the crisp red flame marking my Devourer. Then the next two minutes, I was suddenly halfway there. I didn't spend too much time breaking down these anomalies – analyzing them would only get me killed faster if something found me while I was recording the Scientific Method.

It was Caveman time.

See pretty shiny thing, acquire pretty shiny thing. Use heavy club on anything in my way.

I had finally made my way up to a clearing that I was almost certain held my Devourer, judging by the reddish hue to the surrounding boulders.

Instead of rushing in blindly, I wedged myself into a crevice between a large, split boulder, to debate my next steps. The last hundred feet or so of my walk had been tricky. I hadn't run into anything, but I'd heard a whole lot. Dozens of predators lurking around me, waiting like spiders near a light fixture outside at dusk. Just waiting for a stupid fly to… go after the shiny thing.

I grunted, rethinking my caveman mentality.

So, I knew this area was being watched, and that the moment I grabbed the Devourer – the only crisp light in this whole place – I may as well be sounding an alarm, letting every monster present know exactly where I was.

I hadn't heard from Mordred for some time now – ever since he'd learned the error in calling out my name one too many times, and subsequently been attacked by a clicking, boulder-sized monstrosity. The thing had chased him a long way before I heard an unearthly death cry.

It hadn't sounded human, so I was betting Mordred had won.

I was thankful I'd kept up my spells, but they were taxing me. I wasn't sure if it was simple exhaustion after the fight in the Dueling Grounds, or if it was something about the place itself draining my magic.

Point was, I couldn't keep it up for much longer. And I still needed to find my way back before someone killed me to death. I needed to be sneaky.

I'd momentarily considered making a Gateway or Shadow Walking, but had quickly dismissed it. One, I didn't know the potential repercussions for opening a Gateway here – if it would be a signal fire for every creature within a mile.

Secondly, I had no idea what I would appear next to. What if I Shadow Walked into a den of monsters?

And magic here was a greasy thing. I could feel a thin layer of grime over each spell, like it was smudging my soul. Making me more like the landscape. I had a very bad feeling that using that level of magic here would do something permanent to me. Something I wouldn't like. As I thought about it, I'd seen something like the smudged scenery once before.

In Hell. That probably meant something. But Anubis could have scooped us both up if this was his realm. So maybe something about the two places was just similar, yet also different.

They were both big supporters of death and scary things.

I heard something run past, sounding like a galloping horse, but it was going the wrong direction, so I let out a breath. I needed to hurry.

I poked my head out of the rock and finally glanced into the area where I hoped Devourer was. And I almost fell over.

A giant skeleton sat before me, a spear the size of a bus piercing his ribcage where his heart would have been. It had to have been forty feet tall when standing. But the bones were black, and thankfully brittle, implying it had died long ago.

I swept the rest of the area, checking for traps or any signs of life. Nothing but the dead giant and a couple tall, thin tree trunks, all bathed in the smoky red glow of my Devourer's gem.

I ducked back into my crevice, and briefly imagined Mordred doing the same from the opposite side of the clearing. I almost let out a faint laugh as I visualized us each looking into the clearing when the other was ducking. Instead, I sucked in a breath and stepped out, slowly stalking into the clearing, my eyes alert. The canopy of the two trees slowly materialized into a stork-like body, and a ten-foot-long beak. I almost let out a scream, realizing they weren't tree trunks, but *legs* supporting a *body* that was about five feet over my head.

I also hadn't run screaming.

Because the creature was looking *right at me*, beak slowly swiveling back and forth. I froze and it hesitated, turning to me with more intent. My heart thundered in my chest at a ridiculous thought, and I resumed my slow walk. The creature immediately lost interest, and I almost collapsed in relief. Could it be possible?

It could see things standing still more clearly but had trouble with moving objects.

And judging by how it kept glancing over at the glowing Devourer, it also had an interest in light.

Which meant taking it away was off the table. So was halting to think about a new plan.

So, I continued slowly walking between the legs of the creature, careful not to touch it. Stopping meant death, but it was beyond unnerving to be weaving in and out of the legs of a twenty-foot-tall stork, all the while imagining that ten-foot-long beak stabbing into my spine.

I made two circuits of my slow walk, feeling ridiculous. This thing might not sense motion, but I knew plenty of other things here did. What if they decided to check up on their newly acquired night light?

I made my decision. I could always risk Shadow Walking back to my hiding place in that boulder, or back to the Dueling Grounds. Grab and dash. I carefully watched my steps so I could reach the Devourer and dislodge it without stopping my walking.

My fingers latched onto the wooden staff, and I felt my breath catch. It was vibrating like a tuning fork. Was that an indicator that Mordred was nearby, or just an indicator of how angry it was for missing its earlier meals?

I ran into my first problem when the spear didn't dislodge easily. I let it go to continue my circuit, because even that momentary hesitation had caused the DemonStork to whip its head my way, narrowly missing me with its beak. That close, I got a very personal whiff of its scent. Like moldy berries, of all things. I continued walking, holding my breath as I realized it meant walking directly past its eye, which was now at my head level.

I was only inches away from being able to reach out and touch the melon-sized eyeball, but other than sniff at the air, it didn't so much as notice me. Why did it sniff the air if it couldn't sense something right in front of it? I realized I didn't quite care. Out of direct sight, I circled back for another pass at the Devourer, feeling sweat dripping down my forearms.

I readied myself to try a lot harder, a lot quicker this time, hoping that a few attempts would loosen it enough to tug it free. It was firmly wedged in the giant's pelvis bone, which would have been hilarious at literally any other moment of my life.

My Devourer had kabobbed a giant's family jewels.

I took a slow, measured breath, and my hand latched onto the spear again.

I gave it a hard, forceful yank, and was startled that it came free.

Along with the *entire gods-damned skeleton* of the giant.

The bones crumbled into gravel the size of my head, pouring down towards me in a roaring avalanche of sound, dust, and debris, sending the DemonStork to flapping its wings and cawing furiously as its head darted back and forth like a snake. I realized the potential for an errant bone to pound me into mush or knock me down – pinning me in place, where I had no doubt the DemonStork would finally be able to spot me, now motionless and holding his favorite night light. However, if I tried to keep *walking*, my balance would be off – an easier target for going down if a bone hit me.

But if I stayed *still*, the creature would definitely see me.

So… I stared up at the cascading mountain of bone, planted the spear into the earth so the creature might assume nothing had changed…

And made the rest of my body mimic one of those inflatable Sky Dancer stick figures you see outside shopping centers. You know, the ones that look like they're doing their best seaweed interpretive dance.

I dipped and rolled my hips, flapping my arms slowly, trying to keep in steady, constant motion so the DemonStork didn't spear me. While doing this, I stared up at the crashing, thundering bones, prepared to dodge and duck as needed.

It was a very complicated dance.

Which lets you imagine how surprised I was to find Mordred slipping and sliding, tumbling ass over heels down the pile of bones, having been hiding inside the giant's skull – revealed only after it toppled and cracked open on the giant's ribcage.

CHAPTER 51

We locked eyes – him rolling, grunting and flipping down a waterfall of bones, and me doing my seaweed dance, both feeling properly embarrassed, I would imagine. At least mine was a choice. He just looked like a bumbling idiot, where I was creating *art*.

The DemonStork flapped its wings again, squawking angrily, but seemed appeased to find his night light still in place. Lucky me, it even lowered its head to stare directly into the light from inches away, its beak dragging across my forearm in the process. I held my breath, struggling to keep up my seaweed dance while keeping my arm rock-solid, ready to Shadow Walk in an instant.

This gave Mordred a moment to slowly, smoothly scramble to his feet, gently kicking free of his pile of bones. We locked eyes again, and he grinned at my body-rocking art. Then he began mimicking my seaweed dance. I scowled, and realized we were now having a *couple's* synchronized seaweed dance.

Mine looked better. He was only dragging me down.

The DemonStork hopped back angrily, probably offended by Mordred's unrealistic seaweed dance, and flapped its wings, buffeting a few frigid blasts of air at us. And since I was now in the unique position to look up as it stretched out its wings, I noticed the underside of its feathers were like smoking ice. Had that been... the *source* of the frigid blasts I had experienced while walking here? How many of these fucking nightmares had I walked past without realizing it? Like a typical predator mammal, I had only focused on eye-level and below, never considering an assault from *above*.

But here, there were giants. And DemonStorks.

The DemonStork let out a purring coo, and promptly turned its back on us. I let out a sigh of relief, warily noting the eagerness in Mordred's eyes.

Then I realized something. I must have dropped my illusion spell, because he was staring right at me. When had I done that? Now that I thought about it, I realized I'd dropped the sensory deafening spell also. Because… my magic was almost entirely *gone*. My subconscious had shut it down sometime around spotting the DemonStork, likely sensing that it wouldn't do me any good, and needing to conserve energy.

I was inwardly terrified that I had apparently done this without *thinking*. With so many new, strange powers knocking on my door over the years, I should have been used to strange things like this, but this time it only made me concerned.

I'd think about it later, if we survived.

I was still doing my seaweed dance, staring down Mordred and the DemonStork when I saw him take a smooth casual step closer to me. My sphincter puckered in alarm, and then I saw the DemonStork lift its rear feathers.

And got a birds-eye view of it winking at me with its butt cannon.

Before I could move, it erupted like a mini geyser, and fluorescent green shit jettisoned right between Mordred and I, effectively making a small creek of DemonStork super-shit.

I say super-shit, because it smelled like rotten, acidic swamp sludge, singeing my nose hairs. And it was eating away at the rock, pitting the stone and pile of bones as it sizzled like an egg on a skillet.

Mordred was effectively trapped by the creek of super-shit. Sure, he could try and jump over it, but he would risk being harpooned and eaten by the DemonStork, only to become the next bout of fecal matter in the Dark Lands' Circle of Life.

I would have been fine with that option.

Before he could make up his mind on whether his remaining souls would protect him, I took my own gamble, and began slowly walking back-wards, smiling acidly at him as I kept the DemonStork in my peripheral vision. She squawked loudly and let loose another super-soaker blast of neon feces, narrowly missing Mordred's body this time – saved only by his sudden devotion to the seaweed dance. I almost burst out laughing, but then the creature began following the light, taking its attention from Mordred's predicament.

Well, shit.

I felt like that actor in Jurassic Park carrying the road flare to distract the T-Rex.

The DemonStork squawked angrily, slowly following the light, and giving Mordred the chance to leap over the acidic crap stream.

He also began to follow after me in a casual strut, grinning widely. It was probably the most ridiculous slow-speed pursuit in the history of the world. The DemonStork crushed anything in its path, simply obliterating it under its scaled bird's feet, much like Baba Yaga's House.

We kept this up for some time, and I took note of every time the DemonStork reared up and cawed at some unseen creature, warning it away. Wisely – and thankfully – they listened. Part of me considered how scary some of the local monsters I'd seen were, and that they were all terrified of this DemonStork.

And that, judging by those arctic bursts of wind, I had apparently walked by quite a few of these DemonStorks without realizing it. I shivered involuntarily, watching both the monster and Mordred following me like I was pulling them on a leash.

I needed to get back to the Dueling Grounds.

Sure, I could have used the Tiny Ball in my pocket to get back home – but I would be exhausted and worn out if I did that. Then Mordred would knock on my door, and likely obliterate me. Or I might be lucky enough to bring the DemonStork along with me, forced to tell Dean I had brought home another stray.

No.

I had the Devourer now. I had Mordred right where I wanted him... figuratively speaking.

I just needed to change the battleground.

I studied the DemonStork as I continued walking backwards, hoping she wasn't walking me towards a den of monsters who knew to walk slowly in her view. Maybe I was like the Pied Piper, gathering an army of monsters to follow me, all waiting for that singular moment when the DemonStork wasn't looking to tackle me with a blade to the heart, and then slowly walk away with my corpse, leaving my Devourer for whoever wanted it – that would be Mordred.

So, I gauged my remaining magic, ignored the almost instant pang of depression it gave me, and ripped a strip of my shirt off. The DemonStork cocked her head, splattering another boulder with her acidic sphincter, but continued after me with barely a pause at the sound of ripping cloth. Mordred was staring at me with cold, calculating eyes.

I placed the strip of fabric in my teeth, slowly lowering the Devourer so I could let go of the fabric and douse the light. Mordred's eyes widened in realization and he attempted to pick up his pace. Thankfully, this caught the DemonStork's attention, answering my inner question of whether moving *fast* attracted her the same as standing *still*. I had assumed it would, because natural selection would have likely culled her from their VIP list if not.

Being unable to spot something running and screaming in the opposite direction would really hinder her chances as an apex predator.

I quickly formed a ball of liquid fire and sent it screaming at Mordred's chest. He opened his mouth in disbelief at the weak attack and the fire pelted him, splattering over his torso in a wash of flame. I immediately unclenched my teeth, dropping the fabric over the Devourer's stone.

DemonStork shrieked in outrage, darting a beady eye my way, but not spotting the light from the stone, her attention fixated back on Mordred, who was slowly attempting to put out the fire before he burned alive. DemonStork squawked unhappily, obviously sensing the difference in the quality of the light, and suddenly erupted in a full circle shit show, blasting her digested green eggs and ham in every direction.

Thankfully, I was already ducking around a corner and running for all I was worth, no longer caring about subtlety. Because less than twenty feet away, I noticed the flame of torches that marked the line to the Dueling Grounds.

A thought hit me, then. That the creatures here were obviously scared of fire, or else they would have crossed over the line of torches long ago.

Which meant…

I could have just run around slinging fire from the onset, and it might have worked out.

I told myself that was ridiculous, and nothing could be that easy.

Then I heard the DemonStork shrill in agony and sensed the giant pillar of fire behind me as Mordred lit her up.

"Wizard's fire, Nate. Fucking wizard's fire. It's only, like, the *first spell you ever learned…*" I snarled, sprinting as fast as I could manage, making my way to the line of torches.

Something wrapped around my ankle and yanked me from my feet, sending me crashing to the ground where I banged my head harder than I would have liked. I saw the Devourer skittering across the rock, the strip of fabric concealing its light falling free, basically shooting up a warning beacon for any nearby monsters. Then again, the pyre of flaming Demon-Stork would hopefully catch more attention than my Devourer. I stared up, dazed, seeing the line of torches was only ten feet away, now, as I listened to the sound of slow, measured boots striding up behind me.

CHAPTER 52

I groaned, climbing to my feet as I tried to clear my head. I searched my surroundings for any sign of nearby creatures, or anything I could use as a distraction to make it the last ten feet to the safety of the Dueling Grounds. Unfortunately, I found nothing helpful. I swept the area one last time, Mordred's boots growing closer, and I saw something strange – a very familiar feather lying on the ground. And it wasn't old. My heart dropped into my stomach in horror.

I glanced up sharply at the ring of torches, and saw the crowd of onlookers standing on top of the bleachers, watching in utter disbelief as my Devourer's red light caught their attention. The newbies were probably wondering if this was just a normal night out at the Fight Club.

Asterion looked murderous, fists flexed at his sides, as if he was considering charging in here to bitch slap Mordred. Then again, he was a bull, and my Devourer did have a strobing red light on the tip, so...

I was ten feet away from life. If Mordred killed me there, I would wake up in bed at Chateau Falco.

But if I let him kill me *here*, it was for *real*. Not only was I concerned about my *own* life, but for all the families of Freaks in St. Louis. Mordred would bootstrap them into his army, sending them marching off to Fae and Camelot.

Mordred walked out of the darkness, chuckling wickedly. Right between me and the torches.

Me and the families of St. Louis.

Me and Life.

I felt like I was peering through the veil of death at the land of the living. So close, but so far away. And I was too drained to do anything about it. I felt the coin around my neck and shivered at the thought. I wouldn't go down without a fight, but I was terrified of what would happen if I used it. Did I want the job, or not? It would ultimately come down to the point where I was obligated to take it, my own feelings be damned, because there was no way I was dying without giving it my everything.

"No more clever little games, Temple. Whatever happens out here is permanent," Mordred taunted.

I nodded woodenly, thinking desperately. He was right. Out here, things were permanent. And I now had a very good reason to be concerned.

Or…

I locked eyes with Mordred, and then studied the darkness all around us with a regretful sigh. "Bet you can't make a rainbow," I finally said. A sudden blast of wind decided to whip at my shirt, buffeting my hair. We both froze, checking the area – not forgetting to look up this time – to make sure it wasn't some nearby threat. But nothing else stirred. The creatures were all likely searching the area near the bonfire that smelled suspiciously like chicken.

"Excuse me?" Mordred asked, bewildered.

"We're in a place that seems to reject light." I drew deep on my dwindling magic, letting him see how much it cost me, and that I was running on fumes. A weak, pale rainbow limped to life, dimming rapidly as my power flickered. Then it just winked out with a pathetic puff. The effort left me wheezing and seeing stars. "I'm spent, man," I admitted. "But you have to admit, I got in a few good punches. Made you do a stupid dance. Least you could do is give me something pretty to see before you finish it."

He stared at me, eyes checking me for some deception. But it wasn't a lie. I *was* beat.

"Just make me a fucking rainbow, bitch," I muttered, angrily, prodding him.

Mordred rolled his eyes. "Fine. I'll grant your childish dying wish," he grumbled, seeing I really was as exhausted as I claimed. To be fair, he was, too, especially after lighting up that DemonStork. But he had way more reserves with his remaining Six Souls. He flung his hand out, and made a faint, pastel rainbow, but it puffed out almost as quickly as mine had.

"*Lame*," I said, drawing the word out as I scuffed my boot on the ground. "Make a *real* rainbow. I want to see if, by *yourself*, you're really as powerful as people seem to think. That you're worth losing to. Shout, 'I'm Roy G. Biv, bitch!' as you do it."

He blinked incredulously. "Why on Earth would I do something so stupid?"

I shrugged tiredly. "Humor me. You've got me dead to rights. Give me a laugh as I walk to the hangman's noose." When he still hesitated, I rolled my eyes. "Just like I thought. You're nothing without your precious Nine— oops… *Six* Souls. Without them, you're just a punk-ass, no-talent wizard with daddy issue—"

Mordred snarled, both at the challenge, and at the ridiculousness of the request. "I'll show you the biggest rainbow you've ever seen," he spat, straining as he bloomed with power. I swallowed, realizing two things.

Mordred was no pushover as a wizard – much more powerful than me, and I had considered myself pretty fucking impressive, as did many other wizards I had met in my life.

He was also pretty incredible at making majestic rainbows.

A giant blast of color screamed into existence, about as vibrant and profound as any colors I'd ever seen. Almost like I was seeing raw colors for the first time in my life. Mordred poured power into it like he was holding up the world – having no fear he would deplete himself for my execution. He had his Six Souls for that. The land tried to eat at his rainbow, popping and cracking at the surface to dribble liquid paint in fat dollops on the ground. Mordred poured even more power into it, panting as he fought to make the rainbow brighter, to reduce the pitting on the surface.

He shot me a look, gritting his teeth smugly. Then he shouted at the top of his lungs. "I'M ROY G. BIV, BITCH!" The words echoed in both the Dark Lands and the Dueling Grounds not far away. And then he laughed at the ridiculousness of it all.

I was grinning from ear-to-ear, laughing as well, eyes wondrous as I realized I was probably sitting beneath the biggest, shiniest rainbow the world had ever seen. It was a really good way to die, all things considered.

Mordred finally let go, panting as he placed his hands on his knees, shaking his head. He laughed tiredly, before straightening. "That has to be the brightest rainbow the world has ever seen. Satisfied?"

I began a slow clap, smiling. "Christ, man. I couldn't make one half that bright. You're like, the king of rainbows, or something." I mimed worshipping him, and then sat down with a pained grunt or two, utterly exhausted.

He grunted, watching as the rainbow slowly paled, still refusing to die. "I'll admit, you gave me a scare back there. I underestimated you." He dipped his head slightly.

I shrugged, setting my hands down behind me to lean on them with a dramatic sigh. "Thanks, Roy G. Biv," I replied with a resigned wink.

An icy blade suddenly winked into existence in his hand as he began walking closer. He was smiling at the stupid nickname, chuckling to himself. "This has to be the most bizarre dying wish—"

My unicorn hit him like an airplane hitting a seagull on take-off, complete with an explosion of what seemed to be two-billion black and red peacock feathers – just like the familiar lone feather I had found on the ground a minute ago. The one that had scared the hell out of me, because Grimm was *supposed* to be watching over Alex at Chateau Falco.

Grimm's gnarled, thorny horn ripped into Mordred's stomach so fast and hard and close to me that I could almost feel it in my *own* gut, whipping my clothes and hair about at the sheer force of impact.

The pair kept right on going, shattering through the ring of torches leading to the Dueling Grounds.

And then through the row of nearby bleachers, sending the bystanders crashing and flailing to the ground as the bleachers collapsed into piles of jagged, broken timber. The spectators screamed and shouted, no longer having fun as the errant torches caught the edges of the wrecked bleachers alight with flame.

I ignored their cries and the sudden concussive explosions hammering into the Dueling Grounds. Grimm did that sometimes when he was feeling particularly frisky – riding black bolts of lightning around an area in the same way a dog has the urge to suddenly sprint about like a lunatic after dropping a deuce on the lawn.

And all the while, he was thrashing his horn, tearing Mordred's gut open wider – I hoped.

I stumbled to my feet, eager to take advantage of the opportunity

Grimm had provided to get back to the relative safety of the Dueling Grounds, where I couldn't really die.

"I came in like a wreeeecccccking balllll..." a familiar voice sang from behind a nearby boulder. A young man in the prime of his life strolled into view, scooping up my Devourer with one foot and catching it. I stared at Alex, all the blood draining from my face as I recalled the implied warning I'd heard from Quinn's potted house plant.

It had been talking about this moment. Right now. Grimm had taken Alex here, and now he was in the Dark Lands, where he could actually *die*.

"What are you *doing* here? You were supposed to stay at Chateau Falco where it's safe!" I shouted, jogging over to him, snatching away the Devourer, and spinning him around, desperate to get him back to the Dueling Grounds. To relative safety. I shoved him, ignoring his attempts to argue. "Do you have *any* idea how *dangerous* it is out here?" I hissed, almost incoherent with anger – anger birthed from my fear for his safety. I shoved him harder, both of us running now, as Alex still tried to get a word in edge-wise. I rolled right over him, shouting. "I didn't even want you *near* the Fight Club tonight, let alone out *here* where you can actually *die*!" I roared, shoving him through what remained of the ring of torches Grimm had destroyed.

We crossed the line of safety, and I let out a sigh of relief. But I didn't relent, shoving Alex onward, harder this time, eventually knocking him sprawling on his face as he tripped over some of the bleacher wreckage from Grimm's path of destruction. I placed my hands on my hips, ignoring the groans and cries of the attendees who were trying to claw their way out from the debris. Many of them saw me, cried out in terror, and ran without looking back. I even ignored Grimm's tirade of imaginative curses as he slammed Mordred into the base of the tree, pinning him into the trunk. Mordred was coming out of an apparent daze, and punching Grimm in the head weakly as Grimm thrashed back and forth, tearing the gut wound wider as Mordred tried to draw on his Six Souls to heal him faster than Grimm could gore him.

I stepped over Alex, snarling down at him as I made my way towards Mordred. "When we get home, you're grounded, Mister—" I cut off abruptly, realizing I'd been rambling on autopilot, repeating what my mother had told me about seventy-thousand times.

Then I tensed as I heard a heart-wrenching neighing sound.

CHAPTER 53

I looked up as Mordred grabbed Grimm by the neck, his arms suddenly consisting of vines and roots as thick as tree branches. His legs were firmly rooted to the ground – literally – like two tree trunks. My eyes widened, impressed, despite the situation. He was using some hardcore earth magic to give him the strength to stave off Grimm. I watched, too far away to help, as he heaved, picking up Grimm by the neck, and then tossed him across the ring, destroying the *Carl's Heels* sign.

He noticed I was back within the safety perimeter of the Dueling Grounds – where he could no longer permanently kill me – and his eyes flashed with outrage, his jaws clenching hard enough to actually shatter his own teeth.

"Your turn, Ruin!" Alex shouted at the top of his lungs, interrupting the wizardly Wild West stare-off. "For Kai! For Falco! For Temple! FOR YOUR FAMILY!"

Mordred and I both rounded on Alex, wondering what in the blazes he was shouting about.

And that's when a fuming, crackling, sizzling cloud of pure, celestial piss and vinegar drifted out of the Dark Lands with a loud *burp*.

"That's what I get for eating my food too fast. Now, I have an upset tummy," B growled, bolts of lightning blasting into the ground beneath him as he stretched, growing darker and wilder.

Except… judging by the look of anticipation on Alex's face, *Ruin* was my Baby Beast's fancy new name.

It might say something about me that I momentarily flushed with pride that my kind-of-son had named his first kind-of-pet. Just like I had done with my first kind-of-pet, Talon the Devourer.

Mordred shot a look at Alex, frowning briefly, likely wondering who the fuck he was. Alex grinned back at him. "My Thunder Buddy is about to ruin your whole night, bub."

I burst out laughing.

Which didn't make Mordred any happier, but he was soon distracted by Ruin. The Beast formerly known as B looked to be searching for a mosh pit to break up with his own addition of excessive violence – the world's angriest little thundercloud. His form morphed to that of what I could only describe as a giant Pac-Man, his jaws stretching wide, full of stone, needle-like teeth as long as I was tall. Then those teeth began to grow longer and sharper with new offshoots of spikes and needles growing off the original fangs, like eons worth of crystallization happening in the span of seconds – enough time for him to close the distance to Mordred, unaffected by the blasts of power Mordred was hurling at him like a fireworks display.

Ruin didn't waste time on theatrics or witty repertoire. Neither did he seem concerned as the bolts of power flew right through him without any effect.

He just gobbled up Mordred in one cobra-like lunge, his teeth gouging through some of the earth and tree, causing a thump of twenty trillion toothpicks and clods of sod to explode outwards. I barely threw out a weak shield in time, using mere fumes of my magic, to protect Alex and I from getting splintered to death.

Most of Ruin's teeth shattered on impact, and all was silent for a few heartbeats.

Then the tree began to fall, toppling down in slow motion with a long, drawn out *cracking* sound. Those spectators who had paused their escape to stare in awe at first the unicorn, and then the belching, talking thundercloud suddenly resumed their mass exodus, screaming and running to get out of the way, or ducking into any semblance of shelter they could find. They didn't look half as scared as they should have been. Likely, they considered themselves safe, here at the Dueling Grounds – that if they happened to get squashed by the giant fucking tree, they knew they would wake up safe-and-sound back at home.

Immortal and long-lived types have a strange fascination with danger and carnage. Always pushing the envelope to see how close they could get to kissing the Reaper on the nose without letting him grab them by the cojones.

However, some instincts are hard to break. When you see a massive tree falling right at your face, you're probably going to run rather than give yourself a motivational pep-talk that it won't *really* hurt that badly. The tree thundered down into the last set of bleachers, and I saw a beautiful piece of knitted fabric whip up into the air. It said *TEAM TEMPLE* on it, right below a cute little recreation of my family crest. I couldn't help myself. I began to laugh, running a hand through my hair as I watched it fall to the ground only a few paces away from me.

That cute little old vampire had knitted me a doily!

I knew I'd liked her for a reason.

I waited anxiously for Mordred to come back to life, for one of his souls to by torn from his body.

Nothing happened.

Had we just done it? Had B just ended the battle with one freaking bite? One move?

I felt my Devourer quivering, jolting, and almost seeming to whine, but still, nothing happened outwardly to B or Mordred.

I turned to look out at the remaining faces, spotting Midas, Asterion, Baron Skyfall, the two Chancery members who had been with Alvara, and Drake and Cowan. They stood well back, but obviously had no intentions of leaving before the show was over. To bear witness to the true, full story of what *had* to qualify as the craziest Fight Night ever. Many of them looked dazed, cut up, or even sported cringeworthy wounds. The crappy part was that if they were injured, the only way to make sure they didn't *stay* injured was to kill them, *here*.

That way the Dueling Grounds could send them home safe and sound without a scratch.

And I was fresh out of magic to make those friendly executions quick, which meant I would have to use a sword or something, because defeating Mordred wasn't enough for one night. And it would have to be me, because

I sure as hell wasn't going to let Alex do the honors. Have his memory of his first kills be of his friends and allies.

Even though it wouldn't be *real*, the *memory* would be. And nightmares are born in memory.

I helped Alex to his feet, brushing off his shoulders stiffly like a mother hen. No, a cock of the walk. "We'll talk about this later," I told him in my dad voice. "But... thank you."

He smiled crookedly, realizing that now was not the time to jump and shout for joy.

I was definitely embarrassed that I had chastised him like a worried, boring dad. But... I was beginning to accept that that's just what I was, now. *Maybe not so much the boring bit*, I thought to myself, surveying the carnage that remained of the once lucrative Fight Club.

Midas stormed up to me, shaking his head as he did the same, likely tallying up the costs as efficiently as a calculator. He locked eyes with me, and although he looked glad to see me back out of the Dark Lands...

I had no doubt who would be the first volunteer to kill me tonight to send me back home.

"Good thing you have the golden touch, right?" I said, attempting levity. "Shouldn't cost you a penny," I said. He grunted unhappily, glancing over at the bleachers. I picked up a broken branch at my feet and promptly poked him in the belly while he wasn't looking. "*Boop!*" I cooed in a playful tone.

He jolted instinctively, spinning to snatch the offending branch with his bare hand, and the wood instantly turned to solid gold, too heavy for me to maintain my grip. I dropped it and, of course, it landed on Midas' foot. He cursed loudly, shouting out in pain as he hopped around on his good foot. I winced, taking a step back, holding up my hands. He rounded on me, face beet-red in both pain and outrage.

"Sorry. I didn't think... I mean, to be fair, you kind of overreacted—"

But I cut off when I saw his face suddenly change, staring over my shoulder.

I spun to find B – no, *Ruin* – vibrating like he was having a seizure, arcs of gold, yellow, green and blue ripping back and forth from end to end of his cloudy mass. He began to stretch wider, and I saw that his jaws were slowly opening, as if forced.

I saw one boot, and then another.

Followed by a pair of hands forcing those jaws apart.

Ruin abruptly released his bite, drifting up into the air, his teeth shattering. And all those arcs of power pinging around him exploded in a thunderous blast of multicolored lightning.

And every single fucking bolt found a target.

Midas was obliterated in a heartbeat, and I thanked my lucky stars that I'd instinctively dove out of harm's way, tackling Alex into a pile of wreckage and throwing up a shield of condensed air above us. I'd somehow – perhaps entirely by accident – planted my Devourer into the ground so the blade pointed straight up like a lightning rod.

Power slammed into the spear, but it ricocheted off in a multitude of smaller bolts of power, incinerating the rest of the survivors in the vicinity. The eruptions lasted only a few seconds, but they struck so fast and hard that it sounded like one massive explosion – one growling, earth-shattering kaboom.

I noticed the Team Temple doily lying on the ground beside me, momentarily considering snatching it up as a memento.

"Ruin…" Alex gasped when the noise died down, staring over my shoulder. I turned to look and saw that Ruin was now a cloud as white as snow, no longer over-flowing with energy.

"I got one…" I heard Ruin say in a faint whisper, bobbing up and down drunkenly, and then he suddenly winked out of existence with a faint *pop* like a bubble.

He'd… gotten one. One *Soul*? Holy shit! That meant… Mordred was now down to *Five* Souls!

I turned to see that Mordred had spotted me, and the look on his face told me he was done playing games. No more dying wishes granted. No more words needed. Dr. Bedside Manner was here to tell it like it was.

He hefted two of Ruin's teeth like weapons – one in each hand – and his face was a bloody, furious mask. "This ends here, Temple. Even if I have to drag you back to the Dark Lands by your toes…" he snarled.

I blindly grabbed the nearest stake of sharp wood and locked eyes with Alex. He blinked back at me in confusion.

And then I stabbed him in the heart.

There was no way I was going to let Mordred get the both of us. The least I could do was send Alex home tonight by killing him here and now. Before Mordred dragged him to the Dark Lands with me.

Alex's eyes bulged with pain as he gasped, staring up at me.

And if I hadn't caught that deep, unconditional look of love and comprehension in those eyes, I might have just volunteered to walk into the Dark Lands for Mordred to execute me. Because if Alex had thought for one moment that I had betrayed him...

My soul would have died anyway.

But I saw the love in those brilliant eyes. They were also spiced with a dash of anger at me for sending him to safety rather than letting him fight beside me, but mostly I saw the love thing.

I scrambled to my feet and took a deep breath, surveying the wreckage for a moment, making sure there were no other people Mordred could use against me. Because if so, I would need to quickly kill them before they became leverage. Because Mordred had already displayed he was willing to drag me into the Dark Lands to kill me for good, and letting anyone help me, now, could put them at the same risk.

But, that problem was quickly solved, since everyone had either fled of their own volition or they had already been electro-blasted in Ruin's unexpected suicide bomber explosion. I even noticed one of Asterion's boots smoldering in the center of a clear patch of grass.

I gritted my teeth angrily, hoping Ruin was okay.

Because... the air felt strange, now, like the Dueling Grounds was fighting something. And I had a thermometer constantly reaffirming me of this. My Devourer.

It now felt like I was gripping a live wire, and I didn't dare let it out of my sight. Mordred was scared of it, so I was keeping it close. I was beginning to sense that there was a lot of hangry magic in the air, caused by the Dueling Grounds and my Devourer not being familiar with the term *sharing*.

I knew that if Mordred had his way, I wouldn't find myself in bed tonight. He was going to make me pay for stealing *any* of his souls, let alone *Five*.

Yahn, Alucard, Gunnar, and Ruin had each taken one of Mordred's souls. Talon also scooped one up by default, since I had donated mine to him for his sacrifice. Five Souls down, Five Souls to go. Which meant this was round three.

With hardly any magic to speak of, no chance of even *considering* Fae magic without risking a debilitating flashback, and not much physical strength left to me, I took a shaky breath and knew I had only one last chance. One last *hope*, ironically.

I grabbed the coin hanging around my neck. It melted into my hand, suddenly the interior of my Horseman's Mask. I heard a grunt from Alex, and I looked up in horror to see he was still *alive*. He was dying slowly, not a quick death like I had intended. Damn my aim. He was suffering. *My kid was suffering.* The Team Temple doily beside him was the worst kind of mockery.

I heard Mordred's slow, steady footsteps approaching me, and my lip curled back into an animalistic snarl. I couldn't let Mordred see that Alex was still alive. Couldn't let Mordred bring him out there with us. No matter what.

So, I slammed the Mask over my face just as Mordred grabbed my shoulder from behind.

Alex's eyes widened, knowing exactly what I'd just done, and why I'd done it. To keep him safe, I had…

Chosen to become the Horseman of Hope.

And everything changed…

In.

One.

Eternal.

Instant.

CHAPTER 54

$\mathcal{I}$ felt Mordred's hand on my shoulder, felt his fingers beginning to tighten. I spun and punched him directly in the nose, feeling cartilage crunch in slow motion like the sound of ice breaking on a frozen pond. He dropped onto his ass, sliding a few feet before slamming into some smoldering wreckage. He gripped his face, staring up at me in bewildered confusion. I stared down at my hand instead, marveling at the texture of my skin. Like liquid black and white rock, or raw, uncut diamonds.

"There was supposed to have been a trumpet or something..." I complained, absently. "Typical."

My claws looked pretty intense, too – inches long, jagged black blades extending from each fingertip. I flexed my fingers, rolling my wrist, and wasn't surprised to find that my digits moved and functioned like my normal skin had – it was just as tough as rock, now. I scratched the tip of my claw against my palm experimentally, and it sounded like a knife dragged across stone, but I didn't feel a single flicker of pain.

I glanced back at Mordred to see that his nose had begun to heal. I simply stared at him as I internally assessed some very strange things happening to the rest of my body.

The Mask felt like it was made of a million velvet fingers, caressing my cheeks and nose like it was searching for the most comfortable position, aligning itself to the contours of my face for a perfect fit. As I had experienced before, it didn't seem to weigh anything, or obscure my vision or anything like that. Almost like putting on makeup.

I gasped as both of my shoulder blades suddenly blazed with heat like someone had poured a line of hot wax on them. Just a surprising sensation, not necessarily torture.

Then I felt them tear *open*, making me grunt, stumbling slightly.

Because although that part had been slightly painful, it felt more like a sore muscle getting a much-needed stretch. A pleasant, necessary pain. I still held the Devourer in one fist, but Mordred seemed no longer interested in that as he shook his head incredulously. "That's not poss—"

A low, visceral blast from what sounded like a conch horn the size of a skyscraper split the air, making the very ground rattle, and I hunched over as I felt the Mask grip my face tightly, as if trying to fuse with my skin.

Hope… a voice purred in my ears. *We've been waiting for you… This might hurt a little.*

"Wait, what?" I rasped, spinning left to right, searching for the voice that had somehow been heard over the echoing foghorn like sound in the skies. But I was soon distracted by what felt like a thousand spiders with white-hot, needle-feet suddenly dancing across every square inch of my body. Mordred was scooting away in horror, eyes dancing wildly as he tried to determine who I was talking to, and where the booming horn had come from, like he expected an army of Valkyries to descend upon him. "Who *are* you?" I demanded of the voice. "And *what* might hurt—"

I gasped, then, closing my eyes as I felt every single one of my bones abruptly *pop* like a string of firecrackers. I gritted my teeth, squeezing my eyes shut as the muscles of my body tugged and jerked spasmodically, feeling as if my very body was exploding.

I panted, muscles still twitching as the pain finally began to fade.

When I opened my eyes, I expected to find myself lying on my back, not crouched down and staring at the bloody mask that was Mordred's face. Chunks of black and white diamond grit were firmly embedded into his flesh, and he stared at me with wide, unblinking eyes, totally speechless. Even as I watched, his body began to heal, the gravel popping out in fits and starts, but the wash of blood remained, and so did the terror in his eyes.

I wasn't entirely sure where the gravel had come from, because my hands were still covered in the uncut diamond skin. Maybe – like a snake – I had shed an outer layer or something. I slowly stretched to my feet, raising my arms above my head to stretch out my twitching muscles, and get the blood flowing. To see the result of what I had just experienced.

The pain had faded, and in its place was… a pleasant tingling sensation throughout my entire body. This transformation felt a lot different than last time. And that wailing horn was definitely new. The Four Horsemen had told me it would be a Heavenly chime or a quartet of Holy trumpets or something similar. But that horn had been more savage and primal than cherubic.

And my Horseman Virtual Assistant had been *entirely* unexpected. No one had informed me about that part.

We've been waiting for you… it had said. But who was *we*?

Soon enough, Hope… the voice replied. *Now, it's time to introduce yourself… Your cousins are waiting. They may be a little shy, at first. After all, this is a first for everyone. I'll slow time a moment to let you speak with them…* the voice added casually, as if it was no big deal to slow down time.

I looked up to see the Four Horsemen standing at the edge of the ring. They hadn't been there a few minutes ago, or at least I hadn't seen them lurking about. They had their hoods pulled up, and were staring at me with their familiar Masks. And they looked… very uneasy.

War stared back at me with his red and white samurai mask of molten lava. The spines of his wings were like red-hot branches tearing through his robes of burning coals. No skin stretched between the spines, so that they more resembled fiery branches, and his claws dripped like molten lava.

Pestilence – or Conquest, as he preferred – had chosen not to wear his disgusting, diseased-ridden zombie look, and instead resembled one of those old Renaissance doctor masks, complete with the long, beak-like nose. But his robes were rotten, full of holes and green stains – definitely not a hygienic medical practitioner. His pale wings were sickly, disheveled spines, and they looked infested with insects or bacteria of some kind.

Famine wore his scarecrow mask – complete with bloodstains on the torn and ravaged burlap sack-textured surface – and his robes looked like woven corn husks. Desiccated branches formed claws from his sleeves, and wings like massive cornstalks sprouted up over his shoulders.

And Death, with his traditional bone mask, skeletal wings flaring out behind him, again with no skin between the spines. His robes were a death shroud. Like one flowing, black doily.

They seemed to be studying me just as intently as I studied them. And they did look pretty nervous.

Mordred was staring at me, and it took him about ten seconds to complete his blink. Huh. She really had slowed time…

I paid him no mind, walking past him to meet my brothers. No, the voice had said *cousins*. Maybe she needed a software update.

I flinched as I saw one of Grimm's black and red peacock feathers in my peripheral vision. He was alive! But when I spun, I realized it wasn't Grimm.

It was *me*. My stone spine wings had sprouted feathers identical to my unicorn, just much longer and wider, long enough to brush the ground as I walked, leaving a bloody trail in their wake. I still had the stone spines, but my wings had fleshed out marginally with the feathers. And I suddenly realized where all that gravel had come from. The feathers had broken free of their encasement.

"Upgrade," I mumbled, comparing the feathers to those hanging from my Devourer. Identical.

Like my Alicorn, Grimm.

I narrowed my eyes, deciding to call bullshit.

That voice had made it sound like this moment was some big surprise that no one had known about other than them – whoever *they* were.

So why did I feel like I'd opened up a few Christmas presents early? Grimm, years ago, and my Devourer just recently. Had that been why my final transition had been delayed? That I'd needed the Devourer to complete the transformation into the Horseman of Hope?

In my fascination with my new wings, I hadn't noticed the Four Horsemen crossing the rest of the distance. They stopped several paces away, studying me.

"Rejoice and shit!" I said, flaring out my new wings in a slow twirl, realizing that it was instinctual. I didn't have to consciously think about moving them, stretching them out, or tucking them back. It was almost like I'd always had them.

Callie was going to lose her shit. I couldn't wait to show them off.

Death cleared his throat, dismissing my comment. "Mordred's fighting the time freeze, and despite your pretty feathers, this fight is far from over. In fact, I think he's been holding back. I can feel him pulling deep on his remaining Souls."

I turned to look at Mordred, and saw him standing there with eyes closed, slowly muttering under his breath, like he was praying. I grunted dismissively. "Dudes..." I said, shaking my head, unconcerned. "He's down to Five Souls – Four of those stolen from Hell, and then his *own*. And there are Five of *us*. Are you guys allowed to play, or am I on my own?"

"You smell... different," Famine finally said, leaning closer to sniff at me with his stained scarecrow mask.

I grunted. "Hey, back off, cornstalk. You're going to mess up my feathers." I knew the least about Famine, compared to his Brothers. I'd spent the most time around Death, but I'd also confided in War and Conquest over the past year or so. Even though I didn't know Famine's legend, something about him just seemed to mesh with me. He seemed more easygoing, always quick with a joke, and overall less serious than his Brothers.

The others had sad, depressing origin stories. Maybe Famine had saved a village from starvation and thought to himself, *never again will I let anyone go hungry. I'm going to bake pies for eternity, but I'll pretend to be the Horseman of Famine to throw everyone off.*

"Famine is right," War murmured thoughtfully.

"I'm the *Fifth* Horseman. We're not supposed to be twinsies. You guys are all different," I added, pointing out their attire.

They shared a long look with each other. "Your bell toll was... not what we were expecting," Conquest said, his Renaissance doctor mask cocking like a bird, reminding me of the DemonStork Mordred had roasted in the Dark Land's first ever Burning Man Festival.

"Look. You guys offered me this job. I took a while to commit, but I expected a little warmer of a welcome than this. Time to make up for it. Throw me a party and tell me you're allowed to *play*," I said, pointing a thumb behind me at Mordred.

Death nodded, studying me thoughtfully. "Yes. We're here at the Dueling Grounds. We can play. And I think we will have to play in order to have a chance..." He trailed off, eyes locked onto my Devourer, especially the fact that it was humming in my fist. I was actually grateful for the new stone skin, because it made the vibration of the Devourer more tolerable. Before, it had felt like holding onto a live wire. A current just below the sensation of pins and needles you got when your foot fell asleep. Death looked troubled. "Something *is* wrong, but I can't put my finger on it."

He was the only one also holding his weapon, I noticed for the first time.

I pointed at his wicked scythe. "You have a stick, so I'm keeping mine. At least my Devourer goes with my superhero outfit." Seeing his scythe made me glance down at the brand on my palm, since it was also depicted on my Crest. My brand was still there, but outlined in white crystals against the black. It might have been my imagination, but I noticed a faint, golden light outlining it. My Ichor, or just the sunset's reflection? I dismissed it for now.

The ground let out a slow, rumbling groan, and I turned to find that Mordred – despite the time-freeze – had packed on a few pounds. His body was now wider, thicker, and sporting black veins. His eyes were still closed, so I considered now a perfectly good opportunity to attack.

I hefted my spear, preparing to give Mordred a new throat piercing.

Death suddenly grabbed my wrist, shaking his head. "Let him finish praying. We have time. And we need to talk." Cool air wafted out from his claw, and this close to his skull Mask, I felt like I had opened a freezer door in a steamy commercial kitchen.

I lowered my spear, glaring. At least, I think I was glaring. I wasn't sure how well my facial gestures translated to my Mask. "This guy is an asshole. Trust me."

War cracked his neck, his Mask suddenly rippling with fire. "I'm getting bored just standing around, and I'm anxious to see what…" he studied my wings thoughtfully, "*Victor's Secret Angel* can do," he finally said in an amused tone. "Maybe he can prance around, fanning his fancy feathers while we take down this chump."

I rolled my eyes. "Hilarious. Let's just get this over with. I was ready to physically collapse before this. Not sure how much that impacts my performance, now, but I'd rather not find out by drawing this fight on longer than absolutely necessary. So, can I just stab him in the throat already? I promise I won't lose any sleep about interrupting his prayer. Or killing him while he's frozen in time, or whatever the hell this is," I said, studying their reactions. They gave me no indication about the time freeze thing, which could mean almost anything.

Death ignored me, watching as Conquest sniffed loudly. "Something is wrong. A tension in the air." He sniffed again, and then snorted. "Perhaps a poison of some kind. Some disease. Or something *fighting* a disease."

I pointed at Mordred. "His veins literally just turned black. It doesn't take an ex-doctor to diagnose that he may be sick in some way." But deep down, I knew what Conquest meant. He wasn't talking about Mordred.

Something with the Dueling Grounds itself seemed off. As if it was fighting a battle of its own. Likely because it kept having souls stolen from it, and was getting a little uppity with the new kids fucking up the playground equipment, breaking the cosmic rules that the souls the Dueling Grounds were supposed to *protect*...

Were actually being stolen and sent to *Hell*, rather than returned home with a *body*.

Ruin had one-upped us all by actually *eating* one of Mordred's Souls. At least I hadn't seen a Soul sucked down into the earth like before. Even though it looked like Ruin had kicked the bucket, I'd been around when a Beast died, and there had been a few more fireworks involved with the final *bon voyage*.

Death shook his head at my reference to Mordred. "He's speaking of the Dueling Grounds. She is upset that her sole purpose is being overtaken, invaded. We can't let Hell take any more Souls from her or she's liable to get upset."

Conquest nodded, snapping his fingers. "*That's* what it is! The Dueling Ground's *antibodies*."

I blinked at the two of them incredulously. "Excuse me?"

War chimed in. "Balance," he said, shrugging absently. Like he had just given an in-depth TEDTalk on Dark Matter, and after being asked a very scientific *why* question, had answered with a serious face, saying, *Because.*

Was that why my Devourer had been acting up? Was it *also* pissed at all the free meals it had missed?

Death pointed a skeletal claw at my Devourer. "The Dueling Grounds might be appreciative of you using that instead of letting Hell steal any more Souls than it already has. You know, spread out the thievery a little bit."

I grimaced. "You guys are a bad influence. You're telling me to just rob the Dueling Grounds of a few souls, right *after* informing me that the place is actually a living *entity*, a *pronoun*, and that *she* might take offense." They nodded in unison, seeing no problem with my outburst. I sighed, accepting the duty. I was the gunslinger, they were the cannon fodder. "What about friendly fire?" I asked, thumping the butt of the spear into the ground. "This thing is hungry—"

Death waved a hand in dismissal. "Horsemen are immune to Devourers. We can still fall here, but our souls are safe from your spear."

I stored the Devourer-immunity tidbit away for later, and nodded. "Groovy. You guys ready? I need you to keep him busy while I... prance about," I said, drily, shooting a dark look at War.

He chuckled, and began to drum his fingers against his hip in a steady drumbeat.

Famine licked his lips hungrily.

Conquest – Pestilence – sneezed.

Death just stared at each of us.

Then I heard a faint click in my ears, and Mordred abruptly opened his eyes, no longer frozen in time. His eyes were now solidly black like his veins.

CHAPTER 55

War scanned the area, casually ignoring the berserker Mordred suddenly racing at us.

Like he could see an entirely different scene than us, his eyes locked onto, appraised, and then moved on from various points around the arena. He glanced at Famine, his eyes pulsing once. "Lock in the perimeter. No more of this Dark Lands nonsense," he growled.

Famine nodded, calmly turned his back on us, and then he began skipping away, suddenly wielding a chain with two burning bowls hanging from either end. Black dust dribbled from the bowls, leaving a trail of dead grass in his wake. Staring after Famine made me miss whatever War had told Conquest to do, but I saw the result.

Conquest launched up into the air, flapping his wings as he whipped out a bow seemingly made from the heart of a glacier. It smoked as he nocked a black arrow onto the string, and then he simply faded from view, blending in with the burning sunset surroundings.

War nodded at Death, and the Horseman began swinging his scythe like he was competing for a Taekwondo Forms tournament, spinning it all over the place before slamming the back of the blade onto the ground so the staff stuck straight up. He scrambled up it like a monkey and then crouched atop it on the balls of his feet, bony skeletal knees splayed out. He cocked his head from left to right, and I realized he was checking on Famine – who was still making his circuit around the ring. Death began rocking back and forth on his scythe like it was a rocking chair, creating a cringe-worthy nails on chalkboard *screech, screech, screech.*

I also saw that he wasn't holding onto the staff, because he lowered his hands towards the ground – still rocking back and forth, madly – extending his bone fingers down as if reaching for something. Purple sparks began spitting out from both the ground and his fingerbones, and then the sparks abruptly connected, creating a pulsing purple thread from each fingertip.

Then he began to lift them, slowly, up over his head.

And as he did, I realized he had access to a metaphysical fog machine, because the ground was suddenly covered in thick, roiling fog, as agitated as a sea in storm, and in that fog floated hundreds of ancient skulls – thankfully lifeless.

I almost lost my balance before understanding why. I was standing on *top* of these new clouds of fog. It wasn't fog in the natural sense. Death had just made our battleground a shifting, turbulent obstacle course.

And it was walled-in by Famine's perimeter of black dust.

Mordred snarled, ignoring the uneven footing, and flung out his hands.

Living shadows whipped out like a cat-o-nine-tails from Mordred's wrist, intending to slash across War's chest. War sidestepped minutely, and the whip missed him by mere millimeters. But something about the amused flicker of flame in the Horseman's eyes let me know this was intentional. War suddenly whipped out a great sword dripping with fire, and threw it at Mordred, kneeling into a crouch the moment his weapon left his fingers. The blade sliced right through Mordred's hand, lopping it off in a cauterizing hiss. Mordred screamed – a beautiful melody to my ears.

Everyone was staring down at Mordred's dismembered hand as an arrow of virulent poison slammed into the palm of the detached appendage, pinning it to one of the skulls poking above the fog. Mordred's hand began to rot and decay at a rapid rate, oozing with virulent pus and blisters.

Not knowing what else I should be doing, I had already started sprinting towards the crouched over Horseman of War. My wings propelled me to cover the uneven fog faster, and before I knew it, I was sprinting up War's unsuspecting back and using his head as a launching point – which elicited a surprised grunt.

My wings furled out, and I hurled my Devourer right at Mordred's heart. My wings instinctively beat at the air, lifting me higher the moment I released the spear, reminding me of martial arts.

When punching with the right hand, instructors taught you to whip the left hand back to your hip just as forcefully as you're trying to punch with your right. This concept turns a mildly potent linear punch into a much stronger circular motion, giving your strike a significantly more powerful *oomph* factor.

But the coolest part was that my wings had done it all on their own. Kind of like how you didn't need to think about breathing. You just did it.

Or, in a real-world example, if you see a projectile flying towards your chest, you don't have to consciously tell yourself the exact speed the projectile is flying, what parabolic arc it has, or the local weather status that might affect the projectile's ETA with your heart.

No.

You somehow know to subconsciously calculate all of that and – most often – can at least get your hands in the way in time, if not bat away or catch the projectile.

But in Mordred's unfortunate case, my Devourer totally smoked him.

It ripped straight through his heart and out his back, disproving my theory on subconscious muscle memory. Then again, he'd been too distracted watching his hand rotting away.

Mordred gasped as his wound began to smoke. Not wanting my Devourer damaged, I whistled loudly. My spear ripped out of Mordred's body the same way it had entered, but as the blade left the wound – momentarily illuminating his gory chest cavity with red light – I noticed a tendril of shadow had latched onto it.

As the spear flew back to my hand, the tendril of shadow stretched, growing thicker and darker, stuck to the ruby stone in my blade. It was so dense that I thought it was the strange black poison filling his veins, but as the spear haft hit my open hand, I heard the faint wailing sound of a soul fighting for freedom. I idly wondered why I could hear it now when I hadn't heard any of the others make a sound. Was that a Horseman perk? To be able to hear a soul? I hoped not.

I also heard a loud *slurping* sound, like a straw sucking up the last dregs of a soda.

With a final *popping* noise, the soul whipped into my Devourer fully, and I felt the wooden haft crack alarmingly loud. The Devourer flashed once, bathing the foggy ground in a harsh, crimson light. The flash of light also let me see the wide crack from the base to the tip in the haft of my Devourer. I blinked down at it in disbelief and fear. That couldn't be good.

I heard a gasping wheeze from the distance, and saw Conquest fall from the sky, slamming down into the cloudy floor like a limp rag. His body simply evaporated less than a heartbeat later. I spun, searching for the other Horsemen, wondering what the hell had just happened.

And my heart lurched in my chest to see them all wobbling drunkenly, shaking their heads as if they'd suffered simultaneous concussions. War was trying to stand, but gripping his Mask with one fiery claw as if he'd been hit between the eyes. Famine had finished his circuit, but was tripping and stumbling over his own feet, dragging his burning bowls on the foggy ground. I dropped back down to the fog, pulling Death to his feet, since he had fallen from his crazy perch atop his scythe.

"What happened? I thought you said it was safe to use this?" I asked, alarmed. Had I just killed Conquest?

Death flinched, snapping out of his daze to look for War and Famine. He let out a sigh of relief upon finding them, and shakily bent over to scoop up his scythe. He leaned on it wearily, locking eyes with me.

Well, his eyes were just balls of purple flame, so we just faced each other very intensely for a second. "It doesn't matter, now," he said. "We must hurry. This is much more dangerous than we feared…" And I sensed his gaze latching onto the crack in my Devourer's haft, his alarm doubling. "The Soul must be straining your Devourer. We best get this over with. Better to let Hell have Mordred's souls than to risk damaging your blade, even if it upsets the Dueling Grounds. The Devourer is…" he hesitated, then attempted to turn away. I gripped his shoulder, squeezing hard.

And I almost grimaced in disgust as I watched his legs buckle in pain. I released him immediately, staring down at my claw in horror. What the hell? How had *that* hurt him? Death spun, looking just as startled as me as he stared down at my claw, as if he didn't know the answer either.

"What were you going to say, Death?" I whispered, hearing Mordred reviving behind us. *Four Souls left, now*, I thought to myself. *But at what cost… Killing the Horsemen?*

Death sighed, glancing over my shoulder. "The Devourer is vital to your survival. To all our survival."

"But Conquest—"

"Allies fall in battle," War growled from directly behind me. "We'll cry about it over drinks, later. Now, we *fight*." He saw Famine limping over to us, looking severely shaken at his abrupt loss of strength, or injury, or whatever had befallen the Horsemen when my Devourer ate Mordred's soul.

The three Brothers seemed to snap out of it mostly, and we all turned to see Mordred climbing back to his feet, his chest almost completely healed, now.

Four of us against Mordred's Four remaining Souls.

Mordred shook his head once, staring down at the wound, and I saw him clenching his jaw in fury. He lifted his head and his eyes locked onto me and my Devourer. Then he was running at us, fingers extended in long, dagger-sized claws, dripping with what looked like black oil.

In a blindingly fast blur, Famine dove towards the threat, swinging his scales into Mordred's ankles on the way, making him trip and fall. I felt a sigh of relief to see that the Horsemen could still kick major ass. Famine was back on his feet before Mordred could process what he had tripped over, and immediately began beating the living hell out of Mordred's back with his smoking scales. Black, rotten grains spilled from the bowls on the end of the chains with each blow, and wherever they touched, Mordred flinched, body distorting grotesquely.

I tucked my wings back as tightly as possible and crouched down beside a large charred section of bleachers that must have been too tall for Death's fog to roll completely over. I curled in on myself, using the black stone of my skin to conceal myself in the wreckage while Mordred was distracted by Famine. War and Death caught onto my plan, and began swinging their blades at Mordred, but not before he sent Famine flying with a burst of power, his entire body swarming with black shadows.

Famine flew, tumbling a dozen paces away, only mildly saved by his sudden outstretched wings. War and Death lunged, stabbing and swinging in perfect unison – a flurry of crackling purple lightning and splashes of molten lava peppering Mordred even when the blows didn't land. All the while, they backed Mordred closer to the fire where I hid. And as I watched the chaotic Shaolin weapons fight, I noticed something very strange. Mordred was a misshapen mess, like the Hunchback of Notre Dame.

His back was a massive hump, one arm was long enough to touch the ground – with not an ounce of muscle on it, just skin over bone – and his clawed hand was overly large.

His other arm was massively muscled, but that claw was tiny and stumpy, like a baby's hand. Still black and sporting claws, but almost laughable compared to his bulging bicep and forearm. What had Famine done to him? Starved parts of his body while overfeeding others? That was... disgusting.

Still, Mordred put up a fight.

Death's scythe bit into Mordred's shoulder, tearing right out his back, and I saw Death was using his other hand to wake a pair of skeletons in the fog. Mordred snarled in agony, but somehow managed to notice Death's gesture. I blinked in disbelief as two skeletons abruptly rose from the fog and attempted to tackle Mordred from behind, but Mordred spun in time, grabbed onto their skulls with each hand, and flung them at War, using them as a shield for War's flaming sword that had been intended for Mordred's gut. The magma blade skewered the skeletons into puffs of bone dust.

Christ. Until this moment, I had kind of forgotten that Mordred had been a knight, no stranger to direct combat.

But I noticed Famine's attack had done more than mess with his arms. One of his legs was shorter and bony with malnutrition, but the other was long and strong, making him scuttle around in an awkward shuffle as he tried to fend off War and Death's elemental blades.

Famine came out of nowhere to jump onto Mordred's back, tackling him right into me. I lifted my Devourer at the last moment, and Mordred must have sensed my motion, finally learning that muscle-memory thing.

One problem. He tried to block my spear with his cute little baby claw.

My Devourer tore right through the vile little baby hand and into Mordred's open mouth.

Mordred stared at me with wide eyes, my spear permanently wedging his jaws open.

I leaned forward, flicked him gently on the nose, and said, *"Boop,"* like I had with Midas earlier. Mordred was too busy dying to get overly upset about it like Midas had.

Famine grabbed Mordred by the hair and tossed him backwards.

Except my Devourer remained stuck through his head, yanking it entirely out of my grasp. I cursed, shoving Famine aside as I sprinted after Mordred. I winced as I heard Famine cry out in pain, especially when I heard something *snap* like a bone. But I didn't look back, hoping to retrieve my Devourer before Mordred revived himself.

Because maybe Mordred came to, saw the Devourer, and decided to see what would happen if he broke the ruby. I shivered at the thought, imagining him somehow reclaiming the Two Souls my Devourer had eaten. I whipped out my wings to increase my speed. They pounded at the ground and I was suddenly airborne, wind pelting at my eyes. I glided for a moment before tucking them back in and racing back to the ground like a paratrooper. I landed beside Mordred in a crouch, and didn't waste any time ripping the Devourer from his mouth.

The blade came free, but the departing Soul gripped onto the ruby like a rubber band. I hopped onto Mordred's chest, yanking back as hard as I could. Then I began flapping my wings, pulling as hard as I could. The Soul finally did snap free, sending me cartwheeling through the air as the world flashed an even darker red.

The Devourer cracked and made a splintering sound this time.

Followed immediately by a chorus of groans. War and Death were on all fours, shambling forward like drunk puppies. I stared at them in disbelief. "What is *wrong* with you guys?" I demanded. They were the freaking Horsemen. I'd expected a little more professionalism than this. Were they just rusty?

Famine was simply gone.

Mordred was now down to Three Souls, and Team Temple was also down to Three Horsemen. Dare we continue this insanity?

War and Death looked up at me weakly, the flames of their eyes fainter, practically sputtering. "I don't know what's happening. Mordred must have done something to us," War wheezed, climbing painfully to his feet. Death did the same, actually falling over in the process. I glanced over at my Devourer in horror. It was an angrier, darker red, now. And although the wooden haft was damaged and still vibrating in my grip, it felt more like a satisfied purr. But it looked held together by mere splinters.

Why did it seem happy if it was *breaking*? And why were the Horsemen *dying*?

"We need to finish this. I'm not sure I have much more left in me," Death mumbled, sounding like I had woken him after a three-day bender.

War nodded forcefully. "Yes. We need to end this. Now."

He took two steps towards me, dragging his massive body on the ground, staring at Mordred who was climbing to his feet, looking as healthy as he had at the beginning. Well, Mordred's pain was deep in his eyes, his confidence shaken.

War lifted his hands, and I almost gasped in horror as lava golems of some sort began to climb up from the fog, answering their master's call. Then I heard a final gasp from behind me and the lava golems immediately splashed back under the fog. Mordred blinked over at them, face stretching into a very hungry grin.

I spun to see War suddenly collapse into a pile of embers.

I stared in numb disbelief.

Scratch that. Two Horsemen against Mordred's Three Souls—

Death made a strange gasping sound behind me, and I turned to see him look me in the eyes, the flames in those ghoulish sockets flickering weakly, sputtering like a range stove with no propane.

Then he fell, too – a sound like rattling bones scattering over a marble floor.

I slowly turned at the sound of Mordred's sudden triumphant laugh.

I stared at him, walling off my emotions. The Horsemen had died. Was that for real, or like everyone else at the Dueling Grounds? Had the birth of the Fifth Horseman literally been at the expense of the first Four Horsemen?

"Alright, Chuckles," I growled murderously. This was all Mordred's fault. I needed to avenge my fellow Horsemen. Make them proud.

I focused on my Mask, gripping my Devourer like it was the edge of a cliff. I was a fucking Horseman. It was time to see what that meant. The others had started to do some pretty cool stuff before dying. Maybe I had some cool tricks, too. I drew deep on my new powers, not really knowing what I would find, or what I was doing, exactly. I just focused on my memories of my fallen Brothers...

War...

I instantly felt an ocean of boiling, roiling magma consume my soul, demanding nothing but the complete and utter annihilation of my foes. I smiled as I heard the sweetest song imaginable – the Horns of War.

Famine…

A waterfall of hunger suddenly drowned me in a desperate need to devour every flicker of life within a three-mile radius. An Apocalyptic hunger-pang.

Conquest… Pestilence…

I felt every ache, pain, minor sniffle, memory of a past injury, and any imagined sense of self-doubt, fear, or lack of confidence suddenly evaporate into nonexistence. My life was abruptly wholly and entirely disease free – any and all maladies of the mind and body, simply gone.

Death…

I saw my death in complete and vivid detail, watching my body torn apart a thousand different ways in the span of a baby taking its first breath, and all I could feel was…

A ridiculous urge to laugh at the very concept of fear.

War demanded absolution.

Famine was just fucking hangry.

Conquest had cleansed my soul.

Death had made me fearless.

The Four Horsemen were not dead… They were part of *me*, Nate Temple.

The Fifth Horseman. The Rider of Hope. That nerd with the unicorn.

And I felt… *#WokeAF*, as the Reds would say. Or, hyper conscious of the world around me, to put it in non-millennial slang.

I saw Mordred frowning uncertainly, and I gave him a very slow smile. My arms suddenly blazed with white fire, crackling down my wrists and over my Devourer.

Whatever was left of the wooden haft instantly burned to ashes in that merciless white flame, cleansed of all sins…

Abandoning all hopes of remaining a spear.

But the blade remained unharmed, as did the feathers attached to it. They began to fall, no longer supported by the wooden haft, but abruptly halted at shin level to swing back and forth like a pendulum.

Because the blade and feathers now dangled from a crackling white chain of pure energy – not fire, not ice, not lightning, not air, and not earth – but *all* of those things. And every link of that ethereal chain sprouted an inky black thorn on both edges, as long as a finger, and as sharp as a surgeon's needle.

A spear-whip. Something I could easily adapt to.

The ruby on the blade left a trail of faint crimson smoke with each swing, and I looked back up at Mordred with a promising grin.

"My Brothers were holding me back, Mordred. I think it's time you and I get down to business…"

CHAPTER 56

*M*ordred watched my new weapon warily, as if trying to consider the change in tactics he might need, but also focusing intently upon the ruby. The Devourer had eaten two of his Souls, and if my math was correct, he was sitting on three – Two from Hell, and his own.

He sprinted at me, deciding the odds were better than waiting around. I lifted a hand, and a swath of thorns erupted before him in a column that pierced the black skies above, reflecting the burning sunset in the distance, making them appear to be on fire. My thorns scooped up... nine errant skulls littering the fog, making me smile in appreciation of the symbolism.

Mordred slammed into the wall of thorns and screamed as smoke burst forth from wherever he had been pierced. He was panting as I familiarized myself with the weight of the chained Devourer, swinging it whip quick through the column of thorns, aiming for where I thought his heart was.

The black-blade – limned with white fire, now – tore through the thorns like paper, even though it was obvious Mordred was having issues breaking free of their tentacle like grip – snagged and hooked in dozens of places, as he was.

Unfortunately, I missed, and the white fire incinerated the thorn wall like a magician's flash paper, freeing my target. Mordred scrambled backwards, instantly flinging his own inky black whip at me.

I curled a shoulder, slamming my wing down before me like a shield, the diamond spines piercing through the fog, and stabbing a couple of skulls in the process. Mordred's whip hit my spines and feathers with an explosive hiss that rocked me slightly, but didn't break through.

I arched the tip of both wings up high, and then flapped them at the ground as hard as I could, lifting me high into the air, where I began to circle him. Blasts of his black power flew at me, but – like that Vince Vaughn flick – I managed to *dodge, duck, dip, dive, and dodge* them by tucking my wings in, flaring them out, or swooping laterally, all on reflex.

And all while countering as I hurled my Devourer right back at him, hoping to knock him down for me to swoop in for the kill.

Then he got in a lucky punch by blinding me with a fucking rainbow, of all things. I slammed into it and was stunned to discover it was *solid*. It shattered at the force of my impact, raining down shards of glass as long as my forearm and splashing vibrant multicolored blobs of a paint-like substance down over Mordred, covering him in the rainbow goop like he was prepping for Camelot's first Pride Parade. Several of those jagged shards tore into Mordred, too, making him fall to his knees.

I realized rainbows were apparently sharp enough to cut even my new skin. I tried flapping my wings to get away, and felt a dull ache in my shoulder blades, followed by a flash of pain on my forehead.

Then I began to fall, my Mask suddenly vibrating against my skin, making my vision quiver as I fell.

I managed to flare out my wings at the last moment, landing in a crouch as I grasped my forehead. The moment my fingers touched my Mask, I felt a sharp *pop* like static electricity. I hissed, yanking my hand back, staring down at it. My fingertip smoked where it had touched the Mask.

What was going on? I felt like I was on the verge of some precipice, almost able to see over a mountain, but I'd suddenly sprained an ankle. It made me furious. My power was fading.

Hell, I'd only been fighting for what felt like hours, now. Maybe my Mask was fine, but my body had given up a long time ago, refusing to be dragged into yet another brutal battle.

But I saw Mordred getting to his feet, and I knew it was all or nothing. Before something else happened to my newfound powers. Or before my body simply gave up on me.

I took a deep breath, and tried to call up the thorns again, raising my palms up from the ground as if I was trying to lift a car. My shoulders screamed, my bones grating, and my forehead began to throb as if hit by a hammer one too many times.

I ignored it all, pressing on, and the thorns finally heeded my call.

A wall of impenetrable black brambles growled to life, surrounding Mordred, trapping him, stabbing him, piercing him, hooking him, and drinking down his blood. I watched thorns as thick as my wrist tear through his abdomen and out his back.

I tried to lift my hands higher, watching Mordred splayed out on the thorns, crucified, unable to move anything but his jaws. And they were wide open in a silent scream.

I felt a sharp crack down the center of my face, and the Mask fell to the ground, smoking with white fire. I felt my legs wobbling at the sudden evaporation of so much power suddenly relying on my mortal body, and watched as the thorns began to wither and die. I felt my skin slowly returning to normal, and my feathers beginning to fall to the ground like chopped corn stalks.

Before I could fall, I screamed as loud as I could, trying to jump start my failing body.

And hurled my Devourer at Mordred. The white chain evaporated mid-flight, but the Devourer continued to fly true. And it sliced right through the side of his neck as I fell to the ground, the clouds Death had called up evaporating in an instant, leaving us back on the familiar Dueling Grounds.

I managed to lift my head, and saw Mordred stop moving.

My Devourer flashed once with a deep basso thump and I knew I had done it.

Mordred was down to Two Souls. One from Hell, and his own.

We were almost even, now.

Only, I couldn't quite stand up at the moment.

I took a few deep breaths, and managed to flop over onto my stomach. My arm was still bleeding from the fucking rainbow, and I realized it was actually a pretty serious wound. My Mask lay in front of me, a white line down the center as if it had almost cracked in half. My heart stopped for a moment. What would have happened if it had broken entirely?

What would have happened to *me*? Was I bonded to it in some way?

And how did I fix it? I shoved it into my pocket, and was surprised to find I was still wearing my regular clothes from earlier. I hadn't actually taken stock of what I'd been wearing as a Horseman. Probably something really cool.

I recognized my delirium as being slaphappy, and quickly squashed it. I also realized quite quickly that fixing my Mask shouldn't really be a top priority at the moment, because I heard Mordred groan, his body beginning to heal itself.

I gritted my teeth, managing to climb to all fours.

If I was going to stand a chance, I needed to get my Devourer back.

"It's just a flesh wound," I mumbled, dragging one hand in front of the other, crawling closer to Mordred. "I'm not dead yet," I said, sliding my knees across the ground behind me. "I'll show Mordred… I'll just kill myself and wake up in bed as good as new," I murmured. I needed to slice my throat or something. Oddly enough, I felt an alarming flutter of fear at the thought of slicing my own throat. "Man-up and kill yourself, pansy," I told myself, seriously considering it. Because if I didn't make a suicide run, he might just physically drag me over to the Dark Lands, and kill me there.

Mordred was down to Two Souls, now. My only chance was to end this, now. Fight another day. It just might work.

"Die, here, on my terms, and wake back up at Chateau Falco as good as new. Bring back all the same people for an encore, and deliver a fraction of the ass-whooping we dished out tonight…" I mumbled encouragingly, still dragging my hands and feet. "Still need the Devourer, though," I realized with a depressing whisper.

I lifted my head to judge my distance and get a read on the Devourer's location. I spotted it wedged into a piece of burning wood, recognizable only for the feathers shifting slightly in the flickering flames. Thankfully, they weren't burning. I kind of liked them. The ruby was wedged into the wood, hiding the Devourer's telltale glow, thankfully.

But of the most immediate importance was the pair of boots firmly rooted a few inches from my nose.

"Roy G. Biv…" I wheezed, glancing down at my sliced forearm, "You hit me with a rainbow… You dick," I muttered, my ribs aching from my fall.

He kicked me in the jaw, sending me sprawling.

$\mathcal{I}$ stared upwards, shaking off my tunneling vision. Mordred loomed over me a moment later, his face contorted with anger. I noticed he hadn't spotted the Devourer, thank god. Maybe he assumed I'd already retrieved it. I was only a dozen feet away from it, now.

My hand was folded under my hip, and I felt a tiny bulge. I couldn't help but smile. "Now, now, Mordred, don't do anything rash," I told him, awkwardly reaching into my pocket as if trying to sit up. "We still have that meeting tomorrow—"

He kicked me in the ribs, and I used the force of the blow's momentum to roll further than I should have. Since my hand was shoved into my pocket, my face struck the ground on each roll, but I took it like a champ, gasping and groaning for effect. Mordred took it as an ode to his manliness.

Which suited me just fine, because I now had a great view of the Devourer. It was about ten feet away, and the piece of wood it was stuck in was on the verge of collapsing into a bed of embers, tilted at a steep angle. One push and the entire thing would fall inwards.

Mordred noticed my lack of attention, and his eyes widened, spotting the blade. He stomped onto my chest, cracking a few of my ribs in his attempt to grab the Devourer first.

But swinging my Tiny Ball was faster.

I flung it as hard as I could into the bed of embers. The Gateway burst open, and the entire thing collapsed through it, embers, Devourer, and charred wood.

That's when I realized my error. Mordred could simply reach through and grab it. I pulled deep, trying to wake up my magic long enough to hit him with something, anything that would slow him down long enough for the Gateway to snap closed.

My magic sizzled out with a faint pop, and my world spun, leaving me lying on my face, my cheek on the ground as Mordred closed the distance to the Gateway, five feet away.

I realized I was staring at a body beside the Gateway. A young man with bloody, blonde hair holding a familiar Team Temple doily over his chest. *Alex?* I thought to myself, frowning. But… shouldn't he have been whisked back home after dying? Dead bodies weren't common at the Dueling Grounds. They just vanished upon expiration.

Was I hallucinating? Or had I broken the Dueling Grounds somehow? Did they no longer send you home upon death?

Because that would really put a crimp in my suicide plan.

Mordred was so transfixed with the Gateway, he didn't notice when Alex suddenly opened his eyes.

I almost let out a squawk of disbelief, flinching instinctively. I could have sworn he hadn't been breathing. Had I… made him into a zombie by screwing around with the cosmic rules of the Dueling Grounds? My mind began to run a million miles an hour, peppering me with bizarre and horrifying theories.

Right before Mordred could reach through the Gateway, Alex released his wad of bloody cloth and rammed a spear up into Mordred's gut.

The wizard gasped in surprise, but tried to use his momentum to lean over the blade as if intending to dive or fall through the Gateway, ruptured stomach or not. His arm was already halfway through when it winked shut, cutting him off at the elbow.

Mordred fell down face-first, gasping…

Right into a bed of coals, the poor bastard.

He coughed, choked, and screamed with pain, rolling out of the coals and onto his back, but he was momentarily too injured to get back up. I watched as Alex climbed shakily to his feet. He shambled over, kicked Mordred on the end of the stump arm – ignoring Mordred's instant scream

– and then yanked the spear out of his stomach, almost losing his own balance in the process.

I wheezed a motivational cheer that if anyone would have heard, would have made them weep with love and devotion. But to me it just sounded like a death rattle.

Alex stood over Mordred, wobbling on weak legs. How the hell was Alex still alive? Was I *that* bad at stabbing people in the heart?

Realizing what Alex was about to do, I growled angrily, but couldn't gather the strength to stand, let alone stop him. Now, Alex was *really* in danger. He'd just made himself a target for Mordred, by stabbing him in the gut and slicing off his arm. I knew that the whole stump-kick thing would be the one to really stick in Mordred's craw, though.

Mordred sneered up at Alex, clutching his stump tightly. He was already beginning to heal. "You're too late. Rather than wait for you to take my last soul from Hell, I consumed it *myself*. Thank Temple for evening the odds. My own soul was strong enough to gobble up one from Hell, but didn't stand a chance against all *Nine* of them." He spat blood, chuckling darkly.

That was terrifyingly *interesting*. Mordred had... *eaten* the last of the Nine Souls? Why? To keep the power for himself? Maybe fearing us simply taking it for him, he'd chosen to use it himself. But that meant...

Mordred was down to One Soul... Killing him now would send him home.

We'd done it. Although I hadn't anticipated him coming out of it with one for himself, I guessed I couldn't be greedy. We'd taken Eight of them, after all. Which was more than I'd thought we'd get away with.

Mordred spat out more blood. "Can you even kill, boy? In my day, we learned how to make the hard choices from our first steps. But you children are all weak—"

Alex didn't even hesitate, stabbing him through the throat. Well, it was more of a spastic, drunken lurch, using the tip of the spear to save him from collapsing, and just happening to land it in the center of Mordred's throat. "Shut up," he mumbled, swaying back and forth. Mordred evaporated into nothing, and I let out a sigh of relief as I felt the very air throb in what felt like a similar relief.

The Dueling Grounds were back online, and just as happy about it as me.

Alex shambled over to me, smiling sadly.

"Why?" I rasped. "Why didn't you let him kill me? None of it is real. You didn't have to do it. We were all even. One Soul each."

Alex's smile was even sadder this time. His chest was oozing freely, and dried blood caked his lips and jawline. He'd stained my doily. But his eyes were sure and confident behind the exhausted, pained glaze. "I couldn't let him. Because tomorrow, or some day after, you'd remember the moment Mordred murdered you. Having that flashback at the wrong time could break your resolve, birthing fear and self-doubt. What if it happened at a critical moment?" he asked, voice cracking as his eyes moistened with tears. He almost fell over, but caught himself by propping the point of the spear into the ground at my side.

I winced instinctively, feeling the rush of the blade so close to my ribs.

Alex took a shallow breath, and I could hear a rattle in it, his lungs filling with blood, and a tear for each eye suddenly spilled down his cheeks, washing away some of the grime. "I... need to kill you, Dad..." he whispered, using his muddy, bloody free hand to wipe away the tears.

The crack in his whispered voice broke my heart into a million pieces like a shattered rainbow. He was obviously in debilitating pain. I was astonished he wasn't already dead. But despite all that... *he* was worried about *me*. Not wanting me to have to burden myself with even the *memory* of Mordred defeating me.

And to be honest, he had a point. One I hadn't considered. A memory like that *could* have messed with me, and likely at the worst possible moment. Just like he feared.

I could only hope that Mordred carrying around the memories of us killing him eight times had the same effect on *him*. Even Alex had taken a trophy in that competition.

And Alex had called me *dad*... My *son* had killed Mordred... for *me*.

I shook my head weakly, my own eyes misting up. "No... I can do it myself—"

Alex settled the spear over my heart, ending my argument. "I've only got a few moments left, and no one else is here to guarantee that you die. It has to be me," he said in a firmer tone. Then, he smiled crookedly. "And I couldn't imagine how terrible I'd feel if I botched up murdering you," he said in the driest tone I had ever heard. "Leaving you here... all *alone*... to bleed out—"

"I get it," I muttered, managing a pointed scowl. "Stop torturing me..." I met his eyes solidly, "my Son."

He closed his eyes tightly, cherishing the sentiment.

Then he gasped, coughing up fresh blood. "Mordred is still coming tomorrow... and you're the only one who can save us. I'll be home soon. Sorry it's after curfew..."

I opened my mouth to argue one last time. I could end it myself. I didn't want this on his conscience – even though it wasn't real, wasn't permanent – but he ended the discussion himself, stabbing me through the heart as his own heart failed. I gasped instinctively, unable to breathe.

I felt Alex fall atop me in a bloody hug, and I tried with every ounce of will left in me to ignore the pull of death long enough to return the gesture, to wrap my arms around him, too...

CHAPTER 58

I woke up screaming, my arms hugging an imaginary child who meant everything to me. I blinked, my mind slowly coming back to reality. I could still imagine the blade piercing my heart. Still remember trying to hug Alex back as he died in my arms.

I gasped anxiously.

Alex.

I needed to make sure he wasn't still suffering in the Dueling Grounds, but that he had actually died this time. I jumped out of bed, my legs still not accustomed to upwards mobility, still half asleep. And as I stumbled out of the room, rebounding off the door and into the hall, I realized I was completely naked.

I didn't care. I tore down the hall towards Alex's rooms, shouting his name at the top of my lungs. It was late, so the lights were off, the hall illuminated only by the LED lighting casting areas in warm, soothing hues that gradually changed colors on a continuous timer, bathing the area from white, to yellow, to orange, to red, and on through the rainbow.

I kept on shouting, not caring in the slightest if I woke anyone up. Anyone worth their pay would be on high alert tonight after even one of my allies had returned from Fight Club, raving about the carnage. As I tore down the halls, I was actually kind of surprised that no one had tried to return to the Fight Club to check on us. Then I remembered that there was some kind of time restraint on that – if you had been killed there, you had to wait a half-day or so before you could return.

Still, there should have been armed fucking guards at every corner, or someone waiting in my room for me.

I burst into Alex's rooms, sweeping the area quickly, but saw no sign of him.

I cursed, spun, and ran back out the door. Would he have awoken somewhere else? Or had he returned like me and gone out to check on everyone else, to tell them what had happened?

"If I was Alex, where would I go—"

It hit me in an instant, and I began running.

Ruin. He would go to check on either Ruin or me, and seeing as how Ruin had left the Fight Club in a truly unique way, it wasn't unbelievable to think he might have actually died. Whereas if Alex had woken up, realized he was fine, then he would have assumed I was fine as well, and gone out to check on the other most important person in his life.

I kept on shouting Alex's name as I half ran, half fell down the stairs, saving myself only by grasping at the bannister. Dean stormed onto the landing at the base of the stairs in his night robe, saw I was naked, and grimaced.

Then he pulled out his airsoft gun; for some reason he'd had it tucked into his robe. And it had some kind of bulbous extended magazine filled with about a million plastic BB's.

I blinked at him incredulously. "Really?" I snapped in disbelief. "You work for me! You can't just shoot me—"

He cocked back the hammer and clicked off the safety, cutting me off with the weight of his actions. "Spare the rod, spoil the child," he said in the tone only a well-established Butler could pull off. "I warned you, Master Temple. No more nudity in this house. It's getting quite out of hand." And he pointed the gun at me, unloading without further warning.

I squawked and sprinted for my life to escape the line of fire, hissing at each fiery bite of the damned plastic bullets pegging my ass and lower back. Dean had gotten the automatic version, apparently.

My run was not that of a graceful, long-legged gazelle, because too wide of a stride and he might tag my dangly bits by accident. So, it was more of a stiff-legged speed-walk as I basically pretended to be the fastest wind-up nutcracker toy in the world, keeping my legs straight as I swung my legs as fast as possible.

Dean obviously intended for me to remember the lesson, for he pursued me with a vengeance.

"Dean!" I shouted, alarmed at how fast he was in house slippers. "We're all in grave danger!"

"We're always in grave danger. And you look perfectly fine. I'll have no more of this nudity nonsense," he said in a cool, unflappable tone, unaffected by his swift sprint. "Enough is enough."

I spotted a blanket hanging off a nearby couch and lunged for it. He shot my hand with about seventy-eight BB's, and another sixty-two hit me in the exposed ribs as I desperately tried to swing it over my shoulders.

Finally covered, I held it over my face, rounding on him. I realized it was some sort of tiger skin, not a blanket, and that it didn't reach all the way to the floor. "There!" I hissed. "Happy now?"

He shot me in the pinky toe with another dozen bullets, making me hop on one foot. "Dance, monkey," Dean said in a dry tone, switching targets to my other foot, almost ripping off that pinky toe as well. "Dance," he repeated, not releasing the trigger for a second.

I snarled in both pain and outrage, and spun to resume my sprint for Alex.

I no longer heard him running after me, but as I lengthened my stride, I realized Dean had learned a thing or two about geometry in Butler School. Because he used the marble floor to angle bullets *under* my tiger-skin, and I suddenly felt about thirty-six of the plastic hellfire missiles tag me in the testicula-oblangata, momentarily shutting down my brain and sending me sliding on the floor. I whimpered, tucking my feet under the tiger skin, and rolled out of the sniping Butler's line of sight, gasping.

The sound of bouncing BB's echoed down the hall, but I no longer heard the sound of him pulling the trigger or pursuing me.

I cautiously peeped my head around the corner to see Dean pointing the gun at me from down the Hall. I swore, ducking back to safety, but he never pulled the trigger.

"What's the new rule, Master Temple?" he called out loudly.

"No more nudity in public places," I shouted back, desperate to get him away from me.

"Thank you, Sir. Can I do anything else for you this evening?"

I shook my head in disbelief. "No, Dean, thank you. That will be all."

"Of course, Master Temple. I'll have breakfast ready in the morning. Good night, sir."

"Good night, Dean," I called back, gritting my teeth. I didn't risk movement until I heard him walking away, and I didn't peek out into the hallway until I was sure he was gone.

Then I was running again, this time out the front door.

I had forgotten about the news reporters lurking at the gate, but spotting the blazing array of floodlights they had set up aimed towards my front door, I immediately swore seven kinds of hell. Especially at the gasps of surprise and the sudden explosion of clicking cameras that were apparently rigged to a motion sensor so they wouldn't miss the opportunity to snap a thousand pictures of the local billionaire in his natural habitat.

The streaking, tiger-skin clad billionaire running through his lawn in the middle of the night for a nocturnal hunt.

I might have flinched instinctively at those clicks, my body's fight or flight syndrome instinctively thinking it was Dean and his airsoft gun again. I ran out of view, using the hill to hide my movements as I ran to the pale white tree glistening in the moonlight.

I let out a sigh of relief, almost collapsing to the grass as I saw Alex standing at the base of Carl's Mighty D, discreetly calling out to the tree-house high above, but careful not to alert the press that something was happening.

Too late for that, thanks to me.

But Alex was alive. I took a deep breath, let it out, and then walked over to him.

He was wearing a thick robe, and had a steaming cup of cocoa in his hands. I blinked down at it as I stopped beside him.

He noticed me, gasped, and instinctively reached in for a hug until he saw my outfit. "Ummm..."

I scowled back. "All I could find on short notice. You're lucky Dean didn't find you before you got that robe."

Alex frowned at me. "Dean *gave* me the robe. *And* the hot chocolate. He saw me running through the hall, naked, looking for you. I was crying, so I think he was concerned. Said he would go check on you."

I blinked at him, opening my mouth silently, but couldn't form words. That no good, backstabbing bastard of a Butler.

Alex was frowning. "Didn't he find you? He had a robe ready for you..." he added, inspecting my tiger skin.

I let out another breath. "I thought this was cooler," I snapped. "Is he home?" I asked, glancing up.

Alex shrugged. "I think so, but he's not answering."

"Go away!" a voice shouted from within the treehouse.

And I almost sat down on my tiger skin and cried. B—no, Ruin was alive. But why...

"Come on out!" Alex hissed. "We were scared to death for you. You were a goddamn hero tonight!"

The door to the treehouse creaked open, and out drifted a train-wreck of a cloud. "Ow..." he said groggily. If a cumulous could mimic a one-night-stand's walk of shame, Ruin would have nailed it. I grew alarmed. "B, what the hell? Are you okay?" I asked nervously.

His center mass rumbled distantly, like a complaining growl of thunder on the horizon, and a flurry of multi-colored lightning coagulated from his edges to a single point near his lower edge. He suddenly condensed into a much smaller mass. "Oh, not again," he whispered anxiously, zipping back into the treehouse and slamming the door.

I shared a quick, confused look with Alex before a flash of light from up above caught our attention. And what looked like a hurricane briefly illuminated the tree house from inside. Water abruptly poured down through the crack in the treehouse door, and the windows burst open, rattling from a sudden torrent of wind. We instinctively dodged the falling water, grimacing at a bizarre thought.

Ruin groaned in agony, an all-too-familiar sound. "I don't want you to see me like this. I just want to die," he whimpered pathetically, not really meaning it.

"Did he just..." Alex whispered incredulously.

I shook my head in disbelief, realizing I was about to burst with laughter. "I think so."

Ruin had just... had an accident. IBS – Irritable Beast Syndrome.

Alex turned to me, grinning wide. "That soul he ate must have been expired," he said, chuckling. Then he bubbled over with laughter.

After such a crazily chaotic night, all the death, fear, carnage... to witness Ruin experiencing his first case of food poisoning was just too much. And… just the right amount. Soon we were both cackling, no longer caring about anything the reporters might pick up for the paper in the morning.

We laughed back and forth for a while, exchanging jokes about Ruin's rumbly tummy.

But he was alive. Alex was alive. And if they were alive, my other friends were alive, too. I realized I must have left my cell phone in my room, and that it was probably blowing up with missed calls and texts. But glancing over at Alex – and another waterfall from Ruin's treehouse – I told myself it could wait a few more minutes.

Alex regarded me warily. "Sorry about killing you… And for tricking Grimm into taking me to Fight Night. I told him you were challenging Roy G. Biv. That's really all the push he needed to turn against your wishes."

I grunted, unable to even find the energy to be upset. "That's what friends are for," I finally admitted.

Despite how crazy that sounded, he nodded thoughtfully. "I think I'm beginning to see that." Alex pointed at my neck. "That doesn't look good," he said softly.

I glanced down to find my Horseman's Mask, back to its disguise as a coin, hanging from the chain around my neck. It now featured a jagged white line down the center. I sighed, letting it go, and in the process, got a glimpse of my Family Crest branded into my palm.

It *also* had a jagged bolt down the center – part of the original design. I frowned.

I was getting really sick and tired of these coincidences.

I nodded at Alex. "I'll figure it out later," I told him.

He reached into his pocket, and handed over the Devourer as casually as if he was handing me my mail. My eyes widened and I snatched it away eagerly. The light was still there, but it was very dark now, like a dim, wine-colored night light. The blade hummed slightly, but nothing like it had earlier tonight. I glanced at Alex, the look on my face obviously incredulous.

He shrugged easily. "I needed to let my cocoa cool off, and Ruin wasn't answering, so I walked back to the Drop Zone to pick it up," he said casually, sipping at his cocoa. He let out a pleased sound. "Ah, perfect," he said, licking at his lips.

At any other time, I probably would have swatted the cocoa out of his hands.

Then I noticed the mischievous twinkle in his eyes. "Cocky little shit," I muttered, grunting.

He grinned back, nodding. "Learned from the best. Oh, and I put your satchel in your bedroom's safe like you asked." I let out a breath of relief. The vial was safe.

I rolled my eyes at Alex's smug grin, and then jumped to my feet, suddenly remembering something as I thought about the Devourer. The Horsemen!

"Alex, I need to go check on something. You're in charge while I'm gone. I won't be long, hopefully. I'm sure everyone is going to have a ton of questions. Answer what you can, but try to get everyone to stay in one place so we can make Gateways to get them all here. We need to talk about what happened tonight."

He nodded. "We won. That's what happened."

I grimaced. "We won an intense battle, that's for sure. But the next battle happens tomorrow when Mordred pops over for our meeting. I have a feeling the agenda might have changed after tonight. This is a war, and we need to figure out what comes next. How he'll respond. I'm guessing it will be something awful that none of us would have voted for."

Alex nodded soberly. "You should probably change before you go check on the Horsemen," he said as I was walking away. I turned to look at him, but he had his back to me, sipping his cocoa loudly.

"You... saw it all, didn't you? The Horseman thing..." I asked in a soft voice.

"Oh, yeah. You kicked some serious ass, for what it's worth."

I nodded, studying his back, considering his newfound confidence and rock-solid threshold for doing what needed to be done. While suffering a fatal chest wound, he had watched as the Horsemen went up against Mordred. Seeing how the battle was faring, he had clung to life in order to offer help at the last minute. Ignoring his pain to make sure he was there if I needed it. For as long as he could hold on.

"I think you're going to be very dangerous one day, Alex."

He glanced over his shoulder at me. "Only to the bad guys, Dad." Then he turned back to the tree, humming softly to himself.

Taking his advice, I did decide to change into something a little more respectable.

But I was smart enough to Shadow Walk rather than risking my life in Dean's funhouse.

His hallway of Death by Airsoft.

CHAPTER 59

*I*t took a little bit of effort, but I finally managed to find where the Horsemen were staying. Mainly because I had found a notepad in Othello's room with an address on it, the rest of the page blank.

I strolled up to the unassuming cottage at the end of a quiet street and knocked.

I heard footsteps approaching the door, and my heart rose.

The door opened, and I saw Death staring back at me. My sudden burst of relief died just as suddenly when I really took stock of him. He looked like his namesake, pale and wan. He was using his scythe as a cane.

"Um, what the hell happened tonight?" I demanded, peering past him. "Where are the others?"

"In here," a sniffling voice called out. I frowned uncertainly, meeting Death's eyes.

He shrugged. "Apparently, we caught a cold," he said tiredly.

"I caught it first," the same sniffling voice wheezed before erupting into a hacking cough. Must have been Conquest. "This is terrible! I feel like I'm dying!" he whined.

Death rolled his eyes. "Come on in, Hope," he said, turning his back on me to lead the way.

I followed him, not sure if I should be terrified, or if it was no big deal for them to catch a cold.

I followed Death to the living room to find War, Conquest, and Famine huddled together on a couch, sharing a blanket. It was a rather ridiculous sight, to be honest. Othello was cursing under her breath, shoving an electric thermometer into Conquest's mouth. She noticed me, and snarled, "The man-flu! One little sniffle and they all suddenly think the world is ending!"

I studied her patients, diagnosing that they really didn't look very good. Alarmingly bad, actually. "Well, with these guys, it kind of is *world-ending*, right?"

Othello shot me a dark look. "You wouldn't see a woman acting this dramatic. We know how to handle a weak cough."

I shared a look with Death, who was leaning on his scythe much more openly, now. Practically hanging onto it, his body sagging. "You... didn't tell her?" I whispered, growing alarmed at his rapid rate of decline.

"Didn't tell me *what?*" Othello demanded, turning to Death with a furious look. I appraised the other Horsemen, and realized they all looked much worse than a few moments ago. They had purple rings under their eyes, and their skin was ashen.

Famine began coughing violently, slapping his hand over his mouth. When he pulled it away, his palm speckled with blood. Everyone stared incredulously, even Othello, making her momentarily forget all about her boyfriend's omission.

The thermometer suddenly beeped, saving Death's life. Othello took it out hurriedly, read it, and then dropped the thermometer in disbelief. "One-thirty-nine!" she shrieked. "That's *impossible*. You were at ninety-nine two minutes ago!" She jumped off the couch, eyes widening as she checked on Death.

Famine reached out for a small trinket sitting on the coffee table, a figure of some kind. As his fingers drew closer, it began to smoke, then zapped him upon contact. He hissed, sending himself into another coughing fit.

"Is that... your Mask?" I asked warily.

It was a rhetorical question, because the look in Famine's eyes gave me my answer. I reached up to my neck, realizing that the coin – my Mask – was vibrating so intensely that it was actually hurting my skin.

And growing stronger. I touched it, wincing at the electric current sensation, but it didn't smoke or zap me like Famine's had.

Death abruptly collapsed like a puppet with cut strings. Othello was instantly lifting his head to her lap, terrified. "Jesus, Nate! He's burning up, too! They were fine a few minutes ago—"

Then it dawned on me. "I'm... making it *worse*," I said in disbelief. My Mask was killing them.

And before she could respond, I sprinted out the front door, Shadow Walking back to the Sanctorum at Chateau Falco, not sure how far away I needed to get.

I began to pace, staring down at my phone. I didn't want to call her in case she was busy saving their lives, but I wanted to call her in case she needed help... saving their lives.

My phone finally rang, and I instantly answered. "Are they okay?" I demanded.

"Yes," Othello said, voice shaking. "Back to their horrible... man-flu," she said with forced humor, but the mini-sob ruined it. "Within moments of you leaving..." she trailed off, thinking. "Where are you?"

"Chateau Falco," I told her, still pacing.

She was quiet for a moment. "That seems to be far enough away... At least you're no longer killing them. I didn't believe you were the cause, but..." she sniffed, "you kind of proved that fucking bit, didn't you?" And I could tell she was on the verge of hysteria.

Not just because I had somehow harmed the Horsemen, but that I had somehow harmed... her *boyfriend*.

"What can I do?" I asked.

"You can tell me what the hell—" I heard a rattling sound like she had dropped the phone, and then a heated argument. I also heard three men cheering weakly in the background.

Death came onto the phone, voice soft and thready, but no longer alarmingly so. "Nate... You must find the Four Horsemen..."

I gripped the phone tightly, wanting to snap at him. "I almost *killed* the Four Horsemen a few minutes ago, remember?"

He growled back like an old dog with no teeth. "Find the Mask Maker. He can... explain it better. I honestly... don't even know where to begin..." I could tell the conversation was draining him, the pauses between words growing longer.

"Matthias?" I asked. "I don't have time to go hunting for him. We have bigger problems right now."

Death began coughing – a wet, nasty sound. "No," he wheezed. "There is no bigger problem than this. Your Mask isn't what we thought…"

The phone was snatched away again, and I heard a chorus of weak *boos* in the background, then another round of hacking coughs. "I'm back," Othello snarled. "Sit down before you fall down, Hemingway!" she snapped into the background. "And stop eating the crackers, Famine! They only throw you into coughing fits!"

"Othello, I have to go. I have to fix this."

She grumbled angrily. "Fine. I'll get my answers from these four toddlers," she muttered. "And Nate? You better fucking fix this. Keep your distance until you do. And call first next time! No more unannounced visits!" There was a pause before the line went dead.

I slowly lowered the phone, staring off at nothing, thinking furiously.

Then I began to pace, feeling restless, not knowing where to begin, but I did know if I sat down I would pass out. Not necessarily from exhaustion, but from hyper stress, feeling overwhelmed and uncertain what to do. Death's words slithered through my mind like poison.

Find the Four Horsemen…

Your Mask isn't what we thought…

Find the Mask Maker…

None of that made any sense. I'd almost killed the Four Horsemen just by being in the same room with them. And some very strange things had happened to them at the Dueling Grounds, weakening them. And I'd briefly received some kind of energy boost from them at the end, after they'd… fallen, or whatever it had been.

And the Horsemen couldn't even *touch* their own Masks.

And now my own Mask was damaged. Did it need a recharge or something? Had I strained it in my fight against Mordred? I very seriously considered putting it on anyway, because that voice I had heard inside it sure seemed to have some answers – knew all the fine print of the employment contract I hadn't bothered to read.

I let out a breath. One thing was certain. If I couldn't ask that voice, there really only was one other person who might have an idea of what had happened. The man who had given me my Mask as a birthday present. "The Mask Maker…" I muttered. "That crazy son of a bitch—"

"That's no way to talk about your grandparents," a voice said from the other side of the room.

329

CHAPTER 60

I spun instinctively, calling up my whips of elemental fire and ice. They crackled, singeing the rug as I stared at a figure sitting behind the ancient wooden writing desk.

Matthias Temple. The Mad Hatter. The Motherfucking *Mask Maker*...

He slowly slid a fingertip across the surface of his old desk, smiling to himself at distant memories. He finally sighed and folded his hands in front of him before looking up at me. He looked like a kind, old man, completely unassuming, as if trying to project a peaceful demeanor. But he was a Maker, and he didn't need his hands to make a bad situation worse. "They're dying, aren't they?" he asked tiredly.

"What are you doing here?" I demanded, ignoring his question as I took slow, deliberate steps closer. I was done with coincidences, and I wasn't about to answer his question until I got my own answers for once. Matthias showing up right when I was told to go find him? I hadn't heard a word from him ever since he'd kidnapped my Knight, putting Baba Yaga and Van Helsing into a deep, deep sleep.

His eyes flickered to a velvet bag on the table. The bag was... shaking, like he had caught a pissed off badger or something. "These began rattling in their bag an hour ago. I'd almost forgotten I Made them, to be honest."

I frowned at the bag, then frowned harder at Matthias. "Made..." I said, catching onto the distinction. He nodded very slowly, watching me.

Because Matthias was a *Maker* – a man balancing a symbiotic relationship with a Beast that gave him access to truly unbelievable powers. When he said he *Made* something, the word usually had a capital letter in front of it. He wasn't usually talking about Making sandwiches.

"Where have you *been*?" I asked, changing topics, unsure whether he was a friend or foe.

"Pan chased me around for quite some time. Finally caught up to me and told me he only wanted to help the Knight. Said he knew a cave in Fae where we wouldn't be disturbed, where he could begin healing him. But I'm pretty sure he just wanted to keep an eye on me. Make sure I wasn't a danger to you. I think… he cares very much about you, Nate."

I nodded slowly. Matthias had kidnapped the Knight from Pan, and I hadn't heard from him in a while. Matthias' answer sounded like what Pan would do, though. Taking him to a cave in Fae… where I had been born and raised.

"Pan agreed to let me leave when I showed him this," he said, tapping the velvet bag, and annoying the occupants inside. "So, I'm not a threat to you." His eyes grew introspective for a moment, and he tilted his head slightly. "At least, I don't think I am…" He leaned back with a sigh. "It was probably smart of him to keep an eye on me," he finally admitted, taking no offense in the fact that he obviously wasn't sure he could trust even himself to make the right call at times.

I let out a slow breath, thinking. They had the Knight, and Mordred seemed intent on hunting down anyone with any ties to the Round Table. Also… maybe a Knight would have insight into exactly what Merlin had done to the Table. The upgrades Mordred had mentioned.

I didn't realize I was glancing at the actual Round Table until I heard Matthias grunt. "I was never quite sure what to make about that. It has secrets, I know it… I wasted many years trying to learn them, but ultimately failed. I could sense it was powerful, but…" He sighed, shrugging slightly. "What *isn't* fucking powerful and dangerous inside Falco?" he admitted, grinning.

The house seemed to purr appreciatively, taking Matthias' words as a compliment.

Matthias smiled nostalgically up at the ceiling high above. "Ah, it's good to hear from you again, old girl. Congratulations, by the way. I'd love to meet your boy someday…"

Falco grew noticeably silent, and Matthias sighed sadly.

I, on the other hand, grinned. That had been a big fat, *not likely*, on the celestial magic eight-ball scale.

I turned back to the velvet sack, walking closer, almost afraid to ask. "Is that for me?" I asked nervously, fearing the contents.

Matthias grunted. "That depends on if you have the Devourer. If not, I'm going to toss these to the bottom of the stone ocean next to your Fae Cave and hope for the best," he muttered.

I cocked my head at him, not quite following his meaning. But I did pull the Devourer from my satchel, showing it to him. He winced, his face cast in the dim red glow of the spear's light, like a curtain of blood.

Taking a leap of faith, I held it out to him. "You need to take this away. Mordred wants it more than anything in the world, and if he gets his hands on it, he'll have three of his souls back, making him stronger…"

Matthias lifted his hands, leaning away. "The Devourer isn't the *problem*, boy. It's the *solution*."

I stared back at him, wondering if he was having part of the conversation inside the padded walls of his mind, forgetting to say it out loud. How was the Devourer the solution? Anubis was going to be rightly pissed when he learned I had taken three of his Nine Souls – if he didn't know already…

Matthias noticed my look, and leaned closer. "You need to feed the souls to your new Brothers. Or Sisters, I guess…" he added thoughtfully. "I hear you're quite the ladies' man." He smirked absently, a distant smug pride that his descendant had a way with the ladies.

Allegedly.

I blinked at him. "Are you feeling alright, Matthias?" I asked warily. Because he wasn't making any sense, and he was prone to fits of madness. He'd been locked away so long he'd taken to believing he was actually the Mad Hatter, after all.

"I'm fine. But you may want to sit down for this," he said, and then he casually upended the velvet bag.

Three… Masks fell onto the table, rattling and humming against the surface, and the coin on my necklace suddenly began to bounce and tingle against my chest. I gritted my teeth, ignoring the slight pain, fearful of what would happen if I took it off so close to these… other Masks.

What if they bonded together like Transformers or something. Power Ranger Horseman!

As Matthias fought to build a perimeter around them with items from the drawers, or the stack of books perched on the edge of the desk, to prevent them from skittering off the table, I just stared, feeling nauseated. They kept angling towards me, like I was some kind of magnet. Or perhaps it was my Mask – the coin tingling against my chest.

"And what are these?" I asked in barely a whisper, having a pretty damned good idea what they were, even if it didn't make any sense at the moment.

"Um," he said, corralling one of the more active Masks back towards the center of the desk. "Your new Brothers and Sisters. You have to Make Horseman Masks in groups of Four, you see. Otherwise they won't work." He said all of this absently, more focused on keeping them on the desk, like herding chickens.

He had just Made another set of Horsemen Masks, and had forgotten to mention it? Jesus. No wonder the Four Horsemen were sick. Whatever Matthias had done was fucking with them somehow.

I leaned forward, studying them. I slowly waved my Devourer to the right, and the Masks began shifting that direction. I waved the Devourer slowly to the left, and they seemed to grow more agitated, perhaps annoyed, but they did try to change course. They were varying shades of stone – white, gold, and green – and entirely unique from another. But before I could get a closer look, Matthias finally growled, wincing as he snatched them up and shoved them back into the sack. "That's quite enough of that. Quiet, now," he commanded the velvet sack.

Surprisingly, they did seem to calm down. Slightly.

"They have to be made in Fours..." I repeated slowly. "And you just... forgot to tell me that when you gave me mine... Then you broke up their little family. No *wonder* they're pissed."

Matthias tapped his temple, grinning guiltily. "I was a little out of sorts back then, but I'm much better now." He met my eyes, his face hardening. "Would you rather I had handed them *all* over to you back then?"

Right. I shook my head, waving a hand. I also decided not to give him my opinion about declaring himself *much better now*. We had enough to fight about already. "Is that why they're pissed? Because you broke up the band?"

Matthias shook his head. "Then why are they so... agitated?"

Matthias pointed a finger at my Devourer. "They're hungry for *Souls*.

333

And I'm not sure I've been in the presence of Souls *that* powerful for quite some time. Makes my nose itch being this close."

My stomach began to rumble queasily. "These Masks need souls?"

Matthias shrugged. "That will calm them down for a while, the stronger the better. But what they really need is owners. *Riders.*" He glanced at my necklace thoughtfully. "I think they're a wee-bit jealous of their Brother finding an owner," he admitted with a shrug. "Something woke them up about an hour ago, and I'm guessing it has to do with your concern over the other Four Horsemen. The older *Biblical* Riders," he clarified, frowning. "This is going to get confusing, isn't it?"

I grunted, recalling how my coin had reacted when they'd been dumped onto the table. But now, my Mask was just giving off a faint humming sensation.

"We already have Four Horsemen. The Biblical ones, as you called them. Is this why they're sick?" I asked, pointing at the bag. "Because I'm accidentally replacing them with these?"

Matthias scoffed, waving a hand. "Heavens, no. These don't replace the Bible Thumpers," he muttered, as if I'd said the dumbest thing in the world.

I gave him a very dry look.

He sighed. "Think of *your* Four Horsemen – *these* Masks – as… *cousins* to the Biblical Horsemen." I shivered to hear the words, *cousins*, just like that voice inside my Mask had said. "These Masks were awoken about an hour or so ago, so you did *something* with your Mask. And if the Four Horsemen are suddenly sick, it's definitely related to these assholes. They're leeching power from the existing Horsemen. Jealousy, remember?" he chuckled. "Vengeful little shits, aren't they?" He slapped the table at that, laughing harder.

"Yeah… fucking hilarious. How do I stop these Masks from leeching off the Four Horsemen?"

Matthias stared at me as if I was purposely being daft. "I just *told* you. Feed them. That will calm them down for a while. Give you time to find owners. You need to put the souls from your Devourer in the Masks, or else they will drain the Biblical Horsemen entirely. You woke yours up, bonding with it, finally, so now you're on borrowed time. They won't stop leeching power until you pay them respect, giving them what they want – Riders. Barring that, feeding them powerful souls will buy you more time."

"You couldn't have given me a warning that I needed to start interviews a while ago?" I demanded.

"Consider this your warning. Start interviewing people." He pointed at the Masks. "For your favorite three people. Or most hated three people," he muttered. "Whatever you choose."

I leaned closer. "You're telling me that if I feed these souls from my Devourer into these Masks, that the Four Biblical Horsemen will miraculously be healthy again? Back to fighting shape?"

Matthias thought about it. "Well, I'm not a doctor or anything, but it sounds about right."

I grimaced. Of course. But I didn't really see a negative in it. Getting rid of these souls by placing them into the Masks would mean I could use my Devourer again. That it would no longer be dangerous to carry, fearing Mordred hunting me every time I looked over my shoulder. And like a security blanket, I was feeling pretty damned secure with the blade on my person. Like it had been designed for me, specifically.

Remembering I had found it in Pandora's Armory, and that it matched the unicorn that had bonded with me, I accepted the fact that I was a target in some vast, universal con-game. Sometimes, all you could do was roll with the con, waiting for the moment you could flip the script and turn it back on the con-man.

And anyway, it wasn't like I had much choice. Either throw the Devourer in the deepest section of the ocean where Mordred couldn't find it – and likely end up killing the Biblical Four Horsemen as the three Masks on the table slowly drained their powers to nothing.

Or... feed these *vengeful little shits* the souls I wanted nothing to do with anyway.

"I'm going to need to sleep on this," I told Matthias. "Or at least take a walk to clear my head, making sure I'm not jumping into yet another bad decision." Because I had just considered that Anubis might have a very strong opinion on the matter. I was holding three of his Nine Souls in captivity, and Ruin had eaten one of them as well. Out of Nine, Anubis had only recovered four. That probably wouldn't look good in his eyes.

Matthias watched me uneasily, then glanced at the bag, which had suddenly begun to rattle much more angrily, as if realizing I was delaying their meal. "I... well, I wouldn't wait too long. Right now, you are waving a raw steak in front of a pack of lions, then walking away."

I nodded, watching the twitching bag. "I'm their brother, though, right?"

Matthias gave me a very dry look. "How well did that work out for Cain and Abel?"

I scowled. "Right. Thanks for that lovely image."

"Bad things happen when you use a Mask without a soul…"

"Mordred's still out there. Can't we just… put this Mask business on hold? I've been dragging my feet for years. Why the sudden rush?"

He shook his head. "You woke up your Mask tonight, starting the clock. Now, your new siblings need Riders, or a distraction until you find Riders. Maybe feeding them will give you a year or two. Perhaps three, if you're lucky. I don't quite know. I just Made them," he said, shrugging innocently.

I blinked at him incredulously. Was he really taking no responsibility in this? It was unbelievable.

"It's also considered very rude to wake a Mask," he said, pointing at the coin around my neck, "before you've chosen Riders for the *others*," he said, pointing at the bag. "Anyway, this is all scholarly. No one thought it actually possible. Sure, they theorized about it, but didn't actually believe it. Not after…" he shook his head. "Anyway, you have three big, fat, juicy souls."

I narrowed my eyes suspiciously, but ultimately let it go. He had a point. Souls locked in the deepest pits of Hell had to be incredibly powerful.

"I need you to find out exactly how long I have to decide. And what the consequences are to waiting. What the Biblical Four Horsemen can expect if I don't hand over these souls." Because the more I thought about it, I really needed to check with Anubis, first.

"Well, left unchecked, it will drain the Biblical Horsemen to…" he searched for the right word, then snapped his fingers as loud as a gunshot, making me flinch. "What's that saying? *Ashes to ashes, dust to dust…*" he ventured, quoting the bible.

I grunted grimly, thinking. "But if we're all Horsemen – which makes zero sense, by the way – why are we forced to cannibalize ourselves?"

Matthias was shaking his head. "Balance. Right now, the Biblical Riders have all the juice, all the toys. Your ragtag orphans have *no* toys, and the two squads just ran into each other on the playground. You're similar, but differ-ent. A new branch of the family. You're rivals, in a way. Friendly rivals, perhaps, but on the power spectrum, you're rivals. And right now, you have three berserkers led by an even more unstable Mask," he said pointing at my necklace, "and the orphans are staring down the rich kids. You need to throw them a bone. Feed them the souls. It's not like your Devourer is going to last long, anyway. To be honest, I'm stunned it's held three souls this powerful for so long without fracturing." He glanced at the ruby, and his eyes widened in alarm.

CHAPTER 61

$\mathcal{I}$ glanced down, picking up on the horrified look on his face. It *was* fractured, and a spider's web of cracks were growing even as we watched. "Well, shit."

"You better decide fast, Nate…"

"How?" I shouted frantically.

Matthias scanned the room desperately, searching for anything that might help, well, with whatever unholy communion we were making up as we fumbled along. His eyes latched onto the Round Table, and he grunted, turning back to me with an uneasy smile. "Try Knighting them?"

I leaned forward, hissing. "I don't know their names!"

"Well, *give* them names. That shouldn't be too hard. You're a fucking wizard, right? Merlin did it all the time."

"I'm not fucking Merlin, you twat!" I snapped, panting with fear. Because I realized that Anubis was about to write me my first official warning for my employee file.

Matthias narrowed his eyes angrily at my insult, then he folded his arms, taking a deep breath, murmuring to himself like he was counting to *three*. His eyes considered the Devourer, then the coin around my neck. "You're Hope, right?" I nodded. "So, come up with three other names… Something with balance, something with opposition. Pit them against each other. Maybe that will keep them from the Biblical Riders."

I nodded, taking a deep breath. Matthias upended the bag gently, and the Masks fell out, rattling like a kicked hornets' nest, smoking slightly as they singed the surface of the desk. And, as if the Names were being pulled out of me, I spoke, touching each Mask like a handshake, welcoming them to the world.

"Despair," I murmured, touching the white stone Mask with the tip of my blade. The Mask calmed slightly, pulsing warmer through the blade, and a soul zipped out of the ruby, straight into the open-mouth of the Mask. That one felt very personal, for some reason I couldn't quite explain.

"Justice," I said, touching a golden Mask. I felt a cool, tingling shiver through the blade, and felt like I had just popped a mint into my mouth. The golden Mask also sucked down a soul from the ruby, eliciting another crack through the stone.

The stone began to glow brighter, the red smoke thick in the air.

"Absolution," I said, touching the last green Mask. This one nipped at me playfully through my blade, and gobbled down the last soul.

The ruby crumbled to dust, a pile of lifeless diamond grit.

Despair to oppose and balance Hope.

Absolution to oppose and balance Justice.

I don't know why, but the Names just felt right as soon as I said them. The Masks sat motionless on the desk, now, as if settling down for a long nap to digest their food – like everyone did after a big Thanksgiving meal. I just hoped it was long enough for me to do… whatever it was that I needed to do.

I was relieved to find that my blade was still intact, along with the feathers. No longer a Devourer, but still a powerful blade. Did that make it an Eyeless, like Talon's spear? It didn't have a single nick in it from all my fighting last night. Not a scratch or dent anywhere along the razor-sharp edge.

I frowned, studying the motionless Masks on the desk. "What about *my* Mask?" I asked, remembering that it was damaged. Was that crack related to this business?

Matthias looked up sharply, as if he'd completely forgotten about it. He held out a hand, asking for it. I tugged it off the chain, letting it shift into an actual Mask rather than a coin. It hummed lightly, but no longer the raging vibration it had been doing lately. As if feeding its siblings had calmed it, slightly. I handed it over, hesitating only for a moment. Matthias hefted it as if weighing it, and then lifted it to his ear as if listening to a secret.

Then he lowered it, glancing down at it in surprise.

He lifted it back to his ear, murmuring unintelligently. Then he listened again.

He lowered it much more slowly this time. "It's... well, it's jealous," he finally said.

I threw my hands into the air. "What the fuck does *that* mean? It has a Rider! The others don't!" Of course, I got the petty Mask.

"It means it wants a soul, too. Doesn't want to be left out. You respected her siblings, she feels slighted. She should have been first."

I pointed at the shattered Devourer. "I'm fresh out of souls, Matthias. And I am not going down to Hell to get another. Anubis is liable to lock me up for good when he hears I fed his souls to my new pets."

Matthias handed back the Mask, waving his other hand dismissively. "Just go kill another god. That's all these were," he said, indicating the diamond grit. "Old, dead gods.

I blinked at him in disbelief. The Nine Souls... had been fallen gods?

"You're friends with a bunch of gods, right? Just go ask if one of them will let you kill him. Or her," he added, thoughtfully. "Hell, a Beast would probably do it, too. Someone with a lot of worship power, or just general power will also suffice."

I frowned at that, his words ticking something in my mind. "I think Mordred still has one of the Nine Souls..." I said, thinking.

Matthias grunted. "Yeah, I don't think you have time to take on Mordred again. This needs to happen, pretty soon. Your Mask is dangerously close to cracking. Find a god."

I shifted in my seat, slightly, not really coming up with a convenient way to bring up that topic in my godly social circle. Maybe host a poker night? *Hey guys, anyone want to bet their soul on this hand?*

Something was digging into my hip, so I reached into my pocket. My fingers latched onto the glass vial I had used to tempt Mordred into joining me at Fight Night. I'd retrieved it the instant I'd put some clothes on, fearing to leave it out of my sight.

I pulled it out, studying it thoughtfully. The liquid metal swirled and shifted lazily inside.

I glanced over at the Round Table, considering Odin. I doubted he would be willing to hand over his Soul any time soon. "Hey, Matthias. Does it smell like blood in here?" I asked out loud, not knowing why, but remembering Odin had commented on it, saying the Round Table must be dirty. That it needed a cleanse.

Matthias grunted. "I don't smell anything. Are you bleeding?"

I waved off his concern, tilting the glass vial in my hand absently.

I considered asking Anubis if he had any other Souls lying around, but was pretty sure he was going to filet me for stealing the ones I already had – let alone for feeding them to my new Masks. He'd told me to regrow my ichor, and I could only do that by killing a god. Had that been another hint?

I tilted the vial again, watching the strange symbols floating within the liquid metal.

What had Merlin done to get these runes and symbols to float around inside the liquid metal. He'd made the Round Table, and obviously added that stream of metal for a reason.

I tried to read some of the symbols in the vial, but realized I was just staring at the vial. It was fascinating to watch, like molten metal alphabet soup.

Mordred had hated Merlin, hated how the people worshipped him, loved him.

I narrowed my eyes suddenly, staring down at the vial. At the liquid golden color.

And for the first time ever, I felt like an idiot.

"Motherfucker..." I breathed. "It's Ichor..." Matthias grunted in disbelief, but I felt him leaning over the desk to get a closer look. My Mask began to purr, and I'd forgotten I'd set it on my lap at some point. The crack down the center was prominent, and I knew one solid blow would shatter it.

Merlin... had spelled his own blood, fusing it to the table. That's what all the runes and symbols were. They were incantations, and with him having been worshipped by so many people – as much or more than Arthur had ever been worshipped...

Had Merlin, in his own way, become a god of sorts? Mordred had wanted that power for himself, to replace his Nine Souls...

With no other ideas, and preferring not to ask my godly pals to give me their souls, I popped the lid of the vial off, took a deep breath, and poured it on my Mask...

I heard a very surprised gasp from Matthias...

I heard a very satisfied purr from my Mask...

And I heard the sound of racing feet from the hallway behind us. "Nate!" Gunnar shouted, sounding incredulous. "It's all over the news already. Mordred cancelled the meeting tomorrow. Said he had pressing business out of town and needed to postpone it for three weeks. We fucking did it!"

I felt him approach the table, suddenly noticing I wasn't alone. "What are you two doing— Holy shit! Why is your Mask doing *that*?"

I stared down at it in amazement. "I guess we'll just have to see... Three weeks, you said?" I asked, thinking about Mordred. "That should work. Matthias was just telling me about a vacation spot I really need to check out... But I have a few things to do before I start packing..."

And I began to plan my vacation.

I needed to learn about my past.

I needed to hear my own Manling Tale.

I needed to hear the Legend of Wylde Fae...

Because three weeks wasn't very far away, and memories could be deadly things.

And I knew a little Fae child named Alice who was just dying to hear some Manling Tales...

Nate Temple will return in LEGEND, late 2018... Turn the page to read the first chapter of **UNCHAINED** - *Book 1 in the Amazon Bestselling Feathers and Fire Series - and find out more about the mysterious Kansas City wizard, Callie Penrose... Or pick up your copy* **ONLINE.**

(Note: Callie appears in the Temple-verse after Nate's book 6, TINY GODS... Full chronology of all books in the Temple Universe shown on the 'Books in the Temple Verse' page at the back of this book.)

TRY: UNCHAINED (FEATHERS AND FIRE #1)

$\mathcal{T}$he rain pelted my hair, plastering loose strands of it to my forehead as I panted, eyes darting from tree to tree, terrified of each shifting branch, splash of water, and whistle of wind slipping through the nightscape around us. But... I was somewhat *excited*, too.

Somewhat.

"Easy, girl. All will be well," the big man creeping just ahead of me, murmured.

"You said we were going to get ice cream!" I hissed at him, failing to compose myself, but careful to keep my voice low and my eyes alert. "I'm not ready for this!" I had been trained to fight, with my hands, with weapons, and with my magic. But I had never taken an active role in a hunt before. I'd always been the getaway driver for my mentor.

The man grunted, grey eyes scanning the trees as he slipped through the tall grass. "And did we not get ice cream before coming here? Because I think I see some in your hair."

"You know what I mean, Roland. You tricked me." I checked the tips of my loose hair, saw nothing, and scowled at his back.

"The Lord does not give us a greater burden than we can shoulder."

I muttered dark things under my breath, wiping the water from my eyes. Again. My new shirt was going to be ruined. Silk never fared well in the rain. My choice of shoes wasn't much better. Boots, yes, but distressed, *fashionable* boots. Not work boots designed for the rain and mud. Definitely not monster hunting boots for our evening excursion through one of Kansas City's wooded parks. I realized I was forcibly distracting myself, keeping my mind busy with mundane thoughts to avoid my very real anxiety. Because whenever I grew nervous, an imagined nightmare always—

A church looming before me. Rain pouring down. Night sky and a glowing moon overhead. I was all alone. Crying on the cold, stone steps, and infant in a cardboard box—

I forced the nightmare away, breathing heavily. "You know I hate it when you talk like that," I whispered to him, trying to regain my composure. I wasn't angry with him, but was growing increasingly uncomfortable with our situation after my brief flashback of fear.

"Doesn't mean it shouldn't be said," he said kindly. "I think we're close. Be alert. Remember your training. Banish your fears. I am here. And the Lord is here. He always is."

So, he had noticed my sudden anxiety. "Maybe I should just go back to the car. I know I've trained, but I really don't think—"

A shape of fur, fangs, and claws launched from the shadows towards me, cutting off my words as it snarled, thirsty for my blood.

And my nightmare slipped back into my thoughts like a veiled assassin, a wraith hoping to hold me still for the monster to eat. I froze, unable to move. Twin sticks of power abruptly erupted into being in my clenched fists, but my fear swamped me with that stupid nightmare, the sticks held at my side, useless to save me.

Right before the beast's claws reached me, it grunted as something batted it from the air, sending it flying sideways. It struck a tree with another grunt and an angry whine of pain.

I fell to my knees right into a puddle, arms shaking, breathing fast.

My sticks crackled in the rain like live cattle prods, except their entire length was the electrical section — at least to anyone other than me. I could hold them without pain.

Magic was a part of me, coursing through my veins whether I wanted it or not, and Roland had spent many years teaching me how to master it. But I had never been able to fully master the nightmare inside me, and in moments of fear, it always won, overriding my training.

The fact that I had resorted to weapons — like the ones he had trained me with — rather than a burst of flame, was startling. It was good in the fact that my body's reflexes knew enough to call up a defense even without my direct command, but bad in the fact that it was the worst form of defense for the situation presented. I could have very easily done as Roland did, and hurt it from a distance. But I hadn't. Because of my stupid block.

Roland placed a calloused palm on my shoulder, and I flinched. "Easy, see? I am here." But he did frown at my choice of weapons, the reprimand silent but loud in my mind. I let out a shaky breath, forcing my fear back down. It was all in my head, but still, it wasn't easy. Fear could be like that.

I focused on Roland's implied lesson. Close combat weapons — even magically-powered ones — were for last resorts. I averted my eyes in very real shame. I knew these things. He didn't even need to tell me them. But when that damned nightmare caught hold of me, all my training went out the window. It haunted me like a shadow, waiting for moments just like this, as if trying to kill me. A form of psychological suicide? But it was why I constantly refused to join Roland on his hunts. He knew about it. And although he was trying to help me overcome that fear, he never pressed too hard.

Rain continued to sizzle as it struck my batons. I didn't let them go, using them as a totem to build my confidence back up. I slowly lifted my eyes to nod at him as I climbed back to my feet.

That's when I saw the second set of eyes in the shadows, right before they flew out of the darkness towards Roland's back. I threw one of my batons and missed, but that pretty much let Roland know that an unfriendly was behind him. Either that or I had just failed to murder my mentor at point-blank range. He whirled to confront the monster, expecting another aerial assault as he unleashed a ball of fire that splashed over the tree at chest height, washing the trunk in blue flames. But this monster was tricky. It hadn't planned on tackling Roland, but had merely jumped out of the darkness to get closer, no doubt learning from its fallen comrade, who still lay unmoving against the tree behind me.

His coat shone like midnight clouds with hints of lightning flashing in the depths of thick, wiry fur. The coat of dew dotting his fur reflected the moonlight, giving him a faint sheen as if covered in fresh oil. He was tall, easily hip height at the shoulder, and barrel chested, his rump much leaner than the rest of his body. He — I assumed male from the long, thick mane around his neck — had a very long snout, much longer and wider than any werewolf I had ever seen. Amazingly, and beyond my control, I realized he was beautiful.

But most of the natural world's lethal hunters were beautiful.

He landed in a wet puddle a pace in front of Roland, juked to the right, and then to the left, racing past the big man, biting into his hamstrings on his way by.

A wash of anger rolled over me at seeing my mentor injured, dousing my fear, and I swung my baton down as hard as I could. It struck the beast in the rump as it tried to dart back to cover — a typical wolf tactic. My blow singed his hair and shattered bone. The creature collapsed into a puddle of mud with a yelp, instinctively snapping his jaws over his shoulder to bite whatever had hit him.

I let him. But mostly out of dumb luck as I heard Roland hiss in pain, falling to the ground.

The monster's jaws clamped around my baton, and there was an immediate explosion of teeth and blood that sent him flying several feet away into the tall brush, yipping, screaming, and staggering. Before he slipped out of sight, I noticed that his lower jaw was simply *gone*, from the contact of his saliva on my electrified magical batons. Then he managed to limp into the woods with more pitiful yowls, but I had no mind to chase him. Roland — that titan of a man, my mentor — was hurt. I could smell copper in the air, and knew we had to get out of here. Fast. Because we had anticipated only one of the monsters. But there had been two of them, and they hadn't been the run-of-the-mill werewolves we had been warned about. If there were two, perhaps there were more. And they were evidently the prehistoric cousin of any werewolf I had ever seen or read about.

Roland hissed again as he stared down at his leg, growling with both pain and anger. My eyes darted back to the first monster, wary of another attack. It *almost* looked like a werewolf, but bigger. Much bigger. He didn't move, but I saw he was breathing. He had a notch in his right ear and a jagged scar on his long snout. Part of me wanted to go over to him and torture him. Slowly. Use his pain to finally drown my nightmare, my fear. The fear that had caused Roland's injury. My lack of inner-strength had not only put me in danger, but had hurt my mentor, my friend.

I shivered, forcing the thought away. That was *cold*. Not me. Sure, I was no stranger to fighting, but that had always been in a ring. Practicing. Sparring. Never life or death.

But I suddenly realized something very dark about myself in the chill, rainy night. Although I was terrified, I felt a deep ocean of anger manifest inside me, wanting only to dispense justice as I saw fit. To use that rage to battle my own demons. As if feeding one would starve the other, reminding me of the Cherokee Indian Legend Roland had once told me.

An old Cherokee man was teaching his grandson about life. "A fight is going on inside me," he told the boy. "It is a terrible fight between two wolves. One is evil — he is anger, envy, sorrow, regret, greed, arrogance, self-pity, guilt, resentment, inferiority, lies, false pride, superiority, and ego." After a few moments to make sure he had the boy's undivided attention, he continued.

"The other wolf is good — he is joy, peace, love, hope, serenity, humility, kindness, benevolence, empathy, generosity, truth, compassion, and faith. The same fight is going on inside of you, boy, and inside of every other person, too."

The grandson thought about this for a few minutes before replying. "Which wolf will win?"

The old Cherokee man simply said, "The one you feed, boy. The one you feed..."
And I felt like feeding one of my wolves today, by killing this one...

~

Get the full book ONLINE!

~

*Turn the page to read the first chapter of **WHISKEY GINGER**, book 1 in the Phantom Queen Diaries, which is also a part of the Temple Verse. Quinn MacKenna is a black-magic arms dealer from Boston, and she doesn't play nice. Not at all...*

TRY: WHISKEY GINGER (PHANTOM QUEEN DIARIES BOOK 1)

*T*he pasty guitarist hunched forward, thrust a rolled-up wad of paper deep into one nostril, and snorted a line of blood crystals— frozen hemoglobin that I'd smuggled over in a refrigerated canister—with the uncanny grace of a drug addict. He sat back, fangs gleaming, and pawed at his nose. "That's some bodacious shit. Hey, bros," he said, glancing at his fellow band members, "come hit this shit before it melts."

He fetched one of the backstage passes hanging nearby, pried the plastic badge from its lanyard, and used it to split up the crystals, murmuring something in an accent that reminded me of California. Not *the* California, but you know, Cali-foh-nia—the land of beaches, babes, and bros. I retrieved a toothpick from my pocket and punched it through its thin wrapper. "So," I asked no one in particular, "now that ye have the product, who's payin'?"

Another band member stepped out of the shadows to my left, and I don't mean that figuratively, either—the fucker literally stepped out of the shadows. I scowled at him, but hid my surprise, nonchalantly rolling the toothpick from one side of my mouth to the other.

The rest of the band gathered around the dressing room table, following the guitarist's lead by preparing their own snorting utensils—tattered magazine covers, mostly. Typically, you'd do this sort of thing with a dollar-bill, maybe even a Benjamin if you were flush. But fangers like this lot couldn't touch cash directly—in God We Trust and all that. Of course, I didn't really understand why sucking blood the old-fashioned way had suddenly gone out of style. More of a rush, maybe?

"It lasts longer," the vampire next to me explained, catching my mildly curious expression. "It's especially good for shows and stuff. Makes us look, like, less—"

"Creepy?" I offered, my Irish brogue lilting just enough to make it a question.

"Pale," he finished, frowning.

I shrugged. "Listen, I've got places to be," I said, holding out my hand.

"I'm sure you do," he replied, smiling. "Tell you what, why don't you, like, hang around for a bit? Once that wears off," he dipped his head toward the bloody powder smeared across the table's surface, "we may need a pick-me-up." He rested his hand on my arm and our gazes locked.

I blinked, realized what he was trying to pull, and rolled my eyes. His widened in surprise, then shock as I yanked out my toothpick and shoved it through his hand.

"Motherfuck—"

"I want what we agreed on," I declared. "Now. No tricks."

The rest of the band saw what happened and rose faster than I could blink. They circled me, their grins feral...they might have even seemed intimidating if it weren't for the fact that they each had a case of the sniffles

—I had to work extra hard not to think about what it felt like to have someone else's blood dripping down my nasal cavity.

I held up a hand.

"Can I ask ye gentlemen a question before we get started?" I asked. "Do ye even *have* what I asked for?"

Two of the band members exchanged looks and shrugged. The guitarist, however, glanced back towards the dressing room, where a brown paper bag sat next to a case full of makeup. He caught me looking and bared his teeth, his fangs stretching until it looked like it would be uncomfortable for him to close his mouth without piercing his own lip.

"Follow-up question," I said, eyeing the vampire I'd stabbed as he gingerly withdrew the toothpick from his hand and flung it across the room with a snarl. "Do ye do each other's make-up? Since, ye know, ye can't use mirrors?"

I was genuinely curious.

The guitarist grunted. "Mike, we have to go on soon."

"Wait a minute. Mike?" I turned to the snarling vampire with a frown. "What happened to *The Vampire Prospero*?" I glanced at the numerous fliers in the dressing room, most of which depicted the band members wading through blood, with Mike in the lead, each one titled *The Vampire Prospero* in *Rocky Horror Picture Show* font. Come to think of it...Mike did look a little like Tim Curry in all that leather and lace.

I was about to comment on the resemblance when Mike spoke up, "Alright, change of plans, bros. We're gonna drain this bitch before the show. We'll look totally—"

"Creepy?" I offered, again.

"Kill her."

~

Get the full book ONLINE!

MAKE A DIFFERENCE

Reviews are the most powerful tools in my arsenal when it comes to getting attention for my books. Much as I'd like to, I don't have the financial muscle of a New York publisher.

But I do have something much more powerful and effective than that, and it's something that those publishers would kill to get their hands on.

A committed and loyal bunch of readers.

Honest reviews of my books help bring them to the attention of other readers.

If you've enjoyed this book, I would be very grateful if you could spend just five minutes leaving a review on my book's Amazon page.

Thank you very much in advance.

ACKNOWLEDGMENTS

Team Temple and the Den of Freaks on Facebook have become family to me. I couldn't do it without die-hard readers like them.

I would also like to thank you, the reader. I hope you enjoyed reading *HORSEMAN* as much as I enjoyed writing it. Nate returns in December 2018 with LEGEND.

Callie Penrose releases in September 2018 with her book 5, *SINNER*.

And Quinn MacKenna will return late 2018 in her book 5, *MOSCOW MULE*.

And I have a few more novels and novellas planned for the year, so don't hold your breath…

ABOUT SHAYNE SILVERS

Shayne is a man of mystery and power, whose power is exceeded only by his mystery…

He currently writes the Amazon Bestselling **Feathers and Fire** Series about a rookie spell-slinger named Callie Penrose who works for the Vatican in Kansas City. Her problem? Hell seems to know more about her past than she does.

He also writes the Amazon Bestselling **Nate Temple** Series, which features a foul-mouthed wizard from St. Louis. He rides a bloodthirsty unicorn, drinks with Achilles, and is pals with the Four Horsemen.

Shayne holds two high-ranking black belts, and can be found writing in a coffee shop, cackling madly into his computer screen while pounding shots of espresso. He's hard at work on book 10 of the Nate Temple Series - coming summer 2018 - as well as Callie's book 5 in the Feathers and Fire series for Summer 2018. **Follow him online for all sorts of groovy goodies, giveaways, and new release updates:**

Get Down with Shayne Online
www.shaynesilvers.com
info@shaynesilvers.com

facebook.com/shaynesilversfanpage

amazon.com/author/shaynesilvers

bookbub.com/profile/shayne-silvers

twitter.com/shaynesilvers

instagram.com/shaynesilversofficial

goodreads.com/Shaynesilvers

BOOKS IN THE TEMPLE VERSE

CHRONOLOGY: All stories in the Temple Verse are shown in chronological order on the following page

NATE TEMPLE SERIES

FAIRY TALE - FREE prequel novella #0 for my subscribers

OBSIDIAN SON

BLOOD DEBTS

GRIMM

SILVER TONGUE

BEAST MASTER

TINY GODS

DADDY DUTY (Novella #6.5)

WILD SIDE

WAR HAMMER

NINE SOULS

HORSEMAN

LEGEND (TEMPLE #11) - *COMING DECEMBER 2018...*

FEATHERS AND FIRE SERIES

(Also set in the Temple Universe)

UNCHAINED

RAGE

WHISPERS

ANGEL'S ROAR

SINNER - *COMING SEPTEMBER 2018...*

PHANTOM QUEEN DIARIES

WHISKEY GINGER

COSMOPOLITAN

OLD FASHIONED

DARK AND STORMY -

MOSCOW MULE - *COMING FALL 2018...*

CHRONOLOGICAL ORDER: TEMPLE VERSE

FAIRY TALE (TEMPLE PREQUEL)

OBSIDIAN SON (TEMPLE 1)

BLOOD DEBTS (TEMPLE 2)

GRIMM (TEMPLE 3)

SILVER TONGUE (TEMPLE 4)

BEAST MASTER (TEMPLE 5)

TINY GODS (TEMPLE 6)

DADDY DUTY (TEMPLE NOVELLA 6.5)

UNCHAINED (FEATHERS... 1)

RAGE (FEATHERS... 2)

WILD SIDE (TEMPLE 7)

WAR HAMMER (TEMPLE 8)

WHISPERS (FEATHERS... 3)

WHISKEY GINGER (PHANTOM... 1)

NINE SOULS (TEMPLE 9)

COSMOPOLITAN (PHANTOM... 2)

ANGEL'S ROAR (FEATHERS... 4)

OLD FASHIONED (PHANTOM...3)

HORSEMAN (TEMPLE 10)

DARK AND STORMY (PHANTOM... 4)

Printed in Great Britain
by Amazon